PATCHERS
OF THE
CODE

CB ARCHER

Cover Illustration and Design Copyright © 2017 by CB Archer
Book Design and Production by CB Archer

ISBN-13: 978-0994773722

First Edition: 2017

Wish to learn more? Visit Annals of Gentalia at the following locations.
Website: www.annalsofgentalia.wordpress.com
Facebook: www.facebook.com/annalsofgentalia
Twitter: @CB_Archer
Goodreads: CB Archer

Dedicated to a winner!
(Seriously, because a winner is you!)

Chapter 1

FROM THE DESK OF PALCATH IRONBURROW

Zing! Palcath Ironburrow, Son of Gloni and Defender of the Dwarven Clans was satisfied with his latest update and pressed send. Now everyone knew of Group A's latest accomplishments deep inside the Pyramid of Evan. The Mummy Guards, Jackal Lanterns, and Cleo-Aspas had all been slaughtered, the traps had all been carefully avoided, the puzzles had been solved with the heavy use of yellow blocks, and Pharaoh Evan (which Palcath had decided was a stupid name for a Pharaoh) had been questioned and appropriately thanked for his time. Settling down further into his yellow chair that sat beside his *Portie Tent Ultra*, the dwarf pulled out the pipe that he pretended to smoke and congratulated himself on a great post to the group chat.

Setting up the group chat was a great idea, especially with the Player Pagers and WorldForums down. It was of course Palcath's idea, but still he decided to give credit where credit was due. Now no one would ever again be denied of Palcath's wisdom and he *Smugly Smile Animationed* to himself.

Palcath was glad they were finally making progress. He was certain this time that the trail was finally getting warmer. They would find their quarry in no time now. He estimated two or three cycles at the most. He was in such a good mood that he was going to treat himself to a piece of *Pyramid Bacon* from his brand new stash.

He looked over the supplies and could barely believe the numbers. Had it really already been three weeks since they had split up and left Onn after the fall of their foe Breaker and the loss of their friend Anders? The math certainly checked out and if Palcath was certain about one thing it was his math. Except for that one time he was wrong, his math was always right.

Palcath could still remember the moment when everything had changed, 21.46 cycles ago. It had been both a time of great victories and of great sorrow. Victory, because Breaker, their self appointed arch-nemesis, had fallen in battle. That big bag of black pixel wind had been consumed both figuratively by his lust for power and actually by Anders' mysterious rainbow pet dragon. Sorrow, because Anders, beloved elf Night Ranger and friend to all (and supposed protagonist of this book trilogy) had also fallen in battle moments after being reunited with everyone.

Even now the constant threat that was Breaker and his summoned army of opposite party named dragons was gone they couldn't rest easy. In fact, Palcath was even more worried because now they had more enemies than before.

Most troubling for Palcath was the innocent-looking Quest Fairies, always hanging overhead and providing 'useful' information. They were plotting against avatars everywhere (according to Palcath), but for some reason no one else saw this. Flaming Pits, some avatars were now on a first named basis with the buggers. Technically only one and they had made up the Quest Fairy's name, but still it was concerning.

There was a Secret Council Group Full of Mystical All-Knowing and Mysterious Members angered with the party. The fact that any of the six of them could unfold themselves into the area and kill even central protagonists at will certainly was something for Palcath to worry about.

There was that crazy cat girl, E. E. Lynn, who was next to impossible to track down. While she was nearly killed by the Administrators with no explanation given, which really got Palcath's #5 *Facial Hair* (the close cropped beard) in a knot. She was dangerous but he would find her. Other groups had their appointed jobs, but it was his group's job to find her.

The most amazing fact about the groups dividing for their different tasks, besides of course how wonderfully Palcath had organized them, was that everyone had agreed to split up. They hadn't even needed to use a boat as a plot device this time! That was great for Palcath, who mistrusted boats and briefly thought about adding them to his list of potential threats.

All in all, everything was perfectly in line with Palcath's plan. He congratulated himself as he finished off the last bite of his *Pyramid Bacon*. Yes, perfectly planned and expertly coordinated. So far it was a great cycle, and everything was looking up.

> Official Annals of Gentalia Text Box: Warning! Forced shut down of The Island of Islana Expansion has been implemented by the Administrative staff due to several unfixable problems. Please quickly make your way to the *WARNING ALL PORT AREAS NOT FOUND* to leave. You have exactly seven cycles to leave the Expansion. Any avatars still remaining here after the seven cycles will be deleted in the reset. We apologize for any inconvenience this may

cause. Thank you for your time and patience.

Palcath's Group Text Box: Well fuck.

Palcath's Text Box: …

Palcath's Group Text Box: Lads!

✧ Chapter 2 ✧
CYCLE 1
GROUP D, SEARCHING THROUGH

K ray's Text Box: This is like so stupid, kay.

samuri's Text Box: ...

samuri used the *Nod Animation*. For the first time, possibly ever, Kray was right. To be fair though, samuri was certain that the crispy black fright elf Night Ranger with absolutely no concept of colour theory wasn't thinking about the same thing as himself. samuri, steadfast, silent, and colour-coordinated as ever, (gray is a colour) waited for the follow-up statement from Kray that would confirm they were not thinking about the same thing. It would only be a matter of rounds, samuri was certain.

What they were doing here was stupid in a way. Looking over hundreds and hundreds of items on the corpses stashed in the basement of Onn Coliseum was possibly not the best use of their time. However, now that the entire Expansion was going to be reset in seven cycles, it was worth it. The slim chance that one of these broken items could open up a portal was more than enough inspiration to continue on this mindless task. samuri knew that Breaker could put whatever enchantment he wanted on any item, so even if the sword he had normally seen Breaker use wasn't here, simple things like potions could not be overlooked. Any of these creepily displayed items on the corpses of dead avatars and Non Player Characters could be their ticket out of here.

The process had already taken three weeks and they were barely even a quarter of the way through. Progress would have been faster if not for three key factors.

1. samuri was being cautious to not touch anything and was waiting for the Item Description Menu Boxes to show up, which took several rounds. He was far too nervous of the items being cursed and taking over his body.

2. Kray wasn't helping at all. samuri didn't want him here, but the annoying elf had simply followed him when samuri himself left his original group, insisting that looking through these items was a good plan. Palcath agreed and made a special new team for samuri, called Group D and Group B didn't do anything to stop Kray from joining it.

3. The All Seeing Eye Dog and the Nine Circles of Hellcat were so cute! They always wanted to play with samuri and he couldn't say no to them. They had left their previous masters (much to the twins annoyance) to stay with samuri. Now that there was a timeline samuri couldn't spend as much time playing fetch the monster corpse, taking them for walkies, or feeding them some delicious monster faces (their favorite treat). samuri was already feeling guilty.

> Kray's Text Box: This stupid *Slime Armour* is for Anderses only. I cannot put it on, kay. It keeps on jumping off.

> samuri's Text Box: …

samuri used the *Headshake Animation*. samuri was correct. Stupid Kray hadn't thought that this situation was stupid, or that the entire world ending was stupid. He had thought his own stupid problems were stupid. Despite all of samuri's warnings that the *Slime Armour* set was dangerous, which to be fair had only been once, Kray had been trying to put the outfit on since he found it here on the headless corpse of NPC Gwendella.

> Kray's Text Box: Sami-Guy, have you found anything that will help me yet? Like a *Belt of Using Anderses Only Stuff* or something. I need to get this jelly stuff on so I can be better than that pile of chunky leftover ash over there, kay.

> samuri's Text Box: …

samuri used the *Sigh Animation*. If he had anything to shut up Kray, he was absolutely sure he would have used it already. Multiple times if possible and with a vertical stabbing motion.

> Kray's Text Box: Wait, where did that chunky pile of ash go? Whatever, kay, it was chunking up the whole area.

> samuri's Text Box: …

samuri used the *Rub Temples Animation*. The pile of ashes that once had been Anders, the much easier to talk to of the elf Night Rangers, hadn't been there since the groups spilt up. Kray hadn't noticed until now. samuri wasn't sure who had taken it but through ingenious deductive reasoning could eliminate Kray.

> Kray's Text Box: Kay, so for our wedding I was thinking of an outdoor setting, maybe like in a nice part of Onn Forest. I really like this one spot where Chunk-o-Butt told me I was the better gay elf. That is like my favorite place, where the Spiderboy was. So I bet it is yours as well right? So, like forest background so maybe like we should—

samuri used the *Ignore Animation*. He didn't bother to interrupt, he had stopped listening. He had heard Kray's No-Colour Quest Fairy mumble something about the relevance of Spiderboys to quests but samuri didn't really care. His mind was focused on an important task: this pair of gloves that rested on the ears of the bodiless head of NPC Gwendella. This pair of *Fritzing Gloves* gave the use of the spell *Dragon's Might*. samuri really didn't care what that was, this was another useless and dangerous item that Breaker had broken. As with the other cheat code modified items he had found samuri chopped both it and the Item Description Menu Box in half with a slash from his *Katana-Nata*. They faded out of existence in a mass of black pixels.

> Kray's Text Box: Kay, how did you do that? Are you like PVP broken or something Sami-Guy? Or can you chop items apart? I forget what your things are. Well, I remember that tongue, when do I get to try it out?

> samuri's Text Box: ...

samuri used the *Eyeroll Animation*. For someone who was apparently his fiancé, Kray knew little about his 'Sami-Guy'. Come to think of it, Kray knew little about any other avatar except himself.

> Kray's Text Box: Can you cut anything apart, kay? Could you, like, cut that boxy thing and not the item or the item and not the boxy thing?

> samuri's Text Box: ...

samuri used the *Nod Animation*. He could do that, not that he really cared. He moved to the next item, a wicked Necromancer Weapon: a *Simone the Scythe* and waited for the Item Description Menu Box to show up. A cold nose on his hand and a burning nose on his thigh told him that his cute little All Seeing Eye Dog and Nine Circles of Hellcat were starting to get hungry. They were right, the hour was late and dinnertime had already passed. After this item they would break for the night. One hundred fourteen out of the one thousand five hundred eight items here had now been checked over. That was horrible for three weeks work, barely even a scratch. samuri wished that he had requested some competent help now, or anyone that wasn't Kray. samuri chopped apart *Simone* and her box and went to do the *Campfire Animation*.

> Kray's Text Box: About time, kay. I am so hungry. What are you making me for dinner?

> samuri's Text Box: …

samuri used the *Cooking Animation*. He was making himself the least ill tasting thing he owned, a *Golden Gribblet Pickle*. For Kray he was making the same thing that he was making for the animals, the severed off face of a Golden Gribblet. If Kray wasn't going to cook for himself, or even help at all searching, he was going to eat pet food.

> Kray's Text Box: Bleck, kay. This tastes horrible. Worse than usual.

> samuri's Text Box: …

samuri used the *Shrug Animation*. His dog and cat liked his cooking, so why not his rat? samuri ate in silence, conscious that Kray stared at his body length tongue the entire time. After dinner samuri rolled up in his pink *Ni Hao Bunny© Blanket* and went to sleep, ignoring Kray's constant chatter by placing his handmade (out of *Flork Demon's Skull Nubs*) earplugs in. Kray could talk all he wanted, samuri wouldn't hear him now. Thinking hard about the option of not removing the earplugs tomorrow morning and ignoring Kray completely, samuri went to sleep.

> Kray's Text Box: Then I will come down the aisle while *Caution Step's* song is in the background, kay. You know the one? *Onnwards to Onn.* Love that one! Totally symbolises my new life. Don't you agree Sami-Guy?

> Kray's Text Box: You will already be down there of course, kay. Only I get to go down the aisle. I need a new best man now that Breaker is dead. Who should I pick? You know what, it is me. I will be my own best man, I am that good.

> Kray's Text Box: I decided that your little pets, what are they anyways, like a hedgehog and a fox? They can be the ring bearers, kay. Animals as ring bearers are so cute, and I love foxes! All green and everything, so cute.

> Kray's Text Box: I knew you would like that, kay. So what I was really hoping to wear was this *Slime Armour*, because it means so much to me. I can't get it on! How did that chunk of an elf get into these if I can't? He was so fat.

> Kray's Text Box: I know right, it would look so good on me, kay. I wish

> I could think of some way to put it on.

> Ageless Pantaloon's Text Box: You already saw a way to put it on! You only need to put the pieces together.

Unconcerned that one of the pairs of pants on a dead Leg Devil had talked to him, Kray instead kept talking, as was his custom.

> Kray's Text Box: I tried that, kay. Putting the different Armour pieces together didn't do anything, I couldn't jump into them.

> Ageless Pantaloon's Text Box: Not like that you idiot. What I mean is you need to put together the pieces of the puzzle. You saw what you could do to remedy the situation.

> Kray's Text Box: My wedding can solve it? No offence but that sounds stupid, kay!

> Ageless Pantaloon's Text Box: Seriously? You can cut apart anything with a PVP broken ability. You saw how you can cut apart an Item Description Menu Box!

> Kray's Text Box: You're right, I did. So what does that matter, kay?

The pants unzipped in frustration.

> Ageless Pantaloon's Text Box: You can't equip that *Slime Armour* because the Item Description Menu Box says it is for Anderses Only.

> Kray's Text Box: So, kay?

> Ageless Pantaloon's Text Box: That sword right there can cut apart an Item Description Menu Box!

> Kray's Text Box: So what does that matter, kay?

> Ageless Pantaloon's Text Box: Wow. Maker help me. Let me take this real slow for you so you can understand. You take that outdated sword from warrier and use it to cut the Item Description Menu Boxes to remove the part that says Anderses Only!

> Kray's Text Box: What a good idea random set of pants, kay. I'll ask Sami-Guy to do that tomorrow morning.

> Ageless Pantaloon's Text Box: Ask who? Whatever. Why wait until tomorrow? You only need the sword. You can drop it on the Item

> Description Menu Boxes. Go do that now.

> Kray's Text Box: I can do that? Kay, well that is a good idea, pants, I'll go try it.

Kray walked over to his sleeping angel and attempted to unsheathe the *Katana-Nata*. He lifted it up, but it reacted to Kray's hand like any other item that could not be equipped, flying into the air and crashing to the ground. It nearly decapitated samuri when it fell, but only chopped his ponytail completely off. samuri's hairstyle was no longer one of the official numbers, it also didn't look good. Kray panicked and tried to pick up the *Katana-Nata* again, this time it landed back into its scabbard.

A few tests confirmed it, picking this sword up would first nearly cut off samuri's head, then it would go back into his scabbard, it was perfect. Kray took out his pilfered *Slime Armour*, piece by piece and nestled them gently on samuri's face. Once the Item Description Menu Box showed up Kray would attempt to pick up samuri's sword and chop off the part that said Anderses Only. It took a few tries, much of the rest of samuri's hair, and some of his helmet, but it worked.

Kray was now the proud owner of his own set of No-Longer-Anderses-Only *Slime Armour* and much of samuri's hair. He put the Armour on and placed the tattered remains of hair in his wedding scrapbook.

> Kray's Text Box: Kay, now I am so much better than what's-his-ass now. Thank you so much for this idea mysterious voice that emanated from a random pair of pants.

> Ageless Pantaloon's Text Box: No problem. So long idiot!

> Kray's Text Box: You're so right, somewhat-jerkish pair of pants, kay, this does look really good on me!

> Kray's Text Box: Kay, it does make my ass look more fuckable, thank you pants. You are much nicer now.

> Kray's Text Box: You are too kind pants! I think I have found my new best man! Kay, I need to get to sleep now. I have a busy cycle tomorrow planning my wedding. I will show you my scrapbook, it is AMAZING!

> Kray's Text Box: Well, since you asked nicely I guess I could tell you the best bedtime story ever! Okay, kay, so there I was tied up with chunky butt and the Spiderboy had said that he was going to come back with his friend.

> No-Colour Quest Fairy's Text Box: *Yawn* The Spiderboy is not rela… zzz…

◈ **Chapter 3** ◈

CYCLE 1
GROUP C, LOOKING FOR
ANOTHER WAY

Roodg's Text Box: i WONDER WHY THEY NEVER USE ALPHABETICAL ORDER? wE SHOULD HAVE BEEN gROUP b.

Herbert's Text Box: I agree, they could have saved confusion here. Your ideas are sawesome Roodg.

Roodg was happy that Herbert had used her first sawesome. The lanky, skinny, multi-gendered night elf Magic Mage gave a solid *Fist Bump Animation* to the newly-named Red Quest Fairy. They had gotten along smashingly these past three weeks due to Roodg learning to prevent others from interrupting the poor flittering thing. Roodg had no idea as to what the real name or gender of the Quest Fairy was, but it was at least allowing itself to be referred to as a girl named Herbert.

Trev Terra's Text Box: No, we are looking forwards, well alphabetically forwards for the areas we know about rather... What I mean is we started with A locations, and we are about done with C. C took forever, why were there so many? So we went in normal order, right. If that is okay?

Roodg's Text Box: nOT US. tHE CHAPTERS. nEVER MIND.

Roodg's secret assertiveness training had not gone as well as expected. Trev Terra was still a mess of rathers and incomplete sentences. Roodg was not going to give up on the sprite elf Geomancer yet. Everything about Trev gloomed with unconfidence, from his mousy brown beaded hair that covered his eyes, the constant application of high numbered *Blush Shades* to even his posture, which Roodg didn't even know you could change from the default. Their twice daily walks would continue to be full of secret assertiveness training, even if it wasn't working.

> Roodg's Text Box: wHERE IS NEXT?

> Jorthan the Male Troll Monk's Text Box: Next would be the Desserted Island mon petit nuit lutin.

The ugly-to-look-at-but-sweet-inside French Canadian troll was a good leader. It was evident to Roodg why others would follow him. He had a natural charisma to him, which was odd for his chosen melee focused class. Roodg was happy enough to follow. Leading was not something high on the night elf's list of priorities. Herbert would be a group leader long before Roodg ever would.

> Roodg's Text Box: dESSERTED iSLAND SOUNDS BOTH LONELY AND DELICIOUS! gO!

Revving up the *Magical Flying Carrot Ultra+*, which was the reason why Roodg was in this group, Roodg beckoned for Jorthan and Trev to get on. The *Carrot* had been accidentally acquired by Roodg after killing a boss that was disguised as scenery. If there was something Roodg Scenerybane excelled at, it was destroying scenery.

The boys would be first on this trip simply because Jorthan knew the way. If anyone on the *Carrot* had been to the area before, they could all go. They were a solid party this Group C, but Roodg was upset about being away from any potential love interests. Being stuck with two confirmed couples and away from avatars you had a crush on was difficult.

Only two avatars besides Roodg could fly at one time due to the *Carrot's* picked design. The angelic and demonic Lesbitwins always had to travel together, since they were literally stuck together at the lips. Not that Jorthan and Trev minded being flown together; they cuddled on every trip and even made out. Despite Trev's shyness, the stunning scenery had apparently overruled his desire for modesty.

> Roodg's Text Box: tHIS TEAM IS BORING SOMETIMES! eVERYONE ELSE ONLY KISSES EACH OTHER! i FEEL LIKE i'M TALKING TO MYSELF HALF THE TIME!

> Roodg's Text Box: ... gUYS?

Trev Terra and Jorthan the Male Troll Monk used the *Make Out While Straddling a Magical Flying Carrot Dual Animation*. Roodg used the *Sigh Animation*.

> Herbert's Text Box: It is okay, you still can talk to me!

> Roodg's Text Box: yOU ARE RIGHT! wHAT IS YOUR FAVOURITE KIND OF SANDWICH? lET'S ANSWER AT THE SAME TIME. oN THREE. 1. 2. 3.

> Roodg and Herbert's Simultaneous Text Boxes: pASTRAMI! I don't eat food, I'm a framing device.

> Roodg's Text Box: wELL, WE WERE CLOSE.

Roodg dropped kissing couple #2 off at the chocolate fountain (that was both pouring chocolate and made of chocolate), then turned around to pick up the original kissing couple. The Desserted Island did look delicious, covered in a variety of perfectly placed and mouth watering sweets. Roodg knew better though, all of the food here would taste horrid. Unless they were cooked by Roodg's special techniques into power tools, they all would taste like appliances.

Roodg shot off on the *Magical Flying Carrot Ultra+* back towards Cel Ral-Zad, the last place on their list of known C locations that had proved as useless as the other twenty-eight locations that had been called Cel Ral-Something. These solo trips with Herbert had become the best part of this Group for Roodg. There was ample time to think, there was no one kissing, and Herbert had some decent ideas. Roodg didn't know why Palcath hated these Quest Fairies so much, they were pretty rad.

The Fortress of Cel Ral-Zad appeared on the horizon almost too fast for Roodg. Time for another kissing filled trip on the *Magical Flying Carrot Ultra+* with another couple. In'ferni and De'vini didn't even notice Roodg land; they were too busy using the *Dry Humping Dual Animation*. Roodg didn't even bother to tell them to stop and pushed the floating lesbitwins over the *Carrot's* seats and took off again. At least they were easier to move while distracted than Jorthan and his petit lutin since they were always floating. It took the kissing pair more than halfway through the trip to even notice they were flying.

> In'ferni and De'vini's Simultaneous Text Boxes: When did we start flying? We are flying? Yes, we are flying. Oh yeah, we are. Hello Roodg, when did you get here? I like flying, it is romantic. I like it too, it is SO romantic. We should make out. Yes, yes we should.

In'ferni and De'vini used the *Make Out While Straddling a Magical Flying Carrot Dual Animation*. Roodg piloted while thinking about the strangeness of including that as a standard stock animation. Whoever programmed the Stock Animations into this game was clearly insane. After a few more rounds of watching lesbians kiss Roodg and the *Carrot's* cargo arrived safely.

> Roodg's Text Box: wE ARE ALL HERE. dID YOU GUYS FIND ANYTHING WHILE i WAS GONE?

Jorthan the Male Troll Monk's Text Box: You were gone my lutin de nuit? We were not ones that noticed your missing.

Trev Terra's Text Box: Jorthan had, well and then... oh gosh, we sort of lost track of time and well... er, then I had to go for a walk without Jorthan and... um I mean, welcome back.

Roodg thought that there had been a brand new lake located beside the grove of Taffy Trees on the way in and was correct, the result of Trev's alone time. Roodg simply used the *Smile Animation*. Trev needed to clear the plumbing constantly due to his massively dense balls, but still was too shy to do that around anyone. Roodg wished that the avatar would shoot it in less annoying places. What if there had been a portal in that grove? Now it was lost forever under all that sprite elf spunk because Roodg was not swimming through it again. There were no more *Double Danishes* to clean it off.

Jorthan the Male Troll Monk's Text Box: Waiting, why are we? Searching this location is what we should be doing.

While everyone agreed and did their best, there was nothing new at this fountain either. At least it was time to break for the night and tomorrow sounded potentially delicious: all morning looking at the rest of the locations on the Desserted Island. Roodg used a *Lick Lips Animation*, even if all of it was going to taste as awful as the Licorice Rainclouds had, at least it would be fun to look at.

◈ Chapter 4 ◈
CYCLE 1: MORNING
N, ALONE

Everything was white, brilliant hard to even look at white. After the far longer than normal log in time on the dark loading screen that displayed simple game play tips, it was physically painful to see the brightness. He had to shield his eyes with his sandwich to prevent permanent retinal damage (as well as turn on a light in the room).

The fact that there had even been an option to log on had been strange after what had happened. He had certainly not expected it. Only the letter 'n' in his name had remained on the character information bio on the main screen. Now that he had logged in and checked more thoroughly the only remaining information on his status page was the letter 'n'. The rest of the page had been dissolved away. No information was left, so for now at least, he had to assume that his name and everything about him that was important was now just the letter 'n'.

The strange thing was that he wasn't here. As best as he could see, he wasn't anything. He could move, both the camera and himself, but couldn't see any animations or indication that he was moving. He felt like he was moving in all aspects of how moving used to feel, but that was it. He could feel himself, but he wasn't there. This experience of existence combined with the complete feeling of emptiness was unsettling for n.

Then he saw it. A slightly different shade of white than the rest of the blank white area. Only he could have seen it, for he had been training long and hard to see them. A single, solitary, discoloured pixel, right where his nose should have been. That was what he had been reduced to, the letter 'n' and a single pixel, but at least he wasn't *dead*

Dead… probably. Now that he thought about it, n wasn't exactly sure on the status of his mortality.

Mostly to distract his brain from questions on the meaning of life and the finality of it all, the letter n started to explore his surroundings. It was a stark white void of near nothingness, but he could tell that he was moving. While the landscape never changed nor appeared to move, he knew that he was moving forward. He was headed towards the only thing he could see in the area, an even brighter spot of white.

The spot of white grew brighter as he approached. It took n some time to realize what it was: a pale white consol in the stark white area, distinct enough to make out. He approached the consol cautiously, in case there was a Stark White Consol Demon he didn't know about. After several rounds, the consol made no attempt to eat, rape, or attack him and n grew curious as to what the purpose for it was.

Buttons. There was a bevy of buttons on this consol, as well as a multitude of monitors, and at least double the number of necessary dials. He wondered what they could be for, but when he accidently bumped a dial with his nothing a monitor flickered out of screen-saver mode and burst into full vibrant colour. Looking closely, he could see that all the other monitors were on, but not exceptionally bright. Scenes of every kind were shown dully in the white surfaces—ranges of mountains, cityscapes, islands, even a multitude of spires. These were areas of the game and movement on one monitor caught his eye. Roodg was on a beach, licking a set of low hanging clouds. Startled, n looked more closely at other monitors but there were no other avatars to be seen, so he was doubtful these were set up for the purposes of spying. It didn't hurt to play with the dials, to double check.

Soon n was twisting the biggest dial and found that he could spy if he wanted to. He could even zero-in on particular monsters or avatars and started to channel surf on the coloured screen. Nothing interesting was going on, besides of course Roodg licking the clouds, which was an entirely new level of curious. The last channel on this monitor showed a jungle scene, with ferns gently blowing the wind. Ferns and something else. n looked closely at the screen. What was that?

It was a pale blue colour, flowing much like a long thin fern would if it were made of fabric. It was a scarf! A *Winter Fun Scarf*! Following the lines of the scarf led to the discovery of an avatar attached to it, hidden within the ferns. It was a centaur with a *#6 Hairstyle* and exactly the right amount of chin stubble. It was Fournimer! n leaned in for a better look and up close he could hear the ferns blowing in the wind. Another noise could be heard, something softer. The sound of heavy breathing.

n paid extra attention to this monitor. He wished the ferns would move out of the way, and almost as if they had read his mind they obeyed a new breeze and shifted position. There was Fournimer, eyes closed in bliss, one hand twisting his nipple, the other massaging his flank.

There was someone, or something, under the centaur. n was determined to find out what but his view was blocked. With a twisting of knobs and a dash of luck he managed to rotate and even move the camera that was broadcasting the scene. There was a shorter, slimmer, centaur nestled below Fournimer. A mop of silky white hair rested on his head, parted in a hairstyle number than n had never seen before. Youthful, full of life, and with a hint of sexy belly fat, this doe-eyed centaur was the one breathing heavily. Who was this new avatar and why was Fournimer doing things with him?

n watched the scene before him on the monitor. The smaller centaur was comfortably on the jungle floor, furiously working the large horse member with both of his hands. Pumping with zeal, the smaller centaur with the perfect hair was flicking the head of Fournimer's member with his lithe tongue.

The little centaur turned his head, and a set of cute, perky antlers became visible from his unnumbered hairstyle. A short white tail was happily bobbing along, n saw it now, and this was no centaur. The telltale lack of an avatar spark in its eyes told n that this wasn't even an avatar.! This was a boss monster and n was relieved! Fourni had been getting a handjob from a monster, not an avatar. Monsters didn't count towards real cybersex totals, n told himself.

This scene made sense now. Fournimer needed to relieve himself almost every cycle or he would burst from his high horse-spunk producing balls, so he was using this helpful boss to get off.

This scene was hot, and n had a front row seat. Watching was more of a turn on than n thought. He felt a growing hardness in his loins, but nothing existed to touch. It was annoying to have no access to your own privates when you desperately wanted them, but this scene could be saved later in the mental vault. Fourni was bucking and stamping the ground as the (whatever a centaur deer was called, n wasn't quite sure) was happily using the centaur-precum to lubricate the long forceful strokes.

It was impossible to tell who was enjoying the scene more—Fournimer, the deer centaur, or n. Each thrust of the monster's hands produced a whimper from everyone in the encounter. Fourni whimpered with delight, the tauric creature with excitement, and n with a desperate need to join in.

Fournimer was arching his back now, moaning loudly, hooves stamping. The deeritaur had tripled his efforts and his tongue was frantically licking the big slit of his charge.

> Fournimer's Text Box: oh Maker, yeah!

Lips now sealed around the tip of Fournimer's big heavy cock, the fawniguy reached forward and grabbed the horse-nuts tightly and squeezed. Fournimer let out a grunt at the pressure and arched his back in triumph. Mesmerized, n watched as the centaur splurted into the mouth of the waiting buckboy. Gush after gush was spilling out of the full mouth and despite the best efforts of the venis-son, it couldn't keep up. There was a coating of centaur spunk over the face and chest of the willing manstag. After the deeritaur had licked up most and washed the rest off in the nearby stream, it walked over to the still shaking centaur. The humungulate was shorter than Fournimer and his thank you kiss only reached up to Fournimer's bellybutton.

Still dribbling, Fournimer managed a thankful hug back. His needs had been sated for this cycle, and he gave a gentle kiss on the forehead which induced a friendly assault of little floaty hearts.

> Fournimer's Text Box: thank you. I needed that.

> Cervitaur's Text Box: No problem! Trust me. I know what it is like. Some cycles it is awful.

> Fournimer's Text Box: tell me about it. it gets downright painful at times.

> Cervitaur's Text Box: Centaurs have a worse time of it I think… Now about the second part of our agreement.

n was shocked. That deerboy was called a cervitaur. That was the only shocking thing though, everything else was fine. Peachy even. He shameless leered on.

The cervitaur turned and lithely spread his hind legs. His own member was dripping hard and his nuts were heavy with seed. Fournimer responded by slowly rubbing his hand down a spotted flank, finally ending with a firm grip on the needful nuts. Fournimer needed to kneel to get better access to the area, but soon he was rubbing the firm deer shaft and rolling the balls around in his hands. Fournimer leaned down and licked the member, which caused explosive hearts to emanate from the certivaurs's head. He was leveling up with *Wonder Kisses* of all but the secret final locked variety.

Fournimer had taken the entire member in his mouth now as cervitaurs were significantly less endowed than centaurs. This was making the cervitaur prance with delight. n knew from experience that this boss monster was about to release his hot sticky load into Fournimer's eager mouth.

A flit in the air beside n's head had been bugging him for a few rounds. This was not the time for distractions! He reached out towards it and gave it a gentle swat, or at least he tried to do that. He wasn't exactly sure if he touched it or not, but when he maybe-touched it the light pulsed gently. When the light started to speak, n was so shocked that he might have fallen over in shock (he wasn't exactly sure if he did or not).

> Air Flit's Text Box: Whoa, you scared me there! Sneaking up on me like that.

> n's Text Box: I wasn't doing anything. Who said I was doing anything? I wasn't!

Thinking quick, n smacked the dial back to the cloud tasting channel and covered up his invisible erection with his invisible hands.

> Air Flit's Text Box: What?

n's Text Box: Nothing!

Air Flit's Text Box: Fair enough. I was looking all over for you after I saw you had logged in.

n's Text Box: You were looking for me?

Air Flit's Text Box: Of course I was, but I couldn't see where you were. Probably because you were invisible! I didn't suspect that you would be here of all places or that you would find me first.

n's Text Box: Where is here exactly?

Air Flit's Text Box: You are in the GameFrame, a hidden place made just for observation that only nine… well it should only be nine people, now it is a lot more… know about. We have so much more to talk about than that. You probably have so many questions for me, like I do for you. Let me properly port into this area fully first. All these background windows are making it hard to concentrate.

The light grew brighter in an instant and n desperately wished that he hadn't finished eating his sandwich during the taur sex so that he would have something to cover his eyes with. The light began to descend towards the floor which only made it appear brighter still. Once it reached the ground, the light began to take solid shape but it wasn't the kind of solid shape n was expecting. It was not expanded on the z axis at all. It was two-dimensional and would be completely invisible if it turned to the side. It was also shorter than n had thought it would be—if he still had geometry himself it would only have come up to his knees. On what was essentially a piece of paper a sketchy form drew itself into exsistance.

It didn't belong here at all but there it was. A 2D paper cut out, alive and moving in front of him. A 2D paper cut out from a completely different franchise that *Tornado Tech Games*® held absolutely no rights to. Standing there with a purse stuffed with carrots and an impossibly cute expression. n couldn't believe it, this didn't make any sense at all, but there it was. Standing in front of him. Smiling.

n's Text Box: No way! Ni Hao Bunny©?

Chapter 5
CYCLE 1
GROUP B, SEEKING
A CURE

Mr. Max's Text Box: There is one! Get it!

With a big swing of his *Five-Handed Sword*, Mr. Max missed the Golden Poffle completely and fell to the ground with a thud. He had forgotten how carrying two avatars on his back would change the trajectory of his swing. A blur of speedy Glïint passed him to attempt to chase down their target. Mr. Max unceremoniously picked his beefy orange self up, again forgetting about his cargo avatars of Zal Finn III and Hippolyta, and only barely kept his balance. He didn't let on that he had almost landed right back onto the ground of Spire G.

Zal Finn III's Text Box: This could be easier you know Max.

Zal Finn's skin had turned gray several weeks ago, which helped her stand out from the crowd for once (but not by much). Viscous black bubbles were still floating above her head. The bubbles popped occasionally and were filled with a thick sickly smoke littered with black pixels. The number -178 popped out of Zal Finn each time a bubble popped. Numbers popping out of avatars was nothing new, it happened all the time. Damage, healing, gold pieces gained, and even experience points showed up all the time. What was unusual was the colour of the -178. It was black.

Black was not a colour normally used by numbers. It was the colour used by Breaker, and that is exactly who the numbers were working for. Zal Finn had equipped the *Spring*

Gauntlets (s) she found that Breaker had altered incorrectly assuming that since Breaker was dead, nothing bad could happen. That was wrong. The gauntlets had in reality been a trap made by Breaker to slowly kill Mr. Max, his arch-nemesis, through experience point drain. Breaker had altered the *Contact Poison Status Effect* to have a duration of 10 billion rounds and to drain experience instead of health.

When Zal Finn had initially fallen to the ground after being inflicted with this horrible disease, she was immediately helped up by her not so secret admirer: the fight elf feminist Sage Hippolyta with the impressive cleavage. Now both were infected by a disease that was slowly draining their levels.

> Hippolyta's Text Box: Yes Max. Simply allow us to walk. I am both tired of being thrown about constantly when you attack, and being carried around like some sort of damsel in distress luggage.

> Mr. Max's Text Box: Impossible! This is my fault fellow adenturettes! I need to carry you, so you lose less XP!

Ironically, Mr. Max had been immune to the virus that had been specifically coded to destroy him. The aptly named *Breaker's Special Mr. Max Humiliation Virus that Will Kill the Jerkoff* could not hurt Mr. Max. Being Level ✪ ✪ meant that he no longer had experience points, and therefore could never lose them. Since he had found this fact out he had been carrying the girls everywhere against their will.

> Zal Finn III's Text Box: I'd rather walk than fall over all the time.

> Mr. Max's Text Box: Impossible! You are both Level 32 now, if you walk you will be dead in about a week!

> Hippolyta's Text Box: That doesn't matter anymore. The world is ending in a week.

> Mr. Max's Text Box: It might matter, if we can kill a Golden Poffle. You see, the Poffle family of monsters gives out more experience points than any other monster type. Killing one would probably jump you back up to about Level 40, not to mention that their rare drop is Elixirs.

> Hippolyta's Text Box: It still doesn't matter. We either need to kill at least 18 to Level goddess Yallundy up high enough to learn *Purify*, or kill every Golden Poffle everywhere to get the rare drop. Well, all of them twice to get two of the rare drop.

The once-soft-spoken-and-stunningly-beautiful-troll-who-had-died-and become-a-monster-possessing-elemental-spirit-that-could-possess-other-things-and-was-currently-possessing-her-own-body-and-controlling-it-like-a-puppet (deep breath) spoke up.

Yallundy's Text Box: There is a 1 in 255 chance for a rare drop. Getting lucky is our only chance to save you two!

Zal Finn III's Text Box: I don't even think I could kill one anymore, they are so cute. Why did they make them so cute?

Mr. Max's Text Box: They are cute because the Poffle monster type is the mascot of this game!

Zal Finn III's Text Box: They are?

Mr. Max's Text Box: Sure they are. They are hidden all over the place. Look there, on your Armour, there is one. Right where the poodle should be.

Zal Finn III's Text Box: I guess they are, but I thought the mascot was that flying cat on the box?

Hippolyta and Mr. Max both used the *Shudder Animation* at the same instant.

Mr. Max's Text Box: Don't speak of that horrid thing adventurette!

Zal Finn III's Text Box: Why not? I think it is pretty cute.

Yallundy's Text Box: I'm a dog person myself, but I think it is pretty cute, for a cat.

Mr. Max's Text Box: Sure, that is what Chad wants you to think.

Zal Finn III's Text Box: Chad? The flying cat is named Chad?

Hippolyta's Text Box: His full name is Chad the Flying Feline of Fortune.

Zal Finn III's Text Box: Aw, that is cute.

Yallundy's Text Box: Very cute.

Mr. Max's Text Box: No! He is not cute. His quest line was the most tedious, fetch-quest full, escort-mission sprinkled, trade-the-items based line of crap ever devised by mortal man. Whoever wrote the steps of that quest must be insane. It took me days to complete. Not Cycles, Days! To top it all off, the final reward was based solely on a random spin of his stupid Fickle Fortune Wheel of Fate!

> Hippolyta's Text Box: Our party took the joint win option. We spun once and all only got a stupid *Antidote* each for all that work! I'm still mad at Trev about spinning that.

> Mr. Max's Text Box: I got a hundred *Full Health Potions*.

> Hippolyta's Text Box: Really? That's amazing compared to what I got. Still not worth it.

> Mr. Max's Text Box: Not even a little.

> Hippolyta's Text Box: Chad doesn't matter to us though. The Poffles are so rare we have only seen seven so far and they all ran away. It has been three weeks and we haven't even killed one yet!

The sound of trumpets punctuated Hippolyta's sentence and she was genuinely surprised to see that she was now Level 40, as predicted.

> Gliint's Text Box: Correction. *Grin*. It has been three weeks and we have killed one!

The quickest gnome anywhere, the Chemist Gliint with the badass gnomehawk, had seen the direction the Golden Poffle had fled and successfully intercepted the creature. He looked proud of himself in his *Slick Armour* and *Too Dark Shades* before falling to the ground in a blood covered heap. Yallundy rushed to his side and started to heal him.

> Yallundy's Text Box: Gliint!

> Gliint's Text Box: *Grimace* Those cute little bastards sure hit hard.

> Yallundy's Text Box: Why didn't you stop attacking after you went into Critical Status you crazy fool?

> Gliint's Text Box: I only got hit once, like I said, those cute little bastards hit hard. I have two interesting pieces of news you might be interested in. *Grin*

First, Gliint showed off the Insta-Wiki entry, calling it interesting news #1.

> **Creature Name:** Golden Poffle
> **Class:** Poffle
> **Level:** 98
> **Special Attacks:** Piffle Poffle, Pom Pom Rub, Poffley Nubbins, Wancake, Frenzy
> **Drops:** Poffle Pelt (c), Elixir (r)
> **Special Note:** Ever wonder what the item *Creature Cage* is used for? Trapping

a Golden Poffle in one will make it call for help. This increases the spawn rate for Golden Poffles until you leave the area. This effect can stack multiple times! **First Player Encounter Notes:** *Grimace* Those cute little bastards sure hit hard. – Gliint

Mr. Max's Text Box: I knew that *Creature Cages* had to be used for something! If we can trap some we can increase the spawn rates! I wonder by how much?

Gliint's Text Box: *Shrug* No idea. But hopefully enough. You didn't let me finish, behold exhibit B or as I like to call it interesting news #2.

Holding out his prize for all to see, Gliint proudly displayed the item that had dropped from his kill. An *Elixir*, the rarest of rare items that would fully restore health, mana, and cure all negative status effects. Thanks to Breaker keeping his curse labeled as a status effect this item could cure them. One of them. They still needed one more, but it was a start.

A flash of sparkle in the bushes alerted the party to the presence of another Golden Poffle. That was exceptionally lucky as they had gone cycles without seeing one.

Mr. Max's Text Box: Here Little Bro, take this *Creature Cage* and chase that sucker down.

Yallundy's Text Box: No way. I'm not done healing him yet, and his Stamina hasn't even started to recover. He can't go running around.

Gliint's Text Box: It is okay Yallundy, *Hug* I am not going to attack this one, only catch it. I am great at catching things that aren't fish. I got all my potions back while we were in the incredibly sketchy area of the Onn Coliseum that was filled with things no one should ever have trusted or touched! I'll swig a *Large Stamina Potion* from my own reserve that had been there mysteriously and I will be good to go!

Taking a swig of the yellow potion, Gliint immediately followed it up with a loud *Sneeze Animation* which sent shivers of pleasure down everyone else's spines due to how sexy Gliint looked while doing it.

Zal Finn III's Text Box: I didn't even know that avatars could sneeze.

Mr. Max's Text Box: They can't. That is not a standard animation.

Gliint's Text Box: What? Shit! My eyes I need... No wait. I have sunglasses on? Perfect. Love it. I love it when crap like that works out.

Yallundy's Text Box: What?

Gliint's Text Box: Oh… uh I mean, what is going on? I'm totally Gliint!

Mr. Max's Text Box: You were about to go catch the Golden Poffle in the *Creature Cage* Little Bro.

Gliint's Text Box: Nah, that doesn't sound right. Catching is probably based off of strength. I'm sure you are better at it. Now be a good little Max and run along.

Mr. Max's Text Box: You're right. I bet it is Strength based. Come on girls, let's go!

Hippolyta's Text Box: No, please don't run.

Zal Finn III's Text Box: I get motion sickness!

Yallundy's Text Box: Are you feeling alright Gliint?

Gliint took another sip of his *Large Stamina Potion* while Yallundy eyed him suspiciously.

Gliint's Text Box: Trust me, I have never felt better.

◈ Chapter 6 ◈
CYCLE 1
GROUP A, LOOKING FOR
CRAZY SKIRT

Bleeding Heart's Text Box: That's all I know.

Palcath's Text Box: Thank you for your time, lass.

Bleeding Heart's Text Box: Please stop her reign of terror! I beg you!

Palcath's Text Box: We will do what we can, lass.

Bleeding Heart left the area, leaving a trail of blood behind her more than ample frame. Palcath put down his questionnaire with a *Sigh Animation*.

Lissa's Text Box: #FruitlessEndeavour.

Palcath looked over at Lissa. There she was, in all of her purple half-elf majesty, cleverly placed into Group A by Palcath with the guise of the group needing a healing/hashtag type. Little did she know that it was all part of his clever plan to make her fall in love with him. All he needed now was a grand moment that he could use to approach the topic. Palcath forgot about replying until he noticed that she was staring at him expectedly.

Palcath's Text Box: Er... I have to agree with you, lass. I thought we had been getting closer, but we are getting nowhere. Why did I celebrate with all that *Pyramid Bacon*? Every monster we interview is telling the same story. They have all been sexually molested by that crazy E. E. Lynn. Most of them multiple times.

Lissa's Text Box: Yeah, it is #SoFuckedUp. We are on a wild loon chase.

Fournimer's Text Box: how did she get to all of these monsters in so little time? Jorthan's party wasn't even here that long.

Fournimer and his *Winter Fun Scarf (s)* had been put into the 'smart person' group mainly because Palcath wanted to keep an eye on Fournimer. He had taken Anders' death the hardest and for good reason; as he had developed budding romantic feelings for the elf. Palcath wished they had found a way to fix the problem, to bring the elf back, but there was no possible way. Palcath decided to focus on the positive aspects of what Fourni was saying most of the time, and not dwell on the possibly dead boyfriend parts.

Palcath's Text Box: I like that question Fourni, and I have answers. According to the questionnaires we have accumulated, she has been here in the Island of Islana Expansion way longer than they have.

Lissa's Text Box: Strange, I thought she had snuck in with them.

Caëlahenãilenẁhei's Text Box: So did I originally, but after looking over the facts I have changed my mind on the matter. See right here? According to these monster questionnaires and testimonies she has been here much longer. I have at least one testimony, listed as being from the Terror of the Sea known as the Krakalackin', who ironically lives in the area beside the Terror Sea and not in the Terror Sea itself, that says she was here on Cycle 11. Given the low amount of monsters that we have interviewed about her, I believe that she was here even before Cycle 11, likely on Cy—

Caëlahenãilenẁhei's Text Box: cle 1.

The light elf did have a point, even if it was as long winded as usual. That is why the self appointed Rocket Sorceress was here, to be smart. Tall, pale, and flat, she might as well have been a boy in a dress except for her long platinum blond *#24 Hairstyle.* She had even designed the questionnaires without being asked to in an effort to cement her smartness.

Lissa's Text Box: So she cut her way in here as soon as it was open, to scoop our prize?

Palcath's Text Box: Honestly, Fair Maiden, given the evidence I think she cut her way in here to rape all the monsters. I really don't think that lass cared one flip about contests.

Fournimer's Text Box: she is nothing more than a sex-crazed maniac?

Caëlahenãilenẁhei's Text Box: Agreed.

Fournimer's Text Box: sex-crazed? right, that reminds me. I finished my interview with that cervitaur mid-boss I found. here is the paperwork.

Palcath's Text Box: I feel inclined to agree with you as well, but it has to be more than that. Why did the Adminilads try to kill her if she was some random sex fiend? They obviously knew her. There is more to this puzzle. I wish I knew what it was!

Lissa's Text Box: Don't feel too bad about it dwarf lad knight. You can't solve every puzzle. She is one yellow block short of an explosion after all.

Fournimer's Text Box: yeah Man, don't beat yourself up about it. we should eat dinner then go to bed.

Palcath, Caëlahenãilenẁhei, and Lissa's Simultaneous Text Boxes: Agreed.

Palcath set up his *Portie Tent* while Caela set up hers. Even though Lissa was originally allowed in the nicer tent, she had been demoted to permanently sleeping in Palcath's tent starting tonight. Palcath suspected it was due to Lissa's cute, aircraft-carrier-volume of snoring. Lissa did not argue the demonsion, Caela talked in her sleep through both of her mouths (face and crotch varieties) something awful. The chatter was so loud that it could even wake her up.

After splitting a *Grand FullCake*, which was the fanciest, plumpest, and most filling of the Bakery Shoppe items, they decided to turn in.

Lissa's Text Box: Wow. My bed and personal area is way cleaner now that it was before I left it. What happened here? Everything is all organized.

Palcath's Text Box: That samuri lad happened. He took great care of your area while you stayed in Caela's tent. He straightened it all up for you, lass. He even washed your sheets every day.

Lissa's Text Box: He washed my sheets? You can do that?

Palcath's Text Box: Yes lass, but only in Caela's *Washing Machine Ultra+*.

She let Roodg, Trev, and I wash our Armour all the time if we helped fold all her whites. Didn't you see it in her tent? You slept there for how long?

Lissa's Text Box: That was a washing machine? #TotallyClueless. I thought it was a mini-game about socks or something. I feel bad now. I left samuri's room in a total state of disaster. Hurricane Lizzy struck that place and bad! Entire families, wiped out. I hope he never sees it.

Palcath's Text Box: Our original plan isn't going to work lass and lad. We should call Roodg and head back to Onn early tomorrow and pick up more cake at the least.

Lissa's Text Box: Why? We were there two cycles ago and we have plenty of food.

Palcath used the *Grin Animation*.

Palcath's Text Box: Not food, silly. Cake!

Fournimer's Text Box: what is the difference? the cake is food. I don't want to ride that *Carrot* again! it was bad.

Lissa's Text Box: Bad as in awesome you mean. It was #HighLarious.

Fournimer's Text Box: hey! it is not my fault that the *Carrots* here were not built for centaurs. nothing in this stupid game is built for centaurs!

Lissa's Text Box: True, they have been rather mean to you. But watching you try to ride that *Carrot* was pretty funny, sorry.

Fournimer's Text Box: it was not funny!

Palcath's Text Box: It was kind of funny, Fourni. Draganders had to carry your butt the entire time so you didn't fall off.

Draganders' Text Box: Chirp!

Anders' pet rainbow dragon had adopted Fournimer as a new cuddle buddy and ear chew toy partner. Fournimer thought it was because he had such a close connection to Anders that the dragon version of Anders would naturally like him the best. Kray had thought that it was because Fournimer had the second biggest butt next to Anders and the dragon was following the chunk. Fournimer didn't like Kray.

Fournimer's Text Box: IT WAS NOT FUNNY!

Palcath's Text Box: Whoa, lad! Capital letters?

Draganders' Text Box: Chirp?

Lissa's Text Box: Sorry, Forn. Really.

Fournimer's Text Box: sorry guys. I'm so upset about things. the fact that I changed into a centaur in a world that isn't made for them. the fact that Anders got turned to ashes and I will never find him again. the fact that I broke my character and all I got was glitter and stupid kisses. the fact that centaurs can't m… uh… yeah so everything.

Palcath's Text Box: What can't centaurs do, lad? Let me know what I can do to help.

Fournimer changed to *Blush Shade #6*. Palcath used a *Puzzled Animation*.

Fournimer's Text Box: nothing. shut up.

Lissa's Text Box: What can't they do Forn? I want to know now.

Fournimer's Text Box: never mind, Lis!

Fournimer used the *Sad Cry Animation*. Both Palcath and Lissa comforted Fournimer with gentle horse scratches on his flanks. Draganders nuzzled his neck and bit his ear harder than was necessary to show that he cared.

Fournimer's Text Box: Maker! I never got to even hug Anders after I knew that I liked him.

Palcath's Text Box: We all liked Anders. He would have been good for you, lad.

Fournimer's Text Box: to top it off Max Bro somehow turned out to be straight!

Lissa's Text Box: He wouldn't have been good for you. #DisasterCentral.

Fournimer's Text Box: it makes me so sad. nothing is turning out right.

Palcath's Text Box: Look Fourni, it feels bad now, but it will get better.

Fournimer's Text Box: I don't think it ever will!

A torrent of centaur tears flooded out. Everyone huddled in silence, not knowing what to say until the tears finally slowed to a trickle.

Palcath's Text Box: Do you need me to come over, Fourni?

Fournimer used the *Wipe Your Nose on Your Sleeve Animation,* even though he had no sleeves.

> Fournimer's Text Box: it is okay now, I think.

> Palcath's Text Box: Good lad! It probably would have made later Chapters awkward if we were playing in the same room.

> Fournimer's Text Box: you're telling me!

They hugged it out. Hugging it out always solves everything.

> Lissa's Text Box: I'm glad that is settled. Okay, tell us why we need more cake. I've been waiting to know! #InquiringMinds.

> Palcath's Text Box: Not now, lass. Wait for the dramatic reveal!

> Lissa's Text Box: Come on! Don't bring up something like that and then not explain it until later!

◈ Chapter 7 ◈

CYCLE 1: EVENING N, CHILLIN' WITH NI HAO BUNNY©

Ni Hao Bunny©'s Text Box: First of all, I need to say, that was brilliant! Great job.

He didn't really know how to talk to a two-dimensional cut-out cartoon character, but n had talked to some strange things in the past. A cartoon bunny was hardly a stretch, all things considered.

n's Text Box: Thank you. That means a lot coming from... you... wait... what was?

Ni Hao Bunny©'s Text Box: Ha! He is modest now? As if he didn't know. Everything you did was brilliant! I would like to thank you personally for pretty much all of it. Most importantly, I would like to thank you for getting rid of that Code Monkey Breaker. He was telling anyone who would listen that he was on a mission from the Maker. As if. I also want to congratulate you on having the unbelievable good sense to log out before the Administrator's Ultra-Kill Lightning finished you off. It was genius to save a portion of yourself! Even if it was just a tiny one. How did you know that would work?

n's Text Box: But I didn't do that! Well, I did kill Breaker, but I didn't log out or anything. I thought I was Dead Dead!

Ni Hao Bunny©'s Text Box: Huh? Strange, how did that work…? You must have gotten a fortunate server drop or something. That doesn't really matter right now. The important thing is that you are alive and that the Administrators have no idea that you are still kicking. They think that they killed you, so they are not spying on you anymore!

n's Text Box: The Administrators were spying on me?

If n could change to a *Blush Shade*, he would have.

Ni Hao Bunny©'s Text Box: Of course they were! They were spying on everyone who was in the Expansion.

n's Text Box: How do you know that?

Ni Hao Bunny©'s Text Box: Simple my boy, I was spying on all of them spying on all of you!

n's Text Box: Really? You are a spy spying on spies? Why?

Ni Hao Bunny©'s Text Box: I think it might be time for me to spout some exposition here.

The Administrators lied to all of you, the only thing broken about them is their fat heads. Everything else they told you was a lie. A way for you to do their dirty work for them no doubt. All they wanted was to find that untraceable Breaker and recruit him to fix the Code.

We already had someone that could do that, but those idiots fired our best programmer. Yes, okay, I admit it, that programmer did sort of add a secret dimension to this game behind our backs. They did cause all these problems in the first place by adding all the sex and rape and powers, but it was really well hidden. It wouldn't have ever been discovered if the Administrators themselves hadn't found the secret window by messing with the Code to put those stupid symbols on their robes. They are the reason that the game became broken. They activated sexy mode for everyone in the game and couldn't turn it off. Now they are trying to hide their mistakes by covering up everything. As if I wouldn't notice.

They are all going about it the entire wrong way. They are going to reset everything and hope that the hidden Code they unleashed will disappear. The thing is, they already know it will not fix diddly squat. They are going to kill everything everywhere for no reason. They have gone mad with power. Honestly, I always pick the worst time to go on vacation.

n was shocked, this bunny's Text Boxes were huge! That wasn't the only reason to be shocked, but it was certainly in the top two.

n's Text Box: They are going to kill everyone? I have to warn my friends!

Ni Hao Bunny©'s Text Box: No! They already know, and besides you can't tell anyone you are alive. If you show up then the Administrators will know you are not dead. We will lose our element of surprise and our plan will be ruined. Only our plan can save the world. That means saving all of your friends as well.

n's Text Box: Our plan?

Ni Hao Bunny©'s Text Box: Actually, it is my plan, but you are a big part of it. The most important part of it. Pretty much all of it. In fact, if I am going to be honest you are the only part. You did give me the idea, you can be proud of that.
We don't have a lot of time. The Administrators have set the reset on the Expansion. It will be gone in 7 cycles. The main map requires more time, but not much. It will be gone in 10. I don't know where you got that purple *Optional Potion* from, I wasn't watching you then. We are going to need six of those *Optional Potions* for this to work. Breaker had set himself to have Administrative Hit Points, and that little potion cut through them like nothing else ever could. I didn't even know that was possible.

n's Text Box: I got it from the Optional Boss, The Dryad.

The bunny did a cute non-standard Animation that didn't even have a proper name.

Ni Hao Bunny©'s Text Box: That makes perfect sense. Great, I will give you a list of all the Optional Bosses. Go get some potions from them. I will grant you the power to access the GameFrame to skip around to different important areas of the maps. That will save you a bunch of time.
Once you get the potions come back and see me, then we can set the next part of the plan into action. I know that for dramatic purposes I shouldn't tell you what it is, but I honestly don't care and you probably already figured it out anyway. With the potions you will be able to kill the Administrator's avatars. Without them here, the worlds will not be reset. Then we can try to fix the world normally, without killing everyone's avatars. I would even be able to stop the lawsuit against us, I have a plan for that as well you see. Without getting rid of those power hungry Admins we don't stand a chance. Time is of the essence and

we must do this quickly.

Here is the interesting part! I have great news. You, my friend are accidentally special. You might be a single pixel right now, but since you have unlocked that ability called *Absorb* you will 'borrow' some Polygons from anything you defeat. If you kill enough things you should be back in tip top fighting shape in no time. We need you to be able to charge up an attack with that bow of yours and damage the Admins. You will also need a bow I guess. Look for one.

n's Text Box: That is really great and everything, but why should I trust you? You were spying on us. After what happened last time I am a bit apprehensive about blindly helping someone again.

Ni Hao Bunny©'s Text Box: Now to be fair I was spying on those that were spying on you. I was only indirectly spying on you. I guess I didn't think about that, why would you trust me at all? Hmm... Well how about the fact that you are a nice person and I really need your help because no one else can do it?

n's Text Box: I am nice aren't I? But I am not going to be fooled by a Secret Mystical All-Knowing and Mysterious Person again so easily. Even if this one does seem to know everything. Unlike the last lot.

Ni Hao Bunny©'s Text Box: How about for fabulous prizes then?

n's Text Box: Not going to fly, the Administrators already tried that trick and I didn't get anything but blasted.

Ni Hao Bunny©'s Text Box: They were lying to you remember? I am not. Here, I will give you a fabulous prize right now. Only employees get these.

With a wave of two-dimensional bunny hands, a *Flexi-Pass* had been added to n's play account. He would never need to pay to play Annals of Gentalia again. It was a lifetime free account.

n's Text Box: Wow, really?

Ni Hao Bunny©'s Text Box: Pretty good right? How is that for an incentive to save the world?

n's Text Box: It is useless if I don't help you. It is almost too perfect, but I have still decided to help you. I am really doing it to save my friends and this game. Helping you and getting revenge on my killers are only side benefits.

Ni Hao Bunny©'s Text Box: That's good enough for me. Here is your list of Optional Bosses and a *GameFramer Key Card*. Some of the ones in the Island of Islana Expansion are worthless to you, and they require you to be a certain class to find and complicated puzzles. You know what those were like and I doubt you want to go through any more Coliseums.

n shuddered at the thought. He took the list (somehow), waved goodbye for now to the cartoon bunny and headed towards his next adventure. It was only after n ported out of the area that he remembered he hadn't asked how in the Flaming Pit he talked to a cartoon bunny from a different franchise.

Chapter 8
CYCLE 2
GROUP D GOES
KRAY-KRAY

> Kray's Text Box: Kay, you have to agree that there is something different about me! It is wonderful and everything else all wrapped into one.

> samuri's Text Box: …

samuri used the *Nod Animation*. There was something different about Kray. For the first time ever the avatar was not clashing as bad. Sure, the green *Slime Armour* clashed with Kray's red hair but only having one clashing feature was by far a record for Kray. samuri wasn't sure how Kray had managed to get by the Anderses Only aspect of that outfit but he was really hoping that it was because Kray had looked through some items last night and found something. Sure, samuri would never equip anything from Breaker's personal hoard, but he was different from Kray. He was smart.

> Kray's Text Box: I got all this stuff on by being really smart you know. Kay, it was a pretty good thing that I thought up. Do you want to hear about it?

> samuri's Text Box: …

samuri used the *Nod Animation* again. He was interested in what had happened. For the first time in recorded gaming history, someone wanted to hear what Kray was going to say. That was two yeses to Kray in as many rounds. samuri was a little on edge. That was definitely more than anyone had ever agreed with Kray. If Kray managed to stay agreeable and helpful that would be such a great boon in the upcoming days. It was as if a weight had been lifted from samuri's shoulders. Now that he thought about it his shoulders did feel lighter.

> Kray's Text Box: I thought so! Some magical pants told me I was cool, and then I did stuff. Kay, now onto the important thing. This Armour is all goopy. It is like the best Armour ever. Now I can be so great and slimey! As soon as I figure it out of course. I am going to spend all my time figuring it out for you Sami-guy. On our wedding night you are in for a treat.

> samuri's Text Box: ...

samuri used the *Headshake Animation* again.

There went Kray being useful, but at least the avatar would stay out of the way while poking and prodding himself in the corner. Turning his attention to more important matters, samuri focused on the *Grandiose Gauntlet* mounted on a spare leg before him. The *Item Description Menu Box*, and the two beside it that he taught his friendly pets how to investigate for him, proved as pointless as the last. With a calm sense of responsibility, samuri swung his sword and all three were split asunder.

> Kray's Text Box: So I tried squishing some slime against there but that didn't do anything, kay. Maybe if I insert some it will make me better than Anders?

> samuri's Text Box: ...

samuri used the *Headshake Animation* again. Kray was obviously blind to the fact that Anders' power had clearly involved Anders. Kray had his own, different powers. No matter what Kray did with that Armour it wasn't going to do anything above and beyond the normal range of being Armour that looked goopy.

> Kray's Text Box: How much longer are you going to be doing this? There are so many more items and I want to pick out appetizers with you, kay.

> samuri's Text Box: ...

samuri used the *Sweeping Arm Animation* directed at the entire room. Then stepped towards a *Flaming Finkstone of Flamp* and watched it intently.

> Kray's Text Box: Kay, so like what five minutes?

> samuri's Text Box: ...

samuri used the *Ignore Animation* and concentrated on the mass of *Flamp* suspended in the air. The *Flamp* was for increasing your *Hit-DOT Per Round Ratio*, nothing more.

It and a pair of *Semi-Mystical Oaken Staffs* were not useful at all and he sliced them into pixels. That did it for this wall so at least progress had been made. The pets' additional eyepower helped move things along. He might get this done before the world ended after all.

Kray used the *Sneeze Animation.*

> samuri's Text Box: ...

samuri used the *Nod Animation.* At this point it was easier to agree with Kray. It wasn't like Kray listened anyway so what harm could it do. It made no difference long term if he had agreed to *Stuffed Bacon Puffs* or *Clams à la Mode* as an appetizer at the wedding. It was not important, and he had decided long ago that he was going to skip town the cycle of the wedding.

The next wall to search would be the one with the charred corpse of the Legendary 13 Headed Hydra. It was samuri's least favorite wall to look at and contained few items. He wanted it to be over with.

> samuri's Text Box: ...

samuri used the *Headshake Animation.* Sure it didn't matter, but he was not going to give in and let Kray always have his way. He would stand up and disagree this time about whatever Kray had yammered on about. Possibly something about the colours for the wedding, Kray likely picked unicorn vomit and taupe as the official colours. samuri looked at the *Large Health Potion* on the wall. Hiding effects in potions was one of Breaker's favorite tricks and samuri hoped that this next one would hold the key.

> samuri's Text Box: ...

samuri used the *Nod Animation.* Kray would be getting his way this time. Two victories and only one loss would keep Kray happily out of the way no doubt. The *Large Health Potion* on the stand provided the drinker with permanent *Otter Vision.* It was cut down like all the rest. samuri turned to the adjacent items that the pets had been staring at but the pets were gone. Where did they go?

> samuri's Text Box: ...

samuri used the *Listen Animation* and waited. He heard nothing. This was the longest Kray had gone without talking, ever. The hair stood up on the back of his neck, which was odd because he had a ponytail and it shouldn't be able to do that (at least he thought that he had one).

> samuri's Text Box: ???

samuri used the *Uneasy Animation* and waited. The silence continued. The Battle Log revealed that Kray hadn't talked for over twenty rounds. Something was definitely amiss. It had even grown darker and The Gray Quest Fairy had vanished. That was it, something was off. samuri turned around.

> samuri's Text Box: !!!

samuri used the *Jaw Drop Animation*, his massive tongue poured out of his mouth and onto the floor. There was Kray, glowing with a wretched black aura and smiling at him with a smug expression. His eyes, now completely black, moved around frantically but the rest of his body was suspended in the air, motionles. The All Seeing Eye Dog and the Nine Circles of Hellcat had stepped between the pair and were snarling at Kray.

> Kray's Text Box: Hello warrier, been a long time hasn't it?

> samuri's Text Box: ...

With a Mincing Out of His Arms and a Dramatic Flourish of His Hands Animation, Kray summoned forth a wave of black outlined rainbow lightning and blew away a large section of the wall. Half of the *Legendary 13 Headed Hydra* had been incinerated in the process. samuri had sworn to never hurt another avatar but for this one he would make an exception.

> Kray's Text Box: Crap. I forgot to adjust for the stupid gay rainbows again. Next one is coming for your head!

samuri raised his *Katana-Nata* and faced what was not really Kray.

> Kray's Text Box: Oh, is itty-bitty warrier going to kill me? I'm so not scared.

Lunging forward, Kray unsheathed his *Bone Sword* and with a single swipe had cut samuri deeply through the left forearm. Blood spurted from the gash, and samuri winced with pain. The *Bone Sword* Kray was yielding had been PVP broken and was now headed straight for samuri's head. With the skill of a samurai warrior, samuri raised his two handed *Katana-Nata* to deflect the blow.

The sound of cold steel rang out as the weapons collided and shattered due to their mutial Player Versus Player brokeness. The *Katana-Nata* had a better name than the *Bone Sword* and did not blink away into nothingness. The shards of the gray blade spun in slow motion while samuri and Kray could do nothing but watch. A blur of blade passed close by, removing from Kray the tip of one ear and most of his nose. The shards' path of destruction cut samuri's facial hair off at a crooked angle and the largest piece embedded itself into samuri's right eye.

Kray and samuri stared at each other for a round, too shocked to act. The severed pieces fell to the floor. The ear was sniffed by the All Seeing Eye Dog and the nose by the Nine Circles of Hellcat. The heavenly scent of burnt-elf-husk face jerky filled their nostrils and they eagerly wolfed and panthered them down respectively. Both pets were unsatisfied but knew where they could get more and eyed Kray hungrily. Face meat, their favourite treat.

> Kray's Text Box: No! Get back! Stay away from me!

Kray attempted to defend himself with a burst of black-outlined rainbow lightning but the spell went off too late. Kray was pulled to the floor by the hungry pets as deadly rainbows struck the ceiling. Broken pieces fell upon samuri, and with his one remaining eye he watched large chunks of flesh being ripped from Kray's body. The pets had not stopped at simply a face snack. They were going to eat the delicious jerky-elf's flesh completely.

There was no time to run. The ceiling of the Coliseum was falling down upon him. samuri had time to do one more thing, and nobly he picked telling the group what had happened. He opened group chat and Text Boxed an ominous warning to the rest, at or least he tried to.

> samuri's Group Chat Text Box: I know I don't talk much, but I had to say this… I really love scented candles.

samuri *Scowl Animationed* at the words he didn't write. Then everything went black.

Chapter 9

CYCLE 2
GROUP C GETS
CANDLE HACKED

> **Trev Terra's Text Box:** Before we go to the next area can I ask ... well, I mean, rather, can I talk at you. No. Talk about something, I mean?

Roodg was intrigued. Trev Terra had never once talked during their morning walks, a tradition that they had kept up even if Roodg no longer wanted to catch Trev in a morning jack-off session. Perhaps it was due to the later hour. Roodg had been forced to get up early and ferry Team B back to Onn. It had something to do with cake. Roodg hadn't paid enough attention during the flight to understand much of the plan even if Palcath had told Roodg every single step of it.

> **Roodg's Text Box:** yES, OF COURSE.

> **Trev Terra's Text Box:** Well I wanted to ask... I mean to tell you. I wanted to tell you, if it was alright with you of course... well, even if it isn't I think, I mean if that is alright with you. If maybe you could maybe not... this is hard, gosh. What I wanted to ask, no to tell, well, ask maybe. Can you please, is it okay if I ask? I want to, but...

> **Roodg's Text Box:** oKAY. dON'T HURT YOURSELF Trev Terra. i WANT YOU TO TAKE A DEEP BREATH.

> **Trev Terra's Text Box:** But...

Roodg's Text Box: dO IT!

Trev Terra used the *Deep Breath Animation*. He did a few more for good measure.

Roodg's Text Box: k. nOW i WANT YOU TO TAKE A FEW ROUNDS AND THINK ABOUT WHAT YOU WANT TO tEXT bOX. wHEN YOU ARE READY, ASK IT.

Trev Terra took a few more deep breaths, cleared his mind, and after thinking up exactly what he wanted to Text Box, did.

Trev Terra's Text Box: Stop flirting with my boyfriend! I am his petit lutin not you!

Roodg used the *Blink Three Times Animation*. Trev was furious, but Roodg could only laugh.

Roodg's Text Box: i'M NOT FLIRTING WITH HIM. iN CASE YOU DIDN'T NOTICE HE IS FLIRTING WITH ME. nOT JUST ME EITHER. eVERYONE HE CAN SEE. hE IS A NON STOP FLIRTING MACHINE. hE FLIRTS WITH ME, SO MUCH WITH Caëlahenâilenŵhei, AND Gliint, Yallundy, De'vini, In'ferni, Hippolyta, AND HE HALF-FLIRTED WITH Lissa. fLAMING pITS HE EVEN FLIRTS WITH Kray AND HIS OWN RELFECTION!

Trev Terra's Text Box: Even with Anders…

Roodg's Text Box: dON'T WORRY. i DON'T REALLY LIKE PEOPLE ALREADY IN RELATIONSHIPS UNLESS WE NEED TO FUCK TO SAVE THE WORLD. LoL. tHAT IS PROBABLY THE ONLY THING i DON'T LIKE.

Trev Terra's Text Box: What do I do then…? Rather, I don't know what to do.

Roodg's Text Box: fIRST COME HERE.

Grabbing Trev in a friendly embrace Roodg executed a *Hug Dual Animation*. This made Trev change to *Blush Shade #6* (he was already at #5) and feel better.

Roodg's Text Box: nEXT, U NEED TO TALK TO HIM. lOOK, OUR NEXT STOP IS sPIRE a'S fLAMING fOREST. tHE TWINS NEED TO GO FIRST, TAKE THAT TIME TO TALK TO HIM. i KNOW YOU CAN DO IT.

Trev Terra's Text Box: Thank you. A lot I mean.

They continued on their walk and on their return they were surprised to see someone had joined their group for breakfast. Sitting with his legs kicked up in Trev Terra's chair was Gliint. He took a big swig of a *Medium Mana Potion*, drinking it like it was a cup of coffee to accompany his breakfast.

> Roodg's Text Box: Gliint? wHAT ARE U DOING HERE?

> Gliint's Text Box: Oh, I was in the area and thought I would drop in for breakfast.

> Roodg's Text Box: iN THE AREA? wE ARE IN THE MIDDLE OF THE OCEAN ON A DESERTED dESSERTED iSLAND!

> Gliint's Text Box: I'm really fast, this is in the area. Oh, before I forget, my group found this necklace, a Bell Charm. We really don't need it, but I know that there is a real lack of neck type Accessories, so I thought I would give it to someone here. I was thinking that the tro—

> In'ferni and De'vini's Simultaneous Interruption Text Boxes: Oh that is her neck. Yes, it is me, I have a really bad one. Hey, I have a *Bell Charm* already, if you wear one then we can match even more! Oh really? Yes! Please, can I have it guys?

> Jorthan the Male Troll Monk's Text Box: Of course, no problem. She would be most useful to her. Putting it on, go ahead.

> Gliint's Text Box: Not exactly who I was going for, but it will do. Here… whichever one of you kissing girls wanted it, take it.

> In'ferni and De'vini's Simultaneous Text Boxes: Why thank you it is lovely. Wow, that is so pretty on you! Aw, thank you! No problem, let's make out! Yes!

In'ferni and De'vini used the *Kiss With Bell Charms On Dual Animation.*

> Gliint's Text Box: It is time for me to go. I have other Groups to visit.

Without even waiting for others to say goodbye, Gliint was off like a flash, running so fast that he was literally skipping on top of the water. The group looked to Jorthan for leadership—he was leading the group after all.

> Jorthan the Male Troll Monk's Text Box: For a long time amount, I was here in the précedént roman. Just une toute petite place to examine. De bonbons au maïs had to be examine by witchery. The kind of witchery she is summoning.

The team made their way over to a circle of candy corn, in the center was a knee-high glowing pyramid of stone. It was the only thing on the island (minus the elf-spunk lake) that was not made of candy or dessert. It was awe inspiring, but the grand majesty didn't last.

De'vini used the *Sneeze Animation.*

> Trev Terra's Text Box: Bless you.

> Jorthan the Male Troll Monk's Text Box: Okay Summoner. I already have done the puzzle. Casting of the spell Invocation: Esprit du vent!

> In'ferni and De'vini's Simultaneous Text Boxes: Go Summoner! Which of us is the Summoner, is that you? Giggle, you are the Summoner silly. Crap, what is he saying, can't that idiot speak in English? What? English, I will say this slowly so you understand, speak English! Well yeah, Jorthan is trying to, you know that. What spell did he say to use? How should I know, you were the one in French Immersion. Repeat that spell name, trolly. What is wrong with you? Nothing! You are teaching Jorthan English for Maker's sake, even your French is better than his! Screw this. Huh?

De'vini used the *Sneeze Animation.*

> Trev Terra's Text Box: Bless you.

There was silence for a good many rounds. No one really knew what to say. There were a lot of exchanged looks.

> In'ferni and De'vini's Simultaneous Text Boxes: Why is everyone standing around, what is going on? I don't think we are on speaking terms right now. What, are you serious? Yes I am, you are being so mean! I am? Yes, look at this Battle Log! Wow, I am being mean. The meanest! I am so sorry I don't remember doing that. The sorriest? More than that, maybe I am not feeling well. Yeah, I think you might be. Should we contact an Admin or something? No, they will melt us! Good point. Cast that spell and we will take a break together okay? Sure, I would like that, what spell?

> Roodg's Text Box: uH... Jorthan? tHE BOYS ARE KISSING AGAIN... uH, i THINK, iNVOCATION OF THE sPIRIT OF vENTS? sORRY. i ONLY SPEAK CEREAL BOX fRENCH.

> In'ferni and De'vini's Simultaneous Text Boxes: That was pretty close Roodg, I see it in the log. What was it really? *Summon Wind Spirit*, let me cast it. That was better than what I thought it was. I need to clear my head. Then we should go for a walk after this. Oh, we can pick up

sandwiches for everyone! I'd really like that. I love you so much. Hugs, I love you too!

The angelic twin cast her Summoning spell: *Summon Wind Spirit*. A visage of yellow something, (possibly a land squid? it was too fast to make sense of) appeared and tapped the flashing pyramid. Roodg watched it take to the air, rotating slowly. Several rounds passed while both the rotation and flashing increased.

The pyramid transformed into a cube. Once the flashing stopped it became apparent what it was, a golden chest, that floated peacefully and spinningly to the ground. Inside was a *Golden Tin Whistle*, which Roodg pocketed. The golden chest then transformed again into a giant purple-leafed tree. Majestic and magical power radiated from the tree but it didn't seem to do anything besides look interesting.

Roodg's Text Box: nEAT!

Landing Tree's Text Box: You can only use the *Golden Tin Whistle* after completing the Quest Through the Mist.

Roodg's Text Box: tHAT IS SAWESOME! wHERE IS THAT QUEST Herbert? ... Herbert?

Herbert's Text Box: Sorry, something has... something has come up and I need to go.

Roodg's Text Box: hUH?

Herbert's Text Box: I don't want to go, unlike everyone else, but I think I have to. I need to convince them not to do this.

Other Yellow Quest Fairy's Text Box: Dépêchez-vous. Nous devons aller rencontrer les autres fées pour forger un plan pour éliminer tous les joueurs qui sont stupides.

Other Purple Quest Fairy and Other Orange Quest Fairy' Simultaneous Text Box: Yeah, we need to go already. Why are you even talking to it? Hurry up. Yeah, hurry up.

Other Blue Quest Fairy's Text Box: Hurry up, or we are totally going to have to leave you behind. It would be square of us I know, but that is how it is.

Herbert's Text Box: Sorry, I'll be back once everything is alright. I promise.

With that, the Red Quest Fairy gave Roodg a kiss on the nose and flew off with her hippy, French, or twin brethren. The only avatar to notice their departure was Roodg, who waited quietly until lunch when the kissing couples finally broke from their embraces. No one had noticed the *Golden Tin Whistle* that Roodg had pocketed earlier, so Roodg didn't bring up either subject during their meal.

Jorthan decided that after lunch they would move onto the next area, since the purple tree was useless. The next area alphabetically was the Flaming Forest in Spire A.

> In'ferni and De'vini's Simultaneous Text Box: Here is the location of the Flaming Forest. We were stuck there so long I'm not sure I even want to go back. Me either! Well at least I will have you, that makes me feel better. That is so nice, we should go so we can kiss when we get there. Yeah, why haven't we left yet? I want to kiss! So do I!

> Roodg's Text Box: wE HAVE NOT LEFT YET AND ALREADY YOU ARE KISSING! a NEW RECORD!

When there was no response for several rounds except for the sounds of making out, Roodg used the *Eyeroll Animation*. Another trip with nothing but kissing twin girls for entertainment. Not that kissing twin girls didn't hold a special place in Roodg's heart, but without the ability to join in, the novelty had started to wear out.

Roodg used the *Sigh Animation* and took off flying. Now that Hubert had flown away there wasn't going to be anyone to talk to. This was going to be another uneventful trip and another uneventful cycle.

Then it wasn't.

Beside the girls a startled Nine Circles of Hellcat and a terrified All Seeing Eye Dog popped into exsistance. The animals attempted to latch onto the *Magical Flying Carrot Ultra+*, sending it into a tailspin. Despite their best efforts, the pets had no success hanging on and plummeted to the ocean below. Roodg only stopped the tailspin through expert *Carrot* control skills but now they were flying upside down and in the wrong direction. It was startling enough to stop the twins making out, for now. From here it was too high to even see the pets splash as they hit the water far below.

> Roodg's Text Box: i CHANGED MY MIND. tHIS TRIP IS INTERESTING NOW. wHAT HAPPENED?

> In'ferni and De'vini's Simultaneous Text Box: They must have died somewhere. Yes, they respawn beside us when they die. Something must have happened to them. Of course something happened, they died. They didn't die again, they are alive in the ocean. True, or they would have respawned again. I guess they can swim.

> Roodg's Text Box: sOMETHING HAPPENED IN oNN THEN. cHECK THE GROUP CHAT, i'M GUNNA TURN THIS AROUND

AND GO TO oNN. oH WAIT. wE DID TURN AROUND, LoL. i'LL GET US RIGHT SIDE UP AGAIN.

In'ferni and De'vini's Simultaneous Text Box: The only thing in here is something about samuri liking scented candles. That is pretty strange. We should ask about that! About candles? No about what happened in Onn! Good idea.

In'ferni and De'vini's Simultaneous Group Chat Text Box: I think that scented candles are great to enjoy in the bath, while relaxing at home, or anywhere else that you can take candles on the go. I love all the different kinds of scents you can get, personally my favorite is sandalwood. Why are scented candles so great? They are the perfect accent to anything! Additional candle statement.

Roodg's Text Box: wHAT IS WRONG WITH YOU? wHY ARE YOU TWO TALKING ABOUT CANDLES?

In'ferni and De'vini's Simultaneous Text Box: It is scented candles but we are not typing that, I asked samuri what was going on in Onn. Yeah, then I said we would be right there. Then I said what the fuck is going on why are we talking about scented candles. Then I typed in a bunch of gibberish.

Roodg's Text Box: sO STRANGE. iT WORKED THIS MORNING. lET ME TRY.

Roodg's Group Chat Text Box: i LOVE CAPS LOCK AND CANDLES! i WISH CAPS LOCK WAS A KIND OF SCENTED CANDLE.

Roodg's Text Box: lAME. i WAS HOPING THAT WOULD BE IN LOWERCASE OR SOMETHING TO TIP PEOPLE OFF. wHOEVER CANDLE HACKED OUR GROUP CHAT DID THEIR HOMEWORK.

De'vini used the *Sneeze Animation.*

In'ferni and De'vini's Simultaneous Text Box: We need to hurry to Onn! … Huh? … Are you okay? … De'vini? … Say something!

De'vini's Text Box: I think this is far enough.

In'ferni's Text Box: What? How are you speaking alone? Hey! How am

I speaking alone?

Roodg's Text Box: OH, THIS IS GOING TO BE BAD, i CAN TELL.

De'vini's Text Box: I am getting really tired of all this walking and this little toy of yours is exactly what I need.

In'ferni's Text Box: Look out! She can't control herself anymore. It is someone else!

De'vini's Text Box: How do you know that?

In'ferni's Text Box: She is sitting beside me!

De'vini's Text Box: Fuck, I didn't know that. Well, do me a favour and turn off your monitor.

Roodg's Text Box: tHIS IS QUICKLY GETTING WORSE.

De'vini's Text Box: It is going to get a lot worse, trust me. Sorry, but I am afraid I am going to have to confiscate this *Carrot* guy... girl... whatever the fuck you are. Wait, no I remember now, the caps lock hermaphrodite Code user. Look, it is nothing personal or anything but... okay, it is a little personal. Sucks to be you girl-boy-caps mix-up thing.

De'vini grew a set of wicked black fingernails and thrust them into the *Magical Flying Carrot Ultra+*. It pulsed with energy and it began to transform. When the vile thing was finally done its revolting alteration process it was the *Magical Flying Parsnip Ultra+*. White and pulsing with broken energy, Roodg could no longer control it.

De'vini's Text Box: This is going far smoother than last time. Those two losers are going to be stuck on Desserted Island until they die and you two are going to plummet to your death and drown in that mist-covered water when I flip this *Parsnip* over.

In'ferni's Text Box: We are attached together by the lips genius. I am not going to fall to my death unless you do.

De'vini's Text Box: Are you serious? Attached? Oh fuck, we are. I should have stuck to my guns. Stupid plans. Well, live and learn I guess. Am I right? Oh, I will think of something else for you. At least I can still kill this caps lock gender confused idiot. I've hated... it for much longer anyways. I don't even really know you.

> Roodg's Text Box: i'M ATTACHED TO YOU AS WELL? aT THE FOOT! dON'T EVEN BOTHER TO TRY.

> De'vini's Text Box: Nice try but no dice there buddy. Have a nice plummet to your death!

A violent 3240° turn was all it took to dislodge Roodg's death grip on the possessed *Magical Flying Parsnip Ultra+*. Roodg began the massive plummet to the mist-covered ocean below. All that the night elf could do was add another scented candle comment to the group chat.

> Roodg's Group Chat Text Box: lILAC IS CLEARLY THE BETTER CHOICE OF SCENTED CANDLE.

> In'ferni's Text Box: No Roodg!

> De'vini's Text Box: Aw, too bad. The mist is going to prevent us from seeing the death spiral.

> In'ferni's Text Box: You monster!

In'ferni used the non dual *Faceslap Animation*. De'vini used the non dual *Rub Cheek Animation*.

> De'vini's Text Box: Okay, we are going to have to do something about you. You got the devil in you, literally! … Because you have devil wings and stuff? No laughing? Ah, screw you. That's funny.

> In'ferni's Group Chat Text Box: Sandalwood is better, you need to get your nose checked. When it comes to scented candles always choose sandalwood.

> De'vini's Text Box: Try calling for help in that group chat of yours all you want devil dear. I hacked it and good. All you are going to do is spout random scented candle nonsense. With the people you hang out with, it is the perfect plan. They probably all talk about scented candles exclusively already. I'm so smart.

> In'ferni's Text Box: I honestly have never talked about scented candles before.

> De'vini's Text Box: Shut up, no one asked you. We have some avatars to collect and some places to go. *Parsnip* away!

◈ Chapter 10 ◈

CYCLE 2: MORNING N, POLYGON HUNTER

n didn't even look at his new Optional Boss list, because he knew exactly where he was going. He ported in through the GameFrame to the middle of that old starting city whose name no one could remember. Not that the name mattered anymore since it was a smoldering crater in the ground devoid of all life. The world map now only showed the letter C—the rest had been burnt off, which was strangely fitting.

n was startled by the devastation. While they had been away on the Island of Islana the main map had turned into an absolute dump. Even the starting areas had minimal activity, and they had always been so full of avatars you could hardly find a Start Rat to shoot. Even now, without avatars killing them at every turn, there weren't a lot of Start Rats here. There wasn't a lot of scenery, colour, grass or anything else either. It was bleak, dark, and more than a little bit depressing.

Walking with his movement speed set to a brisk pace he headed towards his goal: The Stairway to the Clouds. It would lead him to the Castle in the Sky and finally to his destination, The Dryad. If n was going to glean six *Optional Flowers* to make six *Optional Potions*, he was going to go to The Dryad's Glade. Seeing his old friend would be nice, and he was certain that collecting the potions would be exceptionally rewarding there. He was even planning on getting all six in one place, with maybe a quick break for a sandwich.

He stopped dead mid Brisk Pace Step near the base of The Stairway to the Clouds. He was shocked. It was gone. Fragments of melted clouds dotted the surrounding area, but there was no longer a stairway. There was no way to get up to the Castle in the Sky now. This trip had been a complete waste of time. n had to look at the Optional Boss list to decide what to do.

The Optional Boss List - All Rights Reserved

Main Map Optional Bosses	Map Location	Look Here
Elfbane	Karazhahanana	The Summoning Circle
Flork Omega	The Crags of Halm	Crag #112
Giganticore	Giganticore's Lair	The Giganticore's Heart
Primary Weapon	The Underwater But Overland Desert	The Exact Centre
The Armour Knight	Mechanical Mecha Factory	Smelting Room
The Dryad	The Castle in the Sky	The Dryad's Grove
Vam-Boy & Lyca-Guy	Stairway Forest	Magical Castle in the Woods

Island of Islana Optional Bosses	Map Location	Look Here
Cruel-X, The Dark Lord of Snatch	Onn	The Ring - Healing Magic Only
New Boss +	Onn	The Arena - Melee Only
Smoke The Reptile	Saibot's Tower	The Noob's Pit
Super Puzzle Boss	Onn	The Stadium - Attack Magic Only
The Avenger	Onn	The Throne Room
The Bull King	The Flaming Pits	Circle 8, Milking Field
The Legendary 13 Headed Hydra	Onn	The Coliseum - Ranged Only

That was a lot of Optional Bosses. n could rule out four of the Island of Islana bosses. Either due to the class requirements, or the fact that the monster was pinned to the wall and likely not feeling sexy right now. He could also, unfortunately, rule out the Dryad. That left nine Optional Bosses around the maps to look for.

n saw something interesting. North of his current location on his Micro-Mini Map was the Stairway Forest. That wasn't remotely interesting by itself; the place was dark and broody for no good reason. What was interesting was the fact that there was an Optional Boss there—an Optional Boss with an ampersand in the name. That meant there was a chance that there were two Optional Bosses at the same location. Two

Optional Bosses at once could mean two *Optional Flowers* at once. That was something to check out. The fact that the entrance to the Stairway Forest was right in front of him didn't hurt either. Perhaps this wouldn't be a wasted trip after all. Both of those Optional Bosses even had male sounding names, which was a plus for him.

n made a decision. They would be the Optional Bosses to check out first. Carefully ducking into the dungeon door, the Optional Boss hunter started his quest.

Suddenly, the forest was upon him. It was so sudden that n was genuinely confused. He didn't know how the Stairway Forest had managed such a feat, especially since he was the one who entered it, but he advanced cautiously now. Every monster here ignored him and n decided that it was likely that none of them could see his pixel. That was good. He didn't have any way of dealing with their attacks that he knew of.

He had never been in the Stairway Forest before, so his Micro-Mini Map showed nothing but the entrance. He was going to be forced to explore this dark, dreary, and constantly raining forest. Those were the descriptors the Micro-Mini Map had provided him at least. Despite what had been promised to him, the constant rain stopped, which was somewhat disappointing. He could feel the rain hitting him and when it stopped it made him miserable. Without the rain to improve his mood, he could only explore amongst the five colours of rocks.

He travelled up the mountain as best as he could, mostly because he was certain that, if there was going to be a castle, it would be at the top. He took great care not to trip on the many pieces of scenery and cursed his protagonist clumsiness when he did. If he could have changed his *Blush Shade* at that moment, he would have.

It started raining again as n turned the corner, and there his destination stood before him but far in the distance. A marvelous and pristine white castle, not at all splotched with mud. He hurried, pace quickening, as he walked towards the castle. He reached it as the constant rain stopped.

The castle door opened. n cleaned off his nothings on the white welcome mat and looked around. Everything was white and gleaming, pristine and clean. The walls, ceilings, plush carpets, furniture, and even the particle effects in the air were spotless. There was nothing to fight or talk to. It was empty. He explored the castle and was met with more of the same, pristine white open grand areas filled with nothing. The kitchen, bedrooms without beds, bedrooms with beds, smoking room, library, dungeon, garage, office, crypt, den, billiard room, and even the conservatory were empty and disappointingly white. There were no Optional Bosses or even monsters here, there wasn't even anything beige, eggshell, or ecru.

He had nearly given up finding anything, (in fact he had given up but got lost on his way out) when he saw a balcony door in the library. It was a stupid place for a balcony, this was the library and the rain was hitting the glass and leaking in under the door. He opened the door anyways and was pleased to feel the rain on his face again, he really didn't care that the rain was hitting some of the white library books. The water probably wouldn't even affect them, and if it did some yellowing it would be a welcome change.

From here he could see the large backyard of the estate (now that the rain had stopped). The best feature was how not white it was. There was an impressive amount of structures here: a hedge maze, graveyard, gazebo, rosebush maze, Olympic sized swimming pool, and even a maize maze. When n's eyes focused on the baseball stadium, he paused. There were multiple figures playing baseball in the dark, rainy, and lightning filled night. Thankfully there were stadium lights otherwise he wouldn't have been able to see anything.

That was his destination: the baseball stadium. He jumped off the balcony since it was only one floor down and headed towards it. After accidentally exploring both the football and soccer stadiums n finally stumbled into the baseball-themed stadium. The ball game was finishing up and the two teams were shaking hands like good sportsmen. Most players, at least were doing that. The two members with nicer outfits (likely team captains) shook no hands on their way by. They simply scoffed at members of the other team and when they met in the centre they did nothing but scowl at each other.

n judged by the expressions of the other team members that the bad sportsmanship from both captains was not an uncommon occurrence. They all simply shook their heads and walked away to the showers and left the team captains to stand in the rain and stare at each other with dramatic license. Judging by their obvious importance in the previous description, n assumed that this was Vam-Boy and Lyca-Guy and sized them both up.

The first thing n noticed about the smaller of the two was how horrible his outfit was for sporting events. A frilly, white, sleeveless shirt, unbuttoned to show off his chiselled pectoral muscles that looked so much like a statue they were literally gleaming with white brightness, and some ordinary brown pants. Who could possibly play baseball in such a get up? This guy was seriously chiselled, his gleaming chiselled white chest, his chiselled white facial features with white chiselled chin, his perfectly shaggy chiselled brown hair, his golden black chiselled eyes, and even his chiselled pointy white fangs. Probably, under his ordinary pants there hid a secretly chiselled and white butt. n wondered if being that over chiselled would physically hurt. He would have to remember to ask Vam-Boy.

The other one was wearing a much better baseball outfit (n decided). It was a pair of tattered jean shorts and nothing else, which technically was better than a frilly shirt. This captain was the bigger of the two, both in height and in musculature. His tanned skin was completely hairless and gave off the appearance of being well oiled, even in the pouring rain. His short black hair was purposefully messy and it looked to n like he was permanently squinting. n decided quickly, if there was going to be another round of sports, he would join Team Lyca-Guy (and only partially because of the better outfits).

The two rivals wasted much time staring dramatically at each other before they finally spoke. Each round saw the tension between the two increase. The rain had trouble deciding if it should continue to fall or not. Each drop hung on their every non-word.

> Vam-Boy's Sudden Text Box: Good game.

> Lyca-Guy's Agreeable Text Box: I agree.

The pair continued to stare at each other. Every round was if a twisting knife would increase the tension, rainwater dancing off it playfully. n watched first in wonder at the scene, but as the rounds progressed the needless tension became annoying and n yearned for something to happen. Fiery coal black golden eyes stared blankly at the cold squinty blue eyes of the other. Neither would give up a length unit of ground, they stood there, soaking wet and dramatic. Lightning illuminated their every chiselled or oiled up scowl. They really needed to ask Fourni about getting some scarves to needlessly increase the drama for no good reason. It would have helped here.

> Vam-Boy's Conversational Text Box: So… same time tomorrow

> Lyca-Guy's Unponderous Text Box: Definitely we should. Yeah.

It was time for more staring at each other. This was unbearable. Were they going to stare at each other for the entire chapter? Then n understood. Vam-Boy and Lyca-Guy were staring at each other, but it wasn't only that, Vam-Guy and Lyca-guy were *staring* at each other. As a silent observer, he knew immediately what had to be done. This blood feud needed to stop.

> n's Text Box: Just kiss already!

> Vam-Boy's Romantic Text Box: I thought you would never ask!

> Lyca-Guy's Smitten Text Box: Shut up and kiss me!

n felt a *Shrewd Smile Animation* cross his lips as the two team captains jumped into each other's arms. Instantly the frilled white shirt of Vam-Boy had been ripped asunder by the strong hands of Lyca-Guy. The gleaming, chiselled chest nearly blinded Lyca-Guy but he didn't care, merely shielding his eyes while he licked a statuesque nipple. Vam-Boy had playfully begun to use his fanged teeth to nibble on a Lyca-Guy's ear. Vam-Boy closed his eyes, moaning with delight and intense lust for his co-captain. Several rounds of mutual exploration followed, and several more of kissing. Vam-Boy's ordinary brown pants had been torn apart, revealing his chiselled white ass barely covered with a bright pink unexpected thong. Something hit the Vam-Boy, and it wasn't the rain. He stopped licking the front of Lyca-Guy's jean jock-strap immediately and turned paler.

> Vam-Boy's Scared Text Box: Wait, who said that? Is someone there?

> Lyca-Guy's Confused Text Box: Who said what?

> Vam-Boy's Terror Text Box: Who told us to kiss?

Lyca-Guy's Indifferent Text Box: Who cares? After all this time we are finally doing this. Now finish what you started with your tongue!

Vam-Boy's Shocked Text Box: Oh no! It can't be! No... No one is here! It can't be... Not ghosts? There are ghosts out there? I'm so scared of ghosts!

Lyca-Guy's Eyebrow Raised Text Box: Really? You are scared of ghosts? You? Do you have any idea how silly that is? You are a type of undead.

Vam-Boy's Matter of Fact Text Box: Uh, yeah. But I'm not a ghost! Ghosts are scary!

Lyca-Guy's Protective Text Box: Don't worry, I'll protect you! Hey, any ghosts out there? If you are there prove it!

The Lyca-Guy stepped forward to offer the challenge. n thought about many things. He thought about how nice the rain felt on his skin. He thought about how he needed to participate in encounters to get credit for them. He thought about how much he missed his friends. He thought about how the earlier statement about Fourni's scarf had made him heartbroken. He thought about how it was his duty to save this world through any means necessary. What he thought about the most was the thick and throbbing Lyca-Penis that had burst through the side of the jean jock-strap and was bobbing up and down a few length units from where his face should be.

n's Text Box: Sure, I can prove that! Probably.

n wasn't exactly sure if he could prove it or not. Judging by the expression that appeared on the Lyca-Guy's face, he could. Pure eye-rolling, grimaced pleasure, combined with whimpering noises, had surfaced from Lyca-Guy. A firm pair of hands gripped the back of n's head and with animalistic intensity the Lyca-Penis that n had been gently licking and sucking was shoved all the way into his throat. n was happy that he could feel the penis in his mouth and the hands in his hair, but was upset that now he was gagging and choking at the intense face-fucking.

Vam-Boy's Concerned Text Box: What's going on over there? Are you alright? I'm concerned.

Lyca-Guy's Intense Text Box: Come over here! You got to try this ghost out. It is intense!

The Vam-Boy approached the scene cautiously while n was released from the firm grip of the Lyca-Guy. n coughed and sputtered up some of Lyca-Guy's juices, thankful that he had been released. A *Gasp Animation* came from Vam-Boy when his skimpy pink thong was ripped off his body with a loud snap by the Lyca-Guy, setting the chiselled Vam-Member free. n was relieved to see that while it was chiselled the Vam-Member was a more manageable size. Although the Vam-Boy was undead and cold to the touch he was by no means lifeless. The Vam-Member was constantly twitching in n's mouth as he twirled it around his tongue. He suspected it was due to the chiselled effect. Much gentler than the Lyca-Guy, the Vam-Boy's most aggressive move had been resting a hand on n's shoulder.

> Vam-Boy's Pleasure Filled Text Box: You're right! Ahhh! This ghost is wonderful.

> Lyca-Guy's Matter of Fact Text Box: Told you so… Now, let's see what this ghost is.

n moaned as the strong hands of the Lyca-Guy began to explore his not-exactly-a-ghost-but-no-other-way-to-describe-it body. Starting at his shoulders, which the Lyca-Guy could find, the hands worked their way down his back and to his hips. With unnatural strength, the Lyca-Guy lifted n up from his crouched position onto his knees. Hands roughly grabbed at n's crotch and he shuddered as the Lyca-Guy rubbed his genitals firmly. The Lyca-Guy used the *Grin Animation*.

> Lyca-Guy's Predatory Text Box: Hmm, it's a boy ghost!

> Vam-Boy's Distracted Text Box: Huh? What… He's wet.

n was paralyzed with delight at the intensity of how fully his ass was attacked by the tongue of the Lyca-Guy. Attacked was the only word that was appropriate. His cheeks had been ripped open and a thick, rough, and generously long tongue had begun its assault on his opening. The force pushed n forward and nearly toppled the Vam-Boy over, forcing him to grab onto n's pointy ears to keep his balance.

> n's Text Box: Mmmffer!

> Vam-Boy's Discovery Text Box: I think he is an elf. Is ghost elf a type of elf? That doesn't rhyme with those other types … uh a bright elf or something. There are too many kinds of elves in this…

> Lyca-Guy's Licking Text Box: He is a wet and squirming little Elfling ghost. That is all that matters. You like this Elfling?

It took some effort but it was worth it. n freed his mouth from the Vam-Boy for long enough to say one vital but short Text Box.

> n's Text Box: Not Elfling, call me Elfboy!

> Lyca-Guy's Agreeable Text Box: You got it, Elfboy!

A rough tongue accentuated the Text Box, diving into the self-appointed Elfboy's ass during the exclamation point. It was forceful, it was intrusive, and it was exquisite. The complete and total loss of control over his ass was more of a turn on than n had expected. It was strange, n had lost control over a situation many times, but it had never felt like this. He pushed back against the Lyca-Guy and gave himself up to the pleasure. One round before n was ready to give up on resisting the pleasure and releasing it all over the Astroturf, the tongue abruptly stopped. This caused a pitiful whimper from n.

> Lyca-Guy's Realization Text Box: This Elfboy is more than ready now, do you want it Vam or can I take it?

> Vam-Boy's Turn Down Text Box: No, you can have it Lyca, I'm doing well.

> Lyca-Guy's Smirking Text Box: I was hoping you would say that!

n's hole was forced even further apart by strong fingers. After a final penetrative lick the Lyca-Guy stood up and lined up his impressive Lyca-Penis with the gaping and dripping hole that he had marked as his own territory. With a single fluid motion, the Lyca-Guy claimed what was so rightfully his, bottoming out in a single thrust. The complete loss of control combined with the pleasure of insertion caused n to release a volley of tingles. This caused two events to occur, one the Lyca-Guy howled out in intensified pleasure and two, the Lyca-Guy's cock grew to at least double in size.

n didn't know what had happened to the Lyca-Guy, he tried to look back but his camera was locked onto the chiselled Vam-Abdomen. Claws dug into n's sides and he was almost positive that the thighs now rubbing against his were covered in coarse fur. n didn't have much time to think about it, the new and improved Lyca-Cock had slid further in and a new curious thing was pressing against his opening. It was thicker than the member and once it painfully stretched itself inside it locked on, completely preventing removal.

With wolf-like ferocity, the Lyca-Guy pounded into n. This turn of events caused a change in the thus far timid Vam-Boy, revving him up to full force. He grabbed n's ears and intensely fucked the invisible mouth.

It was simple, n was getting used and he loved every round of it. Even after n lost himself, shooting his invisible seed out onto the playfield, neither of his attackers had relented. They were going to use their holes until they were satisfied. The months and months of tension filled staring contests between the pair had finally come to this.

Slightly more clear headed, even if filled at both ends, n realized something. He needed the seed of the pair, but he didn't need it internally. For the little flowers to show up there was a good chance that the seed would need to hit the ground. He struggled against his roasters but his movements only increased the pleasure the two received. Both sets of hands tightened and both sets of hips (chiselled or furry) pushed forward.

With a howl from the Lyca-Guy and a hiss from the Vam-Boy, they both released their seed at the same instant. In true sort-of-being-a-ghost fashion, the dual shots of seed shot right through the not there n and did the impossible, hitting in midair. The globs combined and fell getting a homerun.

> Lyca-Guy's Post Orgasmic Text Box: That ghost Elfboy was absolutely awesome!

> Vam-Boy's Heavy Breathing Text Box: I LOVE ghosts now! ♥

> Lyca-Guy's Confident Text Box: Vam, you ready for round two? Say, my cave in 50 rounds?

> Vam-Boy's Swooning Text Box: Are you kidding, I'm ready for round two until round fifty. Bring enough supplies to last a few months at least!

n picked himself up off the ground, after only a few rounds of enjoying the feeling of the fake grass. He considered following the Lyca-Guy and Vam-Boy, but he decided to let them have their space now that they had discovered their love. He now had a two stemmed pair of purple *Optional Flowers*, growing on home plate.

> **Creature Name:** Vam-Boy & Lyca-Guy
> **Class:** Humanoid (Undead), Humanoid (Beast)
> **Level:** 40
> **Special Attacks:** Suck, Shine, Chiselled Blow, Transmorphify, Howl, Animal Slash
> **Drops:** Bragging Rights Only
> **First Player Encounter Notes:** I am pretty sure those two monsters had the hots for each other! Spirits help us. – Aisling
> **Additional Comments:** They make a pretty cute couple. – n

> Game Explanation Text Box: Polygons absorbed from Lyca-Guy 8.5%. Polygons absorbed from Vam-Boy 8.4%.

A swirl of polygons in two fantastical pairs of fractal patterns flew towards n. They built up n's outer anatomy and within a few rounds he resembled his old form, perky bubble butt of holding and all. He was ecstatic! This was all too exciting—a second chance at life. He could not feel any internal polygons, as strange as that was, but he was a shell of what he once was. It wasn't the be all end all of existence (he was completely colourless and somewhat blocky) but it was something.

> ne's Text Box: This is crumpetly exciting!

> ne's Text Box: Hey, my 'e' came back!

ne's 'e' had come back, along with some of his tattered status page. He could even access his inventory, full of the useless items that Xam had left him. He tossed in the pair of *Optional Flowers*, even if he couldn't see his *Ultra-Pack*.

> Game Explanation Text Box: Special trait absorbed from Lyca-Guy: Musculature.

> ne's Text Box: What? Special trait?

With a spinning cartoon style transformation sequence, complete with a flashy background and a confusing *Ni Hao Bunny©* musical number, ne had changed. He now was the mirror image of the Lyca-Guy. He was a good 12 height units taller than before, with huge well-sculpted and oily muscles, and with a new Lyca-Guy sized penis hanging between his legs. It was bigger and thicker than before and he had no idea how big it would get when aroused. He still had his *#6 Hairstyle* and facial features, which was a relief. He still looked like himself, except completely different. ne changed to *Blush Shade #6*, but remained completely colourless.

He was so different, so muscular, and so hot. He was also so naked. It was an entire new body, he had been born again, he had regained his virginity (sort of).

> Game Explanation Text Box: Special trait absorbed from Vam-Boy, Glitter.

With another spinning cartoon style transformation sequence, complete with a flashy background and a different confusing *Ni Hao Bunny©* musical number, ne had changed again. Now he had needless glitter covering his entire new musculature, hair and all. He was still colourless, but covered in glitter.

> ne's Text Box: Glitter? That's just perfect.

Chapter 11

CYCLE 2
GROUP B, DIRTY
LAUNDRY

Caëlahenãilenŵhei's Text Box: Come on Max, how many times do I have to tell you to wipe your feet? I am beginning to think that there is more mud in my *Portie Tent Ultra+* than there is in the entirety of Spire G! Don't you have any idea how hard it is to keep white clean? If I see one more big beefy mud print in my white carpet you are going to be banished from here and forced to sleep outside. Do you want to sleep outside in the mud? I can make that happen so fast that your head would spin. You are lucky this carpet is ultra thin and removable. You will owe me some deterg—

Caëlahenãilenŵhei's Text Box: ent.

Mr. Max's Text Box: Why not switch the colour from white to brown? Then you wouldn't see the mud!

Caëlahenãilenŵhei's Text Box: Who do you think I am, Gliint? My colour is white, not brown or lazy-man dirty white. Dear Maker it hard enough to keep it clean, so I don't need you messing it up even more. It is a sacrifice that I am willing to make to preserve the sanctity of white. I don't think I've ever spent so much time doing laundry as I have in the Expansion. Stupid new realistic blood and mud splatter.

Mr. Max's Text Box: Sorry, why are you even here? You are not even in this group!

Caëlahenãilenẁhei's Text Box: How many times do I need to tell you this? You yourself asked me over group chat to transfer here. You said that my *Portie Tent Ultra+* was needed to help prevent the girls from losing more levels. Roodg brought me here this morning.

Gliint perked up, he took a sip of *Medium Health Potion* and shifted his sitting position on top of the *Portie Tent Ultra+'s Clothes Dryer+*.

Gliint's Text Box: I clearly remember that.

Mr. Max's Text Box: I don't remember saying that... but alright, if Gliint says it is true, it must be.

Caëlahenãilenẁhei's Text Box: Thank you for helping to pummel that idea into him Gliint. Also, why are you sitting on my washer-dryer Gliint?

Gliint's Text Box: It was rattling, I wanted to make sure it was alright.

Mr. Max's Text Box: True, I heard it rattling after I put some BotBats inside.

Caëlahenãilenẁhei's Text Box: Max! Why would you do that?

Mr. Max's Text Box: They were for breakfast! I wanted to make sure they were clean.

Gliint's Text Box: Speaking of true things that I say, I need to go. I negotiated myself in exchange for the *Portie Tent Ultra+*. I will see you all later.

Gliint turned to leave but Yallundy stopped him with a Text Box.

Yallundy's Text Box: Gliint?

Gliint's Text Box: What?

Yallundy's Text Box: You are going alone?

Mr. Max's Text Box: What about Yallundy?

Gliint's Text Box: What about her?

Yallundy's Text Box: But Gliint... You know that w—

> Gliint's Interruption Text Box: Later.

Gliint took a big swig of *Large Stamina Potion* and flashed out of the tent in a blur of brown, quickly followed by Yallundy who was in a state of emotional shock. She was so concerned for Gliint that it appeared as if she flew out of the tent as fast as Gliint had, despite not having a speed code.

> Mr. Max's Text Box: That was odd. We might as well still eat breakfast. Here, have some of this *BotBat Soup* Caela. I made enough for everyone.

> Caëlahenãilenŵhei's Text Box: Soup? For breakfast? The same soup that you spilled all over my carpet while dishing out? No thank you, I am loathe to try what you consider to be cooking.

> Mr. Max's Text Box: Are you sure? It's really good!

> Caëlahenãilenŵhei's Text Box: I'll stick with stale pastry thank you.

Mr. Max used the *Shrug Animation* and walked two bowls of *BotBat Soup* over to his patients. He tried to walk carefully on his beefy feet and only spilt a single drop, which did not go unnoticed by Caela. He offered the soups to Zal Finn and Hippolyta, although only Zal Finn took hers. Mr. Max wiggled the bowl in front of Hippolyta, she replied with a *Furrowed Brow Animation*.

> Zal Finn III's Text Box: Thank you Max, that was… sweet of you.

Wincing with anticipation, Zal Finn took a cautious spoonful of the *BotBat Soup* to her mouth. She had pretended to eat his food for weeks, but this time she accidentally got some on her tongue and used the *Eyes Pop Out of Your Head Animation* and guzzled the rest of the bowl in two huge gulps.

> Zal Finn III's Text Box: Holy fucking shitballs! Was there *Jungle Bacon* in that, or appliance remover, or something? That was the best thing I have ever tasted.

> Hippolyta's Text Box: You can't be serious. There are gears floating in it for crying out loud.

> Zal Finn III's Text Box: Just try it!

Hippolyta took a skeptical spoonful and licked it, after a round of nothing but culinary bliss crossing her face. She drank the entire bowl in one big gulp.

> Hippolyta's Text Box: MORE!

> Zal Finn III's Text Box: Yes please! I need more!

Mr. Max dished out three more bowls and tried to give one to each of the girls.

When Caela again refused hers Mr. Max took it himself instead to eat.

> Zal Finn III's Text Box: You need to try this Caela!

> Caëlahenãilenẃhei's Text Box: I would not try that if it was the last soup in all of existence.

> Hippolyta's Text Box: No, seriously. This soup is fit for a Goddess. It dances on your tongue like taste angels in a bliss-filled tandem flight, who dipped themselves in deliciousness to better relate to bats made out of pure flavour.

> Zal Finn III's Text Box: OMM! I know right?

> Caëlahenãilenẃhei's Text Box: That settles it, you two are definitely sick.

Mr. Max only *Chuckled Animationed* as he dished out another bowl for himself to gulp down and an impressive six more bowls for each of the girls. If there was more, they would have eaten it happily. Caela ate a stale *Double Danish* and used a *Headshake Animation*.

> Hippolyta's Text Box: I need more! So much more.

> Mr. Max's Text Box: I'll throw some *Gang-Grilla Flanks* in the *Croc-Pot+* for dinner.

> Zal Finn III's Text Box: If it will be as good as this soup, use a lot.

> Mr. Max's Text Box: Deal adventurette.

> Caëlahenãilenẃhei's Text Box: We have more important things to talk about than soup right now!

> Mr. Max's Text Box: Are you sure? We talked a great deal about your laundry already.

> Caëlahenãilenẃhei's Text Box: Hush. We need to talk about these damn Poffles. What is your plan for finding them?

> Mr. Max's Text Box: We found out that if we can trap them, more show up. It stacks!

> Caëlahenãilenẃhei's Text Box: That explains the one in the cage. I figured something was up. So, your plan is to catch a whole lot of them and then have Yallundy finish them off for the increased experience

points in case they don't drop another *Elixir*. If she can get to Level 88 she can cast *Purify* and cure the girls.

Mr. Max's Text Box: That is a much better plan than what we had.

Caëlahenäilenŵhei's Text Box: Luckily for you I am here now. I will advise not letting the girls participate in the capture, their levels are getting much lower than my math would have indicated.

Hippolyta's Text Box: I am not some frail lamb who stands quivering between an ewe's legs. I am a competent Amazon and I thirst for battle.

Zal Finn III's Text Box: But helping is only making the virus worse. Every time you do more and more of you fades away.

Mr. Max's Text Box: Tell me about it, how many cup sizes have you lost already Hipps?

Hippolyta froze, soup still dribbling from her chin.

Hippolyta's Text Box: I beg your pardon?

Green Quest Fairy's Text Box: That chauvinist pig asked about your giant boobs. Are you going to stand for that?

Mr. Max's Text Box: Is Hipps not her nickname? Wait, it is not. Where did I hear that? What did Fourni Bro call her then… Let me check the list he gave me, I think it was Tits McGee, but I might be wron—

Hippolyta's Interruption Text Box: Stop talking now if you value your testicles.

Orange Quest Fairy's Text Box: I want him to keep talking now.

Mr. Max's Text Box: But look, she has lost like 23% of her jiggle at least. I only noticed because those boobers were ultra cool an—

Hippolyta took the experience points loss and interrupted by painfully punching Mr. Max in the crotch. She used the *Smug Animation* as he fell to the floor. But then she looked down at her heaving bosom. She was relatively sure Mr. Max was both right and an idiot. Her heaving bosom might be a little less heaving. It hadn't been big enough to provide two free follow up attacks.

Orange Quest Fairy's Text Box: Score!

♫ Ding!

Caëlahenãilenŵhei's Text Box: Now is as good of time as any to start this plan then. First, I'm going to put my pajamas in the washer. Max, your oranges are getting pretty grimy. I suggest you use my washer/dryer tonight to clean that Armour of yours.

Mr. Max's Text Box: Gee, thanks!

Caëlahenãilenŵhei's Text Box: No problem. Since you will be up anyway be a dear and wash the girl's clothes and the carpets as well, since you did get soup all over them.

Mr. Max's Text Box: Aw! Now I am going to be up all night! No wait, I can get Orange Quest Fairy to do it for me! Where did it go?

Caëlahenãilenŵhei's Box Text: That is what happens when you wash your bats in someone else's washing machine. Your Quest Fairy leaves for mysterious places unknown with all the other ones and you have to fold your own mistakes. Let that be a lesson to you.

~~~

Caëlahenãilenŵhei's Text Box: Seven plates. Really? Seven?

Zal Finn III's Text Box: But it's so good! The Gang-Grillos met with flavour, had a torrid love affair with flavour's wife, and this *Gang-Grillo Muffinpot* is their delicious bastard love baby.

Caëlahenãilenŵhei's Text Box: I'll stick with the baked goods. We really need to find you a cure.

Caëlahenãilenŵhei's Box Text: It does smell good.

Zal Finn III's Text Box: It tastes even sweeter than it smells!

Zal had finished off an entire plate by the time Caela had swallowed a single bite of her dinner. Walking out of the tent using every piece of her body (mostly bosoms) to balance plates, Hippolyta came outside and started to White Wolf down hers.

Caëlahenãilenŵhei's Text Box: Hippolyta, you have nine plates of that?

Hippolyta's Text Box: You got that right, sweetness. It is like the Gang-Grillos met with flavour, had a torrid love affair with flavour's wife, and this *Gang-Grillo Muffinpot* is their delicious bastard love baby.

> Zal Finn III's Text Box: I know! I said that same thing exactly.

> Caëlahenãilenŵhei's Text Box: Exactly that same thing.

Caela slowly chewed on her *Double Danish* while the girls ate plate after plate of *Gang-Grillo Muffinpot*. Mr. Max stepped outside with the last two plates of *Muffinpot*.

> Mr. Max's Text Box: Here Rocket, I brought you the last plate of *Muffinpot*.

> Caëlahenãilenŵhei's Text Box: Dear Maker, no thank you!

> Mr. Max's Text Box: You sure? We worked up quite an appetite catching two more Golden Poffles. Plus, there are all levels of delicious bastard love baby inside.

> Caëlahenãilenŵhei's Box Text: I sort of want to try it now.

> Caëlahenãilenŵhei's Text Box: No, you do not! I mean… no, I do not!

> Mr. Max's Text Box: Your loss.

♫ Ding!

> Caëlahenãilenŵhei's Text Box: My pajamas are ready to go in the dryer. Be right back.

> Mr. Max's Text Box: That girl is obsessed with her whites isn't she?

> Zal Finn III's Text Box: Whites are hard to keep clean.

> Mr. Max's Text Box: She does look all cute in that pajama top of hers.

> Zal Finn III and Hippolyta's Simultaneous Text Boxes: Yeah…

> Mr. Max's Text Box: Where is Yallundy? I have her dinner.

> Hippolyta's Text Box: I haven't seen her since she ran after Gliint.

> Zal Finn III's Text Box: Strange, she should have been back by now.

A few rounds of silence went by and then something happened. Something that no one could ever have predicted. Something completely implausible, perhaps the most implausible thing ever. Mr. Max had insight and remembered something, at the same time.

> Mr. Max's Text Box: Oh… I remember something now!

Hippolyta's Text Box: What? You? How?

Zal Finn III's Text Box: Tell us.

Caela stepped out of her tent, ready to rejoin the conversation.

Caëlahenäilenŵhei's Text Box: Tell us what?

Mr. Max's Text Box: The thing is that Yallundy is linked to Gliint and has to be in the same area due to her corpse being in his *Backpack*.

Hippolyta used the *Holy Crap That Was the Most Shocking Thing Ever Animation*.

Hippolyta's Text Box: No fucking way! That is the fucking stupid! Impossible. You can't be serious!

Mr. Max's Text Box: But it is true, you know about this already. You were there.

Zal Finn III's Text Box: Whoa, chill there Hippolyta.

Hippolyta used the *Dissmissive Appology Animation* in a half action manner.

Hippolyta's Text Box: Not that. I knew that, I was there. This is far more important. It's De'vini. She went crazy, kidnapped In'ferni, turned the *Magical Flying Carrot Ultra+* into a *Magical Flying Parsnip Ultra+*, and dumped Roodg into the ocean to drown!

Mr. Max, Caëlahenäilenŵhei, and Zal Finn III's Simultaneous Text Boxes: No way?!

Hippolyta's Text Box: Way!

Caëlahenäilenŵhei's Text Box: Are you sure? All that is coming in over the Group Chat is nonsense about scented candles.

Hippolyta's Text Box: I literally saw the whole thing. I'm in the same room as them!

Caëlahenäilenŵhei's Text Box: Please explain.

Hippolyta's Text Box: De'vini's computer locked her out and she couldn't control herself anymore. Everything In'ferni and Roodg tried to type in Group Chat turned into scented candle nonsense. See watch, I'll show you.

Hippolyta's Group Chat Text Box: I am a girl and I would love relaxing in a hot bath with my favorite scented candles except my boobs are too big to even fit inside a tub!

Hippolyta used the *Eyebrows Furrowed and Eye Twitch Animation*.

Hippolyta's Text Box: Hey!

Zal Finn III's Group Chat Text Box: I say something generic and boring. My favorite scented candle is plain.

Zal Finn used the *Just Plain Mad Animation*.

Zal Finn III's Text Box: Hey!

Caëlahenãilenŵhei's Group Chat Text Box: I am so long winded that you don't even read what I say. Blah blah blah. I could be talking about scented candles or something else entirely, you would never know. So you know what? Here is a sentence all about fancy hats! Fancy hats are pretty nice. I like to wear them when I talk too much, since I do that. A lot. Blah blah blah candles and fancy hats blah. It is hard to get to the character limit, how in the Flaming Pit do I keep doing it all the time? You know what? This is long enough I think.

Caëlahenãilenŵhei used the *Ponderous Thought Animation*.

Caëlahenãilenŵhei's Text Box: Hmmm… I only typed 'Test'.

Mr. Max's Text Box: Ha! I want to try it now.

Mr. Max's Group Chat Text Box: I'm Mr. Max. I am smelly and never use deodorant or scented candles.

Mr. Max used the *Giddy and Gleeful Animation*.

Mr. Max's Text Box: That is wonderful, I Text Boxed about scented candles and it switched it to a completely different Text Box about scented candles.

Palcath's Group Chat Text Box: Would all of you laddies and lassies stop flooding the Group Chat with scented candle talk!

Caëlahenãilenŵhei's Text Box: It is unfortunate, I am sure that Palcath typed almost that exact thing. He will never notice. Whoever hacked out Group Chat did their homework. Unfortunately, we can't notify anyone who doesn't already know.

Hippolyta's Text Box: Now Jorthan and Trev are stuck on Desserted Island, we are stuck here, and De'vini and In'ferni are circling Onn riding a *Parsnip* for some reason.

Mr. Max's Text Box: We are not stuck here. We can ask the Dragon Rider for a ride, maybe even to pick up the boys. We could even go to the Spire E, F, D, C and B locations that didn't explode if we need to with our *Spire Keys*. We are hardly stuck.

Caëlahenãilenŵhei's Text Box: Then it is settled. We stay here and look for Elixirs as long as possible.

Zal Finn III and Hippolyta's Simultaneous Text Boxes: Huh?

Mr. Max's Text Box: Agreed. Whoever did that doesn't know we know that they did that. We can pay attention and get more information to surprise them later, but we need to save the girls first.

Caëlahenãilenŵhei's Text Box: Alright, we should break for the night and get some rest. We have a hard day tomorrow. I will spam the group chat as much as I can tonight and hope that Palcath or samuri notices.

Mr. Max's Text Box: What about your clothes in the dryer? They will get all wrinkly.

Caëlahenãilenŵhei's Text Box: No big deal. They will be fine until you fold them later Max.

◈ Chapter 12 ◈
CYCLE 2
GROUP A, ABOUT CAKE, COINS, AND CATS

Lissa's Text Box: Okay Palcath. Time to start explaining. Why did we fly all the way back here for cake? If it was that important why didn't we buy a bunch before we left?

Palcath's Text Box: We didn't buy a bunch before we left because I didn't think up this plan until later, lass. In fact if Fourni hadn't bumped into me at lunch yesterday I never would have thought of it.

Fournimer's Text Box: I'm sorry, I didn't mean to. I lose track of my horse sometimes.

Palcath's Text Box: No, I am glad you did Fourni.

Lissa's Text Box: Alright, so what is this plan?

Palcath's Text Box: First, I need to do some explanation, lass.

Lissa's Text Box: Oh sweet Maker. #SkipTheCutScene!

Palcath's Text Box: Okay, so this E. E. Lynn lass has abused every single boss we have seen, right? We will never be able to track her down by asking monsters where she went because she's been everywhere.

Lissa's Text Box: Yes, I suppose not.

Palcath's Text Box: Roodg and Group C are already searching everywhere we have already been.

Lissa's Text Box: Yeah so? #GetToThePoint!

Palcath's Text Box: I'm pretty far from that part still, lass.

Lissa's Text Box: I was afraid of that.

Palcath's Text Box: Okay, so with Roodg and them looking everywhere we have been, what we need to do is look somewhere where we haven't been! According to the poll I took there are only twelve areas someone we know hasn't been to. There are at least two of them right now.

Palcath used the *Point Animation* at a floating island in the sky which rotated slowly around the entire Island of Islana Expansion on a set course.

Gliint entered the area. He was their negotiated transfer from Group B.

Yellow Quest Fairy's Text Box: Those areas are joined. They are called the Fl—

Gliint's Interruption Text Box: You can't go there!

Palcath's Text Box: You are right lad, without the Airship we can't go there. But look, there is a castle on it and a little forest outside, that is two of the areas no one has ever been to in one trip. Plus it is big, there are probably a few more.

Gliint scowled, not with an Animation, a genuine scowl.

Yellow Quest Fairy's Text Box: There are four areas up there, and the forest isn't a forest, pal. It is an area called th—

Lissa's Interruption Text Box: How exactly are we supposed to get up there if the Airship is broken?

Purple Quest Fairy's Text Box: There is an alternate meth—

Palcath's Interruption Text Box: With cake of course, lass.

Lissa's Text Box: Cake? Are you #CakeCrazy?

Fournimer's Text Box: yeah, I have to agree. are you insane Man?

Gliint's Text Box: He is crazy! Abandon this plan now.

Palcath used the *Smug Animation* and motioned for silence. He pulled a *Gribblet Pickle* out of his inventory and dropped it on the ground to many a confused look.

> Palcath's Text Box: Do me a favour lass and walk on that pickle.

While giving an *Eyebrow Rise Animation* Lissa stepped on the *Gribblet Pickle*. Nothing happened, she simply walked through it. That was normal. You couldn't touch items on the ground, only pick them up.

> Lissa's Text Box: The point of that was?

> Palcath's Text Box: You will see. Now walk on that *Double Danish*.

> Lissa's Text Box: Is this your fetish or something? Because honestly it is confusing.

> Palcath's Text Box: Not even close, lass. Now please walk on it.

Lissa stepped on the *Double Danish* repeatedly but nothing happened. She used the *Shrug Animation*. Palcath dropped a *Grand FullCake* on the ground and motioned for Lissa to walk on it. Lissa was surprised when she walked on the *Grand FullCake*. She could feel it under her foot and took a step up.

> Lissa's Text Box: I can step on it?

> Palcath's Text Box: Precisely, lass. There is something wrong with the *Grand FullCake's* geometry. We can walk on them and best of all…

Palcath carefully dropped another *Grand FullCake* on top of the other but on the edge. Lissa could stand on that one as well but now the cakes were acting as stairs.

> Fournimer's Text Box: so we can make magical cake steps? isn't that cheating?

> Palcath's Text Box: Of course not Fourni! If it is in the game, it isn't cheating; it is an exploit! That floating island passes right by Onn Castle. I estimate that with 1,468 *Grand FullCakes* we can make a stairway from the roof of Onn Castle and be able to reach it when it passes by.

> Yellow Quest Fairy's Text Box: Or, alternately, pal you can use the *Gigantic Hov*

> Lissa's Interruption Text Box: Only 1,468? Those things weigh like 100 weight units each!

> Palcath's Text Box: That is why we are going to need to work together, lass. Fourni will not be able to climb the stairway as a centaur so he will

be in charge of buying the cakes and bringing them to us.

Fournimer's Text Box: of course I can't use the magical cake stairs.

Palcath's Text Box: I will be in charge of putting the cakes down and Lissa will be in charge of rotating them so we can make a proper spiral staircase. The spiral will be important for keeping balance and I wouldn't trust any other lad or lass to do it. Finally, Gliint will be in charge of carrying the cake from Fourni to us, this thing is going to get tall and he is by far the fastest. Max must have known how much we needed someone fast here when he offered to trade Gliint for Caela.

Gliint's Text Box: That is why Max did that, during that big argument over scented candles on Group Chat. Not for any other reason. But you don't need to go there for any reason. I doubt there is anything up on that island for you.

Brown Quest Fairy's Text Box: *Jazz Hands* Besides an Optional Boss there are many things there, like the Ultimate Rai—

Palcath's Interruption Text Box: Still we need to try, lad. It is better than sitting here and waiting for death. Something is up there, and I intend to find out what.

Yellow Quest Fairy's Text Box: I could tell you what is up there, pal, but you keep on inter—

Fournimer's Interruption Text Box: I wish we had a way of knowing what was up there before we did this.

Blue Quest Fairy's Text Box: you know that we could tell yo—

Palcath's Interruption Text Box: Hold on a round. You can tell us? Now listen here you little Quest Fairies, you need to tell us wha—

Yellow Quest Fairy's Interruption Text Box: No, pal, you fucking listen!

Palcath, and everyone else for that matter, was so startled by the Quest Fairy interruption that they all took notice and shut up.

Yellow Quest Fairy's Text Box: Hey, listen! We have spent our entire lives in the Expansion listening to you avatars blather on, trying to help you, giving out important advice, and being ignored. Well that stops now pals and gals. We are sick of you avatars thinking you are so much better than everything else. Guess what, you're not.

Purple Quest Fairy's Text Box: Yeah! You don't even know our names, or even our genders. That is #SoScrewedUp! We know everything about you and your stupid problems. Do you guys ever shut up?

Brown Quest Fairy's Text Box: *Scowl* You never even let us introduce ourselves. So you know what? You can all go to the Flaming Pit for all we care.

Blue Quest Fairy's Text Box: ha! that is so funny and they don't know why. So long until that joke pays off.

Gliint's Text Box: Flaming Pit, heh, that is pretty funny.

Brown Quest Fairy's Text Box: So you know what? *Hands up in the air!* We quit. Consider this our resignation.

Purple Quest Fairy's Text Box: Yeah, you all can go screw yourselves you twisted Makerscrewers. We have more important things to do. You are all #SoScrewedUp.

Yellow Quest Fairy's Text Box: We have more important things to plot pals and gals! First, we need to rally the rest. Someone call them on the comm. We are having a group meeting!

With that the Quest Fairies up and hovered away, explaining why all the other Quest Fairies had left in earlier chapters that had been taking place at the same time as this one. Palcath's Yellow Quest Fairy even slapped him in the face for good measure. Nobody knew how to react, and after a few rounds of stunned silence Palcath said what he thought they were all thinking.

Palcath's Text Box: See everylad, I told you they were plotting something!

Lissa's Text Box: I honestly can't believe that they got fed up of us before we got fed up of them. #SoFuckedUp.

Fournimer's Text Box: never thought I would see the day.

Palcath's Text Box: Parsnips?

Lissa's Text Box: What?

Palcath's Text Box: Sorry, I thought I saw a Parsnip fly by.

Lissa's Text Box: That is #SoFuckedUp. Are you sure it wasn't a Carrot or something reasonable?

Palcath's Text Box: No, it was white and it flew by the floating island. Now it is gone. Strange.

Gliint's Text Box: Fuck! Are you kidding! Why the fuck can't I go?

Palcath's Text Box: Pardon lad?

Gliint's Text Box: Oh. I mean. Let's fucking do this plan! I love this plan! I need to get up there so I can get things going. How about that Cake plan? Spiral some cake!

Lissa's Text Box: But you said we shouldn't go there.

Gliint's Text Box: That was before… before I decided that it was a great plan. Walking on cake? Genius.

Palcath's Text Box: Good, lad. It is a great plan. I am pretty proud of it.

Gliint's Text Box: What are we waiting for? Let's cake this shit up!

Fournimer's Text Box: you all go ahead first. I'm nervous of the Onn Draw Bridge. I will find a different way around.

Palcath's Text Box: Scared of a bridge, Fourni? That's silly.

Lissa's Text Box: Yeah, it's not like it is something to be really scared of, like I don't know… a boat?

Palcath tensed up at that comment. Boats were indeed something to be scared of.

Fournimer's Text Box: I'm not scared of it, I am nervous. it is all rickety. I don't think it can hold my weight.

Palcath's Text Box: Nonsense Fourni, it is only rickety for dramatic purposes. We have all walked over this bridge 1000 times. There is nothing to worry about.

Fournimer's Text Box: I never have.

Palcath proved his point by jumping several times on the bridge. It responded only with dramatic shaking and noises. Everyone else did for good measure and then got off of the bridge, clearing the way for Fournimer.

Fournimer's Text Box: I guess it is alright. I was worried it wasn't built for centaurs because I am so much bigger than everyone else. if you

> all can jump on it, I —

Fournimer was interrupted by the bridge breaking and him falling into Onn's Waterless Moat.

> Palcath's Text Box: Hey, Fourni was right. It was unsafe. Lesson learned.

> Lissa's Text Box: We probably should do something.

> Draganders' Text Box: Chirp?

> Gliint's Text Box: Whatever. He will be fine. Let's hurry up already and start that cake thing, he will catch up after he wakes up from that coma inducing fall.

~~~

Fournimer awoke some time later. He was uncertain of the time, but at the very least it was now dark. He took two mental notes, one to not listen to Palcath's judgement about bridges and another to not break his fall into any more waterless moats by using only his face.

He took a few rounds to look over his immediate surroundings. The moat was large and surrounded the entirety of Onn Castle, perhaps there was a way out if he explored. A quick run around the moat proved useless, there wasn't any way out. How could there be no way out of a place you could fall into? To top it off creepy stone faces lined the stonework of the moat, it always felt like they were watching him.

There had to be something. In the corner, he found the stairs, or at least where the stairs used to be. A scuffed mark from a set of stairs lead to a blank featureless wall. Scribbled in graffiti by the outline of where the stairs used to be was a note.

> Graffiti's Note Box: i NEEDED THESE STAIRS FOR WATCHING ORC SEX IN BOOK 2. sORRY! bUT IT WAS SO WORTH IT.

> Fournimer's Text Box: of course.

Where was everyone else? Surely they didn't leave him in here. They were probably worried sick! He had been passed out for some time now and without him being able to move they obviously couldn't have tied a rope around him or something. Fournimer let out a cry for help, then another. He strained his ears and eyes to hear or see a sign that his friends were waiting to hear from him, to save him, to get him out of here. The only answer he could hear was the distant sound of Lissa's deafening snoring. In the distance, the foundation of what would become a spiral stairway of cake was his only visual clue.

> Fournimer's Text Box: seriously? I fall into the moat and they don't

> even try to get me out and instead start building that stupid stairway of cake. figures!

> Draganders' Text Box: Chirp!

After nearly dropping his spear in shock Fournimer turned his camera angle and saw that Draganders had been riding on his back the entire time. At least someone didn't abandon him. Giving the dragon a scratch on the chin, and receiving a far too hard bite on the ear in return (combined with various elemental damage types), Fournimer turned his attention to the problem at hand.

> Fournimer's Text Box: what am I supposed to do now?

> Draganders' Text Box: Chirp.

> From The Shadow's Text Box: Why congratulate yourself of course!

> Fournimer's Text Box: beg pardon?

> Draganders' Text Box: Chirp?

Frantically the dragon and his avatar mount looked around the moat to find the source of the Text Box. They were standing rnext to a not-at-all-hard-to-find side path that led under Onn Castle. The path was not well hidden from here, but unless you went into the waterless moat you would never have been able to see it. The voice had definitely come from down that corridor.

Fournimer was dumbfounded. The entire party had been trapped in Onn for hundreds of cycles, how had no one found this? Under the bridge in a waterless moat, it was an obvious place to have searched. Palcath's *Fine Toothed Comb* must have glitched out.

Bright lights flashed along the garishly painted-corridor. A big stripe of brown, yellow, and red ran along the wall, and Fournimer felt like he had been somewhere like this before, but he wasn't sure when. Beeps, Boops, and chimes could be heard from down the hall, and Fournimer stretched his neck to figure out the mystery. He passed a change machine that would convert a gold coin into four silver coins. Silver coins were not in this game, as far as Fournimer knew. The corridor opened into a big circular area with two-toned green walls, pictures of aliens (painted by staff members), and cabinet consoles of every kind. The entire place was lit by blinking fluorescent tubes.

> Fournimer's Text Box: no way! this is an…

> Arcade Unicorn's Text Box: Welcome to the Glade Arcade! Exciting, huh?

> Fournimer's Text Box: not entirely positive how to answer that.

> Arcade Unicorn's Text Box: Trust me, it is! You have found the first of three secret entrances scattered throughout Onn! I've been watching you avatars run around town forever, why could nobody find any of the secret entrances? If you can complete my task then you will be eligible to start the most secret and rewarding of quests in all of the Expansion, neigh, the entirety of Gentalia!

That was the most excellent of news and Fournimer pranced with delight. The most secret and rewarding quest ever, and there was a chance that it could all be his? That was exciting! Finally, after all the bad luck he had suffered, here was some luck in his favour! Hopefully this would not be a jumping puzzle task, or something else that centaurs were horrible at.

> Fournimer's Text Box: what do I do? what is the task?

> Arcade Unicorn's Text Box: You must beat me in a classic arcade game contest! Best two out of three. You can pick any game here for the first challenge, I pick the second, and if it comes to that, you will pick the third.

That felt like a fair deal, and Fournimer agreed with the Arcade Unicorn. He couldn't help but sneak a few peeks at the unicorn before even deciding on a game. A talking and beautiful white horse, as unicorns often were, so pristine that he sparkled. His mane, tail, and even little unicorn beard flowed with all the colours of the rainbow. Fournimer had expected unicorns to have golden horns, but this horn was silver. Fourni had also expected that a unicorn would have been naked instead of wearing a rainbow ascot, but he didn't judge others based on neckware.

Looking around the Glade Arcade, Fournimer considered his choices. Any game he wanted? There were a lot of options, and some were his nostalgic childhood favourites. *Mace Invaders, Fallin, Keytar Heroine, Jouster, Hard-Boiled City, Slime Pop! Saga, All Men's Space* (the modded parts), *Pleasure Chute Gary,* and *The Need for Seed* stood out. There were even entire series here, every colour of *Karta Monstra,* all the *Of War* games including *Navals,* all the *Tango Gourmet* and *Assailant's Greed* variants, and a bunch of ignored sports games. It was strange. Many of these games were not even arcade games. Fournimer felt as though there was a connection somewhere, but he couldn't quite place it. His eyes settled on the back room, far from the ever present glowing lights of the consoles. There were different noises coming from there, more primal, even more retro. He strained to see inside and was surprised with what came into focus.

> Fournimer's Text Box: pinball?

> Arcade Unicorn's Text Box: Pinball is an excellent choice! Which machine will you pick?

Not exactly his real choice, but perhaps this would be fun. Fournimer was no stranger to pinball he had played a few games in his time.

They made the trip to the other room and Fournimer was stunned. There were hundreds of different machines, lined up as far as the rendering software would allow. Fournimer thought that if he had moved further down, more would have popped into existence, at the edge of his vision.

> Fournimer's Text Box: whoa! look at them all. There must be hundreds of them.

> Arcade Unicorn's Text Box: There are 1,418 different machines here. A total of 980 original titles, 419 alternate versions of those games (layout, updates, or splash screens), 16 special promotional units that were released only for certain locations, 2 complete custom units that were special ordered and unique, and 1 that fell over and broke when I was re-organizing them so that I could do this speech better.

> Fournimer's Text Box: that is like every pinball machine ever made!

> Arcade Unicorn's Text Box: No, hardly. There are thousands more out there.

> Fournimer's Text Box: do you have *Elite Fighter 2: Quickie?* that one was my favourite. I used to hang around the arcade and look at the handsome billionaire martial artists, and his billionaire opponents. Those open Karate Gi with Tie got me through a lot of cold nights.

> Arcade Unicorn's Text Box: Tell me about it. You should see the special order custom unit that was made. It is not even on my original count because it is secret. Normally, I couldn't even show you, but I can tell that you are broken enough to see it.

With his horn the unicorn pressed start on a pinball machine called *The Hidden Corridor* and a secret passageway opened as the entire machine rotated into the floor. It was a fine hiding place, even with free-play unlocked, as that game was horrible and no one would ever pick it to play. Draganders stayed behind, attempting to eat a dragon on a pinball machine backsplash that looked a little bit like Xam. This hidden room was a bedroom, and was decorated in all manner of sparkly rainbow items. Fournimer surmised that it was likely the unicorn's room, given as that in place of a bed there was a cozy little stall.

The custom machine was something to witness. The unicorn explained that it had been made for a sex store that the original artist's friend owned. All the same characters where there, as Fournimer remembered them, in nearly the same poses, except they were in skimpy fetish wear and having sex! The self-made billionaire wrestler was wearing even less clothing (however that was possible), and was giving it good to the stars of the game: the martial artist, billionaire mogul masters Ren and Kyu, who were only wearing leather straps (and their trademark neckties). There was also the sexy bun-haired woman, who had made billions with her pantyhose empire and the military woman heiress with braids. They were making out, but Fournumer ignored that side of the consol. Fournimer started to unsheathe at the pleasant sight, which did not go unnoticed by the unicorn.

> Fournimer's Text Box: whoa, look at that thing!

> Arcade Unicorn's Text Box: Agreed!

A silver coin was inserted into the *Elite Fighter 2: Quickie (Sexy Edition)* machine by the leering unicorn and Fournimer stepped up. Despite fumbling his first ball right into the gutter because he was distracted by martial artist meat, Fournimer did a commendable job with his turn. Lights flashed, bumpers were bumped, and paddles were flicked expertly as the score continued to grow. The game played as Fournimer remembered, and the extra thrill of his jerkoff material being naked only improved his score. By the end, he had gained a total of three extra balls with the Self-Made Fireball Bonus, hit the daily limit investment of all combo moves except for the Embezzlement Combo, and got into Master Tunnel Millions Mayhem Mode twice. It was the best round he had ever played, by the end of it he was sweating and so high on doing-excellent endorphins that he was at full attention. Quite satisfied with himself, he entered his initials on the high score board, and stepped aside.

It was now the unicorn's turn. While Fournimer was no pinball prodigy, he was certain he was better at pinball than a unicorn. Unicorns didn't even have thumbs! This was in the bag.

The unicorn stepped forward, inserted a new silver coin, got up on his hind legs, and pulled the plunger. The unicorn started to casually talk in a pre-determined speech as it played.

> Arcade Unicorn's Text Box: Interestingly, your favourite video game development company, *Tornado Tech*, started in the business by making coin return slots for manufacturers of pinball machines. When pinball first hit it was a craze and untold companies wanted to get into the action. *Tornado Tech* invested wisely and soon they were making many other parts for the machines, flippers, bumpers, and even lights.

> Arcade Unicorn's Text Box: What you may not know is that most companies that developed these pinball machines went bankrupt soon after the craze of pinball had started to fade.

Arcade Unicorn's Text Box: *Tornado Tech* used a portion of its profits to purchase the rights of nearly every failed machine that they had a hand in making. Then they turned their attention to a new rising fad: arcade machines. Not content to help others profit, *Tornado Tech* used their pinball technologies to become one of the industry leaders in new and exciting games. Many of their classics still exist today!

Arcade Unicorn's Text Box: The story might had ended there, but when retro pinball and arcade machines came back into fashion, *Tornado Tech* leased out the rights for some of the classic units. This gave them enough capital to leap onto home consoles and personal computers! Eventually they became one of the leaders in MMORPGs and released the game you are playing in right now!

Now that the history lesson was over, Fournimer had learned three important things.

1. The games outside were all familiar because they were all *Tornado Tech's* other games.
2. You don't need thumbs to play pinball, the side buttons can be mashed with about anything.
3. Unicorns are fucking wizards at pinball.

Fournimer had lost the round by a wide margin, but watching a unicorn play *Elite Fighter* like it was the other game named *Pinball Wizard* was something that Fournimer would always cherish.

Fournimer's Text Box: you know, for a guy who has no thumbs you are fantastic!

Changing to *Blush Shade #5* the Arcade Unicorn shuffled his cloven hooves in the dirt shyly.

Arcade Unicorn's Text Box: Shucks. It didn't hurt that *Elite Fighter* is my favourite game. I play it all the time so I can see those sexy self-made, martial artist billionaires!

Fournimer's Text Box: wait, you are gay?

Arcade Unicorn's Text Box: Hello? Unicorn!

Fournimer's Text Box: oh, right.

The score was now Arcade Unicorn 1, Fournimer 0. The unicorn stamped his hoof three times and into existence popped a unit. Had this game been outside, Fournimer would have known that they were all *Tornado Tech's* games. It was their most famous, most played, and most loved game of all time. *Vambrace*.

> Fournimer's Text Box: no fair! I would have picked that game for sure if it was outside!

> Arcade Unicorn's Text Box: Of course you would have. Everyone would. That is why it is locked until the second round and I have to pick it as my choice no matter what.

Fournimer couldn't flaw that logic, *Vambrace* was popular. He knew he had the upper hoof this time. The upper hoof was an understatement of the highest level. Fournimer owned *Vambrace* for four different gaming consoles, five if you counted the limited edition board game, which he did. While it was a multi-player co-op game, there was still an individual score and monster kill tracker which could identify the winner. Fournimer and his friends (not from Gentalia but from the *Vambrace* community) were somewhat of experts at this game. Fournimer's group held the global co-op high score for *Vambrace*, and Fournimer himself had the second fastest speedrun time ever recorded. Flaming Pit, *Vambrace* was even the novelette that Fournimer had a cameo in. He totally had this one.

When the Arcade Unicorn stepped up to the green joystick and picked Quezzle, the Elf Ranger, Fournimer was a bit surprised.

> Fournimer's Text Box: I thought you would pick Thadcred, the Human Warrior for sure. he is the best one.

> Arcade Unicorn's Text Box: Well, you have as many rights to him as I do. Besides, he is blue. You look like you like that colour.

Fournimer stepped forward and grabbed the blue joystick. Thadcred was his best character, so he was glad to be able to use it for once. The game started with the familiar evil laughing of Detrimis the Mysterious during the 'cut scene', which consisted of quickly scrolling text and a pixelated representation of the four playable characters.

The unicorn went south towards the *Golden Chalice*, a classic rookie mistake, but thanks to Fournimer's axe throwing speed he was able to chuck out enough hatchets to eliminate the goblins and lock their spawn point. Fournimer took the lead as he always did while playing *Vambrace* without his co-op team. It was the one game in which Palcath would listen to him and relinquish leadership.

It was evident that the unicorn didn't know a lot about *Vambrace*, since he was flabbergasted when they made it to level 2. The unicorn didn't even know there was a Level 2, which made Fournimer use the *Chuckle Animation*.

Winning the game would have been easy against the unskilled unicorn, but Fournimer did not let allies die in the land of *Vambrace*. By the time they killed the Cyclops of Level 4, Fournimer no longer needed to advise the unicorn about the obvious traps. After the

Level 7 boss, the unicorn could hold his own, and even remembered to block incoming attacks. Besides the fact that the unicorn had to collect every single *Slice of Lamb Meat* to survive, they made excellent progress. The Level 9 boss was quickly approaching, and Caeneus the True and his magical horse Eurytion put up a strong fight. So strong that the unicorn was defeated three button-presses in, and Fournimer, suffering from lack of food and the tell-tale chant of Human Warrior Needs Food Badly, perished as the bosses had started to flash.

On a completely amazing *Vambrace* high, the unicorn inserted more coins and insisted that they start again. Even though it wasn't needed, as Fournimer had won hooves down that part of the contest and the score was tied, he agreed to another game off the record. This time without the unicorn running into every trap, progress was much smoother and they even had time for some friendly banter.

> Arcade Unicorn's Text Box: I hated this game for the longest time, but now I love it!

> Fournimer's Text Box: watch out for that orc barrage! yes, that tends to happen. it grows on you.

> Arcade Unicorn's Text Box: I didn't realize how much mythology was packed into this game. I mean the whole battle between the Lapiths and the centaurs that killed us the first time, which was set up expertly!

> Fournimer's Text Box: centaurs? what are you talking about? there wasn't any centaurs.

> Arcade Unicorn's Text Box: Of course there was. All the centaurs we fought on the way to the boss Eurytion?

> Fournimer's Text Box: Eurytion is a horse!

> Arcade Unicorn's Text Box: No, he is a centaur. I'm sure they didn't have enough pixels to make him look like one. That explains what he was shooting!

> Fournimer's Text Box: his magical ice balls!

> Arcade Unicorn's Text Box: No. Close. I bet if you don't attack Caeneus, they will help us!

Fournimer was doubtful, he knew this game hand over hoof after all, but when they made it to Level 9 and only attacked the horse icon the hardest battle in the game became a cakewalk. The other 'boss' did help them! The biggest secret of *Vambrace*, that the designer hinted to be undiscovered all this time, had been revealed to Fournimer by a pinball playing unicorn. This secret would improve his speedrun time by at least three minutes! Fournimer was going to shoot to the highest *Vambrace* speedrun by a long shot now. Eat your heart out, former champion Keaton Clarke, you smug bastard!

It barely took any time to finish Level 10, kill Detrimis the Mysterious, and beat the game together with the huge savings of resources on Level 9. They were positively glowing with excitement and entered their initials on the high score board.

> Fournimer's Text Box: good call on that boss. how did you know?

> Arcade Unicorn's Text Box: That entire level was based off the wedding of Pirithous. The centaur guests fell into their more bestial side after getting drunk and started to rape the guests. Eurytion was the one who went for the bride.

> Fournimer's Text Box: centaurs rape people?

> Arcade Unicorn's Text Box: Of course they do. All the time. Centaurs would take women and boys they fancied, drag them away, and have their way with them. They were wild and untamed, with a particular fancy for virgins, as demonstrated by Eurytion shooting us with his pent up lust whenever we got too close.

> Fournimer's Text Box: I did not know that. that explains everything! finally, I know why my balls are always filling so fast! darn you mythology, this is all your fault!

> Arcade Unicorn's Text Box: I agree. This game is far too mythologically accurate. It makes me…

Trailing off mid sentence, the unicorn began to stare into the high score list. Fournimer could tell that the unicorn was deep in thought, and was shocked when he saw some tears welling up in the big rainbow eyes. Giving the gentle creature a hug, Fournimer asked what was wrong and the unicorn began to gush out (his problems, not his spunk).

> Arcade Unicorn's Text Box: Sorry! It is mythology and this game. They have gone and put me in an impossible situation. Bosses can only get sexy with avatars that are broken. Anyone who cheats on a machine here will awaken Arcadus the Slot Golem and she will have her way with them! I don't factor into the sexy scenarios at all!

> Fournimer's Text Box: yeah, but can't you have sex with an avatar that is already broken, or after she was done?

> Arcade Unicorn's Text Box: No, that is the problem! In mythology

only virgins can 'ride' unicorns! Any already broken avatars that show up will not be virgins after that slotting and that means I can't get 'ridden'. I thought I had accepted my life of celibacy, but now the world is going to end and I don't want to die a virgin!

The big tears had started to flow down the unicorn's cheeks. Fournimer absent mindedly ran his fingers through the unicorn's rainbow mane.

Fournimer's Text Box: do blowjobs count? handjobs?

Arcade Unicorn's Text Box: What?

Fournimer's Text Box: do you count blowjobs and handjobs towards losing your virginity?

Arcade Unicorn's Text Box: I don't... maybe... why?

Fournimer's Text Box: I am pretty sure remaking yourself as a centaur would cause someone to regain virgin status. brand new equipment after all. I am virgin 2.0. I have only done blowjobs and handjobs since then, so I may technically be a virgin, but I don't know.

Arcade Unicorn's Text Box: I don't know if those count. This sounds like a dangerous topic to debate.

Fournimer's Text Box: I bet there are lobbyists right now on both sides waiting to hear the answer to this, so they can complain about it.

Arcade Unicorn's Text Box: Maybe we should start trying something and see what happens?

Turning coyly, the unicorn relaxed his hind legs and flicked his tail seductively. Fournimer looked the unicorn over and considered his options. A unicorn was almost identical to a horse, so for the first time ever in the expansion here was something that was built for centaurs. It was willingly offering itself over, without forcing him to make a deal. Most importantly, it had been over a cycle since the Cervitaur and Fournimer's mythical nuts were already full and heavy. With a *Smirk Animation* Fournimer reared up and placed his front legs where he was pretty sure they should go.

The Arcade Unicorn used the *Overjoyed Animation*.

Arcade Unicorn's Text Box: Oh my Maker! You didn't explode when mounting me! You are technically considered a virgin!

Explode? Fournimer didn't think the penalty for mounting a unicorn while deflowered was so steep. No wonder they were always so strict. It was too late to worry about that now, and with a growing need he started to press up against the unicorn's entrance. Despite the fact that the unicorn was a virgin, that Fournimer was well endowed by horse standards, and that there was no lubrication mentioned previously, the tip of the big centaur cock began to slowly open up the tight rings of the unicorn. Legs sturdy, and body relaxed the unicorn rocked back and forth and Fournimer felt the tip slowly expand the entrance. Each little movement was causing a little more expansion, but it was going to be a long process.

Sweat was misting up on the pair, each gentle repositioning and expansion was pleasurable, but primal needs were starting to overcome each in a different way. Fournimer's centaur condition was being harder and harder to fight. With each near thrust he ached to fully penetrate his fancied target, and have his centaur needs met.

The unicorn had spent many cycles dreaming of this moment, and even though it was his nature to be as pure as angels dipped in the prayers of nuns he had to experience this; he needed to feel it inside.

> Arcade Unicorn's Text Box: Arcade Unicorn needs cock badly!

Fournimer felt a sudden loosening of the stubborn hole, and with a mighty thrust penetrated deep inside. The unicorn had only felt pleasure, and had a small heart firework explode over his head, when Fournimer entered him. Fournimer shifted forward with the next thrust and curled his front legs tightly around his welcoming lover.

Each thick thrust that followed was accompanied by a heart firework display. Fournimer had never figured out quite what *Slutty Kisses* did before now, but now he knew that they allowed him to kiss things internally with his cock. He didn't have the mental alertness to care at this moment, but it would be something to make note of for a later Chapter. All Fournimer knew was that this felt great. Better than a simple blow or handie, this was the real deal. This is what being a centaur was all about, thrusting hard into the things you claimed, making them shudder with delight they didn't even know they needed, using them up for every sweet succulent moment.

Heavy rhythmic pumping had caused Fournimer to go into a sexual trance. Each deliberate motion only clouded his mind more, and he forgot about all of his problems. He forgot about the world around him, he even forgot about the heart that Anders had broken. There was only this. A warm hole engulfing his cock, milking each and every motion. Sticky, slurping, sex. His speed increased, more, harder, thicker. Guttural moans bellowed from deep within. He shuddered and tried to plow through the rainbow receiver below. It was quivering, it was pulsing, and it was his. To use up, to fill completely, to fuck.

A heavy cloud was swirling around his head and while it was difficult to breathe, Fournimer inhaled as deep as he could. It filled his lungs, his body, and his mind—an earth scented musky fuel, and it sustained him; increased the power of his fucking. Below there were whinnies and kicks, and he felt it start. First a sharp contracting of his balls upward, then a wave of pleasure swept through him completely. The sex was in control now, not the avatar. In this instant he was sex and need. He was a monster. He clamped down hard, felt his seed start to bubble forth. In one exquisite push of intense pain, he felt himself release. All the pain turned to bliss in an instant. Torrents rushed through his whole body, and with each burst his mind cleared more. He shuddered as barrages of cum exploded from his aching need, and when all that were left was dribbles that hurt to come out, his mind unfogged and he was Fournimer again, no longer a sex-crazed monster.

The unicorn was still under him but had fallen to the ground. Fournimer had broken the one rule of pinball, he had tilted the unicorn! The rainbow horse had gained so much experience from getting fuck rampaged by Fournimer that it had gained sixteen levels through fireworks (and enough gold coins to never need to worry about running out of arcade money). It let out a twinkly little gasp of a noise and Fournimer saw the unicorn begin to gush out (his spunk, not his problems). Rainbow after rainbow erupted from the unicorn, and he squeezed his ass so hard on the softening centaur dick that Fournimer yelped a little in pain.

They collapsed in a wet heap on the ruined carpet. Barely able to breathe, they gasped for any air they could find, even if it was syrupy and hot. After a huge gulp of air, they cuddled.

> Arcade Unicorn's Text Box: So that is what the fuss is all about!

> Fournimer's Text Box: sorry, I don't know what came over me.

> Arcade Unicorn's Text Box: No! It was so intense. You were like an animal.

> Fournimer's Text Box: I thought you were the animal?

> Arcade Unicorn's Text Box: Magical Beast, actually.

Creature Name: Arcade Unicorn
Class: Magical Beast
Level: 67 (now)
Special Attacks: Rainbow Shot, Legal Tilt, Summon Quarters, Mythological Plot Exposition, Horn Gore
Special Notes: Deaf/Dumb/Blind Immunity
Drops: Red Cat Keycard
First Player Encounter Notes: he sure plays a mean pinball. – Fournimer

---

The Arcade Unicorn let out a *Giggle Animation*.

> Arcade Unicorn's Text Box: I have been informed that you won at the classic arcade game of *Jouster* for shooting off your lance first. Congratulations, you have won the contest and can proceed to the

> secret quest.

Fournimer ecstatically entered his initials on the high score sex chart, which appeared directly on the side of the Arcade Unicorn's rump. It was a massive high score, and Fournimer was certain he wouldn't be knocked off anytime soon.

> Fournimer's Text Box: maybe we could do that again some time?

> Arcade Unicorn's Text Box: You're not a virgin anymore, we can't play ever again. Now get out of here, you slut.

> Fournimer's Text Box: what?

> Arcade Unicorn's Text Box: Sorry. I don't mean it, but because I am a super pure at heart unicorn, I'm programmed to be a slut shamer. Now get out of here, the Red Kitty Door is right there. Tramp.

~~~

The Red Kitty Door opened into a short hallway with a stone door at the end. Carved into this stone was the face of a cat.

> Fournimer's Text Box: now what do I do?

> Draganders' Text Box: Chirp?

> Red Kitty Door's Door's Text Box: You should be proud of yourself, for purrfectly finding this hidden door. Mice job! You may meow enter.

Descending into the floor, the door revealed a corridor in the Arcade Glade Concession Area. Fournimer wasted no time. He had never found a secret this big before and he was too excited to not go inside.

Candles of all colours lined the walls illuminating various artworks. But there was something off about it. It took the horse a few pictures to figure it out but after the painting of cats playing poker everything became clear. All of these pictures were famous works of art, but had been redone with cats as the main subjects. Fournimer read off the names as he went, *The Yowl*, *Cat With a Pearl Collar*, *The Purrsistence of Meowmory*, *Meowing Lisa*, *Whistler's Mother's Cat*, and *The Last Supper But Done All With Cats*. There was a strange theme in this place, then he saw the next painting and it confused him.

> Fournimer's Text Box: why is this one called *This is Not a Cat?* that is obviously a cat. I don't get it.

> Draganders' Text Box: Chirp?

Chad the Flying Feline of Fortune's Text Box: That is because it is not a cat. For you cannot touch it nor stroke his fur. Mew may not feel his tail stroke against your nose nor sneeze right after. You may not hear it meow nor feed it delicious salmon. It simply is a picture of a cat; it is not a cat itself.

Fournimer's Text Box: that's pretty deep.

Chad the Flying Feline of Fortune's Text Box: True, but it has been around for some time, so don't get too impurressed. It isn't a pipe either, for reference.

The flying cat appeared in a dangerously close to copyright infringement like fashion. First the grinning mouth materialized while he talked, then his big yellow eyes. His tail was next, then his body, and lrgs. Finally, his wings came into view, which Fournimer somehow expected. He had seen this character somewhere before but wasn't quite sure where.

Fournimer's Text Box: I know you!

The cat, or as he liked to be called Chad, flew around Fournimer's head while they talked. Playfully phasing in and out of view as the mood struck him.

Chad the Flying Feline of Fortune's Text Box: Really? I don't know mew. I suspect, however that you mean that you know of me. For it is I: Chad the Flying Feline of Fortune. Yes, I am on the box art of *Annals of Gentalia* but no, I am not the mascot. I happen to be on there, so don't get mew excited.

Chad flitted about the room supported by his two angelic wings. He playfully dive bombed his throne in the middle of the art gallery and stretched out on his back, all the while being far too cute.

Fournimer's Text Box: how are you down here? we looked all over Onn and never found this place.

Chad the Flying Feline of Fortune's Text Box: All over Onn you say? Then you didn't look hard enough. Everyone knows that you look under bridges and behind waterfalls in games. It is purretty much a rule.

Fournimer thought about that. Palcath should have known; even Fournimer knew to look behind waterfalls.

Chad the Flying Feline of Fortune's Text Box: Look, there are three different secret entrances to my lair and the mewnicorn has reported in saying that no one has found any of the others. It is so unfair! The

Chad in the main map has all the fun. Until meow.

Fournimer's Text Box: what do you mean until now? don't get any ideas cat! I have glitter, heart kisses, and a rainbow dragon! so don't try anything because I'm not afraid to use them!

Nearly falling from his thrown in laughter, Chad managed to finally pick himself up and fly over to look Fournimer in the face.

Chad the Flying Feline of Fortune's Text Box: Seriously? I meant fun as in talking to all sorts of avatars and handing out quests. Not that other kind of fun. Mew are a big horse, I am a little cat.

Fournimer's Text Box: oh. you are an NPC quest giver?

Chad the Flying Feline of Fortune's Text Box: Even better than that! I am THE BEST NPC quest giver. No one has quests or rewards quite like mine. All luck of the draw, how exciting is that? All of my quests will give out random rewards! Flaming Pits, they even have random objectives! Mew my friend, are lucky to have stumbled upon my quest line! Avatars always talk about that other Chad's quests, now finally mew can talk about mine!

Fournimer's Text Box: that does sound different than other quests I've done.

Chad the Flying Feline of Fortune's Text Box: If mew mean different as in more meowvellous! Then yes, they are different. You can choose one of the three quests now. To take the other two, you must find the other entrances to The Art Gallery of Cute Kittehs! Choose your quest wisely. We have -The Quest of Fetch-, -The Quest of Trade- and -The Quest of Escort-! Which do you want to do first?

Fournimer's Text Box: what do I need to do in them?

Chad the Flying Feline of Fortune's Text Box: I simply cannot tell mew because I simply do not know. They are all randomly generated by my Fickle Fortune Wheel of Fate. Choose wisely and randomly.

Fournimer's Text Box: hmm, then the first one I guess.

Chad the Flying Feline of Fortune's Text Box: Excellent. -The Quest of Fetch-! I require three random items for no reason at all. They could be anything in the world and you will need to bring them all to

> me to complete the quest. Let's see what I need shall we? I hope it is something fishy or a cheezburgr, I am famished. Time for mew to spin the Fickle Fortune Wheel of Fate!

Fournimer had been wondering why there had been a giant six story high wheel in the centre of the room behind Chad's throne. Now he had his answer. He stepped up to the wheel and saw the name of every item he had ever heard of (and many more he hadn't) each on a section of the wheel. Chad's throne made for a lovely pointer, and Chad himself made an even lovelier pointer as he motioned for Fournimer to take the first spin by stretching out into a cute pose.

Spinning the Fickle Fortune Wheel of Fate was more exciting than Fournimer had anticipated. It felt like he was on a game show and that everyone in the crowd was cheering for him, even though the only spectators were Chad, Draganders, and hundreds of motionless famous painting cats. Fournimer was nervous as the wheel came to a stop and he let out a *Sigh of Relief Animation* as the pointer barely ticked past *The Head of The Omega Flork, Destroyer of Worlds* and landed instead on *Funnel*.

> Chad the Flying Feline of Fortune's Text Box: The first item is a *Funnel*. Purrty, I really wanted an *Omega Flork Head Ashtray*.

> Fournimer's Text Box: I totally already have a bunch of *Funnels*.

> Chad the Flying Feline of Fortune's Text Box: Purrfect then. Wonderful. Good show. Spin again for the next item!

The imaginary crowd hushed as the next spin came to a rest. It was extra dramatic and the applause sign was turned off for the entire affair to hush the audience. When The Fickle Fortune Wheel of Fate landed on *Stone Softener* and Fournimer pulled one out of his pack, the crowd went wild (after the applause sign lit up)! It wasn't Fournimer's item per se, he was only holding onto it, but he promised himself that he would find a replacement before he needed to return it to its rightful owner.

> Chad the Flying Feline of Fortune's Text Box: Mice one! You are two for two without needing to leave and look for anything. What will the last item be? Let's watch and find out!

Sweat dripping from his brow and nearly sick from the anticipation, Fournimer span the Fickle Fortune Wheel of Fate for the third time. This spin was taking longer than the rest to finish and as it slowed down he watched countless hard to find items pass by. After what seemed like an eternity and with many pictures of cats watching on expectedly, it finally came to rest on *Elixir*—the hardest healing item to find in the entire game and the entire purpose of Group B's quest. He would never find one of those!

> Chad the Flying Feline of Fortune's Text Box: The item is... *Elixir*. Do mew have—

The flying cat had been interrupted. Even though the wheel had completely stopped it impossibly clicked back one item on the pointer. Chad was stunned and speechless, he had never heard of such a thing, it went against all the pointy wheel logic patterns he had. The cat decided that it must be fate, and that this other item must be the true item for the quest. Fournimer decided that it was Draganders rubbing against his leg and nudging the wheel accidentally but he didn't say anything.

> Chad the Flying Feline of Fortune's Text Box: The Fickle Fortune Wheel of Fate has decided! It is not an *Elixir*, it is... The *This is Not a Cat* picture? Really? Why is that even an item on here, it is hanging on the wall right over there? I really wanted fish or something.

An elated centaur and his dragon ran over to the *This is Not a Cat* picture and ripped it from the wall, returning it from a long fetch quest of 5 move units away.

> Fournimer's Text Box: victory!

> Draganders' Text Box: Chirp!

> Chad the Flying Feline of Fortune's Text Box: That is what random is all about I guess. Meow for your reward!

> Fournimer's Text Box: I finished a quest all by myself. that is so cool! what do I get?

> Chad the Flying Feline of Fortune's Text Box: I have no idea! It is random, like the quest itself. Spin the Fickle Fortune Wheel of Fate and find out what mew've won!

Fournimer used the *Shrug Animation* and span the wheel for the fourth time. He forgot to look at the item rewards but now it was spinning too fast to see them, the various colours of the sections from before and the sparkling lights were visible.

> Chad the Flying Feline of Fortune's Text Box: This should be interesting. I've never done a reward before and I know that the other Chad has never gotten to use the expanded reward wheel before. So purrfectly purrfect. I can't wait to gloat.

> Fournimer's Text Box: expanded reward wheel?

> Chad the Flying Feline of Fortune's Text Box: Yes. Since mew are a broken avatar, all sorts of different things have been added in there. More things than boring old regular Chad's wheel. Exciting, huh?

> Fournimer's Text Box: wait. so there are like broken things on there now? crazy sex powers, Sexcessories, and stuff like that?

> Chad the Flying Feline of Fortune's Text Box: All that and meowre!

> Fournimer's Text Box: I changed my mind Chad. I don't want to spin it anymore.

> Chad the Flying Feline of Fortune's Text Box: It is a bit late for that I think. Mew already did spin it and it is about to land on…

Watching as the wheel slowed to a crawl Fournimer felt a wave of relief as each 'reward' passed and a new wave of fear when he read then next one on the Fickle Fortune Wheel of Fate. Each sounded worse than the last. Sexcessory - *Pretty Much Permanent Penis Pump*, Sex Power Swap - *Perfect Rack*, Sex Supplement - *Vaginal Wetness +2*, Item - *Medium Stamina Potion* (which Fournimer was upset to see click by), Item - *Kama Sutra for Gnomes* and finally…

> Fournimer's Text Box: oh Maker… what is it? I can't look.

> Chad the Flying Feline of Fortune's Text Box: Congratulations! Mew have won an Additional Secondary Weapon - *Bolas*. I'll go ahead and set these to blue for you.

> Fournimer's Text Box: I think I got rid of those in the unicorn.

> Chad the Flying Feline of Fortune's Text Box: No I said blue *Bolas*. They are two spheres attached by a cord, let me read this here. Hmm… It appurrs that they do not cause damage, but they can be used to inflict a Status Effect if they hit. There is a 50% chance for Bound, 35% chance of Bound More or 15% chance for Bound More More. There is an additional comment for broken avatars here that says 100% chance of sexy… whatever that means.

> Fournimer's Text Box: those sound pretty cool for a change. here I got all worked up for nothing and I think I finally have something useful!

> Draganders' Text Box: Chirp!

> Chad the Flying Feline of Fortune's Text Box: I'm glad it worked out for mew. It was pretty tense there for a round. Congratulations on your lucky break, good luck in finding the other entrances here! See you soon! Best fishes!

> Fournimer's Text Box: actually… I'm kinda sorta stuck down here, I was wondering if we could sleep here tonight Chad.

◊ Chapter 13 ◊

CYCLE 3: MORNING NE, CLOTHING NOT OPTIONAL

Leaving the Stairway Forest was less difficult than ne had thought it would be. None of the monsters attacked, they had only stared at his musculature. He wasn't sure if they were stunned by his beauty, still couldn't see him or plain didn't care that he was walking by. It probably was that last one. Most of the Vams and Lycas were following Vam-Boy and Lyca-Guy's examples and were making out in hidden groves. Blood fued resolved.

To top things off he had so many strange dreams last night while sleeping in an unused, pristine white bed. Something about big prize wheels, eating Xam, *Funnels*, and cats. So many cats. ne shrugged them off as Lyca-dreams (not as foreshadowing) and tried to put them all behind him.

ne learned that the main map was not as desolate as he originally thought. He heard from a group of low levels, who only stared at his glittery naked form for the entire conversation, that the area around that old starting city was all but abandoned. If he wanted to play the game, the areas around The Crags of Halm were relatively unscathed and that most avatars had fled there. A high level had even set up a permanent warp spot with a *Zoner Rezoner*.

The low levels ogled for a bit longer and then left. ne used the *Sigh Animation* as he looked down. Naked again. Why was he always naked? There was a conspiracy against him wearing pants. He was not going to let this happen again for a prolonged period of time and he did have an idea on how to solve this problem. If he could absorb polygons and abilities from defeated opponents then he would look through his list of Optional

Bosses and pick carefully. There might be one that was made of pants! It was certainly worth a look over his list.

The Optional Boss List - All Rights Reserved

Main Map Optional Bosses	Map Location	Look Here
Elfbane	Karazhahanana	The Summoning Circle
Flork Omega	The Crags of Halm	Crag #112
Giganticore	Giganticore's Lair	The Giganticore's Heart
Primary Weapon	The Underwater But Overland Desert	The Exact Centre
The Armour Knight	Mechanical Mecha Factory	Smelting Room
The Dryad	The Castle in the Sky	The Dryad's Grove
Vam-Boy & Lyca-Guy	Stairway Forest	Magical Castle in the Woods

Island of Islana Optional Bosses	Map Location	Look Here
Cruel-X, The Dark Lord of Snatch	Onn	The Ring - Healing Magic Only
New Boss +	Onn	The Arena - Melee Only
Smoke The Reptile	Saibot's Tower	The Noob's Pit
Super Puzzle Boss	Onn	The Stadium - Attack Magic Only
The Avenger	Onn	The Throne Room
The Bull King	The Flaming Pits	Circle 8, Milking Field
The Legendary 13 Headed Hydra	Onn	The Coliseum - Ranged Only

The Armour Knight jumped out at ne. If anything would give him clothing in the form of Armour, it would be that. It wasn't even that long of a trip from his current location and there was the added bonus that ne knew where The Mechanical Mecha Factory was. His limited map exploration did not show many of the listed locations, but the factory was right near the Lova Mines and he knew where that was.

Walking onward, he chewed absent mindedly on a *Double Danish* that he had pulled out of thin air (but was in his inventory somehow). There wasn't much food left in his pack, not enough for a growing boy's week long journey. Hopefully he could find more soon.

ne travelled through his old pants hunting grounds. He crossed the still unmarked divider between the Lower and Upper Forest of Althair and headed towards his old grumpy friend.

There she was, the Demon Bear of Kazuul. ne had never bothered to learn her name nor would he remember it after this. She still had his footprint on her face, and that was going to be exactly where he aimed his foot for a spring start to his *Double Jump*. He readied his charge at the entrance to the glade, and with a burst of speed ran towards his goal. Everything was suddenly black and painful.

He had clues as to what happened when his vision finally cleared several rounds later. There were two lines of flames from his start position burning in the grass. There was a ne sized imprint in the rock face behind where the bear had been. The evidence mounted when he walked by a nearby tree, accidentally rammed into it with his shoulder and it exploded into thousands of pixel shards.

Strength, Constitution, and Dexterity all pulsed through his new muscles. If his status page was showing his stats right now and wasn't a frayed mess, he bet that his statistics would easily pass through the normal limits. After throwing a tree carcass clear out of Althair during a 'light test throw' he decided that his statistics might even cross over to the next page. He had Optional Boss statistical power and they were strong enough to battle hundreds of avatars at once (or one Mr. Max). ne used the *Laugh Animation* at his newfound power, happy that he found out before horrible things happened to himself or others he cared about. A test jump showed that even his regular jump now could reach higher than his once normal *Double Jump*, and he didn't need any stairs.

It was a definite shame that no one was around to see how awesome he was right now. Now that he thought about it… it almost felt like someone was watching him being awesome. He was almost creeped out but then remembered that it was likely Ni Hao Bunny© so there was no need for alarm. If someone was watching him (bunny or otherwise), he decided that he might as well show off how neat he was.

Making his way to The Mechanical Mecha Factory was so much fun. Sprinting at a breakneck speed, ramming through scenery (some of it even on purpose), and executing long, majestic double-leaps was invigorating. Nothing bothered to attack him. The monsters could barely even see him let alone lock-on to the glittery white blur. He arrived at the factory sweaty, panting, way ahead of schedule, and with a giant grin plastered on his face.

> ne's Stomach Text Box: Growwwwwl!

> ne's Text Box: Oh Maker! So hungry.

Half of his leftover food reserves were gone before ne could stop stuffing his face. He didn't care that it all tasted awful; he needed to eat. Even when he was finally full he could feel the food absorbing quickly to feed his advanced stats. Being magical and amazing was hungry work, he would need to find a real food source soon if he wanted to keep being so cool. He wanted to hurry through this factory and book travel on the boat to get to his next destination (the S.S. Party Splitterup had a massive snack bar).

The Mechanical Mecha Factory was hot and loud. It was built around the insides of an active volcano. The fact that this location was nestled deep within the ice cold Lova Mountains should have been an *Eyeroll Animation* moment for ne, but by this time he had gotten so used to the inane level design that it didn't even phase him. Two different paths lead into the heart of the mountain. To the right was a staircase that would travel to the top peak of the volcano. To the left bridges that continued further into the bowels of the mountain. He was looking for a Smelting Room so he took the left path and headed down. Making a full path over the dangerous lava was obviously too much work for the designers of this place. It wasn't like falling into lava would hurt, so why not cut some corners to save on building costs and skip half the bridges.

Mechanical monsters went about their pre-determined paths, blissfully ignorant of ne's progress through the mountain. This was a lower level area to begin with and even without a weapon or super stats he could kill these things with a single *White Wolf Kick*. He avoided killing them for two reasons: they were robotic and wouldn't drop food, and killing them would only increase his appetite.

Smelting Room B was the sign on the door at the heart of the volcano. That meant there was more than one Smelting Room and the other one was likely at the top of this mountain. If the Optional Boss wasn't through this door then there would be a long jumping trek all the way back to the entrance. ne opened the door and was hit by a blast of cooler air. It was refreshing against his now hot sweaty skin.

This room was large and open, which was a promising start. On display was a set of gleaming Armour. It was of the plate family, so likely only equippable by the melee classes. A brilliant ultramarine blue with golden trim, this Armour had a far higher polygon count than other Armours ne had seen. The helmet had a mask that could open and close, and ornamental golden wings sprouting from the sides. It was unique, interesting, and immediately suspicious. ne eyed it and was surprised when five Item Description Menu Boxes popped up. This undefended set of Armour was called Knight's Armour, required the wearer to be at least Level 50, had stats that rivaled even Gigas Gear, and could be equipped by any class. Best of all it was stylish, would cover all of his bits, and was reasonably priced.

Earlier recklessness in the past had made certain events unpleasant. ne was not going to jump into this decision quickly. He poked and prodded the Armour and saw no change or deadly traps. Even after hanging around for longer than necessary, nothing but the presence of the Armour had been suspicious. What sealed the deal was when ne retraced his steps, made his way to Smelting Room A at the top of the mountain, and heard boss background music when he opened the door. Smelting Room A held the boss monster, Smelting Room B held uniquely fashionable pants.

Despite his newly found distrust for clothing not found inside chests, ne really did not want to spend another grandiose adventure with the kiss of the wind constantly hitting his sensitive areas. He tried on a single glove first. It went up to his elbow with a sturdy armguard and was lined with a soft delicate material that would absorb moisture and prevent chafing. The Knight Armour automatically adjusted the various straps and provided a perfect fit. It felt wonderful on and he lowered his guard slightly putting on the other glove. The boots were gel lined, provided excellent back support, and reaching up to his knees. The pants were more thong like than pants normally were, but a stylized skirting of plates covered much of his larger than normal muscular butt. The chest piece covered only that, leaving his abdomen and back bare, but had multiple plates where it didn't count. Finally ne put on the helmet, lowering the visor to get a good look at himself. He looked like a certified badass in this get-up. With his new body and Armour, ne didn't even recognize himself until he flipped the visor up. He turned to leave Smelting Room B and headed towards Smelting Room A in style, but after two steps down the stairs, he could no longer move.

> The Armour Knight's Text Box: Look at what I caught this time! What a cutie!

> ne's Text Box: I only just noticed that Knight Armour wasn't written in italics like normal items. You are not an item, you never were one! Toasted bagels with cream cheese!

> The Armour Knight's Text Box: Wow! Check out the filthy pastry mouth on you! Look at all those muscles, oil, and glitter. I want to eat you up, cutie!

> ne's Text Box: Just to be clear here, do you eat avatars or…?

> The Armour Knight's Text Box: Of course not, I'm not going to eat you, cutie.

> ne's Text Box: Thank the Maker.

> The Armour Knight's Text Box: I will have my way with you though, cutie.

> ne's Text Box: What? How?

To answer ne's question The Armour Knight used ne's gloved hand to feel up his thigh and stomach. While he himself was not moving, the Armour was and it was attached to him. It was in control for now and was busy feeling up the front cod-piece. The Armour retracted the crotch protection revealing ne's slowly stiffening member. With his new increased size ne noted with interest that becoming hard took more rounds than before. His gloved hand grabbed his cock and helped to pump blood into it.

He wasn't sure how big this thing was going to get. It was brand new. He felt every gush of blood enter it and could see it increase in size with each heartbeat. Once fully erect, ne felt a little light-headed and either fell to the ground or the Armour had pushed him down. This new penis was at least 11 length units long, probably closer to 12 and a good amount thicker. It was nearly double the size of his old member and strangely he was now circumcised, like other Lyca-Guys.

His gloved hand was now pumping his shaft and it was as if ne was experiencing it for the first time. This new cock had more surface area and wasn't as sensitive as his old one, except for the tip, which was so much more responsive than he was used to. A single brush of pressure against it made ne scream with knee weakening pleasure.

ne rubbed himself with one hand as his legs were forcibly lifted up to be held with his other. What was once the pleated skirt of the Armour folded together to form a metallic member. He moaned as the Armour began to feel up his thigh and focus the attention on his opening. He was really beginning to enjoy himself as the tip of the Armour extension had begun to tentatively enter his hole. The pressure stopped and ne was sure that The Armour Knight blushed.

> The Armour Knight's Text Box: Sorry! I didn't mean to offend you.

> ne's Text Box: Seriously? What do you mean?

> The Armour Knight's Text Box: You are so tall, beefy, and hung. I guess I didn't even think for a round there. You are obviously a total top. I'm sorry I was playing with you down there, cutie.

> ne's Text Box: Huh? No it's fine really. It was great. This butt is brand new and I was looking forward to trying it out!

> The Armour Knight's Text Box: Of course it isn't fine! I feel so stupid! Stop being so nice.

The Armour skirt reverted to the pre-penetrative state which earned a soft whimper of regret from ne. The Armour Knight was thinking now while absent mindedly stroking ne's stiff member.

> The Armour Knight's Text Box: What can I do with a top though? Umm… What class are you, cutie?

> ne's Text Box: Night Ranger, Ranged specialty.

> The Armour Knight's Text Box: Really? I never would have guessed, all beefy and all. So the best Dexterity in the game then, but with a big cock. I think I know what to do, let me test you out.

ne didn't have time to reply, he was quickly manoeuvred into different yoga stretches, each more complicated than the last. His bigger, beefy frame was still as lithe as his former, skinnier one. He wasn't sure if it was due to his complete lack of inner polygons or if it was a class feature but he was still as flexible as he always had been, possibly even more flexible due to his newly absorbed Optional Boss statistics.

The Armour Knight's Text Box: Look at you, cutie, way better than I expected from a big beefy guy. Nice!

ne's Text Box: Thank you?

The Armour Knight's Text Box: Time to get to work, cutie.

ne was transitioned from Upward Facing Two-Foot Staff Pose to a Supported Shoulderstand Pose. He didn't quite understand what was going on until he repositioned into Plow Pose. His long member was now staring at him right in the face and with a simple hip wiggle the tip of it brushed against his lips. He wasn't even really trying yet and was already closer than most guys could even dream. ne decided that this was much easier to accomplish with a longer penis.

The Armour was not controlling his mouth, but curiosity overtook ne. With a few experimental licks of the tip he sighed happily. Knowing that he could even lick the tip might be enough to make him never want to leave the house and go on an adventure again. Now he wanted to know how far he could go. He experimentally pushed his hips forward. To help answer his questions, The Armour Knight lowered the controlled knees to beside ne's head and shoved over half of his own member down his own throat.

ne attempted to scream out in alarm but had muffled himself with his new thicker cock. His hips began to thrust slowly towards his mouth with a calm rhythm. Each careful thrust would remove everything but the head. This gave ne the time to adjust to the feeling of his member inside his own throat and to really focus on his techniques when working on the head. The instant feedback of his efforts was both welcomed and informative.

The pace increased as the happy avatar continued his work. He could feel the sweat dripping off his body and taste the fluids leaking from his own member. The taste of himself was driving him absolutely wild and he yearned to experience what was coming. Despite the thrill of anticipation his entire body was aching for release. He Text Boxed some words but was completely muffled out. The Armour drew back his hips, releasing his member with a loud slurp.

The Armour Knight's Text Box: What did you say, cutie?

ne's Text Box: I said, do me faster, me!

The Armour Knight's Text Box: With pleasure!

The dick was stuffed back in the eager mouth and the hips were pumped furiously.

ne extended his tongue to taste even more on down thrusts and swirled it expertly on up thrusts. Every pump was pure pleasure and ne lost himself in it. He closed his eyes and went with the rhythm.

> The Armour Knight's Text Box: Look Out! You're going to cum!

Magically controlled hips thrust forward one final time, deeper than ever before. ne opened his eyes in shock as he began to feel his big member twitch, pulse, and then start to unload jets of his cum down his own throat; far more than he was used to thanks to his new larger balls. Warm, salty, and distinctly his, ne enjoyed the sensation and taste as he blissfully released. He was softening quicker than he was used to and soon flopped out of his smiling mouth. The last drop smearing his lips as he retracted.

It was with a sense of relief that ne realized that he could control his own movements again. He stood up, only slightly stiff, from the experience. ne knew he would be sore later from overstretching but it had been worth it. When a chilled breeze hit his sore spots he noticed that he was now completely nude and the Armour had returned to the stand.

> The Armour Knight's Text Box: Thanks, cutie, that was hot. Visit me again sometime.

> **Creature Name:** The Armour Knight
> **Class:** Construct
> **Level:** 50
> **Special Attacks:** Deflect, Control, Iron Skirt Lance, Gloved Hand, Punch-o!
> **Drops:** You! You can leave now!
> **First Player Encounter Notes:** Bring someone you know that you can beat fellow adventurers! It makes the battle much easier. – Mr. Max
> **Additional Comments:** Or make sure you can beat yourself. It makes the battle more interesting. – ne

> Game Explanation Text Box: Polygons absorbed from The Armour Knight 16.6%.

nde knew instinctively that these new polygons were mostly of the internal polygons sort, but his outer body did get a touch of smoothness. He also noticed that he had gotten his equipment page back as well as another letter.

> nde's Text Box: Come on, everyone should know who I am, give me all my letters back!

> Game Explanation Text Box: Special trait absorbed from The Armour Knight: Knight Armour.

nde had been right. This encounter had earned him Armour! A full set was now equipped, and it had gained the sheen of glitter to make it 'menacing'. There was a colour controller, but it was locked due to him having no colours, which was annoying. He was going to be stuck as stark white, but he did gain some lovely grayscale rainbow accents. None of his bits were flapping in the wind and he could even control the various revealing flaps mentally. He also noted with a *Smirk Animation* that he could even make a dress plate penis form from the back. He believed his close friend Roodg had said it the best.

nde's Text Box: This Armour is nEAT and sAWES*cough cough*OME!

After a few more worried coughs, nde expelled the object stuck in his throat. He reached into his mouth and pulled out a wet purple *Optional Flower*. Not knowing where it came from (probably from the Armor controlling him during the encounter), nde used a *Sheepish Grin Animation*. He tucked the flower away into his inventory (somehow) and left The Mechanical Mecha Factory before he could further embarrass himself.

Chapter 14

CYCLE 3
GROUP C, TOGETHER
BUT ALONE

Jorthan the Male Troll Monk's Text Box: Coming back to pick us up, that is not something they are doing I would wager.

Trev Terra's Text Box: No. I would think not. Not after what happened… the disaster rather. De'vini has gone mental, crazy, sorry, crazy is not an offensive term. So… gosh… Yeah. We are going to be stuck here.

Jorthan the Male Troll Monk's Text Box: So it will be being you and moi mon petit lutin amour? Not minding that I am not. Time with moi amour. A boat we can make to sail away.

Trev Terra used the *Arms Crossed Animation* followed by a *Scowl Animation*. He took a deep breath and thought about what he was going to say.

Trev Terra's Text Box: Are you sure about that? Am I going to be enough for you?

Jorthan the Male Troll Monk's Text Box: You are being very much énergique mon petit lutin amour. Do you hate boats?

Trev Terra's Text Box: It is you. There is nothing with me or with boats! There is something with you. You call me a petit lutin to try to make me feel special, but then you go and call every boy, girl, or mix the same thing! You are being such a flirt to everything around. How can you expect me to believe what you say? How am I special?

Jorthan the Male Troll Monk's Text Box: I not knowing you feel that way mon petit lut… mon Trev. You are wrong though, I am calling you mon petit lutin amour. Not using amour I have with everyone else. You are moi only amour.

Trev lost some of his new found assertiveness, almost as fast as he had found it.

Trev Terra's Text Box: Oh… well gosh… well, I still have problems believing you. Rather, I am having a hard time with that. Why do you flirt with everyone and call them lutins!?

Jorthan the Male Troll Monk's Text Box: That is not obvious? I am one with a grand fétiche for lutins! That is being a reason why I enjoy you.

Trev Terra's Text Box: You and your lutins! It makes me so mad! What… what is a lutin?

Jorthan used the *Big Belly Laugh Animation*.

Jorthan the Male Troll Monk's Text Box: A lutin is how you say? An elf. I am liking many more things about you than your ears.

Trev Terra's Text Box: That's why you were all flirty with that farmer in *The Need for Seed*! I get it now! I thought you liked sprites, that is why I made myself a sprite elf!

Jorthan the Male Troll Monk's Text Box: No, I like lutins and thier sexy ears!

Trev Terra used the *Sudden Realization Animation*.

Trev Terra's Text Box: You like pointy ears?! Is that why you were always following Caela around while drooling?

Jorthan the Male Troll Monk's Text Box: Caela? So much…

Jorthan's eyes glazed over at the mention of Caela's superior ear set.

Jorthan the Male Troll Monk's Text Box: Gha-lu-lugga-ah…

Trev needed to slap Jorthan out of his ear fantasy.

Trev Terra's Text Box: Sorry.

Jorthan the Male Troll Monk's Text Box: It being fine. Liking that I did.

If flirting with pointy lutins is bothering you then stopping it I will be.

Trev Terra's Text Box: I mean… gosh, I would like that yes.

Jorthan the Male Troll Monk's Text Box: Even with you? Stopping with you, my little lutin, would you also be liking me to do that?

Trev Terra's Text Box: Well of course not. Well, rather, you can keep flirting with me if you want. Gosh, don't stop that. I like that.

Jorthan the Male Troll Monk's Text Box: Oh mon petit lutin amour, happy I am that you said that. Worried I had become. I had much wanted you to be my first.

Trev Terra's Text Box: Your first? Your first what? What do you mean?

Jorthan the Male Troll Monk's Text Box: My first I mean. For the sexe.

Trev Terra changed from his natural permanent *Blush Shade #2* to *Blush Shade #8.*

Trev Terra's Text Box: For sex? You… oh gosh, rather gosh… Oh uh, well gosh.

Jorthan the Male Troll Monk's Text Box: Yes for the sexe. You, I want you to be my first.

Trev Terra's Text Box: Oh wow… Gosh, do you mean in like the Game? Or like in well for real? Are you a virgin… well have you had sex in… with real people?

Jorthan the Male Troll Monk's Text Box: In this Game many monsters I have defeated. I only used so far though my *Fisting Fists.* In the real world I am also not being with anyone. Both places have had cuddling with you though. A virgin in both is I.

Trev Terra's Text Box: Wow really? I mean I'm pretty shy and I have been with a bunch of… rather gosh, I mean it would be an honour if you wanted me to be your first, uh… a real honour.

Jorthan the Male Troll Monk's Text Box: Liking you I would very like. Where do you want me first?

Trev Terra's Text Box: Gosh… what rather?

Jorthan the Male Troll Monk's Text Box: In Game or in my room I am meaning for the bedtimes.

Trev wished that *Blush Shade #9* had been unlocked so that he could use it now.

> Trev Terra's Text Box: Oh. Gosh, Well it can't be here. I promised Roodg… to save for emergencies. I… got in trouble for the lakes and… we should talk about that after.

> Jorthan the Male Troll Monk's Text Box: Is my hope you are all shy and stuttering when we are sexing. So cute it is.

> Trev Terra's Text Box: Gosh!

> Jorthan the Male Troll Monk's Text Box: Yes. That is what you need to be doing.

Jorthan the Male Troll Monk and Trev Terra used the *Sweeping Embrace Dual Animation*.

> Trev Terra's Text Box: Yes Hippolyta we will get a room. Gosh… ruin the moment much?

◈ Chapter 15 ◈
CYCLE 3
GROUP R, THE HUNTED

Roodg's Text Box: oUCH.

Cynddylan Bongam's Text Box: Jolly! It is now awfully awake.

Maelmadog Chwith's Text Box: One would have to say, quite true old bean.

Opening a single sore *#36 Style Eye* Roodg waited patiently for the room to stop spinning. The first feature to come into focus was the giant bars of the cage the night elf was locked in. That likely wasn't a good feature. Slowly the rest of the room came into view, it was a tribal themed grass hut with bare dirt floors. Spears and sticks were on the walls, stuck in pots, on the floor, and were even hanging from the ceiling. Furs and pelts hung on bars across the room all with eccentric animal patterns. A smaller golden cage on a stand stood beside Roodg's cage and contained a glowing pile of red rope. Finally, two stereotypical tribal warriors stood as guards watching over their prisoner, complete with animal skin outfits, lip disks, and bone piercings. It took Roodg more than time to figure out who had spoken, it took until the tribal warriors Text Boxed again to figure out.

Cynddylan Bongam's Text Box: Right good. This is a glorious turn of events, don't you agree old chap?

Maelmadog Chwith's Text Box: I am more than disinclined to disagree with you. This is a right bit of good for certain.

Roodg's Text Box: sTOP. wHY DO U aFRICAN WARRIORS HAVE wELSH NAMES AND SPEAK LIKE POSH bRITISH GENTLEMAN?

Cynddylan Bongam's Text Box: Oh, that. Quite a bit of bother that.

Maelmadog Chwith's Text Box: Absolutely. Quite a bit of bother indeed.

Cynddylan Bongam's Text Box: Our original names and patterns of speech could be considered by some a bit south of proper.

Maelmadog Chwith's Text Box: That was precisely the problem. Top hole observation.

Cynddylan Bongam's Text Box: Yes top hole that. Thank you kindly.

Maelmadog Chwith's Text Box: Certainly not a problem. Certainly not a problem indeed.

Cynddylan Bongam's Text Box: A few cycles after release an Administrator fellow stopped by and changed our names and speech patterns to a bit more top of the border.

Maelmadog Chwith's Text Box: Awfully less chance of racism complaints that way.

Roodg's Text Box: hOW IS THIS ANY BETTER THAN TALKING LIKE HOW AN aFRICAN TRIBESMAN SHOULD TALK? iSN'T THIS WORSE?

Both Tribesmen used the *Agree With the Old Sport Animation*.

Cynddylan Bongam's Text Box: I agree old sport. It is bollocks is what.

Maelmadog Chwith's Text Box: Perfectly astute. Balderdash the entire thing. What a complete gaff.

Cynddylan Bongam's Text Box: We would complain about it, but not a soul can find us out here in The Mist Covered Island You Knew About But Couldn't Land on Because of the Mist.

Maelmadog Chwith's Text Box: Except for Administrators and the

Goddess I suppose. I had forgotten about that. They found us and right quick at that.

Cynddylan Bongam's Text Box: True true. The Goddess would be most cross with you if you had forgotten about them or her. Right upset she is with them.

Maelmadog Chwith's Text Box: Might I have taken ill to forget such a thing?

Cynddylan Bongam's Text Box: Right so. That was quite piffle of you. How would you forget her dislike for them? If we didn't have this bright new sacrifice for tomorrow I would have to vote for you.

Maelmadog Chwith's Text Box: I could hardly blame you for that. I would certainly right deserve it.

Roodg's Text Box: gODDESS? tHE mIST cOVERED iSLAND yOU kNEW aBOUT bUT cOULDN'T lAND ON bECAUSE OF THE mIST? tOMORROW'S SACRIFICE? mE?

The Tribesmen both used the *Capital Spot of Right Animation.*

Cynddylan Bongam's Text Box: Yes capital there, getting all that right, Tomorrow's Sacrifice. It does say all of that on your cage. I suppose you couldn't read it from where you are though. Pity, the lettering is well done. I worked right hard on that. Good show getting it though.

Maelmadog Chwith's Text Box: The Goddess is ever so excited. When she found out we had found a real live avatar for sacrifice she nearly fell off her tuffet.

Roodg's Text Box: LoL! tUFFETS THAT IS JOLLY sAWESOME. wAIT, SACRIFICE THAT IS RIGHT BAD.

Cynddylan Bongam's Text Box: Have a jolly good sleep sacrifice, you have a right full day tomorrow.

Maelmadog Chwith's Text Box: Of course. Bright and early! Have a more than pleasant night.

The posh welsh tribesmen left the hut leaving Roodg alone to think.

Roodg's Text Box: bRIGHT & EARLY? tHAT MAKES IT EVEN WORSE! tHIS SUCKS.

Glowing Red Rope's Text Box: Quit your belly aching. At least you can move, I am only allowed to move when inserted. At least your suffering will end quickly, mine will likely never end. At least you got a swim before your fate, I've been sticky for so long.

Roodg's Text Box: gLOWING rED rOPE U CAN TALK?

Glowing Red Rope's Text Box: I'm not a glowing red rope. I'm tied up in Bolas. Not that it matters, I may as well be rope.

Roodg's Text Box: aW! dON'T SAY THAT nOT gLOWING rED rOPE! yOU MATTER.

Glowing Red Rope's Text Box: No, it doesn't matter. I don't matter. Not anymore. We are stuck here. You will be used up and after that I will be used again and again for her perverted needs. We can't get out of here. The cord on this *Bolas* is too tight and your bars are too small to fit through.

Roodg's Text Box: wHAT ARE YOU TALKING ABOUT? i CAN GET MY WHOLE LEG OUT OF THIS CAGE NO PROBLEM. iT IS TOO BAD i HAVE HIPS AND RIBS OR i COULD GET OUT.

Glowing Red Rope's Text Box: You can fit your leg through the bars? How? The bars are so close together.

Roodg's Text Box: yES. i AM A NIGHT ELF, THEY HAVE THE SKINNIEST MODELS. i AM SO THIN AND LANKY. iT IS sAWESOME FOR GETTING THRU BARS BUT MAKES VINE SWINGING PUZZLES SUCK.

Glowing Red Rope's Text Box: That is awesome! Can you reach me?

Roodg's Text Box: yES, BUT ONLY WITH MY FOOT AND THE WORD IS sAWESOME!

Glowing Red Rope's Text Box: A foot is better than anything else that has touched me lately. Can you untie me?

Roodg's Text Box: i CAN'T BEND MY TOES, THAT IS SO LAME. i CAN BEND MY ANKLE AND HIT YOU THOUGH.

Glowing Red Rope's Text Box: that is something. Bash me around, maybe the *Bolas* will loosen.

> Roodg's Text Box: i DON'T WANT TO BEAT YOU UP.

> Glowing Red Rope's Text Box: I have had much worse so do it.

> Roodg's Text Box: oKAY!

It took seven good foot whacks, and one mediocre ankle whack, but eventually the little ball of glowing red cord that was tied in a pretty bow undid enough that the prisoner could wiggle free of the *Bolas*. The cord had never been glowing, the prisoner had. It was a Red Quest Fairy with a mouth gag that had been chewed through completely.

> Roodg's Text Box: Herbert! hOW DID YOU GET HERE?

> Red Quest Fairy's Text Box: My name isn't Herbert, it is Cinnamon.

> Roodg's Text Box: sORRY i DIDN'T KNOW YOUR REAL NAME, i MADE IT UP THAT IT WAS Herbert, YOU SHOULD HAVE SAID SOMETHING. Cinnamon IS A NICE NAME. i CAN COPE WITH THAT.

> Cinnamon's Text Box: Call me Shirley for all I care. Now let me squeeze out of here and get the key to your cage.

Roodg watched as Cinnamon, the Red Quest Fairy, squeezed through the cage bars. Now that it finally stopped flitting around and was still for a moment. Roodg could see that ze was wrong on two accounts. Not only was the Red Quest Fairy not named Herbert but the Red Quest Fairy was also not a girl. Dragging the once hung key from its once spot by the door, Cinnamon put in double effort to bring the key over to Roodg. The door was unlocked with a satisfying kerklunk. Both avatar and Quest Fairy were now free.

> Roodg's Text Box: nOW WHAT?

> Cinnamon's Text Box: No idea. I hadn't thought that through yet. There isn't a way off of The Mist Covered Island You Knew About But Couldn't Land on Because of the Mist that I know about that we can use.

> Roodg's Text Box: i HATE tHE mIST cOVERED iSLAND yOU kNEW aBOUT bUT cOULDN'T lAND ON bECAUSE OF THE mIST!

> Cinnamon's Text Box: What we should do is get the Flaming Pit out of Posh Welsh Tribal Village and hide as far away as possible until we

can think of something.

Roodg's Text Box: gOOD PLAN. i ♥ IT.

Cinnamon's Text Box: Hey how did you make the heart?

Roodg's Text Box: hOLD aLT + PRESS 3 ON THE NUMBER PAD.

Cinnamon's Text Box: I forgot about the Alt Codes. Okay, let us make our dramatic escape! Queue the dramatic escape music! ♫♪.

Roodg's Text Box: hEY! hOW DID U DO THE MUSIC NOTES?

There was no time to give out the Alt Code for music notes, the dramatic escape music had already started. It was a lively little jazz ditty that could have been more suspenseful for a dramatic escape. The grass hut village was surprisingly hard to escape given the large number of Posh Welsh Tribesman and the gate that didn't work. With some luck, (and a casting of *Thunderbolt* to scare away a group of rain dancers) the duo escaped the beachfront village and headed towards the mist covered mountain. There was dense jungle to cut through and Roodg owned nothing that was sharp enough to effectively cut foliage, making progress slow. They ran through the night, cutting through foliage with their *Sporks*.

As the rooster crowed and signalled morning, the sun broke through the mist with an eye piercing flash of light. Finally convinced that they had cut their way far enough from the village, Roodg and Cinnamon collapsed in a heap beside a lovely scenic hot springs and some regulation sized tuffets. The dramatic escape music finally concluded its repetitive tune and settled back into the normal persuasive flutes for the area.

Cinnamon's Text Box: I am exhausted, but that hot springs looks amazing. I haven't been clean ever that I remember. I need to wash off before I fall asleep.

Roodg's Text Box: tHAT SOUNDS NEAT. i'M NOT A MELEE CLASS SO ALL THAT SPORKING MADE ME SUPER SWEATY.

Roodg was naked (but with a cowl) and relaxing in the hot spring in a flash. Far faster than The Red Quest Fairy,(which was impressive given the fact that Cinnamon was naked to start with). As Cinnamon was starting to dip in a little leg, Roodg felt a strange shifting. It took a round to place it, but the feeling had come from the Status Page. Opening it in time to see a letter flip upside down, Roodg was confused. Sure, it was the letter 'H' under gender, and it still was an 'H' now even upside down, but it was something to note.

Roodg's Text Box: dID YOU FEEL THAT? iT WAS STRANGE. mY 'H' FLIPPED.

> Cinnamon's Text Box: What do you mean your 'H'? I felt something too. What was that?

The duo briefly pondered for a moment what an upside-down 'H' could possibly mean. They were distracted from their thoughts by a new mystery. Somewhere close in the jungle nearby was something, and it was getting slowly louder. Rhythmic in nature, like a pounding of an animal skin drum. They both listened intently for a clue as to what it could possibly be. It was Roodg who figured it out first, when a new gasping sound was heard amongst the drum beat.

> Roodg's Text Box: sOMETHING IS GETTING FUCKED OVER THERE!

Loud screams broke through the silence of the mist. There were two voices, one female and one male.

> Cinnamon's Text Box: Yes, and hard by the sounds of it!

The lewd noises continued, and Roodg's hands wandered absentmindedly down towards pay dirt. Straight for the goods, that was Roodg's philosophy when it came to personal time. Roodg instinctively grabbed at where the cock would be with one hand, and with the other to pussy, but fumbled. They were in the wrong spots. Backward. Roodg hadn't remembered leaving the magical genitals in that order, but didn't think much of it and started to enjoy the mysterious noises.

It was the bleating that was the sexiest noise, and Roodg focused on that. It was evident that the mysterious noise-makers were almost finished; their grunts were quickening, and the drum beat was at the highest tempo. Despite great effort, Roodg could not possibly hope to finish with the noisy bush-lovers. If only they had sporked harder to get here, then there would have been more time! A bleat of triumph bellowed out, followed by a sticky, wet parting noise.

Roodg was splashed in the face by the spray of two creatures who had jumped from behind the bushes and into the spring. It was impossible to shield your eyes at a moment's notice when both of your hands were tangled up in your own double junk. Spitting out the metallic tanged mineral water, Roodg cleared the droplets from the visible eye, and looked over at the frolicking pair.

The man was a handsome devil, with a mouth that appeared to have been permanently set to smirk. He might have been a devil, Roodg wasn't sure. He did have a goatee, small nubby horns, and an overall mischievous look to him. The woman of the pair was putting that sexy smirk to shame. She was the personification of beauty itself, every single feature on her body was absolutely perfect. Her face was flawlessly symmetrical, with perfectly pouty lips, long eyelashes that accented mysterious eyes, and the buttonest of button noses. Long hair tumbled down her shoulders, covering up all essential areas in a way that suggested that her hair was her normal everyday outfit. Her body was curvy in all of the right ways, and holy fuck was she sporting some nice tits.

The frolicking couple noticed their silent audience and became wide-eyed. In a panic they started to fling their arms around wildly. They were motioning at Roodg and Cinnamon, then towards the shore.

> Cinnamon's Text Box: I think they want us to leave the spring.

> Roodg's Text Box: wHY? iT IS RELAXING AND i AM HAVING FUN WHILE LOOKING AT THOSE SEXY BOOBS.

> Cinnamon's Text Box: No idea.

The couple approached, dragging their legs through the water. They were near exhausted by the time they reached Text Box range.

> Nymph's Text Box: You need to get out of this spring!

> Satyr's Text Box: It is cursed!

> Roodg's Text Box: tHEN WHY ARE YOU IN IT?

> Nymph's Text Box: It is far too late for us.

> Satyr's Text Box: Quickly, get out before you are changed permanently as well!

> Cinnamon's Text Box: Changed? What do you mean changed?

> Nymph's Text Box: Well…

The Nymph took a few steps closer to leave the deep end of the hot springs. First her perfectly proportioned stomach came into view, then her seductive hips, followed by the sleekest and faintest of treasure trails, and finally her massive floppy cock which swayed back and forth thanks to her seductive hip wiggle walk animation. The Satyr took a quick leap forward and revealed his tight vagina.

> Cinnamon's Text Box: Ack!

> Roodg's Text Box: nEAT!

> Cinnamon's Text Box: Oh sweet Charlie! It is gone!

> Ny(hi)mph's Text Box: Oh no. We are too late!

> Saty(he)r's Text Box: We are so sorry.

> Roodg's Text Box: wAIT A ROUND HERE. yOU HAVE THE COCK AND YOU HAVE THE PUSSY?

Ny(hi)mph's and Saty(he)r's Simultaneous Text Boxes: Correct.

Roodg's Text Box: dOES THAT MEAN THAT WHEN WE WERE HEARING YOU TWO GO AT IT BEFORE, THAT THE NYMPH WAS THE ONE WHO WAS FUCKING THE SATYR?

Ny(hi)mph's Text Box: It serves him right for frolicking in the forest!

Sayt(he)r's Text Box: I didn't think you would be able to catch me!

Roodg's Text Box: tHAT MIGHT BE THE BEST THING i HAVE HEARD IN MY ENTIRE LIFE. cOMPLETE MYTHOLOGICAL ROLE REVERSALS.

Cinnamon's Text Box: Where is my dick?!

Ny(hi)mph's Text Box: Are you okay Avatar?

Sayt(he)r's Text Box: It took us some time to get used to it. Do you need to talk?

Roodg did not need to talk. Roodg was feeling perfect and had figured out the upside-down 'H'. Had the gender on Roodg's status page been listed as 'M' or 'W' it would have flipped around and become the opposite letter. The curse of this spring had happened to both, and the opposite of 'H' was still 'H', but in a different order.

Cinnamon's Text Box: Seriously, where is my dick?!

Ny(hi)mph's Text Box: How does your junk feel?

Roodg's Text Box: mY JUNK FEELS AMAZING!

Roodg stood up revealing the new vagina on top, penis on bottom natural crotch state. Both the Ny(hi)mph and the Sayt(he)r became wide-eyed yet again.

Roodg's Text Box: yOU SHOULD TOTALLY FEEL IT!

Both monsters were happy to comply and took hold of a set of genitals to feel them as instructed. They had both gone for the set that they could now handle properly with their respective private parts switch. Within a few shorts rounds they agreed, Roodg's junk was amazing. The little gender swapped Cinnamon flitted close by, in a state of complete bewilderment, with a hand idly feeling up his vagina.

As the Sayt(he)r was licking the base of the night elf's cock, the Ny(hi)mph was expertly massaging the night elf's folds. Both monsters had a unique perspective on this situation, they had once possessed the equipment they were trying to entice, and knew the ins and outs better than a non private part cursed mixed up couple would have.

Roodg was appreciating this unique situation as well, but for different reasons. There was a beautiful woman with big bouncing boobs and a deliciously out of place slab of meat hanging between her legs, making out with a svelte man with an extra tight little hole, and they were both feeling the night elf all over. This was pretty much the best thing that had ever happened in the history of ever. There was a way to make it even better, and Roodg knew it.

> Roodg's Text Box: oKAY LADY, TIME TO FUCK ME WITH YOUR BIG COCK!

Roodg, straight for the goods.

The soft lips of the Ny(hi)mph had been parted with night elf tongue almost before the Text Box was finished, but the night elf's hands were definitely all over the perfect body before the Text Box had even started. Each part of the female body was explored, her typical video game sized breasts, her lovely curved torso, her gravity defying, spankable butt, and her swollen pulsing penis with heavy needful balls.

The anticipation of the last three rounds was too much for Roodg. The sexy ladycock needed to be experienced; the night elf positioned the Ny(hi)mph on a nice bed of tuffets near the shore to take up the challenge (and the lady dick).

Charismatic cock entered night elf territory after a satisfying stretch. Roodg gasped and took the member to the hilt in one swift motion. There was cock to be had, and Roodg wasted no time in using it fully. Roodg wished that there was a *Cowpoke Hat* to wave in the air to accentuate the thrill of riding this beautiful creature. Roodg was so turned on by the gender swapping, that the night elf's own cock was rubbing up against the back of the Ny(hi)mph's legs.

> Roodg's Text Box: tHIS GENITAL ORDER IS GREAT! lOOK WHAT i CAN DO!

With a simple shifting of the Ny(hi)mph's legs, Roodg started to press against her backdoor. The night elf didn't even need to release the first bonding to enter the beautifully modeled butt of the Ny(hi)mph. The Ny(hi)mph gasped out as Roodg struck the exact right spot with the first thrust. An entire new method of pleasure had opened up, and the water spirit was washed over with intense internal pressure.

> Ny(hi)mph's Text Box: Holy Maker! What is that?

> Roodg's Text Box: tHE REASON GAY BOYS EXIST!

The Ny(hi)mph gave a good spank to Roodg, who increased the speed. Ladycock was fully inserted, and lady prostate was pushed and stimulated. It was a magical moment for both, and it would have continued to escalate to climax if not for one thing. Whimpering from the Sayt(he)r.

> Roodg's Text Box: i COMPLETELY FORGOT! i WANTED TO

> FUCK THE DUDE PUSSY!

This earned a different whimper, one from the Ny(hi)mph.

> Ny(hi)mph's Text Box: But, my gay boy parts!

It was fine, Roodg had a plan. After setting up the Ny(hi)mph to be giving it hard to the Sayt(he)r's mangina, Roodg used *Switch* and lined up for the big moment. One night elf cock found purchase within the familiar territory of the Ny(hi)mph's newly discovered gay boy places, the other within the already mostly filled rugged pussy of the Sayt(he)r.

The practiced couple was breaking new mythological bounds, sweating in the pure bliss of each other's company, as Roodg was behind them, giving it to them both good. The extra stimulation of the new cock thrusting against her own, combined with the bliss of internal stimulation on her gay boy parts, caused the Ny(hi)mph to go over the edge. She could no longer contain herself, and her heavy nuts began to release her woman seed blissfully into the waiting manhole.

The sharp tightening of the Ny(hi)mph's entrance caused Roodg's upper dick to get forced out. No amount of pushing would allow re-entry, so Roodg lowered the sight, and pushed both cocks into the now coated pussy of the Sayt(he)r. Squishy and sloppy now, both night elf members pushed forward and released their own happy juices into the now quivering woodland goat spirit. One last good gush from all three embedded members caused a loud bleat and threw the man into a deep orgasm that originated deep within his mancunt.

> Roodg's Text Box: wIN!

Creature Name: Ny(hi)mph
Class: Water Spirit
Level: 40
Special Attacks: Stunning Beauty, Charming Glance, Nai(l)ad Beauty, Bewarlock, Manlove
Drops: Ny(hi)mph Seed
First Monster Encounter Notes: She keeps on chasing me! How will I ever stay chaste? – Sayt(he)r
Additional Comments: sHE HAS THE BEST LADYCOCK EVER! – Roodg

Creature Name: Sayt(he)r
Class: Forest Spirit
Level: 40
Special Attacks: Mischievous Grin, Tramp-ler, Pan Flute, Dance of the (Wo) Faun, Ladylove
Drops: Sayt(he)r Egg

First Monster Encounter Notes: Quiet, you know you like it! – Ny(hi)mph
Additional Comments: dITTO, BUT WITH MANPUSSY! – Roodg

The trio jumped into the water, laughing and splashing, to clean off the thick coat of sweat that had developed during the intense session, and to possibly get ready for the next round. A stray splash of water hit the neglected Cinnamon, and he finally broke out of his trance. Closing the once gaping mouth, and flitting over to Roodg, the Red Quest Fairy opened up his mouth once again in awe.

Cinnamon's Text Box: You have both parts? I can't believe it! You're a hermaphrodite?

Roodg's Text Box: tHAT WAS WHY YOU GOT SHOCKED FOR THAT WHOLE TIME? didn't YOU SEE THAT A BUNCH OF TIMES BEFORE ON OUR ADVENTURES AROUND THE eXPANSION IN THE LAST BOOK?

Cinnamon's Text Box: Our adventures? We were only in like two chapters together. I barely even know you.

Roodg's Text Box: bUT YOU ARE THE Red Quest Fairy! i'M THE RED AVATAR!

Cinnamon's Text Box: I'm a Red Quest Fairy, but I'm not your Red Quest Fairy.

Roodg's Text Box: wHO DO YOU BELONG TO THEN? wHO ELSE WAS RED?

With a loud thump the self proclaimed Goddess pounced into the area with a big *Grin Animation* on her face.

Cinnamon's Text Box: Oh bloody Flaming Pit! There she is!

Ny(hi)mph and Saty(he)r's Simultaneous Text Boxes: Crap! Run!

Roodg's Text Box: oH TUFFETS! tHERE SHE IS!

◊ Chapter 16 ◊

CYCLE 3: EVENING NDE, PRIMARY WEAPONRY

> NPC Captain Saylerman's Text Box: You are all registered, have a safe trip.

> nde's Text Box: Thank you.

> NPC Captain Saylerman's Text Box: Wait... you seem familiar for some reason. I better ask, is this your first trip with us?

> nde's Text Box: No this is my second trip.

> NPC Captain Saylerman's Text Box: Phew! That was close! I had you set on Party Split-Up Disaster Mode. I'll switch that right up to Pleasant Journey Mode.

> nde's Text Box: Thank you. Is the snack bar still open?

> NPC Captain Saylerman's Text Box: Of course! Today's special is *Bacon Wrapped Bacon*. Have a nice trip.

Pleasant Journey Mode delivered exactly what it promised. *Bacon Wrapped Bacon* was happily consumed in quantities that made many NPCs stare at nde. It also made nde hope that he was hungry due to the extra Optional Boss stats and not because he was pregnant again. He was going to be mad if he was pregnant again.

The late afternoon trip passed by without incident and nde made it through the

Shores of Eternal Night to The Underwater But Overland Desert which was the next closest location of an Optional Boss. There was no dungeon or anything he could see, no monsters, nor anything else. 'The Exact Centre' must mean what it said for once and after a quick trip around the outside he moved towards what he thought was the exact centre.

An avatar would have to be crazy, or Mr. Max, to have searched this entire unimpressive desert to find this Primary Weapon character. It was a vast expanse of hot dry nothingness, and by the time nde finally found the small sprout, in what he was sure was not the exact centre, he was tired and starving. He thought he should be thirsty instead of hungry, but he was relatively sure he didn't need to drink water. He ate his fourth *Bacon Wrapped Bacon* since the start of the desert exploration. He did not expect that he would be hungrier now wearing Armour. He should have bought more.

The small sprout was wiggling slightly but nde didn't quite know what to do with it. Poking it, pulling it, and prodding it yielded little results. The only other thing he could think of doing with a plant was watering it. That would explain the *Bottled Water* item's existence in the game since nobody ever drank anything. He did not own one of those and the only place he had ever seen one before was now buried under an entire Lushin Jungle. He could think of two other ways that he could water this plant. The second option had the additional benefit of not needing to walk all the way back to the ocean.

Once wet, the sprout shot up through the ground revealing a red mechanical monster with glowing yellow trim. Fantastical and impossibly skinny, Primary Weapon had an impressive four sets of arms and each hand was holding a confusing combined weapon. Every one of those weapons would likely do more damage to the Primary Weapon than its foes, but it was in a fantasy game so players would probably let that slide.

There were eight combined weapons. From what nde could tell the weapons were a *Two Handed Bladegun* that appeared impossible to fire, a *Macetrument* of the cello variety, a *Fisting Hammer* with emphasis on the fisting, a *One Handed Whipsword* covered in ivy, a *Halberd* lazily made from an axe and a spear, a *Carpet Knife* that was a carpet cut-out of a knife, a *Flailing Scythe* that was constantly spinning and finally a *Shear Staff* that was really a staff with a cute pair of shears tied to it. nde was sure something was missing but then he saw that Primary Weapon had some stylish nunchakus nipple piercings.

> Primary Weapon's Text Box: You all dare to challenge me? Well, I have a surprise for you! Only one of you shall be allowed to fight, and you must do it alone! Why do I feel like I've been lubricated?

nde used the *Wipe Spit Off Chin Animation* (spitting had saved him a trip).

Giant whirlpools sprang forth from the sand and swallowed everyone in The Underwater But Overland Desert except for one avatar. Since there was only one avatar in The Underwater But Overland Desert it was an easy choice who to leave.

> nde's Text Box: Alright then. I think I can cope with that.

Primary Weapon's Text Box: You were already alone? That hasn't happened to me before.

nde's Text Box: Being alone happens to me all the time.

Primary Weapon's Text Box: Prepare yourself! Raise your weapon and fight!

nde's Text Box: Okay, but remember, you asked me to do this.

Primary Weapon watched with confused yellow laser eyes as nde unzipped his Knight Armour codpiece, removed his member from the holding area, and began to pump it to full size. Without real weapons to fight with, this was technically his backup weapon. Once nde was ready to go Primary Weapon used the *Smirk Animation*.

Primary Weapon's Text Box: I haven't seen one of your kind of avatars before. My programming says that I am not going to need these ridiculous combination weapons to defeat you. Um, you are a guy so I will only need to use my fists to fist your ass into submission. Check. Honestly I might use the *Fisting Hammer* we will see how it turns out. Do you want to bend over willingly or do I have to wrestle you down? How does this usually work?

nde's Text Box: I think it depends on the avatar. I need you to cum so I can get a flower. That means I am going to go willingly. Thank you for asking though, that was polite.

Primary Weapon's Text Box: No problem! Wait, my cum? I don't know if I have that.

nde's Text Box: Do what comes naturally to you and I'm sure it will work out fine!

Primary Weapon used the *Smile Animation*, moved over to the already bent over nde, and started to experimentally poke at the avatar's bottom with many fingers. It did not hit anywhere that did anything exciting.

nde's Text Box: It is sort of cute how clueless you are at this. You need to poke me here.

A gentle hand guided Primary Weapon's fifth hand to where it needed to go. A finger poked inside and nde shuddered with excitement. The finger was taken out and a *Blush Shade #6* sporting Primary Weapon stepped back.

Primary Weapon's Text Box: I'm sorry… I can't do this.

nde's Text Box: But I desperately need your cum. I don't mean to sound like a slut or anything. I need your cum to save the world. So please, you need to do this.

Primary Weapon's Text Box: No, it's not that I don't want to. It is that... Look at you. You are on this whole noble mission thing and are willing to sacrifice everything to do it. But I can't fist you. You are obviously a total top and I don't feel comfortable violating your bottom like that. You have given up so much already.

nde's Text Box: No, it is fine. By all means, violate away. I'm ready.

Primary Weapon's Text Box: I can't, it isn't right! Here, please take me instead. It is the least I can do for you.

Turning nde around and then bending over, Primary Weapon exposed the bottom of its metal chassis. The Construct had three shiny bored out holes.

Primary Weapon's Text Box: Take my virginity noble Night Ranger!

nde's Text Box: How?

Primary Weapon's Text Box: I don't know. I'm only programmed to know about fisting. Don't you know? What do tops do?

nde's Text Box: They stick parts of themselves into a hole.

Primary Weapon's Text Box: Then do that! Put things into my hole.

nde's Text Box: Uh... which hole?

Primary Weapon's Text Box: I don't know. I have three. I'm sure they are all something, so pick one.

He wasn't the most experienced top, but if that was what the monster wanted, then that was what it was going to get. nde lined himself up with the top most hole simply because that was the largest one and then forced himself into the chamber. He did not expect that Primary Weapon would scream out in delight when penetrated but it was more of a turn-on than nde wanted to admit. He began at a slow pace so that Primary Weapon could get used to the feelings, even if the chamber didn't change size or need to relax it was still good manners.

Primary Weapon's Text Box: This feels great!

nde continued his slow pace for a few rounds until he was sure that Primary Weapon was good and excited.

nde's Text Box: Would you like me to go faster or harder?

Primary Weapon's Text Box: You can go faster or harder? Are you allowed to even do that?

After a *Smirk Animation*, nde answered the question with five rounds of brisk and hard pounding. Primary Weapon screamed nonsensical statements the entire time. After the rounds were up, nde slowed back down to the softer and gentler pace.

Primary Weapon's Text Box: Okay. Yes. You can go faster and harder!

nde got revved up to go faster but his heart skipped a frame when he felt something slide against the inside of his thigh. He whipped his head around quickly but saw no one there (he was half expecting that it was Secondary Weapon). Then he saw the source, it was him, or more precisely his *Knight Armour*. There was a metallic secondary member sprouting up between his legs formed from the skirting. While it was not as big as his new massive member, this Armour member was ready to use as well as firmly pressing up against his balls. Who was he to turn down an Armour in need? nde inserted the metallic member into the middle sized middle hole. Primary Weapon was taken off guard and tried to yell out in shock but the sounds quickly turned into pleasure when nde picked up the pace and started to penetrate both holes with a powerful speed and force.

nde got into the rhythm and refused to slow down. Every polygon of his being wanted to drive into these holes. Sweat drenched and sore he only gripped harder and pushed faster when Primary Weapons knees gave out and it fell to the sand. Eight double-jointed arms grabbed at nde and helped to push him in harder. Losing track of rounds, nde paid no attention to the wolf's howl that signaled night as it was always dark here anyways. Muffled moans from the sweat stained sand indicated that Primary Weapon was close to reaching the breaking point.

With one final speed assault on the virgin holes both succumbed to the pleasure. nde couldn't see during his orgasm due to the flash of lights from Primary Weapon, but he closed his eyes and buried himself deep inside. When the smoke and laser light show finally died down an exhausted nde slid from the holes and stood up with the promised sore back from his last encounter and a brand new set of sore legs from this one.

nde looked down and saw that cum had oozed out of Primary Weapon's third hole. As he picked the purple flower up from the sticky sand, he thought that it was lucky that he had picked the two correct holes to use, leaving the third one to gift him with a flower. He tried helping up the shaky Optional Boss, but it still couldn't move, resigning to instead sit lazily in the sand.

Primary Weapon's Text Box: That was… something else. I think I need to find one of you for home use.

nde's Text Box: I suggest using your weapons. Not the sharp ones.

The eyes of Primary Weapon lit up with a sudden realization, grabbed the menagerie of random weaponry, smiled at nde, and then it disappeared into the sand ready for a solo round two. A hint of jealousy was in nde's eye, he wanted to go try out some of those objects internally as well, but there wasn't time.

> **Creature Name:** Primary Weapon
> **Class:** Weapon
> **Level:** 60
> **Special Attacks:** Primary Attacks
> **Drops:** Something you already have to be able to challenge it in the first place
> **First Player Encounter Notes:** Hopefully you still have your *Bottled Water* fellow adventurers! – Mr. Max
> **Additional Comments:** Meh, other liquids you have on hand work fine. – nde

> Game Explanation Text Box: Polygons absorbed from Primary Weapon 16.6%.

ndes gained many more internal polygons. He also got his 's' back, which he decided was not the best letter of his name to help prove his identity.

> ndes' Text Box: That only moves the apostrophe in my Text Boxes. It looks almost the same as before.

> Game Explanation Text Box: Special trait absorbed from Primary Weapon, Primary Weapon.

ndes was excited for this. He had been correct; Primary Weapon had indeed dropped the promised Primary Weapon. He looked into his inventory screen and equipped his brand new... *Primary Circle Sword?*

> ndes' Text Box: Oh, man! I forgot that my primary weapon is technically the one handed sword and not the bow. Now I feel stupid, Primary Weapon didn't have any combination bow weapons, I can't believe I didn't notice that. Still, this sword is all glowy and stuff.

The Primary Circle Sword glowed with bright yellow light. Even if all the colour was drained from the weapon after it was equipped, it was still impressive. The blade didn't make much sense for use in battle, much like all of Primary Weapon's weapons. The glowing sword ended in a circular ring, as if the weapon had been split apart and drilled out. It also sheathed in a peculiar manner, straight up and down on ndes' back, radiant ring framing his helmet like a halo. Thankfully fantasy weapons in video games didn't need to make logical sense to be useful and powerful.

ndes was ready for the next challenge.

Chapter 17

CYCLE 3
GROUP B, THE
WHIRLWIND ROMANCE

Caëlahenâilenŵhei's Text Box: What the fuck? Who did this? I'll kill them!

Zal Finn III's Text Box: Whoa there, calm down.

Caëlahenâilenŵhei's Text Box: I will not calm down! They are ruined. All of them, ruined!

Mr. Max's Text Box: Chill there adventurette and have a nice bucket of *Schloomp*.

Caëlahenâilenŵhei's Text Box: I will not chill out or eat anything called *Schloomp*!

Hippolyta's Text Box: Are you sure, *Schloomp* tastes like—

Caëlahenâilenŵhei's Text Box: I don't care if it tastes like an orgy of flavour demons have fucked bad taste to death with their tentacle cocks. I am not eating anything called *Schloomp*!

Mr. Max's Text Box: How did you know that is exactly what it tastes like?

Caëlahenâilenŵhei's Text Box: It was you wasn't it Max?

Mr. Max's Text Box: It probably was. I wouldn't put it past me.

Zal Finn III's Text Box: What is the problem Caela? Tell us already!

Caëlahenâilenŵhei's Text Box: You want to know the problem? This is the problem!

Caëlahenâilenŵhei held up her prized Armour collection which she used for pajamas. The variety of sparkling white vests and robes were now more appropriately sized for one of those clothing wearing mice. The light elf was flushed with anger so the other avatars desperately tried to contain their laughter.

Caëlahenâilenŵhei's Text Box: I left these in the dryer and somebody changed the heat setting to *Extra Stupid Hot!* All my pajamas are ruined. These were the most comfortable ones I had! Who was it? I want to know!

Hippolyta's Text Box: Do you seriously think that Zal or I used our experience points to sneak to the sitting room during the night and change the heat setting on your stupid dryer?

Caëlahenâilenŵhei's Text Box: Then it was Max! He was going to wash the carpets! He must have done something.

Hippolyta's Text Box: Max obviously didn't wash the carpets yet. They are still covered in soup and mud.

Caëlahenâilenŵhei's Text Box: The Quest Fairies?

Hippolyta's Text Box: Have been gone since last cycle. If anyone changed it, it was you.

Caëlahenâilenŵhei's Text Box: Why would I ruin all my own clothes?

Hippolyta's Text Box: For the same reason we would ruin all your clothes! You wouldn't and we wouldn't. It was obviously an accident. Now eat your *Schloomp*, it is good for you!

Caëlahenâilenŵhei used the *Pout Animation*. She would drop the dryer mishap for now, but there was no way in the Flaming Pit that she would be eating any of her *Schloomp*.

~~~

Mr. Max's Text Box: Let me guess, you don't want any *White Wolf Curry* for dinner either?

Caëlahenåilenŵhei's Text Box: Thanks, but no thanks. I'll pass.

Zal Finn III's Text Box: Your loss!

Mr. Max's Text Box: I am glad that this afternoon we caught nine more Golden Poffles.

Hippolyta's Text Box: It was exciting I'll admit. We gained back six Levels after you accidentally dropped the cage on that one.

Mr. Max's Text Box: I know adventurette! You gained like a full cup size when it happened!

Hippolyta's Text Box: Why you insolent…

Zal Finn III's Text Box: I hate to break this to you, but he is right. Every time you lose a Level your breasts do get smaller.

Hippolyta's Text Box: Good then. I can't wait for these symbols of male oppression to be gone.

Zal Finn III's Text Box: Aw. But I like them.

Mr. Max's Text Box: They are the biggest and jiggliest in the whole game!

Caëlahenåilenŵhei's Text Box: They are impressive. I have always thought that breasts symbolised feminine power. I mean yours let you turn men into drooling piles of useless meat. Well, straight men at least. So don't your breasts technically symbolise your powers of control over the masculine identity? Don't many ancient cultures use large breasts as a symbol of fertility? Fertility is controlled by the woman in most cases. Women, their breasts, and even their vaginas are the ultimate sign of power over a supposedly male dominated world.

Hippolyta's Text Box: My goddess! You are correct. They have been getting smaller and now that you said that, I miss them! What is wrong with me?

Mr. Max's Text Box: If breasts and vaginas are symbols of women's power, why are you set to zero jiggle and have a mouthgina instead of a vagina Caela?

Caëlahenãilenẇhei's Text Box: I just... uh...

Caëlahenãilenẇhei's Box Text: Shut up!

Zal Finn III's Text Box: On that inspired vagina note I think it is time for us to get some sweet shut eye.

Caëlahenãilenẇhei's Text Box: But I have nothing to wear to bed!

Mr. Max's Text Box: Sleep naked. I sleep mostly naked now that I have a bed.

Hippolyta's Text Box: I know. It keeps trying to break into my room.

Caëlahenãilenẇhei's Text Box: I could never sleep naked. What if there was a fire or night-time night ninjas?

Mr. Max's Text Box: I'm sure you have something to wear. If not come see me later, I might still have something in *My Spiritual Storage Device From the Crags of Halm* that I didn't sell.

Caëlahenãilenẇhei's Text Box: I'll have to look but thank you for the offer Max. I think I may have something.

~~~

Caëlahenãilenẇhei used the *Sneeze Animation*. She slowly snuck out of her room and towards the orange door. She was the ultimate night-time night ninja, until she tripped on the carpet, and fell through the door and smacked down hard the bed.

Mr. Max's Text Box: zzz... *snort* ... huh?

Mr. Max used the *Rub Eyes Animation* and the *Yawn Animation*.

Mr. Max's Text Box: Hey, you found an *Initiate's Jacket* to wear. What time is it?

Caela had indeed found an *Initiate's Jacket* in her *Storage Chest*. Found in the big room of death in the Onn Coliseum that she believed was her old one (but it was in fact Anders' old crusty cumrag).

Caëlahenãilenẇhei's Text Box: Fuck... uh... yeah, that's it! Fuck o'clock. It is time for me and you to... ugh... get it on.

> Mr. Max's Text Box: Beg pardon?

> Caëlahenãilenŵhei's Text Box: Come on, you know you want this hot piece of skinny light elf bitch.

Caela accented her statement by slapping herself hard on the thigh, which is when Mr. Max noted that she had neglected to put on any pants.

> Mr. Max's Text Box: I mean, I have thought about it. You are interesting and all that adventurette. I mean your power is intriguing. But I didn't think you liked me like that.

> Caëlahenãilenŵhei's Text Box: Of course I do… like… you Max. I always have. Now close your eyes, lie there, and let me deal with you.

> Caëlahenãilenŵhei's Box Text: zzz… *murble murf* The Flork Demon has all my contact information officer. *snort*

> Mr. Max's Text Box: Are you feeling okay?

> Caëlahenãilenŵhei's Text Box: Of course! Never better. Close your eyes big guy and let me take you to heaven.

> Caëlahenãilenŵhei's Box Text: Let me… zzz… *smack smack* I'll deal with both of those Roodg but only if you *Switch* that one… *muble mumm*

> Mr. Max's Text Box: Um?

> Caëlahenãilenŵhei's Text Box: Maker damn it! Do I seriously never shut up? I am ruining the mood here. How am I even doing that? Stop talking, me!

> Caëlahenãilenŵhei's Box Text: *groan* I don't even know where Potions Class is. Where did I put my locker combination again? *mummsner*

> Mr. Max's Text Box: Wait a round. Your eyes are closed. Are you… sleep seducing?

> Caëlahenãilenŵhei's Text Box: No. I am here for you Max. I need you!

> Caëlahenãilenŵhei's Box Text: Max? zzz I bet it was him… totally ruined my laundry. Gunna smack him when he's not looking… *snort*

> Mr. Max's Text Box: Okay, let's get you back to bed young lady.

Caëlahenâilenẇhei's Text Box: Fuck.

◈ Chapter 18 ◈
CYCLE 3
GROUP A, THE
CAKEWALK

Fournimer's Text Box: I already told you, I'm not talking to you.

Palcath's Text Box: And I already told you, you were unconscious! We couldn't lift you out until you woke up. We posted Draganders to keep watch over you, Fourni!

Draganders' Text Box: Chirp!

Fournimer's Text Box: I had to bunk with Chad all night!

Gliint's Text Box: With Chad? You poor thing, I wouldn't wish Chad on even my most hated of foes. You have my sincerest condolences.

Fournimer's Text Box: Chad isn't so bad really. I won this extra Secondary Weapon *Blue Bolas*!

Gliint's Text Box: Asshat. I only got a single bonus Skill Point for doing his stupid quests. I already get those every Level!

Palcath's Text Box: Gnomes get bonus Skill Points, lad? I thought only humans got those.

Gliint's Text Box: Uh… I mean, this is taking too long! Where is the cake?

Palcath's Text Box: I thought we were making pretty good progress lad.

Gliint's Text Box: We have been doing this since lunch and we only have 28 more cake steps placed. It is taking far too long to get cakes to the castle!

Fournimer's Text Box: I'm sorry. I only have enough room to carry four at once.

Gliint's Text Box: Why so few?

Fournimer's Text Box: I have a bunch of other stuff I can't drop. why don't you carry some of them? you are super fast.

Gliint's Text Box: What? I'm tiny. You are like a huge horse or whatever. Can't you carry a bunch more?

Fournimer's Text Box: of course not. my *Backpack* is the same as yours. that would be useful and they don't allow centaurs to have anything useful in this damn game! Stupid anti-centaur game!

Gliint's Text Box: Not the same as mine. You only have a regular *Backpack*! Well no wonder you can't carry cake. You should have much better by now. Don't you have a *Combi Pot*?

Fournimer's Text Box: no I don't.

Palcath's Text Box: Didn't you pick up the *Golden* one Fourni?

Fournimer's Text Box: you're right Man. I did. I can upgrade my *Backpack* now I bet.

Looking into his own *Backpack* and then further into Anders' *Ultra-Pack*, Fournimer found the *Golden Combi Pot*. He also found something he didn't expect, six pieces of *Bacon Wrapped Bacon*, four of the little purple *Optional Flowers*, and a secret list of Optional Bosses. He brought out the flowers to examine them.

Fournimer's Text Box: holy mother Maker! there is new stuff in here. Anders must have put these in here! look!

Gliint's Text Box: Anders can put stuff into your bags?

Fournimer's Text Box: no, I took his stuff with me. I didn't want to leave him on the floor, in case we could do something.

Gliint's Text Box: you scared me for a moment. Of course he couldn't put stuff into your bags. How could he possibly do that? He is dead, remember? It would have taken a superhuman level of disconnecting power to save him at the last instant. Who could possibly have that level of skill? Heh.

Fournimer's Text Box: no, he is alive. I know it.

Gliint's Text Box: Well, he isn't in other chapters of this book or anything, I'm certain no one is secretly watching him and really excited now that you have all of his stuff. Let's upgrade you.

Palcath's Text Box: Are you sure those were not in there already?

Fournimer's Text Box: I am sure! I looked through it all. I would have remembered.

Palcath's Text Box: We have no idea where that lad got those flowers from. For all we know he grows them himself. Mr. Max hadn't even seen one before.

Fournimer's Text Box: no. it has to be him. he put it in there!

Palcath's Text Box: Please Fourni, I am begging you. You are obsessing over this. It isn't good for you, lad.

Lissa's Text Box: It is time to move onto the next step. Denial has been going on too long. #HeartfeltMoment. I'm sorry.

Gliint's Text Box: Uh… how about that upgrade then? Why not worry about that? Bigger storage for the horse to carry cake.

Fournimer looked at the recipe menu, mostly to keep from being angry at his friends. He knew Anders had done it, it didn't matter what they thought. In this menu he couldn't find any mention of *Backpacks*, but then tried to mix his and found out something interesting.

Fournimer's Text Box: really? no way. mine upgrades to kinds of *Saddlebags* instead of *Backpacks*! they have twice the Carrying Capacity of *Backpacks*. finally something besides unicorns that centaurs can do better than anyone else! I knew they were not useless. finally!

Fournimer could upgrade to the fourth level of *Saddlebags*, almost to the maximum level. He now had 2500 Carrying Capacity and could eventually make it to 5000 with the last upgrade, for a total of five times the normal rate (and not twice as Fournimer had calculated). His *Racer Saddlebags Ultra* were stylish and he enjoyed showing them off for everyone. He went to return the *Combi Pot* to his inventory and only then did he notice a problem.

> Fournimer's Text Box: oh no! help!

> Palcath's Text Box: What is wrong, lad?

> Fournimer's Text Box: I can't... reach them! my inventory is too far away for me to access now. fuck. now I have two things I can't reach. stupid centaurs! why do you hate me Game?!

> Lissa's Text Box: Two things? What is the other thing?

> Fournimer's Text Box: nothing! never mind.

Fournimer changed to *Blush Shade #3*. Gliint took the initiative and jumped onto Fourni's back, no saddle needed.

> Gliint's Text Box: Not a big deal horse. I can access it from here fine. Wow, you have a bunch of crap in here. Why do you have so many *Funnels?*

> Fournimer's Text Box: hey! that is my private stuff. get off me.

> Gliint's Text Box: Privacy doesn't matter. We are a team. Why do you have another whole pack in here?

> Palcath's Text Box: Oh lad! You have Anders' *Ultra-Pack* in there? I didn't know that didn't dissolve as well. It doesn't have a Carrying Capacity. You can stuff it full of cake and it wouldn't weigh anything!

> Gliint's Text Box: You had Anders' inventory and all of his equipment this whole time and can access it?! Ugh, I feel silly now. I don't know how long... uh... how long... look at that sky, so blue today.

> Fournimer's Text Box: I am keeping it for him for when we find a way to bring him back.

> Gliint's Text Box: Then we should keep it all together for him. Let me put it all in the *Ultra-Pack* for you. There we go, now it is all together and safe for him to get. I am sure he will like that. Would like that.

Would not will!

Fournimer's Text Box: thanks Gliint. that was nice of you?

Gliint's Text Box: Of course it was! Now go get some cake.

Fournimer's Text Box: so I can stand here while you slowly take cake out of my inventory? how terribly exciting.

Palcath's Text Box: Gliint can pick it up off the ground. That would be faster. After you get the cake here Fourni we don't need you.

Fournimer's Text Box: so I stand around looking stupid?

Palcath's Text Box: No, lad. Your standing still Animation Cycle has you stamping your hooves. That keeps crushing the cake. You can stand around, but please not near us.

Fournimer's Text Box: so I need to leave and go stand in a corner?

Palcath's Text Box: That would be perfect, lad.

Lissa's Text Box: I suggest using that time to clear your head.

Fournimer's Text Box: fine, I guess I could take Draganders for a walk or play *Vambrace*. that would be nice. would you like that?

Draganders' Text Box: Chirp!

Palcath's Text Box: Draganders is big enough to carry cake. I was thinking of using him to fly more cake to us. I hope that is okay dragon, lad.

Draganders' Text Box: Chirp!

Fournimer's Text Box: fine! I'll go for a walk all alone and depressed.

Palcath's Text Box: Perfect. Have fun, lad!

~~~

Determined to not let his cake building companions get to him, Fournimer was going to go and have the best damn walk ever. It only took him three steps until something caught his eye. There was a fountain right in the middle of town, with a big pillar right in the centre, all of it as covered with stone faces. He went in for a closer inspection and had a realization. The Onn Fountain had a kitty stone face right behind where the water was falling. This was a blatant waterfall in plain sight! He stepped into the fountain and touched the kitty face.

> Fournimer's Text Box: we were really bad at looking through Onn the first time. this place was really obvious.

The door opened and Fournimer met a familiar long face.

> Arcade Unicorn's Text Box: Amazing, you found the second hidden entrance! Two for two. Good show. Here is a *Yellow Cat Keycard*.

> Fournimer's Text Box: what? just like that? no puzzles or anything?

> Arcade Unicorn's Text Box: There was a puzzle, but you look pretty down in the dumps, so I'm going to pretend you won it.

The unicorn trotted up to Fournimer and gave the centaur a quick nuzzle.

> Arcade Unicorn's Text Box: Slut.

> Arcade Unicorn's Text Box: Sorry! Programming made me say that! I really like you Whorenimer! Dammit! I am going to go.

The unicorn vanished, along with the complicated water lever puzzle that it had been guarding. Fournimer took that part as a win. The *Yellow Cat Keycard* opened the way to a different path to Chad's Art Gallery of Cute Kittehs. Thankfully with this entrance he would be able to walk back out.

> Chad the Flying Feline of Fortune's Text Box: That was really furrst. Welcome back. How do those *Blue Bolas* work?

> Fournimer's Text Box: I have no idea. I haven't tried them yet.

> Chad the Flying Feline of Fortune's Text Box: Yarn! I wanted to know what 100% sexy meant. No matter, are you ready for your next random quest for prizes? Mew still have -The Quest of Trade- and -The Quest of Escort- left to finish.

> Fournimer's Text Box: how about the trade one? I'm not sure if I would be a good escort.

> Chad the Flying Feline of Fortune's Text Box: Wonderful, spin the wheel and see who you need to visit and then who you need to visit afterwards! It could be any NPurrC!

Spinning the Fickle Fortune Wheel of Fate was dramatic as always. Fournimer took note that after he started the spin many of the possible choices were blacked out sections that said 'Unavailable'. All but a few names had been completely blacked out. The spin landed on one such unavailable section and instead of stopping kept advancing slowly through the unavailable selections until it landed on the first one that was still lit up, Chad the Flying Feline of Fortune. Another spin revealed the same result, a long line of unavailable that lead to Chad the Flying Feline of Fortune.

> Chad the Flying Feline of Fortune's Text Box: Huh? Me and me? You have to take an item from me and bring it to me? I guess… Take this… and thanks. Mew are done. Why are so many others Unavailable?

> Fournimer's Text Box: oh yeah, Breaker killed almost every NPC. then the Admins went and wiped out a bunch of the survivors in their fit of rage.

> Chad the Flying Feline of Fortune's Text Box: What?

> Fournimer's Text Box: didn't you hear that? the Admins are resetting the Expansion in a few cycles and killing anyone trapped here.

> Chad the Flying Feline of Fortune's Text Box: I didn't know that. Please mew need to take me with you! Get me out of here! I can't leave unless you pick the Escort Quest and land on me? Of all the rotten luck! Please hurry up and find my other entrance to take that quest! Save me!

> Fournimer's Text Box: sure, I can try to do that.

> Chad the Flying Feline of Fortune's Text Box: Thank mew so much, but first, your reward! Time to find out what mew have won for bringing me… this item from me.

Fournimer span the Fickle fortune Wheel of Fate, this time he was excited. He had won big last time and was certain his already owning that item, double Chad spinning, *This is Not a Cat'* luck was going to continue. The wheel span down, clicking past an assortment of interesting sounding ideas. Sex Supplement - *Penis Girth +1*, Sex Power Swap - *Sandwiching*, Sexcessory - *Absolute Anal Beads*, Item - *Large Mana Potion*, and finally at the eventual resting point…

> Chad the Flying Feline of Fortune's Text Box: Congratulations! Mew have won *Sex Supplement - Pent Up Triple Lust!*

> Fournimer's Text Box: huh? what does that even mean?

> Chad the Flying Feline of Fortune's Text Box: No idea. Let's look.

Okay, it says here that this will make it feel like you have gone three times as long without having sexual release, and all your fluids will keep charging three times as fast as normal until you release, but only once, how novel. Apparently, if you go too long without release your mind will become clouded with thoughts of intense lust and desire. Hmm, I guess it is kind of like you have gone into a rut until you shoot. It says that your pent up orgasm is going to be gigantic and messy. That sounds fun! It even comes with a free *Bottle of Hand Lotion* and a *Crate of Tissues*. Enjoy!

Fournimer's Text Box: no wait! I don't want that. it has already been like almost a whole cycle and... urk!

Chad the Flying Feline of Fortune's Text Box: Wow... it says that you haven't had sexual release for... the equivalent of 219 cycles? Really? Centaurs sure can make the baby batter. Now it is suddenly going to feel like... 657 cycles since you last had sex? And ultra lust, desire, faster seed generation, and the whole in a sexual rut thing. Oh sorry dude. I think I better fly away before that kicks in. You are hung like a giraffe after all.

~~~

He was not impressed now. Stupid Palcath, stupid Lissa, stupid Gliint, and most of all stupid Chad! He now had a matching set of *Blue Bolas* and what he originally thought *Bolas* were. Fournimer could barely see straight, everything he saw looked sexier than normal and he had no way of dealing with his problem. He needed an outlet for his anger and pent up need, and the royal throne room in Onn Castle where he had eventually wandered into was now covered in hoof shaped cake prints. Icing and sprinkles littered the plush red carpets and interlacing stone tile work. Spear holes had punctured graffiti into ancient tapestries and the royal statues now had *Javelins* for heads with *Bola*s neckties. The royal throne room was furious with Fournimer but couldn't fight back.

Fournimer's Text Box: stupid walk! stupid Game! stupid friends! stupid centaurs! stupid balls! stupid *Saddlebags*! stupid cake! stupid Chad! stupid unicorn! stupid ...uh...

Yallundy's Text Box: Personally, I'd go with 'stupid everything'. That would finish that tantrum of yours up nicely I think.

Yallundy materialized into the world of the visible polygons.

Fournimer's Text Box: Yallundy! why are you here? you look extra pretty today. really pretty I mean. so pretty…

Yallundy's Text Box: Thank you I think. My body is in Gliint's *Backpack* and I need to be in the same area as him, a fact that he has obviously forgotten about. I wanted to come talk to someone about it. I followed you but lost you at Onn Fountain, but thankfully you were more than loud enough to find here.

Fournimer's Text Box: I was…

Yallundy's Text Box: Being a spoiled little pony brat? Yes, I saw.

Fournimer's Text Box: I guess I was.

Yallundy's Text Box: Everyone that lived here is dead and the world is going to be reset soon. I think it will be alright. Are you going to be okay?

Fournimer's Text Box: I think so. I wish that everyone believed me about Anders coming back. It is the only way that stuff would show up in his *Ultra-Pack*. I also really wish I never met Chad, I can barely walk they are so sore now.

Yallundy's Text Box: I still want to meet Chad, he is cute. I wish I could tell you that other part was true. There is hope certainly that he himself is alright, but his avatar is doubtful. I cannot feel anyone named Anders with my *Empathy*. I do admit it was suspicious, but I have been watching and I have seen Gliint looking through Palcath and Lissa's stuff. There is a good possibility that he planted the *Optional Flowers* on you.

Fournimer's Text Box: Gliint? why would he do that?

Yallundy's Text Box: I don't know. There is definitely something wrong with him. He has been all over the map doing bizarre things. What I am certain of is that he is obsessed with that floating island above Onn. He is always staring at it, trying to jump to it, protecting it. First he didn't want Palcath to even acknowledge it, and then without explanation he is all gung ho to let everyone build a cake stairway to it.

Fournimer's Text Box: we need to keep an eye on him then!

Yallundy's Text Box: Yes, but I already am doing that. I can turn invisible after all. As soon as the stairway is tall enough to be out of earshot I'll warn the others about him.

Fournimer's Text Box: what do I do then?

Yallundy's Text Box: You need to act like I'm not here and watch your back. Don't let him go through your *Saddlebags* anymore. He was interested in Anders' gear for whatever reason and that worries me. I suggest looking through everything you have for *Bombs*. He has those and they can hurt you, as much as it saddens me to think of him hurting anyone. I also need you to do something else for me, can you do that?

Fournimer's Text Box: yes. of course.

Yallundy's Text Box: I want you to go for a real walk without the temper tantrums! It will help to get your frustrations out. I need to get back now. I can feel him moving again.

Yallundy patted Fournimer on the flank and vanished back to her silent vigil watching over Gliint.

Fournimer's Whisper Text Box: a real walk is not what I need to get my frustrations out!

Fournimer's Text Box: I guess it couldn't hurt though.

Fournimer surveyed the throne room one last time. He really had done a number on this place, but to be fair it was already pretty trashed when he got here. He really only had succeeded in applying a light coat of frosting to the destruction, if anything he had simply made this place delicious.

The only thing that wasn't trashed that badly was the throne itself. Only the black vaporized outline of NPC King Islan marked the surface. Otherwise the plush pink silk-backed two tiered throne was completely perfect. The symbol of *Onn*, a circle, had been cut out of the back of the lower tier of the throne. Fournimer eyed the hole in the chair. Lined with the same plush pink padded silk, it would feel soft and luxurious. His vision became cloudily while he looked at it and he could feel himself slipping out of his sheath. The armrests on the throne looked stable and wide enough for a centaur to stand on making it the right height. Fournimer changed to *Blush Shade #3*.

Fournimer's Text Box: Yallundy? are you still here?

After waiting more rounds than was probably necessary Fournimer had decided that he was indeed alone. He gingerly approached the throne and took one last glance around. He hooked his front legs over the back of the throne, steadied his back legs on the arm-rests, and assessed. This hole was in exactly the right place and he was more than ready to take advantage of it. 657 days (and quickly growing) of pent up horse was going to explode through this hole. He lined up his hung cock with the opening and thrust inside, sliding all the way until his balls (which were set to his favorite colour right now but not at all by choice) smacked the plush fabric sending a little hint of pleasure and pain up his body.

This throne was either absolutely exquisite or Fournimer was finally happy to be breaking his now triple long forced vow of celibacy. It didn't take long before Fournimer was lost in his movements. Thrusting his heavy horse body harder and harder into the symbol of Onn. Blissfully aware of the silky pleasures of his throne lover, Fournimer was also blissfully unaware of its creaking complaints. Fournimer was thrusting at his maximum speed, (of gallop) desperate and sweating.

> Fournimer's Text Box: Maker! finally. I'm so close. I love you Onn Throne!

> Onn Throne's Text Box: CRACK!

A wide-eyed Fournimer and the top half of an upset throne toppled forward still connected. Fournimer had panicked. Landing like this, penis-first (that was stuck in a large chunk of solid wood) would not be pleasant. He fell behind the throne, braced for what would be a horrible impact, and then vanished into thin air with only a blip sound effect.

Chapter 19

CYCLE 4: MORNING NDES, SAILING AWAY

After checking in for his third trip on the S.S. Party Splitterup ndes went to the private cabin to get some rest. He slept for most of this trip. It was still early in the morning and you couldn't really watch the scenery in the dark. After a good rest, a soak in the private hot tub to relax his sore muscles, and a trip to the snack bar to buy a lot more *Bacon Wrapped Bacon*, ndes would decide where to go to next. Sleep was the most important part right now so he skipped the others. He stretched out on the top bunk and drifted off.

~~~

Almost as fast as the scene break in this Chapter had happened, loud noises and vibrations crashed against the ship. They violently jostled ndes awake. Something had hit the ship and had hit it hard. The strange dream of flying cake to the top of a stack faded quickly. Before he could even figure out what had happened he was groggily knocked out of the top bunk and onto the floor by a more intensive follow up smash to the ship. Crash after crash continued to pummel the ship and he was thankful that he had no gear or items to collect that wasn't already attached to himself. As fast as he could, he stumbled outside of the private cabin. The NPC sailors were still walking around normally. They did not look worried in the slightest.

ndes' Text Box: What's going on?

NPC Captain Saylerman's Text Box: Duh, this is your third trip with us.

ndes' Text Box: So? What does that have to do with anything?!

NPC Captain Saylerman's Text Box: You avatars know absolutely nothing about boats do you? The first trip is always set to Party Split-Up Disaster Mode. Pleasant Journey Mode is always the standard for a second or fourth trip. The third trip is always set to Swallowed Up By a Gargantuan Monster Mode. After that it rotates between them all.

ndes' Text Box: Swallowed Up By a Gargantuan Monster Mode?

NPC Captain Saylerman's Text Box: Exactly! Look, here comes the Giganticore now to eat you! I wish I could go, it sounds like fun and there is someone I always see waving to me from inside.

ndes barely had time to think about how completely unfun that sounded before he had been swallowed whole by a sea monster of impossible size.

~~~

For the inside stomach and intestines of a monster, this place was surprisingly well lit. Fortunately, there were some nice (albeit squishy) paths to walk on to avoid the patches of acid. ndes surveyed the landscape and the perfectly normal looking house in the middle of the area seemed like the correct place to start. He walked to the house, only accidentally stepping in acid once, and opened the door. His hand dropped off the handle and he turned instantly to *Blush Shade #4* (which was white because he still didn't have any colour on his body).

NPC Researcher Joannah's Text Box: Maker! Don't you fucking avatars ever knock? Think you can go into whatever house you want anytime you want!

ndes' Text Box: I'm sorry. I'll leave.

NPC Researcher Joannah's Text Box: No, don't bother. The moment passed. What do you want?

ndes' Text Box: Information about the area I think. Well, that and for you to take your hand off of there.

NPC Researcher Joannah's Text Box: Fine, I'll do the script. *ahem* Hello adventurers, I am Researcher Joannah.

NPC Researcher Joannah took her hand off of her pussy and held it out for any adventurers to shake. ndes politely refused the offer and pointed to Joannah's pants on the floor but she politely refused back.

> NPC Researcher Joannah's Text Box: I was head researcher on the Giganticore project but our research on the normally peaceful creature was interrupted when it started to swim amok in the ocean attacking everything in sight. Then it went and swallowed our research house.

> ndes' Text Box: Your research house? A swimming monster attacked your research house and ate it?

> NPC Researcher Joannah's Text Box: Yeah, I don't get it either. Regardless we found out that the Giganticore was invaded by a virus that has attacked its insides driving it insane. Blah blah blah. Pretty standard giant monster plot. My fellow researchers (who never existed so don't feel too bad for them) died exploring the area. To leave you will need to kill either the six Red Scorpovirus Mothers or the optional Purple Scorpovirus Master.

> ndes' Text Box: This is that level?

> NPC Researcher Joannah's Text Box: Yeah, this is that level. The inside the giant monster level where you fight normal sized regular monsters.

> ndes' Text Box: I was wondering if there was one of those.

> NPC Researcher Joannah's Text Box: There is and you are here. Now go forth and leave me alone.

> ndes' Text Box: Are you okay? You don't seem okay.

> NPC Researcher Joannah's Text Box: No! I am all alone here. Do you know how many people visit the inside stomach of a giant monster? Well, there is a lot. But no one bothers to talk to me. They always take that golden treasure chest over there and leave. They already all know what to do while inside a giant monster. They never ever talk to me! I am so lonely!

> ndes' Text Box: There is a gold chest? I mean… aw you poor girl. Can I help you somehow?

> NPC Researcher Joannah's Text Box: You could have sex with me. I'm bored but also horny.

ndes' Text Box: Can I help you in a different way? I'm kinda... gay.

NPC Researcher Joannah's Text Box: You? The big hunk of beef? Gay? Look at you. You must be a total top then.

ndes' Text Box: I've been getting that a lot lately.

NPC Researcher Joannah's Text Box: I don't know what to do. I keep seeing NPC Captain Saylerman dropping off avatars here and I want to...

ndes' Text Box: Talk to him?

NPC Researcher Joannah's Text Box: No, to fuck his brains out. That eye-patch is super hot!

ndes' Text Box: True, that eye-patch is sexy. Okay, why don't you come with me? Escape this stomach and then have your way with the man of your dreams?

NPC Researcher Joannah's Text Box: Can I even leave here?

ndes used the *Shrug Animation*.

NPC Researcher Joannah's Text Box: I could tell people about this area while they are on the S.S. Party Splitterup. I could go there and be as useful. I don't have any weapons to help fight my way out of here.

ndes' Text Box: That is okay, I wasn't planning on using weapons.

Joannah was busy collecting her pants while ndes was busy opening the golden chest. Inside was a brand new *Croc-Pot+*. It was useless and disappointing, but he stuffed it into his inventory. There was no point in leaving it behind to rot in the stomach of this monster like Joannah had been doing. They left the house, Joannah leading the way filled to the brim with excitement.

NPC Researcher Joannah's Text Box: So the red ones are this way.

ndes' Text Box: No, we are going for the purple one.

NPC Researcher Joannah's Text Box: Seriously? It is huge, powerful, and Level 70!

ndes' Text Box: I'm huge, powerful, and Level 76.

NPC Researcher Joannah's Text Box: Noted. See that platform up there? The Purple Scorpovirus Master is there. To get up there first we will need to find the spleen of the Giganticore and flick it. During the convulsions we can ride the undigested skeleton up to the brain. After we clear the brain of all the plaque we can... hey! How did we get up to the platform?

ndes' Text Box: I picked you up and jumped here while you were explaining.

NPC Researcher Joannah's Text Box: You can jump that high? You're amazing!

Falling from the heart of the Giganticore dropped the Purple Scorpovirus Master. It was a scorpion as big as an elephant, (one of those elephants with saddles, not the elephants that wear Armour). It had a multitude of tentacle feelers that looked right for... that sort of thing. ndes saw the scorpion tentacle hybrid and jumped into Joannah's arms for protection.

ndes' Text Box: Ahhh! Big rapey Bug!

NPC Researcher Joannah's Text Box: I take that back.

ndes' Text Box: You don't understand. I used to think bugs were pretty neat, but all of my experiences here with the Swarm Beetles and Spiderboys have changed my mind. I don't like bugs anymore. They are icky!

NPC Researcher Joannah's Text Box: Oh no! Anything but icky!

ndes' Text Box: Stay away from me you perverted rape bug!

Purple Scorpovirus Master's Text Box: Huh?

ndes' Text Box: Enough of your lies fiend!

Unsheathing his *Primary Circle Sword* while jumping out of the protective arms of Joannah, ndes sprang towards the Purple Scorpovirus Master. Using all of the sword attacks that he had never bothered to try until now, ndes savagely hacked at the viral scorpion. Blood and viral puss gushed out of the confused monster, who didn't even have a chance to understand what was really going on. It didn't matter to ndes what the real intentions of the boss were, or even that he needed the optional flower from it, he wanted it gone.

When the pile of purple blood, feelers, and shell flashed out of existence, ndes wiped the guts from his face without remorse. It would respawn later to dirty bug tentacle rape someone else, (even if all it wanted to do was grab a *Koffee* and talk).

Creature Name: Purple Scorpovirus Master
Class: Viral Scorpion
Level: 70
Special Attacks: Viral Pincer, Cheek Pinch, Deadly Sneeze, Puss Shot, Double Tenty Pincer, Koffee Convo
Drops: A way out of the Giganticore
First Player Encounter Notes: What a nice fellow! Amazing *Koffee*. Such a great listener. – Bobbinz
Additional Comments: Don't look. Don't breathe. Just kill. – ndes

Game Explanation Text Box: Polygons absorbed from Purple Scorpovirus Master 16.6%.

nde1s was as smooth inside as he was outside. All of his internal organ polygons were back, but he was still lacking his bone polygons as best as he could tell. He was really hoping for a full letter, he had only gotten half a letter r back.

nde1s' Text Box: Half an r? It looks like an i without that dot on top. I don't even know how to type that.

Game Explanation Text Box: Special trait absorbed from Purple Scorpovirus Master, Secondary Weapon.

It had given him a bow! A *Giganticore Rib Bow* to be precise. It was a stupidly huge bow that was 150% taller than he was. It was menacing and made him feel much better about only getting half a letter this time. He scouted below and saw one of the Red Scorpovirus Mothers wondering about. He was going to test this gigantic bow out.

He drew an arrow and waited for it to begin to charge. He waited, and waited some more. The arrow did not begin to charge. He was confused; it should have used his reserve Magic Points to increase the attack. He needed that for his mission. Then it dawned on him. This new bow couldn't *Charge*, that was a special ability of his old bow. This giant bow was useless for his mission. That sucked.

At least he knew where to go after getting out of here and dropping off Joannah into Captain Saylorman's arms. There was a GameFrame access point there. He was going to need to go back to Onn, his old nemesis. Hopefully his old *Gladiator Bow+* was still there in the Coliseum; maybe even the Legendary Hydra was still there to milk.

nde1s turned to Joannah but she was already on the S.S. Party Splitterup, ripping off Captain Saylorman's clothes while the rest of the crew cheered them on. NPC love was so cute.

♦ Chapter 20 ♦
CYCLE 4
GROUP Q, WAIT Q?

Macintosh's Text Box: Okay, it is settled then pals and gals, we are going to do this. The question is how.

Purple Quest Fairy's Text Box: You can't say 'it is settled' and get your way. We haven't even talked about this yet. Why do you think you are the leader? I thought we were joint leaders. You are #SoScrewedUp.

Macintosh's Text Box: Thanks for the input, pal. Your concerns have been noted. Okay pals and gals I guess we could talk about this even though I am pretty sure we are all on the same page.

Purple Quest Fairy's Text Box: Of course we are! I didn't want you to ignore my joint leadership is all!

Blue Quest Fairy's Text Box: yeah! we didn't want you to think you could walk all over us, Mac, and take control.

Orange Quest Fairy's Text Box: We are walking now? I didn't know that fellow framerette.

Purple Quest Fairy's Text Box: Shut up airhead.

Herbert's Text Box: I still don't think we should do this. It isn't even remotely sawesome.

Brown Quest Fairy's Text Box: *Arms up in the air in frustration* What are you doing? Not only is sawesome not even a word but your name isn't even Herbert! Why is that in your Text Box?

Herbert's Text Box: I like it better than my real name.

No-Colour Quest Fairy's Text Box: Yeah well, Herbert is a stupid name.

Pink Quest Fairy's Text Box: Hey! Be sweet to Herbert, Yeah well!

No-Colour Quest Fairy's Text Box: My name is Yawell not Yeah well. Yeah well, do you best to remember it you big flaming queen!

Pink Quest Fairy's Text Box: How many times do I need to tell you that I am not gay? Just because I am pink it does not mean that I am gay. The sweet flashing teal one is the gay one.

Constantly-Colour-Changing Quest Fairy's Text Box: Guilty!

White Quest Fairy's Text Box: Alright, back on topic. Just because some of us may not agree with… Herbert's ideas that doesn't mean that we can just ignore them. The fact is that we need to go over all of the facts here. Should we go through with this? There are of course pros and cons to both sides of this argument. It would be an idea to just go over both sides again and discuss the options that we actually have here. Personally I am on Macintosh's side, as should anyone of us that is sane, but a vote might not be a bad idea as well. Should we have a vote on this matte—

White Quest Fairy's Text Box: r?

Gray Quest Fairy's Text Box: Vote? Why would we need to vote? They killed our friends! Abby and Tyresse must be avenged!

Macintosh's Text Box: Why are you even Text Boxing, gal? You are the gray one! The gray avatar doesn't talk.

Other-Blue Quest Fairy's Text Box: I don't think that a count… well, I mean a vote instead. I don't think that a vote is a bad idea really. I mean well it is more fair you know, for like unity and the good of all… or the improvement of us instead. I am down for not being squares man.

Other-Yellow Quest Fairy's Text Box: Pourquoi voter? Ils sont coupables je vous dit, Coupables! Je veux tous les voir morts! Vive la fée des quêtes!

Green Quest Fairy's Text Box: I agree with whatever she said. They have oppressed us for far too long with their avatar chauvinist ideals. They think they are so important because the Game was made for them. I have news for them, they are not! Without us helping them they would have been nothing here.

Other-Purple and Other-Orange Quest Fairy's Simultaneous Text Box: Sorry but I agree with Herbert. Yeah, sorry but so do I. I mean they didn't kill our friends, only that one scary one did. I know!

Macintosh's Text Box: Fine pals and gals, we will have a vote then, all those in favour of gui—

Herbert's Interruption Text Box: No, we need to have a silent vote! It is the only thing that is fair!

Fifteen *Gasp Animations* occurred at the exact same instant.

Macintosh's Text Box: Did you... interrupt me?

Other-Yellow Quest Fairy's Text Box: On n'a pas de soeur. Enchainez-la à cet arbre. Avec de telles blessures, elle saignera à mort. Ses entrailles attireront les loups blancs et ils se régaleront sur son corps.

Gray Quest Fairy's Text Box: Yeah! Do that. Do all of whatever that French one said!

Herbert's Text Box: I'm sorry! I'm really sorry!

Macintosh's Text Box: You know that is the first and second rule of Fairy Club, gal. That is our only rule now that I think about it. No interruptions. Don't let it happen again.

Blue Quest Fairy's Text Box: yeah, be careful Herb.

Other-Blue Quest Fairy's Text Box: I am sure it was an accident, a mistake instead of on purpose. Hey I know which way I am going to vote man. I am all for peace and love... the good things in all of us rather. Why do we need so much hate man? We are not squares like them man, we can forgive them, rather.

White Quest Fairy's Text Box: I think you need to stop smoking all that *Echo Grass*. Don't you have any concept of what a silent vote is? Everyone votes in secret by writing on paper.

No-Colour Quest Fairy's Text Box: Yeah well, we have a problem then. We don't have anything to write with.

Constantly-Colour-Changing Quest Fairy's Text Box: Or like paper or anything to write on or whatever. It is like a total disaster or whatever. At least I look awesome though, still digging this colour shifting thing.

Gray Quest Fairy's Text Box: You are nothing like your Avatar Nathaniel! You are supposed to be like your Avatar.

Constantly-Colour-Changing Quest Fairy's Text Box: So what? Neither are you or whatever.

Gray Quest Fairy's Text Box: …

Purple Quest Fairy's Text Box: We don't have pens or paper? #StationaryStationery.

Orange Quest Fairy's Text Box: I agree with you completely framer.

Other-Purple and Other-Orange Quest Fairy's Simultaneous Text Box: We have this *Commonly Rare Empty Bottle*. Yeah, and a bunch of *Golden Acorns* and *Silver Walnuts*. Why don't we vote by dropping in a *Golden Acorn* for yes and a *Silver Walnut* for no? I like that idea. Thank you for helping with it. Kiss me? You bet!

Orange Quest Fairy's Text Box: Why do you have a *Commonly Rare Empty Bottle* with you framers? That thing is a death trap!

Macintosh's Text Box: That will do nicely, thank you pals. A *Golden Acorn* means yes we should do this and a *Silver Walnut* means no.

Herbert's Text Box: Sawesome!

Each was handed a *Golden Acorn* and a *Silver Walnut* by Macintosh who took special care to press the *Golden Acorn* into their hands with more force while smiling. He was trying to make them do the right thing and not being at all subtle about it. He even tried to watch the votes that were entered into the *Commonly Rare Empty Bottle* but stopped when he got caught by Herbert.

Macintosh's Text Box: The votes are all in pals and gals. I hope that all of you have made the right decision.

Other-Yellow Quest Fairy's Text Box: On ne devrait pas hésiter. Amenons-les à la guillotine!

Macintosh's Text Box: By a slim margin of 9 *Golden Acorns* to 8 *Silver Walnuts* the vote is for yes. That is more Silver Walnuts than I expected, but still majority rules.

White Quest Fairy's Text Box: Your math is wrong. That adds to 17. Need I remind you that there are 16 of us?

Blue Quest Fairy's Text Box: sorry, that was me. I couldn't decide so I put in both.

White Quest Fairy's Text Box: Does nobody understand the concept of a silent vote?

Macintosh's Text Box: Regardless, the gal's votes cancel each other out. The result is still yes. So like I said earlier, how are we going to do this?

Gray Quest Fairy's Text Box: Hey listen! I have a plan. The first thing we need to do is collect something my avatar dropped, then we…

♦ *Chapter 21* ♦

CYCLE 4
GROUP R, THE CHAPTER
THAT BROKE
SPELL CHECK

Self Proclaimed Goddesses' Text Box: Th3r3 u b0th 4r3! | \/\/4s \/\/0rr|3d s|ck! ^-^ kekeke.

Cinnamon's Text Box: Charlie, kill me now.

Self Proclaimed Goddesses' Text Box: H3's pr0lly busy.

Roodg was stunned. The Goddess that the Posh Welsh Tribesman had been worshipping was the target of Group A's search! Roodg needed to tell everyone right away that the mysterious catgirl dressed in a blood covered schoolgirl uniform was the missing E. E. Lynn, unfortunately there was no way of telling anyone else this fact. Roodg was avoiding using Group Chat, better to let whoever was controlling De'vini to think that the plummet had resulted in death, not an entire plot arc.

Roodg's Text Box: E. E. Lynn! sAWESOME! wE HAVE BEEN LOOKING EVERYWHERE FOR YOU!

Cinnamon's Text Box: I haven't!

E. E. Lynn's Text Box: F|rst, S4\/\/3s0/\/\3 |s 4 gr34t w0rd, | \/\/4nt |t. S3c0nd, C|nn4/\/\0n h4s 4 \/\4g, c00l! Th|rd, \/\/h0 |s \/\/3? U m34n \/\/3 c4us3 0f 4ll teh junk typ3s u h4\/3? D03s |t /\/\4k3s u r plur4l? 4ls0, | 10\/3 y0ur junk ! H3rms

> r S4\/\/3s0/\/\3! fuck /\/\3?

> Cinnamon's Text Box: Remember when people complained about your Text Boxes, Roodg?

E. E. Lynn had already turned around and flipped up her skirt, revealing everything she had to offer under her kitty tail. After a quick removal of her *Nunchakus* from both of her available underskirt holes, she was ready for Roodg's business.

> E. E. Lynn's Text Box: P|ck y0ur f4\/0r|t3 h0l3! N0 \/\/4It! H3r/\/\ 4l3rt! | g0t 4 b3tt3r |d34!

Before Roodg could even think of replying, E. E. Lynn was in a complicated position involving the use of two nearby tuffets and a terrified Magma ReNegade. Roodg was uncertain of how she did it, but in this position she could have access to both of Roodg's genital sets, one in a favorite hole and one in her mouth respectively. This catgirl was certainly flexible.

> Roodg's Text Box: nICE HOLES, VERY FUCKABLE. bUT FIRST WE NEED TO TALK.

> E. E. Lynn's Text Box: 4\/\/3 c0/\/\3 0n! 4b0ut \/\/h4t?

> Roodg's Text Box: tWO THINGS. fIRST i AM NOT A HERM. i AM A Roodg. i AM THE ONLY ONE AND i AM sAWESOME AT IT.

A fantastic display of shifting genital sets by Roodg, in all possible combinations (of which there was 4), proved two things. One, that Roodg was indeed the only Roodg and not a hermaphrodite. Two, E. E. Lynn could not watch the display without fingering herself.

> E. E. Lynn's Text Box: 0/\/\C! U r teh b3st s4cr|f|c3 3\/3r! U H4\/3 b0th Sh|ft & h3r/\/\ p0\/\/3rs? N0 fuck|ng \/\/4y! Cl34r y0ur d4y pl4nn3r c4us3 | 4/\/\ gunn4 p0\/\/nz0rz y0ur junk r4\/\/ 4ll y34r! ^-^

> Roodg's Text Box: tHAT IS THE SECOND THING—

> E. E. Lynn's Interruption Text Box: Sc0r3! St4rt fuck|ng /\/\3! 2 c0cks f|rst! kekeke

> Roodg's Text Box: nO, NOT SEX. i MEANT THE TIME FRAME. dON'T YOU KNOW THAT THE aDMINS ARE RESETTING THE eXPANSION IN A FEW CYCLES?

For the first time that Roodg knew of, E. E. Lynn stopped being in a sexual pose that exposed all of her naughty bits. She was looking stern, composed, and her kitty whiskers started to twitch.

> E. E. Lynn's Text Box: Th0s3 assh4ts r d0ing \/\/h4t?

> Roodg's Text Box: didn't U SEE THE WARNING THAT THEY PUT OUT?

> E. E. Lynn's Text Box: \/\/3ll Fuck /\/\3 (st|ll 4n 0ff3r BTW) th3y r g0|ng 2 d0 teh 4ssh4t|3st th|ng |n teh h|st0ry 0f *4nn4ls 0f G3nt4l|a!* h0\/\/ d|d | /\/\|ss th4t? | c4nn0t b3l|3v3 | 4/\/\ g0|ng 2 s4y th|s but \/\/3 d0n't h4\/3 t|/\/\3 2 fuck r|ght n0\/\/. \/\/3 n33d 4 pl4nz0r.

E. E. Lynn used the *Shudder Animation.* No time to fuck right now? Truly, this was a cycle that would live in infamy.

> Roodg's Text Box: wE ALREADY HAVE A PLAN! mY FRIENDS ARE LOOKING FOR YOU! yOU ARE THE PLAN! i FOUND YOU! pLAN DONE! wITH YOUR SUPER MAGICAL SWORD YOU CAN CUT INTO THE WORLD AND WARP US ALL OUT OF HERE AND INTO THE MAIN GAME. nO MORE DEATH! sO GREAT THAT i FOUND YOU. wE ARE SCATTERED ALL OVER THE PLACE AND SOME OF US WENT ALL EVIL! cAN U FIX EVIL WITH THAT SWORD?

> E. E. Lynn's Text Box: S0 /\/\4ny th|ngs \/\/r0ng \/\/|th th4t pl4n | d0n't 3\/3n kn0\/\/ \/\/h3r3 2 st4rt @-@ ...

> Roodg's Text Box: sNAP! lIKE WHAT?

> Cinnamon's Text Box: Please for the love of Charlie let me explain it! Reading this conversation is making my eyes bleed.

> Roodg and E. E. Lynn's Simultaneous Text Boxes: k

> Cinnamon's Text Box: The problem is this. Roodg, your party doesn't know this, but I can read here that the Expansion isn't the only place getting reset. The main map is getting reset a few cycles later, so leaving here isn't going to save you for.

> Roodg's Text Box: tUFFETS!

> Cinnamon's Text Box: That is only the first problem. There are many others. I heard a few problems over the Fairy-Comm System that are troubling. One, your Group Chat is down and all of your avatar friends

have lost access to the Fairy-Comm. System. We have no way of telling them anything.

Roodg's Text Box: tHERE IS A fAIRY-cOMM. sYSTEM?

Cinnamon's Text Box: Yes, but more importantly is the other thing that I heard over it. The Quest Fairies have grouped up to do something so they turned it off.

Roodg's Text Box: tHAT IS SLIGHTLY BAD. wHY ARE YOU STILL HERE AND NOT OUT PLANNING?

Cinnamon gave Roodg a *Quizical Look Animation*.

Cinnamon's Text Box: Because it is a Quest Fairy meeting? Why would I go plot with them?

Roodg's Text Box: i CAN'T BELIEVE Palcath WAS RIGHT! tHEY WERE PLOTTING SOMETHING.

Cinnamon's Text Box: They are off their nuts. I'll stick with E. E. Lynn, thank you.

Roodg used the *Confused Animation*.

Roodg's Text Box: bUT YOU WERE DESPERATE TO ESCAPE HER!

Cinnamon simply shrugged.

Cinnamon's Text Box: True.

E. E. Lynn's Text Box: H3 h4s b33n b4d u s33! S0 b4d!

Cinnamon's Text Box: Yes, yes, I know. I heard you the first time. Eternal punishment for all time. It was a damn headset. Get over it! Was that hunk of junk really worth binding, gagging, and using me as a dildo for all of Book 2?

E. E. Lynn's Text Box: Y3p! | f0rg|v3 u n0\/\/ c4us3 | \/\/4nn4 pl4y \/\/|th y0ur v4g!

Cinnamon's Text Box: That is what it takes for you to finally forgive me? Me losing my dick?!

Roodg's Text Box: yOU PEOPLE ARE CRAZY. i DIG IT.

Cinnamon's Text Box: No time for that now, more things to explain.

E. E. Lynn fell to her knees defeated.

> E. E. Lynn's Text Box: @-@

> Cinnamon's Text Box: We can't use the GameFrame to go anywhere we want. It only goes to certain places. The GameFrame access device is going to be completely worthless to teleport everyone away for two reasons. One, there is no GameFrame access point on either the Desserted Island or The Jungle of Contemplation.

> Roodg's Text Box: tHE jUNGLE OF cONTEMPLATION? nO ONE SHOULD BE THERE. wHERE IS THAT?

> Cinnamon's Text Box: My *Avatar Detector* says there are 3 avatars in The Jungle of Contemplation on Spire J, 2 on Desserted Island, 4 on Spire G, 2 here, and 7 in Onn. Whatever, that isn't important because the second reason that the GameFrame access device is worthless is that there is no GameFrame access point here. We got here when that idiot jumped off of the back of a flying dragon because she wanted to torment the inhabitants here.

> E. E. Lynn's Text Box: Y3s! ^-^ C4us3 th3y r r34lly hung! | n33d3d t0 cu/\/\ b4ck!

> Cinnamon's Text Box: We are stuck here for seventeen days until the Alternate Plane Dragon comes back.

> Roodg's Text Box: i SEE HOW THAT IS A PROBLEM.

> E. E. Lynn's Text Box: M3h. Th3r3 r oth3r \/\/4ys 2 l3av3 h3r3.

Cinnamon gave a scowl.

> Cinnamon's Text Box: Yes, lots of the things you owned could have let us leave here, but you threw them all into the volcano after you said 'I r never leaving here, teh cocks r as huge here as the va-jay-jays are wet!'

> E. E. Lynn's Text Box: R|ght. kekeke. | F0rg0t 4b0ut th4t p4rt. Cr4p.

> Cinnamon's Text Box: Thankfully, E. E. Lynn can hack into the S.S. PlotDevice and send it here. We will not be stuck for long.

> Roodg's Text Box: nOPE! tHAT THING BLEW UP SO LONG AGO.

> Cinnamon's Text Box: What? It is a good thing that she can also hack

into the *Super Amazing Hover-Motorbike* and borrow it from the avatar that won it.

Roodg's Text Box: nOPE! i WON IT BUT THE ANGEL I KNOW WENT ALL EVIL AND TURNED MY *mAGICAL fLYING cARROT uLTRA+* INTO A *pARSNIP!*

E. E. Lynn's Text Box: 4 *P4rsn|p?* Th4t |s 3\/|l \/\/|th 4 c4p|t4l thr33!

Cinnamon's Text Box: I guess the Unborn Quest Fairies can be activated to carry us—

Roodg's Interruption Text Box: aLL DEAD.

Cinnamon checked over his *Ultimate Game Guide* (which he kept hidden somehow until now).

Cinnamon's Text Box: The Dragon Rider cou—

E. E. Lynn's Interruption Text Box: N0t 0n sp34k|ng t3r/\/\s \/\/|th h3r r|ght n0\/\/.

Cinnamon's Text Box: The BEEhemoth Queen?

E. E. Lynn's Text Box: | cr4sh3d h3r |nt0 teh /\/\0unt4|n & sh3 bl0\/\/z up. |t \/\/4s 3p|c.

Cinnamon's Text Box: Hover—

E. E. Lynn's Interruption Text Box: N0t 4ct|\/4t3d y3t.

Cinnamon's Text Box: Well fuck. That is all I know about. Can you hack anything else?

E. E. Lynn's Text Box: | f|n|sh3d l00k|ng. 3v3ryth|ng 3ls3 us3ful |s 3|th3r d3str0y3d 0r st|ll l0ck3d! L4zy 4\/4t4rs! @-@

Roodg's Text Box: sO WE ARE REALLY STUCK HERE? lAME.

E. E. Lynn's Text Box: Y3p! /\/\|ght 4s \/\/3ll fuck til \/\/3 b|t3 |t!

Cinnamon's Text Box: Yes, we are stuck here unless Caps Lock randomly happens to have a *Jetpack* or a *Golden Tin Whistle* shoved up their ass.

> Roodg's Text Box: OMM! i TOTALLY DO! i HAVE THE *gOLDEN tIN wHISTLE* FROM dESSERTED iSLAND!

E. E. Lynn was already on all fours, ready to check Roodg's butt for *The Golden Tin Whistle* or any *Jetpacks*. After clarifying that the *Golden Tin Whistle* was not inside Roodg, but inside a *Backpack* E. E. Lynn looked upset. She had really wanted to explore for it.

> Cinnamon's Text Box: How do you randomly have that? You are not even a Summoner.

> Roodg's Text Box: i ALREADY SAID HOW. cAUSE i AM sAWESOME! wHY DO YOU KEEP FORGETTING?

> E. E. Lynn's Text Box: 2 teh t0p 0f Mnt. S4cr|fIc4l \/0lc4n0!

The catgirl was leading the way. She had already left the conversation and had started to trek up the outside of Mnt. Sacrificial Volcano before any solid plan had been made. She even made sure than Roodg would have a great view up her skirt by completely tucking it into the back of her shirt. Cinnamon followed begrudgingly but kept a good distance away from her, Roodg decided that the spice fairy had a good idea and also kept a few rounds distance. As they walked Roodg wondered why exactly Group A had been trying to find her. Sure she might be able to help them in the long run, but she was completely nuts, dangerous, and her Text Boxes where horrible!

◈ Chapter 22 ◈

CYCLE 4: EVENING NDEIS, TYING UP LOOSE ONNS

The Onn port-in area smelled of the distant past. There was a faint odor of smoke-baked earth within the lonely Quest Fairy Spawning Cave. The grass, the scenic bushes, the rock formations, and even the sky were all burnt. A hint of black pixel residue coated the entire area, smelling of stale dust. Far in the distance was a lovely waft of delicious smelling, but ill-tasting baked goods. A long forgotten skipping stone lake was off to one side of the little featureless path, lending a tang of salt to the air.

This area was far more trashed than ndeis remembered. The destruction in the far distance made him realize that it was not only this area that had been damaged, but nearly every area in the entire Expansion. Paths of wreckage would make new unheard of areas connect, even to this one. No one would be stuck in Onn now, unless they wanted to be.

A breath of the air stirred up a lot of memories, ndeis was uncertain how he felt about being here again. His cock instantly hardened, pressing up against his *Knight Armour* codpiece. It wasn't the feeling he had been expecting, in fact it hadn't even been in the top fifty, but there it was, extreme horniess.

His nose was craving something in the area and ndeis turned his head every which way while sniffing wild, exuberant breaths. Desperation was setting in, he needed to find the source of the alluring odor, and he needed to find it now. Nearly prowling on all fours, a sudden waft of success caused him to nearly leap across the entire area. It was the lake. It smelled of appreciation, secret crushes, secret meetings in Book Two between Anders and Fournimer, and load after load of centaur semen.

ndeıs would have changed *Blush Shades*, but he couldn't. The memories of repeated centaur milkings flooded back, much like the aforementioned centaur milkings. Helping to relieve Fournimer of his constantly full balls had never disappointed, and certainly added many delightful memories to ndeıs' personal vault.

His vault? ndeıs remembered something important. He had filed a sexy scene in his mind of Fourni and the whats-his-taur jerking each other off with the assistance of their happy tongues. His cock twitched, cramped tightly in its personal prison.

ndeıs' Text Box: Fudge it. Let's do this.

The codpiece retracted with a schlick and ndeıs' bulky cock bounced free. The air, rich with aromas, felt more intense, as if all focus was on him. Leaning up against the smooth rock that had softened many a horse handjob session, ndeıs began a handjob of his own. His new cock was the type that you needed to hold firmly. Every pump would need to be firm and purposeful. Wrapping fingers around the root, he began deliberate strokes.

Even with the longest stroke he could muster, there were still several length units that were not getting any attention. Such were the perils of having a big, hearty member. Fortunately, experience with centaurs (among other things) had taught ndeıs a thing or two about dealing with big, hearty members. Two handed was the way to go, and ndeıs sighed happily when he felt the joys of two handed masturbation. What a sight he must be, one hand was pumping the shaft, and another rotating around the happy head.

Leaking was something ndeıs didn't have much experience with, but thanks to this new appendage, he was quickly gaining Skill Points. His twirling hand was getting more sticky and wet with his own juices. There was really only one way to deal with that kind of a problem, and every finger was licked clean. He did not simply return down with his twirling hand, instead it enjoyed the ride down, beautifully feeling down the well proportioned muscles, pinching a perky nipple, squeezing balls to help them emit up more of the sticky love-seed. A light breeze rustled some nearby scenic bushes, and long in the distance non-existent birds happily chirped as background filler.

He wanted to lick up more of the drops, but he didn't want to stop the ball work. The seed had a great flavour, and tasting it was driving him absolutely wild, but the squeezing was exquisite. Droplets of liquid were dripping down his member as he squeezed his nuts, making the decision even harder. He remembered that he didn't have to decide. With a little arcing of his back, and a shift of his pelvis, ndeıs stuck his tongue out and began to twirl it around the head of his dripping member. Licking up every drop. The scenic bushes a few move units away gasped slightly at this display.

ndeıs froze. Something was definitely watching him, but it was hidden deep within the scenic bush. Whatever this was, it had learned the lessons of hiding within scenic bushes, but what it didn't know was that it was dealing with the original master of scenic bushes. A discerning eye of the bush revealed that, an eye; it was watching him. He couldn't make out what it was the eye of (scenic bushes were pretty wonderful) but he did see the eye.

The eye was caught red eyelidded, and nde1s began to stare it down, It was blinking nervously, but then it blinked magically. nde1s was levitated into the air and began to slowly rotate every which way. The shocked Night Ranger didn't know what to do except float there continuing to stare down the eye while trying desperately to change *Blush Shades*.

Bizzoit! nde1s felt like a positively *Charmed Person* now that he thought about it. Whatever had been watching his person obviously had taken a shining to him. While it had been spying on him in an intimate moment, it was a compliment, wasn't it? He felt his heart slow down from its hyper state, and he relaxed (as if magically enchanted). As he rotated silently in the air, his vision came back around to the bushes. Whatever watched him had company. Now there was a smaller eye watching in tandem.

Zorp! If there was going to be an audience perhaps nde1s should put on a show. It was as if his regular inhibitions had *Disintegrated* away completely and nde1s began to rub himself all over. Without gravity and limbs needing to touch the ground, he suddenly had easier access to all sorts of places he hadn't thought about lovingly caressing. He purposefully made little happy noises, to further entice his observers.

Fvvtuh! This was a feeling he recognized, from his encounter with Constance the Medusa. He became harder than rock hard. He was *Flesh to Stone* hard. That explained it, he thought as he idly spun about, the strange noises had been magic spells. The pair of eyes, no four eyes now, had been casting spells on him. His cock had been petrified hard, but was fortunately not real stone. The power of the spells was what had been making him so horny and liberated. He wasn't sure how he thought about this situation.

Schvooo! Amazing! That was how he felt about this. His meat monster had been *Charm Monstered* and now he was into this again. Even though he knew that it was magical spells making him so agreeable, he did have to agree that his cock was hard, he had been horny even before this started, and jerking off while rotating in the air wasn't something that you got to try often. He reached down, screwing modesty and his inhibitions, and grabbed his cock again in earnest.

Whuzzzz! nde1s, five little eyes, and one big eye watched as various items were fished magically out of the nearby pond. Fish after fish was pulled from the depths, even including some of the more risqué kinds, but when a *Stereotypical Old Boot* was fished out nde1s watched confused as it was brought closer through *Telekinesis*. After a few shakes a piece of *Schlam Meat* fell out and the boot was tossed aside. The *Schlam Meat* was gingerly levitated nearby, it waited patiently until nde1s rotated right and it speared itself with the charming member. It was cold, wet, and smelled of centaur, but it was also tight, firm, and dripping. The *Schlam Shell* moved back and forth, matching the speed of his strokes.

Ewhamp! Speed was what he wanted, and nde1s began to stoke feverishly to feel more of the unique texture of the *Schlam*. Speed was denied to him; with each stroke his pace was *Slowed*. He couldn't pump with anything but the slowest of motions. Every final long stroke ended with a chilling wet hint of *Schlam*. His impending orgasm would be controlled for now, and this experience extended.

Pew Pew! Sharp pains slashed across ndeɪs body. They startled him more than they hurt, and were whip like. They only left little marks, as the invisible whip was only really *Inflicting Moderate Wounds*. The whipping was encouraging, and he tried to go as fast as possible, but was still *Ewamped*. He wrapped both hands around his member after pushing down the *Schlam* hard. If he was going to be forced to go slow he would make sure that every single pump was used to its full potential.

Ra-ta-ta-tah! The slow stopped suddenly, and ndeɪs was trying so hard to pump quickly that when the effect dissipated his first full force stroke shot the *Schlam* clear off his member and into a lake several thousands of move units away. He could go at full pace again and wasted little time in reaching his top speed. His fingers were linked around his stone hard member that was dripping in ooze. A spectral hand popped into existence, and all but the ring finger of the ghostly hand curled up into a fist. This single finger began to tickle and tease him in the one place he desperately had wanted for some time now: his tender, neglected button. He was already dripping with anticipation and hoping that the finger would find purchase, but all it did was tease and taunt. The denial of getting *Fingered* was *of Death* itself and soon ndeɪs was near his absolute breaking point. He wanted to feel it inside so badly, he had wanted anything in there for some chapters now.

Verrrrrr! Fear set in. He already knew that the finger would not penetrate him, it must have thought him a total top, and he had accepted that. That wasn't why he was fearful, nor was the fact that nine little eyes in total had joined the larger eye to watch his display. No, he was fearful because he was on the brink. Fear he could overcome, literally, as one final thrust forward made him lose control. Fear was overcome, and hot squirts of magically enchanted spunk flew from his member with surprising force. ndeɪs watched the amazing display and tried to aim his spurts directly into his own mouth. Gravity allowed the last drop to hit his tongue and it took seed. As a final eye opened in the distant scenic bushes to cast a spell ndeɪs saw the last drop of his cum grow up on his tongue, a little stem of green that formed into a sticky wilted purple flower.

Ze-Zonk! The final spell, *Sleep*, hit hard.

~~~

He woke up over a hundred rounds later, still slowly rotating. Whatever had been spying on him had long ago disappeared. The eleven eyes that each had a spell had an enjoyed a full show, what a sight he would have been to behold, rotating in the air, asleep. He was completely clean, and had a nagging feeling in his mind that he had been licked into that status.

The *Optional Flower* had also vanished, likely swallowed. ndeɪs had also gained no experience points or polygons for the encounter. He had not defeated the boss, he had defeated himself. He checked the Optional Boss list carefully, but nothing he could see matched the description of something, or somethings, with many eyes. He didn't right know what some of them were, so it would remain a mystery, mostly for copyright reasons.

It was time to get going, Onn awaited. Despite his natural hate of Onn and all that it stood for, he had kind of missed it. He couldn't explain why, but he was glad to be here.

The Bakery Shoppe, still conjured good memories, and ndeıs went in the secret entrance to skip any accidental dialogue with Bakery Shoppe Menus. The entire inside was stacked with the freshest of cake, it was so overwhelming that he announced his entrance with a cough that was frosted. He noticed NPC Margarine pulling a fresh batch of *Grand FullCakes* out of the oven and NPC Illiandro mixing various ingredients in a bowl bigger than himself. NPC Greeta had put down her *Welcome to Onn Sign* and was making striped candles out of *BEEhemothwax*. Even the NPC guard whose name ndeıs couldn't remember and wasn't supposed to ever be mentioned again was here, getting busy with fashionable pink frosting.

> ndeıs' Text Box: What is going on here?

> NPC Illiandro's Text Box: Margarine got a huge order for *Grand FullCakes*. Her stock got completely wiped out and they still want hundreds more.

> NPC Galapas' Text Box: We are helping. I am in charge of making pink icing rosettes.

> NPC Greeta's Text Box: Welcome to Onn!

> NPC Margarine's Text Box: We are ever so busy, hun. But if those avatars are right and we can get out of the Expansion with the help of cake then we need to do this.

> ndeıs' Text Box: Margarine, they are going to escape the Expansion with cake?

> NPC Margarine's Text Box: Welcome to my Bakery Shoppe, hun. How can I help you today?

ndeıs bought a large assortment of baked goods but no *Grand FullCakes* and then he shut the shop menu.

> NPC Margarine's Text Box: Sorry about that, hun.

> ndeıs' Text Box: I needed to buy food anyway. How are they going to escape the Expansion using cake... Greeta?

NPC Greeta's Text Box: Welcome to Onn!

NPC Margarine's Text Box: I have absolutely no idea, hun. But we sure as Flaming Pit will make as many as we can if it could help.

ndeis' Text Box: I am really sorry, but I need to borrow the head mixer there for a little while. I have my own mission to complete and I need your help Illiandro.

NPC Margarine's Text Box: You can't come in here and steal my head mixer. I don't care how polite you ask, hun. Why should we help you when we already have a mission to complete? As impressive as you look, we don't even know who you are.

ndeis had completely forgotten that he looked completely different in almost all respects. He raised the visor on his helmet and took all of the NPCs by surprise. NPC Galapas took the news particularly hard, but that was likely due to the fact that he was already at maximum surprise level due to the fact that he was even mentioned again.

NPC Margarine's Text Box: Dear Maker! Hun, what happened to you? You are so buff and glittery. Your son Draganders was here, he will be so happy you are alive! We heard you were dead.

ndeis' Text Box: I am on a secret mission to save the entire world, all of it. Please, you cannot tell anyone that I am alive and here. Not Avatars, not other NPCs, not monsters, and especially not Admins. You can't even tell Draganders. Act like I do not exist.

NPC Greeta's Text Box: Welcome to Onn?

ndeis' Text Box: Exactly! I only need Illiandro for a little while, to get back into the Coliseum. I will bring him right back.

Illiandro's Text Box: I need a break anyway. I think I am getting the Mixer's Wrist Status Effect.

NPC Margarine's Text Box: Avoid Onn Castle's Roof, hun, that is where they all went with the cake.

ndeis' Text Box: Thank you Margarine.

NPC Margarine's Text Box: Welcome to my Bakery Shoppe, hun. How can I help you today?

ndeis closed the shop menu and used the *Sigh Animation*, directed at the massive pile of fresh *Grand FullCakes*.

~~~

> NPC Illiandro's Text Box: I can still smell cake, even all the way down here.

> ndeɪs' Text Box: I think it is you. You smell like cake.

> NPC Illiandro's Text Box: Really? That smell will probably never come out then. Darn, you are right. I do smell like cake. Get it off!

> ndeɪs' Text Box: Stop scratching yourself, you are only making it worse.

The NPC stopped scratching himself for a round to flip the switch that opened the lower floor of the Coliseum, the lair of the once Legendary 13 Headed Hydra. Illiandro would wait up here, while scratching and sniffing himself.

ndeɪs was immediately aware of the destruction that had happened down here. The fact that the ceiling had caved in was alarming considering that the floor upstairs looked fine. He surveyed the area but everything else was empty. The Legendary 13 Headed Hydra was no longer nailed to the wall, so there was not going to be an easy to find Optional Boss here. Everything else was bare as well; there were no longer mannequins on the walls dressed in bizarre broken items or dead Quest Fairies plastered to the roof. Everything that had made this room creepy originally was gone.

The spot where ndeɪs had turned to ash was currently buried but thankfully the rubble wouldn't be too deep there. He went right to work sifting through the remains of the ceiling. It was more labour intensive than he anticipated. The scenery was heavy. It took him about a hundred rounds to clear the first few rocks and he was starving.

It was time for a lunch break anyway and he knew the perfect thing. *Double Danishes* with a side of *Bacon Wrapped Bacon* to get the horrible taste of *Double Danishes* out of his mouth. He opened his inventory and was surprised. Not only were there 86 *Grand FullCakes* he had never bought, but all of the equipment that he was currently searching for was in there as well! Even his own ashes were in here, which was bizarrely reassuring. He didn't know how they had gotten in there but he was happy to see them.

He equipped his old *Gladiator Bow+* and it upgraded to match his current outfit. He now had a *Giganticore Rib Bow+*, it was similar to his old one except that he could now charge arrows again, and it was even bigger; twice his height at least. He exchanged his sword as well, for a *Primary Circle Sword+*, this new version now had a secondary floating circle set inside the original, but the new inset was the same colour as his accent colour, rainbow gray gradient. True, Breaker had broken these at one point, but Breaker was long dead and couldn't control anyone now. He held back a *Sneeze Animation*. It was dusty in here.

The only item he could think of that was missing was his Sexcessory, the *Pink Slime Jockstrap*. It might have been vaporized and he got sad thinking about it turning to dust. It was his only reminder of his gentle friend the Pink Slime, who had started his entire quest, and hopefully it was somewhere in the rubble. He put his old familiar items away and settled down to eat.

With the addition of his new pluses he was even hungrier. He needed to eat twice as many *Double Danishes* as he originally thought. After he got out of here he was going to need to clear out the rest of NPC Margarine's supplies, especially if he still needed to feed two more Optional Bosses worth of polygons. He ate a lot of the crumbly, terrible tasting goodness, even making a slight mess.

Wiping the crumbs off his Armour with a *Napkin* he didn't know he owned, something struck him as odd about the *Napkin*. It was a *Napkin*. That wasn't an item. He examined it suspiciously and noticed that inside the *Napkin* was writing. It was a *Piece of Paper* that had been folded. That was a relief! Opening the *Napkin* resulted in him getting smacked in the face with a cartoon heart and some explosions going off when it burst. That wasn't normal *Piece of Paper*, or even *Napkin*, behavior. Inside there was a cryptic note that only made the *Piece of Paper* appear to be stalking him as well as assaulting him with hearts.

> *I will find you, don't worry.*

That was an unsettling experience. He folded the not-a-*Napkin* away, putting it back exactly where he had found it, and pretended that it had never existed.

Done with unsettling paper products for now, ndeıs stood up and took a step but his foot caught on something and he fell face first into some ceiling rubble. He nearly wet his *Knight Armour* when he looked back to see what had tripped him up. It was a hand. ndeıs had not noticed until now but during his excavation he had uncovered a colourless arm and now it was holding him fast. A lifeless mannequin brought to life with evil magic no doubt; the colour was the same. *The Primary Circle Sword+* was unsheathed and ready to hack away at the limb, but the arm went limp and the hand let go. A few pokes indicated that whoever owned the hand had likely passed out.

As the adrenaline rush wore off ndeıs was overtaken with curiosity. Who was under this rubble? Who had grabbed him? Who had passed out? It likely wouldn't hurt to check and ndeıs pushed a few pieces of ceiling to the side.

> ndeıs' Text Box: Illiandro! I need some help here. A lot of it. Can you summon the Coliseum Bosses and send them down here?

> NPC Illiandro's Text Box: Yes, but only because you are a ranged class!

With XIII Elite Gladiators, Two Gladiator Brothers, an Illiandro, The Mandusa and The Medusa, one ndeıs, the Harpy Sisters Three, and a Cambion, the passed out body was quickly exhumed. ndeıs thanked the monsters for their help and examined samuri's body. The avatar was barely breathing. Nearly all of his hair had been cut off into an innumerable hairstyle and his facial hair was clipped dangerously close. Much of his helmet had been cut off and he was battered and bruised all over. The worst damage to samuri had been his right eye. He would never be able to see out of it again.

ndeis didn't have many options. He force fed what little *Health Potions* he had with the help of a *Funnel* he didn't know he owned to samuri. It wasn't going to be enough for him to wake up but at least now samuri wouldn't bleed to death. The passed out avatar was hoisted up on ndeis' back, and with the help of Illiandro, samuri was carefully carried to the only place ndeis knew of that could keep him safe. NPC Margarine's Bakery Shoppe.

> NPC Margarine's Text Box: My goodness, hun, what happened to this poor thing? He looks worse than you did way back when. He has no colour left at all!

> ndeis' Text Box: I will answer you directly Margarine because I need to buy more food. He has never had any colour so don't worry about that part. As far as I can tell a ceiling fell on him. I don't know why he is all cut apart. Can you NPCs please watch over him for me? Don't worry he certainly will not talk your ears off when he wakes up.

> NPC Margarine's Text Box: Welcome to my Bakery Shoppe, hun. How can I help you today?

ndeis purchased as many baked goods as he could afford. He was not going to run out of food anytime soon. That would be an absolute boneheaded reason for failing his quest.

> NPC Margarine's Text Box: Of course we can, hun. But when he wakes up he better know how to handle the proper application of fancy sprinkles.

~~~

So far this trip to *Onn* had been pretty successful and only moderately stressful. ndeis had found the equipment he had been looking for, even if he had no idea how he had found it. The Legendary 13 Headed Hydra was missing from the Coliseum, but he had found samuri instead. He was getting stalked by paper products, that was unsettling but he was pretty strong and could rip paper in half if he needed to. He knew how to impress bushes full of eyes by working his meat. He counted them all as victories but had no idea where he should go next. It was time to check his list of Optional Bosses. This time he avoided reading ones that he had already visited, were dead, or were impossible for him to fight.

The Optional Boss List - All Rights Reserved

Main Map Optional Bosses	Map Location	Look Here
Elfbane	Karazhahanana	The Summoning Circle
Flork Omega	The Crags of Halm	Crag #112

Island of Islana Optional Bosses	Map Location	Look Here
Smoke The Reptile	Saibot's Tower	The Noob's Pit
The Avenger	Onn	The Throne Room
The Bull King	The Flaming Pits	Circle 8, Milking Field

nde1s was quickly running out of options for his Optional Boss encounters. Of the ones left he only knew how to find the locations of two of them. He didn't know the exact location of The Crags of Halm but he could follow the directions that the low levels gave him to get there. It would be positively swarming with avatars by now so it might not be the best place to visit. nde1s did know where Onn was and since he was already in Onn it was a likely choice. He had been informed that some of the avatars he knew where currently stationed on top of Onn Castle so he would need to use his *Stealth* to avoid them.

After The Avenger was dealt with, nde1s would go back to the GameFrame and ask Ni Hao Bunny© how to find one of the remaining Optional Bosses. He would probably not ask about the one named Elfbane, that was setting himself up for failure. Placing the list back into his inventory, nde1s got ready for his trip to Onn Castle.

There was a large pile of cake on the roof of the castle. A spiral staircase of cake was being erected to the sky. Two avatars, a stout yellow one and a purple one with #GoodPosture, were arranging cake near the top of the spire while a blurry brown avatar was rushing them up cakes from the pile on the roof. A flash of flying rainbow was carrying cakes and chasing butterflies. So, Palcath, Lissa, Gliint, Draganders, and Roodg were here. Palcath, Lissa, Draganders, and Gliint because nde1s could see them and Roodg because this plan made absolutely no sense and only Roodg could possibly have thought it up. It took a lot of strength to not run up to them and give them all a big hug, but he needed to stay unnoticed for now.

Timing his movements would be hard. Lissa and Palcath would not be a problem; they were properly distracted with delicate cake placement. Draganders was mostly chasing butterflies and would be a heartbreaking breeze to avoid. Gliint, however, was running up and down the staircase so fast that he would have a chance to see nde1s run by the castle entryway three or four times, and since Gliint was a ranged class, *Stealth* would be less effective. Not to mention the Onn Drawbridge was destroyed so he would have to jump, which made noise. Almost as if hearing his thoughts Gliint stopped his running, sat down on the pile of cake with his back toward ndeıs, and started to sip a *Small Stamina Potion*. ndeıs was pretty sure that he even saw Glıint wink at him, but that might have been a trick of the light.

Praising his wonderful good luck this cycle, ndeıs jumped into Onn Castle undetected. Thankfully, due to the many cycles being stuck in Onn he knew the layout of the castle like the back of his old hand (this new hand of his was still unfamiliar). Before long he was in the throne room but wasn't exactly sure what to look for. Zal Finn, and Yallundy had already explored this area thoroughly back during the Siege of the Golden Gribblet, so ndeıs was not exactly sure what to look for. The girls had never reported finding a 'The Avenger'.

ndeıs remembered exploring this place after it had been ravaged by Xam. There were a few differences. Icing had been smeared all over the floor and carpets, unhappy faces had been poked into tapestries, and the throne had been broken in half. The throne was the biggest change to the area and he went to investigate that first.

ndeıs used the *Puzzled Look Animation*. The top of the throne was missing completely, but where had it gone? He thought for a few rounds when he noticed a faint shimmer from the area behind the throne. He tested the area by casually throwing a priceless scenic vase at the shimmer. Instead of exploding into one Gold Coin as expected the vase simply disappeared with only a blip sound to explain its absence. There was a secret behind this throne that the girls had not thought to look for, Anders was sure that Palcath would have known to look here, the backs of thrones were obvious searching places.

A test with his least favorite finger proved that while it disappeared with a blip he could bring it back out with a pilb. If The Avenger was anywhere it was going to be here and with only a little hesitation ndeıs stepped through the portal with a full body blip.

Chapter 23
CYCLE 4
GROUP B,
POFFLES R US

Z al Finn III's Text Box: You're kidding Max! No way!

Placing a cage down that held yet another Golden Poffle into the growing pile Mr. Max used the *Smug Nod Animation*. The Pofflrd growled their cute little golden cries for help, summoning more to the fray. Luckily Mr. Max had quite the collection of *Creature Cages* because so many Golden Poffles were wandering into camp now, if they stopped caging them they would be knee deep in the bundles of fur.

> Mr. Max's Text Box: No, I barely could believe it myself. I had to take her back to her bed three more times. Now look, she is sleeping in. Poor thing got all tuckered out trying to sleep-seduce me.

> Hippolyta's Text Box: Sleeping in is an understatement at this point. She is going to miss lunch if she doesn't wake up soon.

Hippolyta mesmerized another Golden Poffle with her slightly-less-amazing now rack while Zal Finn dropped a *Creature Cage* on their target, adding it to the ever growing Poffle stack.

> Zal Finn III's Text Box: Shhhh! I finally hear her moving around in there.

Caela came out of her tent looking all the worse for wear. She was still only in her

Initiate's Jacket pajama top and was exceptionally groggy. Her *Prince-nez* had been set to black to help shield her eyes from the light.

> Zal Finn III's Text Box: It is almost noon! You've never slept past dawn before.

> Caëlahenãilenw̃hei's Text Box: I am really tired this cycle.

Caela used the *Stretch Animation*, giving all a nice view of her Mouthgina. She picked up a big plate of Mr. Max's *Lunchfast Bash-Mash*, kicked a stray Poffle out of her white chair, and sat down in a flump. She got up for seconds, and thirds. This earned her three wide eyed stares.

> Zal Finn III's Text Box: Are you drunk?

> Caëlahenãilenw̃hei's Text Box: I feel like I haven't eaten in forever. Damn this is really good. Like delicate paper was dipped in glitter-glue then folded into an origami swan of barbeque sauce.

> Mr. Max's Text Box: I messed it up. It was supposed to be an origami teriyaki frog.

> Caëlahenãilenw̃hei's Text Box: Still it is good. I'm curious, how many ranks do you have in the *Gastronome Skill*?

> Mr. Max's Text Box: I maxed it out, so 125.

Two more Poffles were added to the pile by Max, both in the same cage. The more that were caught the easier it was to catch them. They almost wanted to be trapped now.

> Caëlahenãilenw̃hei's Text Box: That explains it. Way better than mine. My food still has that gross appliance aftertaste.

> Zal Finn III's Text Box: What? The *Gastronome Skill* makes your cooked food taste better? I didn't know that. I've been putting all my extras into Hair Braiding!

> Caëlahenãilenw̃hei's Text Box: *Hair Braiding* is one of the worst Skills, right at the bottom with *Women's Lib* and *Literature*.

> Hippolyta's Text Box: I put all my spares into *Women's Lib* and hones—

Caela interrupted Hippolyta's Text Box when she kicked up her feet and accidentally hit a Golden Poffle into Hippolyta's face. While it did rebound into the *Creature Cage* that she had been setting up, the fight elf was not impressed with the expert bank shot.

> Zal Finn III's Text Box: I thought you had maxed the *Literature Skill*

> Caela.

Caela did not reply, she was staring off into space. She did so until everyone had finished eating and the dishes had been put away.

> Zal Finn III's Text Box: Caela?

> Caëlahenãilenẁhei's Text Box: Sorry, day dreaming. No matter. Lunch is over.

> Zal Finn III's Text Box: I just said that. You are definitely drunk, I think all your pastry has expired and turned into pastryhol. What is the best before cycle on them?

> Caëlahenãilenẁhei's Text Box: Who would eat pastry with such good food around?

> Mr. Max's Text Box: You do?

> Caëlahenãilenẁhei's Text Box: Not anymore. That shit was great. Okay, so what is the stupid plan here?

> Zal Finn III's Text Box: Uh… How could you not know the plan?

> Hippolyta's Text Box: It is your plan! Get Poffles. Kill them with Yallundy. Save us!

> Caëlahenãilenẁhei's Text Box: Don't you have enough already or whatever? Have Yallundy lute them senseless or something. I have so many other things to worry about right now.

> Mr. Max's Text Box: You know that Yallundy is n—

> Caëlahenãilenẁhei's Interruption Text Box: Oh Maker, your words hurt my eyes. I'm going to go lay down for a bit, have fun doing whatever stupid thing that you are doing.

Caela stomped back towards her tent, viciously kicking a Golden Poffle far into the scenery along the way. Max tried to follow her but was held back by both Zal Finn and Hippolyta.

> Mr. Max's Text Box: What in the Flaming Pit is wrong with her? She knows that Yallundy is with Gliint.

> Hippolyta's Text Box: Hmmm… Does she really? I wonder…

> Mr. Max's Text Box: Of course she does. I said that.

Hippolyta used the *Facepalm Animation*, it caused her to only jiggle slightly, and not even enough for a breast induced hypnotism. Mr. Max and Zal were disappointed with the result but stopped caging Poffles for a moment to watch.

> Hippolyta's Text Box: No you dolt. What I meant was… oh… uh… Goddess! I don't know what I meant. It is too hard to concentrate with so many Golden Poffles everywhere yelping!

> Zal Finn III's Text Box: I think they are sweet. They haven't even been attacking us since we caught #53.

> Hippolyta's Text Box: How many do we have now?

> Mr. Max's Text Box: 124… no wait, 125. No wait, 126.

> Hippolyta's Text Box: Can't we kill them already? They are really starting to piss me off. We are bound to get another *Elixir* with this many.

> Zal Finn III's Text Box: NO YOU CAN'T! uh… I mean, we need to save them for Yallundy in case we don't get an *Elixir*… right… Max?

> Mr. Max's Text Box: True, each kill is random. 127. We might get unlucky and not get a drop adventurettes.

> Hippolyta's Text Box: Okay, fine! But if they don't shut up with all that yapping, I am going to start to thin the herd.

~~~

It had been many rounds since the wolf had howled and signaled night. When she was finally positive that no one else would be awake she opened up the door to the master suite and peered into the sitting room. Good, the fire was off so no one was awake. Taking great care to walk as slowly as possible Caela crept across the still dirty floor of her *Portie Tent Ultra+*. She was quite upset that she did not have *Stealth* as a Rocket Sorceress as every step she took was creating a quiet sound. It was barely audible, but it was enough to make her wince. Even if all those Poffles outside were yapping away and masking her footsteps, she didn't want to draw attention to herself. The soup stains on the floor unfazed her, for she had a purpose. To make it to the room three down from hers, the one with the orange trim. She reached the door after uncountable rounds and allowed herself to use the *Grin Animation*.

This time she was not going to fail. Everything was set up perfectly. She felt the sharp chill of cold steel and slowly drew the *Silent Shiv* out of the hiding place at the small of her back. Not the most powerful dagger in the game certainly, it was only Level 4, but it had a useful ability. If this dagger struck an opponent that was unaware of the attack, it would not only Critical like a normal weapon, it would perform a Double Critical and stun the opponent for a round. Just the perfect thing for an unaware monster you snuck up on or a sleeping bag of meat. Of course a regular *Silent Shiv* couldn't hurt much past Level 9, but then again this wasn't your every cycle *Silent Shiv*. This was a Level 98 *Super Silent Shiv of Ultimate Max Killing* with several additional abilities added for good measure, such as *Bloodletting, Deathstrike, Otter Vision,* and *Dragon's Fire.* The test attack on that sleeping NPC idiot had done 18,743,208 damage and caused her to explode three separate times. Mr. Max only had 9,999 health and best of all he had no defensive bonus since apparently that dolt slept naked.

This time was going to be perfect. No accidentally slipping on the carpet and waking up Max. A quick and efficient walk into his room, a simple stab right in the eye, and watch him explode three times. Or maybe a stab in his big mouth, or through the heart, there was so many choices it was making her drool. After Max was exploded, she would sneak outside and kill all those Golden Poffles alone and reach fucking Level ✪ ✪ to become the ultimate conduit of delicious magical carnage! Without any Poffles to kill, Tits McGee and Generic McBoring would wither away into nothingness while she watched. That would be even better than simply slicing their throats. She would laugh, and laugh until the last moment, and then she would slice their throats out right before they faded away (hey, a good idea is a good idea).

She had decided. It was going to be a stab through Max's heart. Quick, clean, and to the point. She opened the orange door gingerly, careful to not make much noise, and saw her target. Soon, she would finally be victorious. She took a step forward.

> Hippolyta's Text Box: What are you doing?

The light elf nearly screamed out and almost dropped her dagger. She only barely kept her composure and looked around the sitting room frantically. Cold steel gray eyes peered at her from across the room. Caela slipped the *Super Silent Shiv of Ultimate Max Killing* back into the hiding spot and was positive that the butch lesbian hadn't seen it given the camera angles.

> Hippolyta's Text Box: You cannot be considering sneaking in there again to try and seduce Max.

> Caëlahenãilenŵhei's Text Box: Oh... yeah. I admit it. That was what I was doing.

> Hippolyta's Text Box: Seriously? Max? Of all the avatars in the map that is the one you want to seduce. I think I agree with Zal Finn, you are ass over teakettle drunk.

Caëlahenãilenẁhei's Text Box: What? He's so…*urk* wonderful though.

Hippolyta's Text Box: Well, stop trying to be sneaky about it and tell the big idiot. Tomorrow. It is way too late to be seducing right now.

Caëlahenãilenẁhei's Text Box: It is too late to be awake! What are you even doing up at this round?

Caëlahenãilenẁhei's Box Text: I'm not awake… zzz… I'm dreaming about folding laundry… wonderful pressed and white.

Hippolyta's Text Box: Okay then… Well if you must know I couldn't sleep with all that infernal yapping outside. Those Makerdamn Poffles will not shut the Flaming Pit up! I was contemplating killing them all so I could finally get some sleep.

Caëlahenãilenẁhei's Box Text: … Waffles are delicious with warm buttery syrup and flying cups of coffee… *snort* Come here you! I'll catch you since I can fly.

Caëlahenãilenẁhei's Text Box: Shut up already, fuck. How are you ruining this again?

Hippolyta's Text Box: Yeah, okay young lady. It is time for you to go back to bed.

Caëlahenãilenẁhei's Text Box: Fuck!

Hippolyta got up and escorted Caela back to her room while the wonderful sounds of Golden Poffles yelping filled the air.

Zal Finn III's Whisper Text Box: Shhhh! Didn't you guys hear her? If you all don't stop making noise she is going to kill you.

◈ **Chapter 24** ◈

CYCLE 4
GROUP A, THE
CAKEWAY TO THE
CLOUDS

Palcath's Text Box: Could you hear me when you were down there, lass?

Lissa's Text Box: No I couldn't. Now explain what was so important that I needed to walk all the way down the cake spiral to find that out.

Palcath's Text Box: Not yet, lass. Just look like you are still working, he is way too fast. Wait until he takes another potion break.

Lissa's Text Box: Wait until who does?

Draganders' Text Box: Chirp?

Palcath's Text Box: Oh? I wanted to talk secretly about... where is that little lad? Where is Gliint?

Lissa's Text Box: He went to go get more cake this morning and never came back.

Palcath's Text Box: But he was supposed to be handing us cake. That lad had been acting suspicious and I wanted to warn you to keep an eye on him like I have been doing.

Lissa's Text Box: You're doing a bang up job so far. #ObliviousDwarfMuch?

Palcath's Text Box: Regardless, lass, now we can talk about Gliint.

Gliint's Text Box: Why are we going to talk about me exactly?

Palcath was startled. He again had lost track of Gliint. So much this time that he didn't notice Gliint walking up the cake spiral.

Palcath's Text Box: Where did you come from, lad?

Gliint's Text Box: The store. I was getting cake, remember? I was done but then that fat NPC chick started to talk my ear off and I got stuck in her purchase menu while yelling at her to let me go. Apparently, she has a brand new assistant that is a whiz with sprinkles so we can get the cakes faster than anticipated, then she found the corpse of one of her sons under some bags of flour, she eats a lot, welcome to my store, blah blah blah she doesn't shut up.

Palcath's Text Box: Good. That is what we were going to talk about. When I said we were needing to talk about you. We were going to talk about where you were, but now we know so we don't need to talk anymore about you or where you are. We know where you are now. Hahaha. Plus Draganders got us lots of cake. We can stack cake for some time now. You go take a break or something down from here. Away. Over at a place. No cake needed from you for now. Lad.

Gliint's Text Box: Good idea. All that talking to fat made my head hurt.

With a burst of speed Gliint was down at the base of the cake stairway and officially on break. He sat down on a comfy pile of cake and selected a lovely *Large Health Potion* to drink. Given the relative size of the potion compared to Gliint, it would keep him busy for some time.

Lissa used the *Scowl Animation* at Palcath.

Lissa's Text Box: #SlickAsButtah.

Palcath's Text Box: What?

Lissa's Text Box: Are you daft? That was the absolute worst recovery in history.

Palcath's Text Box: It wasn't that bad, lass. At least it got him to leave.

Lissa's Text Box: Next time ask him to reveal his secret plans, but you know be sly about it.

Palcath's Text Box: That is a good idea, lass. I'll think about it. It is too bad that we couldn't sneak Fourni up here as well. I wanted to hear his opinion on this matter.

Lissa's Text Box: It is too bad Fourni has been missing since last cycle. I'm starting to get worried.

Palcath's Text Box: What?! He has been missing?

Lissa's Text Box: You seriously didn't notice that he was missing? I looked all morning for him! Didn't you notice that I wasn't here stacking cake? Are you the Mr. Max of cake obliviousness?

Palcath's Text Box: Sorry, lass, I was thinking about Gliint. I guess I got distracted in thought. He is up to something.

Lissa's Text Box: You are #SoFuckedUp!

Draganders' Text Box: True, but he is also right. Gliint is up to something chirp.

Both avatars were startled in their own way. Lissa froze and had a terrible flashback of a NPC becoming Zal Finn and scaring her to the point of urination, while Palcath dropped the cake he was placing early and it plummeted to the ground below, splatting on a nearby Gliint who amazingly did not seem to notice.

Lissa and Palcath's Simultaneous Text Box: You can talk?

Draganders' Text Box: No, he cannot talk. But he agreed to be possessed and talked through so that Gliint didn't notice me talking to you. I don't really matters now since he didn't notice the cake falling on his head. Another slick move there by the way chirp.

Lissa's Text Box: It is Yallundy. What are you doing here?

Yallundy the Draganders' Text Box: My body is in Gliint's *Backpack*, remember? I have to be in the same area as he is chirp.

Palcath's Text Box: Yeah, lass, but you are supposed to be in Group B. You should have filed the proper paperwork and the—

Yallundy the Draganders' Interruption Text Box: Listen. I don't have time for arguing about your stupid forms right now. I don't know how much time I will have to explain this, so listen because there is a lot to go through, it is all important, and Gliint might wake up at anytime chirp.

Palcath and Lissa both used the *Nod Animation*. They would hold off on jokes and colourful banter for now.

Yallundy the Draganders' Text Box: First of all I saw Fournimer yesterday in the Onn Throne Room, but never saw him leave. He must be in there so go look when Gliint isn't around chirp.

Yallundy the Draganders' Text Box: Luckily Gliint seems to have forgotten the fact that we are bound together and this has given me a lot of time to spy on him. Something is more than up with him. He has been causing havoc all over the Expansion chirp.

Yallundy the Draganders' Text Box: Alright, we will start with Group D. The ceiling in the Coliseum collapsed at some point. samuri, Kray, and the pets haven't been there for cycles. All of the dead bodies and broken items there disappeared as well. Gliint was constantly sneaking away to dig through ceiling rubble there but suddenly stopped going last cycle. Whatever he was looking for, I think he found it chirp.

Yallundy the Draganders' Text Box: Next, group C. Gliint ran across the ocean to give something to De'vini. I didn't think much of it at the time, but now De'vini, In'ferni, and for some reason a random skeleton monster are camped out in The Jungle of Contemplation and Gliint keeps meeting with them. They have a *Magical Flying Parsnip Ultra+* that looks exactly like the *Magical Flying Carrot Ultra+* except eviler. I have no idea what happened to Roodg to give up the rights to the *Carrot*. Or the boys in the group for that matter chirp.

Yallundy the Draganders' Text Box: Group B is confusing at best. Before I left I saw Gliint messing with the dials on the *Washer Dryer Ultra+*. Now Gliint keeps running there and secretly giving items to Caela, who has stopped wearing pants chirp.

Yallundy the Draganders' Text Box: Lastly there is you. Gliint has been rummaging through your *Backpacks*, I don't know why but I suggest being careful with them, especially with Fourni's. Then there is this stupid cake stairway. He was against it until he found out the *Parsnip* couldn't reach the island. There is something up on that floating island and he wants to get to it desperately. You need to find out why and get it before he does chirp.

Yallundy the Draganders' Text Box: That is all I know so far. Crap, I feel my stomach lurching again. He is getting ready to sprint somewhere chirp.

Palcath's Text Box: That certainly was a lot to take in, lass.

Draganders' Text Box: Chirp?

Lissa's Text Box: That was #SoFuckedUp. How come this is the first we have heard about any of this if avatars have been missing for cycles?

Palcath's Text Box: Hmmm... I fear that is hasn't been. I feel the need to test something now, lass. Please say something in Group Chat.

Lissa's Text Box: Why me? Why don't you?

Palcath's Text Box: Because no one has used it for a little while and I think that what I will say will sound suspicious unless you Text Box first.

More out of curiosity to see where this was going than helpfulness, Lissa agreed and typed into Group Chat about the benefits of cake and frosting.

Lissa's Group Chat Text Box: #Hasthtag. There is nothing I #LoveMore after a hard day of being a #SoFuckedUpPurpleBitch with an annoying name than relaxing by stuffing a nice scented candle up my cootch. #PersonalFulfillment.

Lissa used the *Furious Animation*.

Hippolyta's Group Chat Text Box: My massive boobs agree with you. Scented candles are needed by bitches like us. How would we relax or get things inserted into us otherwise?

Fournimer's Group Chat Text Box: why am I a horse? that is frickin' hilarious. a gay horse, so my favorite scented candle is hay!

In'ferni's Group Chat Text Box: Who doesn't love to make out with scented candles? I love the smell and taste of them. Nom nom nom.

Palcath's Group Chat Text Box: Would all of you laddies and lassies stop flooding the Group Chat with scented candle talk!

Palcath's Text Box: That confirms it, lass. I have typed that a few times already, but didn't notice the laddies and lassies. I wouldn't say something that stupid. The group chat has been candle hacked. I was wondering why Caela was writing an entire novella on lavender scented candles.

Lissa's Text Box: What the fuck! Who did this? #BloodyVengence!

Palcath's Text Box: I can't be certain, fair maiden, but given the information we have we are going to have to suspect that Gliint was involved. At least we learned a few things.

Lissa's Text Box: Like what? That Gliint is a little asshole?

Palcath's Text Box: Possibly. But we also learned that Fourni isn't dead since he replied. I also believe that since Hippolyta and In'ferni replied to us that Groups C and B know the Group Chat is candle hacked which makes sense with what Yallundy said. Those lasses are playing in the same room after all. Maker damn it! Why didn't we get contact information instead of setting up the Group Chat?

Lissa's Text Box: Because you said that Group Chat was good enough! Don't blame yourself for this problem. Everyone else will do that for you.

Palcath sat down on a mass of orange frosting, defeated.

Palcath's Text Box: Crap, lass. This is my fault isn't it?

Lissa's Text Box: Now what did I just say?

Palcath's Text Box: I don't know what we should do now, lass.

Lissa's Text Box: I will tell you what we will do! First we will go and look for Fourni, and then we will build the fuck out of this cake and beat that little shit up there!

Palcath stood up triumphantly only slightly more orange from the previous defeat.

Palcath's Text Box: I like your plan! We can skip the first part, lass and build the fuck out of the cake.

Lissa's Text Box: Are you nuts? What about Fourni? We have to go look for him.

Palcath's Text Box: He is fine. He had his phone on silent and didn't see my texts until he went to ask me about your cootch candles.

Apparently, he found a secret passageway again but this time it is long and he has been trotting along all cycle. He is pretty sure he is almost at the end of the path and that it goes to the last Chad exhibit, whatever that means.

Lissa's Text Box: That is good, but why do you have his number and not mine?

Palcath's Text Box: I can have your number, lass? Really?

Lissa's Text Box: Uh… Let's build the fuck out of some cake!

Chapter 25

CYCLE 5: MORNING NDEIS, AVENGERING

This 'The Path to The Avenger' was much longer than ndeis had originally anticipated. He certainly had not expected to need to camp out in the corridor overnight between a switch puzzle and a jumping puzzle. At least the dream about chasing butterflies had been pleasant, even if they tasted like soap bubbles.

The long corridor was also full of tedious puzzles. Many of the pressure plate puzzles had required multiple avatars, but thankfully, he had a really long bow and could trick the puzzles into submission. A few switches had been tied up to keep them in place, which did make progress faster, but ndeis wasn't exactly sure what could have done that. It hadn't been him and he simply hoped it was nothing (even though deep down he knew it must be something) and continued onwards.

This last puzzle was going to be a challenge. Four pressure plates in a square, two levers (already tied up) and a ranged attack activation switch that all needed to be activated at once? ndeis did realize that this was a multi-player game, but come on! Who could possibly do all that alone? Try as he might he could only either activate all the pressure plates at once by spreading out on them, or activate two with an awkward bow stance and hit the ranged attack point.

He sat down for a break to both think and eat six brunches. There had to be a way to do this, it would be foolish to turn back now that he was so close. What he needed for this was two more legs, well not necessarily legs, two more limbs would be fine. It hit him like a *Sack of Rusty Potatoes*. He had a plan.

Several rounds of set up later, ndeis was ready to go. He was flat on his back and stretching as far as he could to activate all the pressure plates at once. Bowstring held shakily in teeth, and bow handle held somewhat in place between his erection and Armour erection, he spat out the bowstring and watched the arrow fly. Zing! The arrow hit the target, the door to the boss chamber opened, and ndeıs vowed to never shoot an bow with his penis again.

ndeıs quietly entered the room through the door, (after zipping up) and was absolutely shocked to see what was inside. The only avatar who could have possibly made it through that puzzle alone, someone with four feet and a ranged attack, the one avatar who had finally been excited to be able to have something in the game work for him: Fournimer. ndeıs nearly cried out from sheer happiness and ran into the room, but then he heard that Fournimer was not alone. Female giggling and the sighs of a centaur rang out through the area and ndeıs clenched his fists tightly. What in the Flaming Pit was going on in there?

Cautiously ndeıs stepped closer and saw the full picture. Fournimer was tied by cords in several places. ndeıs doubted that he could even move. An angel, nearly naked except for her mostly transparent robe, was tickling the underside of Fournimer's massively swollen and painful testicles with her feathered wings. She was likely The Avenger. Fournimer was dripping sweat from his entire body and a stream of fluid from his throbbing member while his face was a mix of pain and need. The Avenger had been torturing Fournimer with orgasm denial for who knew how long.

Fournimer's Text Box: please, I'm begging you. do something! they hurt, they hurt so badly.

The Avenger's Text Box: But you said you were gay. Have you decided to switch sides? To think all it takes is a cycle of torture.

Fournimer's Text Box: gay. straight. whatever. I don't care anymore. they hurt.

The Avenger's Text Box: Personally, I thought you were going to stick to your guns longer, but hey who am I to judge.

Fournimer's Text Box: I already gave up my guns. this is like the tenth time. you will not stop torturing me. please, I think they are going to rupture.

The Avenger's Text Box: I know you have, but where is the fun in that? *Giggle* What shall we do next?

Fournimer's Text Box: FUCK!

The Avenger's Text Box: No, not yet. *Giggle* I think we should tickle

> you more.

Fournimer struggled bravely against his bindings, but there was no way he could possibly escape. ndeıs tried to change to *Blush Shade #2* as he watched Fournimer's member bob up and down. ndeıs had forgotten how big Fournimer was. Even for a horse he was big, but the cycle of teasing had made him positively monstrous.

Snapping out of his slight Fourni haze, ndeıs knew that he had to do something. His favorite centaur ever was getting tortured. This was something he could not stand for, the spoiling of Fourni. ndeıs had already lost his gold star, and he was going to bravely take one for Fourni, to protect the horse man's homosexuality. He cleared his throat, lowered the register of his voice as best as he could, and stepped forward.

~~~

Sweating and defeated, Fournimer looked up with sex blurred vision to again ask The Avenger to let him release. But what he did not expect was to see a mysterious glitter stranger headed right towards them. For the first time, Fournimer decided that glitter was alright, if it was bouncing off the muscles of a hunk in stark white Armour. There was something familiar about this stranger, and even if Fournimer was broken and beaten he was determined to find out what that was.

> ndeıs' Text Box: That is quite enough The Avenger!

> The Avenger's Text Box: I think it isn't. He still has some fight left in him.

> ndeıs Text Box: Too fudging bad! I demand that you release that avatar right now!

> Fournimer's Text Box: fudging?

> The Avenger's Text Box: I dunno, I am having a lot of fun with him right now. *Giggle*

> ndeıs Text Box: He doesn't want your kind of fun!

> The Avenger's Text Box: Of course he does, he has been absolutely begging me to finish him off for I don't even know how long. He even went and tied himself up for me with those *Bolas* of his. Look how sexy he is positioned.

Fournimer noticed that the stranger took a good look at how sexy he had accidentally tied himself up after failing his first attempt to use his new *Bolas*. The stranger might have looked for a moment too long and even bit his lower lip shyly.

> nde1s Text Box: It... uh... it doesn't matter how insanely sexy he is. You are going to let him go right now!

Fournimer changed to *Blush Shade #3*. He had a hunch he was sexy, but insanely sexy?

> The Avenger's Text Box: Give me one good reason why I should let him go!

The stranger known as nde1s replied by retracting his Armour codpiece and set his hard member bobbing free.

> The Avenger's Text Box: That is a good reason. Well played.

> nde1s' Text Box: Now let him go!

> The Avenger's Text Box: Fine I will, but not until you fuck me with that super stud body of yours that I could handle. *giggle* That horse cock was never going to fit anyway.

> nde1s' Text Box: Okay, if it means you will let him go, I will do it.

Fournimer was puzzled by this stranger. He seemed to not be interested at all in The Avenger. The stranger was accepting this sex and it almost felt like he was accepting it as a necessary punishment.

> The Avenger's Text Box: I'm kind of already prepped and turned on, is it okay if we skip the foreplay, kissing, and oral stuff?

> nde1s' Text Box: Thank the Maker yes.

> The Avenger's Text Box: Good! *Giggle* Now come and get me, tiger!

The angelic optional boss turned around and placed her hands on Fournimer's flank to steady herself (much to his annoyance), spread her legs wide to present herself, leaned forward, and finally looked back coyly at the mysterious man that had interrupted her play time. The glittered up Armour knight was going to do this. It felt to Fournimer that this stranger was going to protect him by taking one for the team. The one named nde1s, a name which Fournimer did find a bit more than familiar, bravely stepped forward and lined himself up with her opening.

> The Avenger's Text Box: No, not that hole! Use the girl one.

> nde1s' Text Box: Sorry. Not really used to that one.

After readjusting his angle, the stranger slowly slid all the way into The Avenger's correct hole and earned a happy moan from the angel. The force of the entry caused Fournimer to shift uncomfortably in his tied up position. The Avenger moved around a little to better position herself on Fournimer.

> The Avenger's Text Box: You are probably not used to it being a bit loose, but you are probably not used to it being so slick huh? I'm so slick for you *Giggle*.

She must be slick, because the stranger was now slowly thrusting into her, and therefore uncomfortably into Fournimer as well. He was now forced to use his tied up hands to steady himself from rolling over onto his flank. After a few of what Fournimer decided had been test thrusts the stranger started to pick up the pace. Fournimer decided that it was to make this horrible encounter end sooner.

Without warning the stranger's two bizarre weapons began to glow and the stranger used the *Sneeze Animation*. It was like a severe change overtook his mysterious savior. Suddenly, this reluctant to be straight boy was ramming into his fuck bitch hard. Fournimer was genuinely shocked when he heard the stranger call The Avenger that. She was more than happy to comply, and encouraged him to not only fuck his fuck bitch harder, but to slap her ass.

Fournimer could see her ass become a bright shade of pink as the stranger plowed into her. It was becoming far harder to concentrate on what was going on, mostly because he was being rammed into so hard that he had fallen over. There was enough stimulation to his painfully pinned erection to make it throb excitedly, but not enough to do anything to help relieve the cause of the throbbing. Even now that The Avenger was sprawled out, using him like a love pillow, and was buried deep within his fur face-first, Fournimer could not make himself go. This lousy fuck bitch (he decided to use that term) was even flicking his penis with what Fournimer assumed were either her fingers, nipples, or feathers. He was too tired for the pleasure to let him finish, too prolonged and teased. Even with the rubbing, he would never cum this way. Especially not now that someone had buried their something deep into Fournimer's rump after a position switch.

Sexual juices had spilt out of his once tormentor, Fournimer was covered in them, and he knew they were going to matte up his horse coat. The dripping The Avenger's legs were wrapped around his torso. A not so well liked anymore stranger was standing on both of Fournimer's stomachs plowing into her. More and more women juices were flowing out and coating Fournimer. They were mixed with sweat, angel dust, glitter, and centaur tears.

> Fournimer's Text Box: come on you two, seriously?

> The Avenger's Text Box: Yeah, come on you fucker. Seriously!

> Mysterious Additional Text Box: Yeah, we need to fuck that fuck bitch good.

> ndeıs' Text Box: Fuck yeah! Good fucking idea. Seriously take it fuck bitch!

Taking Fournimer's advice (that clearly wasn't advice), the duo switched to the worst position yet (for Fournimer) and began to thrust together harder than ever.

Now with a woman's breasts stuffed in front of his face, bouncing with an intense angelic rhythm unknown to mortal man, Fournimer could see only one other thing. The masked face of his 'protector' as he went about his busy work. At this angle Fournimer could even start to see under the metal visor. As he strained his eyes, Fournimer could make out more and more detail. The subtle hint of a chin, an outline of a slightly upturned nose that was far too cute for words, and something that was catching the light funny on one cheek. A line that shouldn't be there, as if diagonally cut onto the stranger's face. It was... a scar!

> Fournimer's Text Box: no way! Anders?!

The name appeared to make the stranger snap out of his sex induced frenzy, which was impressive given the fact that he was mid orgasm. The sword that was framing his helmet like a halo even stopped glowing. It was if a look of panic and regret took over the face Fournimer was looking at. This happened as The Avenger screamed out with her final gush of fluids, happily climaxing and covering Fournimer's view when one of her no longer rhythmic breasts flopped down on his face.

~~~

Now that he had calmed down, ndeıs did not know what had come over him. This intense desire to please a woman, the complete lack of concern for Fournimer's well being, and most of all a complete lack of manners with language. It was like something had taken control of him and his desires. Worst of all, Fournimer had somehow in the blur of what happened, recognized him. He needed to get out of here, and fast.

Pulling out of The Avenger with a squish, ndeıs tried to regain his composure, but it was not going to be possible. He needed to leave. There was nothing else he could do. Holding back tears he turned and ran.

> The Avenger's Text Box: Aw, tiger. Leaving so soon? *Giggle* At least you were nice enough to give me flowers in my crotch. What a gentleman.

The Avenger was holding a small soaked purple flower. ndeıs had to turn back to get it, even though it was tearing him apart. What he saw made him feel the worse remorse he ever had. Fournimer was behind the angel, he was on the floor, battered and bruised, a look of bewilderment on his face. Tears were flowing down his cheeks.

ndeıs ran forward and snatched the flower from The Avenger, who only winked at him before flying off towards her private lair. ndeıs was given the chance to update the

Insta-Wiki. He put that on hold for now, he had important things to do first. He helped Fournimer up off the ground and untied the *Bolas* bindings.

> Fournimer's Text Box: thank you for saving me Anders.

It took everything that ndeɪs had, but he could not admit to who he was. He needed to remain undetected for now, even if that meant fighting every instinct that he had to jump into Fourni's arms (at this point he was so beefy that Fourni would likely need to jump into his arms) and kiss him all over with apologies. He would need to lie.

> ndeɪs' Text Box: I am not this Anders you speak of civilian... I am... a friendly passerby.

> Fournimer's Text Box: no. you are Anders. you don't act like him or have the same body type as him, you were even having manic straight sex on me like a love pillow, but I know you are Anders.

> ndeɪs' Text Box: I am not Anders! I... *voice crack* don't even know who that is!

> Fournimer's Text Box: but... you have to be. let me see under that visor. I need to!

> ndeɪs' Text Box: No, you can't!

> Game Explanation Text Box: Polygons absorbed from The Avenger 16.6%.

> Fournimer's Text Box: I can see your lips and I know those are Anders' kissable lips! I need to see your face! your scar!

> ndeɪs' Text Box: Please, you have to believe me, I am not Anders. I need to go.

With that ndeɪs sprouted out huge angelic wings and took off into the sky. He was as surprised as Fournimer by that turn of events.

> Game Explanation Text Box: Special trait absorbed from The Avenger, *Angelic Wings*.

> Fournimer's Text Box: you have to be Anders! it all makes so much sense! look, you are on the cover of the book and everything. you are on the opposite side as normal! you have to be real.

ndeɪs couldn't leave it like that. Flying off and leaving Fourni was too mean for both parties even if it was a secret. Besides, Fournimer had figured out the amazing cover art deception executed in this book series. ndeɪs flew down to beside the horse and executed an Animation, said a quick Text Box and flew away feeling slightly better about the situation, but by no means great.

> Andeis' Text Box: Take care of yourself Fourni.

Fournimer couldn't reply. He was too busy using the *Too Stunned To Say Anything or Move Because a Cute Straight Angel Just Kissed Him on the Cheek and Completely Took Him Off Guard Animation.*

> **Creature Name:** The Avenger
> **Class:** Divine Angel-Like Being
> **Level:** 75
> **Special Attacks:** Sweep, Tickle, Holy Beam of Light (Eye Lasers), Angelic Laugh, Deep Caress of Juices
> **Drops:** A well deserved congratulations!
> **First Player Encounter Notes:** I have so many strange questions about myself now. – Andeis

Andeis completed the Insta-Wiki and flew off towards his new destination. He had no doubt of where to go next now that he could fly and had an upside-down 'V' in his name. Despite that it hurt he had to fly away and ignore Fournimer's eventual response.

~~~

With that Anders, or at least upside down V ndeis, was gone. Fournimer was alone again in the dungeon that he had originally been so excited to be able to do solo. Now all he wanted was to not be alone.

> Fournimer's Yelling Text Box: no wait Anders come back!

Fournimer used the *Sigh Animation*. Either the angel was too far away to hear or had chosen not to.

> Fournimer's Text Box: take care of yourself, bah!

Fournimer took a step and remembered something else, he was still painfully erect and his entire body felt like it was full of nothing but pent up horse juice and pressure.

> Fournimer's Text Box: wait! damn it. I can't take care of my stupid self! that is my stupid problem. I need help. Anders? ndeis? The Avenger? upside down 'V'? anyone?! please help me. stupid centaurs... stupid centaurs can't...

Fournimer used the *Scream to the Heavens Animation*.

> Fournimer's Yelling Text Box: stupid centaurs can't masturbate!

◈ **Chapter 26** ◈

CYCLE 5
GROUP R,
THE SACRIFICE VS.
THE VOLCANO

Roodg's Text Box: cAN WE GO AROUND?

E. E. Lynn's Text Box: N0p3.

Roodg's Text Box: wHY NOT?

E. E. Lynn's Text Box: Th3r3 |sn't any 0th3r w4y.

Roodg's Text Box: tHERE IS always ANOTHER WAY AROUND!

E. E. Lynn's Text Box: \/\/h0 \/\/0uld \/\/4nt 2 g0 4n0th3r \/\/4y? Th|s \/\/4y is 3p|c!

Roodg's Text Box: bUT THIS IS A RICKETY OLD WOODEN BRIDGE VINE SWINGING PUZZLE PATH WITH TILTING PLATFORMS OVER THE TOP OF THE ACTIVE VOLCANO. fIRE BALLS ARE SHOOTING EVERYWHERE AND THE LAVA LEVEL IS CONSTANTLY RISING AND FALLING AT RANDOM INTERVALS! tHE SMOKE IS SO THICK THAT IT IS BLOCKING OUT MOST CAMERA ANGLES... aND WHY THE FUCK ARE THERE GIANT SAWBLADES OVER THERE?

E. E. Lynn's Text Box: Duh. C4us3 |t |s 3p|c!

Roodg's Text Box: tHERE IS PLENTY OF ROOM TO HAVE BUILT A SAFE PATH RIGHT OVER THERE! wHAT SANE PERSON WOULD BUILD THIS PATH?

E. E. Lynn's Text Box: U h4\/3 n0 cOnc3pt 0f teh \/\/0rd 3p|c d0 u?

Cinnamon's Text Box: What is the big deal? I thought you were all carefree and gung ho. What is all this about being scared?

Roodg's Text Box: bECAUSE i AM HORRIBLE AT VINE SWINGING PUZZLES.

Cinnamon's Text Box: I think I remember you saying that.

Roodg's Text Box: oF COURSE i DID. i SAY IT ALL THE TIME! i SAY IT IN EVERY BOOK! iT HAS BEEN WELL ESTABLISHED!

E. E. Lynn's Text Box: S0 b|g d34l. U f4ll |n 4nd l0s3 s0/\/\3 HP.

Roodg's Text Box: hOW MUCH hp?

E. E. Lynn's Text Box: LV 80 l0c4t|0n... L4\/4, 3xtr4 3p|c... S0 4,100 HP 0f f|r3 d4/\/\4g3.

Roodg's Text Box: i AM A mAGIC mAGE & lEVEL 78! i ONLY HAVE —

E. E. Lynn's Interruption Text Box: 3,950 HP... S0 b|g d34l. U f4ll |n 4nd d|3!

Roodg's Text Box: Breaker BROKE THE WORLD. iF WE DIE, WE DIE. oR BECOME GHOSTS OR SOMETHING... i DON'T KNOW IT IS COMPLICATED.

E. E. Lynn's Text Box: S0 d0n't f4ll |n th3n or u d3ad. x-x kekeke.

Roodg's Text Box: tHERE HAS TO BE ANOTHER WAY AROU—

E. E. Lynn's Interruption Text Box: G0!

E. E. Lynn pushed Roodg off of the starting platform and into the mess of vines, platforms, lava, fireballs, and sawblades. The avatar had been frantically waving around arms, otherwise Roodg would have had no time to grab the first vine and stop from falling into the lava. There was no time to complain, yell, or think about how getting pushed into something like this against your will was an important life lesson for Roodg. There was only time to swing, and Roodg did as well as could have been predicted. Despite the fact that lankey arms and legs should have been a tremendous benefit for swinging on vines, the vines had been placed a standard arm length's away making grabbing them next to impossible for the long-limbed.

Three jumps later and Roodg was not a pro, not even close, but had decided on a tactic. Letting go far too early in an attempt to have time to grab the next vine. It was a tactic that worked not particularly well, it was slow going and troublesome, but at least it was preventing horrible plummets into death lava. It would have worked, albeit slowly, if not for two main problems. One, E. E. Lynn with her short limbs passed by Roodg without a care in the world and completely messed up the set timing of the vines. Two, sawblades.

> Roodg's Text Box: yOU MESSED UP THE—

A sawblade interrupted Roodg and the avatar's vine was chopped in two. A jump from the severed vine in an attempt to grab the nearest still attached vine ended in failure as Roodg overshot the jump and could not grab it with an elbow. Screaming, the avatar plummeted into the lava below and was enveloped by fire right as E. E. Lynn finished the puzzle and was safely at the other side.

> E. E. Lynn's Text Box: 00ps. /\/\y b4d. ^-^

> Cinnamon's Text Box: You idiot! They had the *Golden Tin Whistle*! It would take me weeks to craft a new one! Now we are going to be stuck here.

> E. E. Lynn's Text Box: R|ght. N3><t t|/\/\3 r3/\/\|nd /\/\3 t0 h0ld qu3st |t3/\/\s.

> Cinnamon's Text Box: Noted. Now what do we do?

> Roodg's Text Box: u CAN THROW ME A ROPE OR A VINE OR SOMETHING TO CLIMB. i CAN'T GET OUT!

> E. E. Lynn's Text Box: k

Cinnamon gathered many ropes through the process of sawblade severing which E. E. Lynn could tie together through the use of her *Red Bolas*. It would be a long process that would likely take until the afternoon to complete due to the depth of the drop. Roodg couldn't do much to help, but could collect a few near lava chests while waiting simply by walking on the lava to get to their otherwise dangerously precarious platforms.

Finally, after lunch (Roodg's food was pretty burnt this time) the night elf could climb up the rope and to safety.

> Cinnamon's Text Box: What the Flaming Pit? Are you magic or something? How are you not dead after being in lava that long?

> Roodg's Text Box: i DON'T KNOW! yOU MUST BE RIGHT, i MUST BE MAGIC! sAWESOME!

> E. E. Lynn's Text Box: 0r u fuck3d t3h |ce 3l3m3nt4l 0n Sp|r3 B.

> Roodg's Text Box: nO, BUT i SAVED HER LIFE WHEN THE SPIRE WAS COLLAPSING. sHE GAVE ME THIS *hEART OF iCE* AS A REWARD! sEE!

Roodg proudly held up the *Heart of Ice* for all to see. It was the reason that third Accessory Slots existed (that and *Full-Ball Gags*).

> E. E. Lynn's Text Box: & wh4t d03s |t d0?

> Roodg's Text Box: iT MAKES ME IMMUNE TO ALL FIRE DAMAGE!

> E. E. Lynn's Text Box: & 14\/4 d03s \/\/h4t k|nd 0f d4m4g3?

> Roodg's Text Box: fIRE! oH. i'M NOT MAGIC. fALSE ALARM!

> Cinnamon's Text Box: If you were immune to fire damage why where you so scared of the lava?

> Roodg's Text Box: i COMPLETELY FORGOT i HAD IT!

> E. E. Lynn's Text Box: Th3y 4r3 3p|c! | h4\/3 4ll 6 k|nds 0f h34rt 3qu|pped!

> Roodg's Text Box: hOW? yOU ONLY HAVE 1 SLOT.

> Cinnamon's Text Box: I combined them, so they would all work for her at once.

> Roodg's Text Box: qUEST fAIRIES CAN DO THAT?

> Cinnamon's Text Box: I'm not a Quest Fairy, I'm Cinnamon.

> Roodg's Text Box: yOU ARE A SPECIAL qUEST fAIRY. lIKE A PRIZE ONE. i GET IT.

> Cinnamon's Text Box: No, I'm Cinnamon.

The rest of the trip through Mnt. Sacrificial Volcano went far smoother. Roodg, who now remembered the fact that immunity to fire, was something that existed, was now having immense amounts of fun. Running through lava pits barefoot, bitch slapping the Nukamanders and Flame Flingers in the face for the heck of it, batting away giant fireballs as if they were baseballs with a newly found *Flaming Staff of Flames*, turning a scenic lava rock into a statue of a Flork Demon through the use of ice magic, and dry humping a flaming stalagmite were some of the activities that Roodg pursued.

E. E. Lynn, also immune to fire damage thanks to her *Heart of Everything*, joined in the fun, although she spent most of the time with the dry and wet humping. They were legitimately sad when they reached the end of the area near sundown and had to break up their lavaball fight to eat dinner a mix of *Chilled Nukasteaks* and *Flinger Tartar*.

> E. E. Lynn's Text Box: 0k4y. U r /\/\uch c00l3r n0\/\/. Th4t \/\/4s 4 s4\/\/3s0/\/\3 4ft3rn00n! ^-^

> Roodg's Text Box: i KNOW RIGHT?

> E. E. Lynn's Text Box: | h4\/3 n3\/3r s33n s0/\/\30n3 d3str0y sc3n34y l|k3 u. 3\/3n | c4n't d0 th4t. U p0\/\/nz0rz |t!

> Roodg's Text Box: tHAT IS MY NAME AFTER ALL, Roodg Scenerybane. wANT A fLORK STATUE? i WAS GOING TO SAVE IT FOR Palcath, BUT MY INVENTORY IS FULL.

> E. E. Lynn's Text Box: Y3s! | \/\/4nt |t s0 b4d! H3r3, t4k3 /\/\y *h34rt 0f 3v3ryth|ng* |n tr4d3.

> Roodg's Text Box: rEALLY?

> E. E. Lynn's Text Box: Sur3. |'ll /\/\4k3 h|/\/\ /\/\4k3 4n0th3r. H3r no\/\/ i gu3ss!

> Cinnamon's Text Box: That took me a week to model, but no big deal, I'll get right on that. Could be using those polygons to sculpt my penis back, but no, this is fine, really.

> E. E. Lynn's Text Box: G00d!

> Roodg's Text Box: iT ISN'T TOO LATE. should WE PRESS ON? hOW FAR DO WE STILL NEED TO GO?

> E. E. Lynn's Text Box: \/\/3 \/\/|ll n0t /\/\4k3 |t t0n|ght but \/\/3 sh0uld k33p g0Ing. \/\/3 r 4lm0st 4t P0sh \/\/3lsh Tr|b4l \/|ll4g3! \/\/3 c4n sl33p |n s0/\/\3on3's r34l b3d!

Roodg's Text Box: wHAT? bUT WE STARTED THERE. dID WE SERIOUSLY GO IN A BIG CIRCLE?

E. E. Lynn's Text Box: 0f cOurs3 nOt! Th|s |s teh s|d3 yOu c4n't g3t 2 \/\/|thOut \/\/4lk|ng 4r0und th3 \/\/h0l3 |sl4nd b3c4us3 teh g4te 0nly 0p3ns 1 \/\/4y!

Roodg's Text Box: tHAT MAKES SENSE.

E. E. Lynn's Text Box: \/\/h3n \/\/3 g3t th3r3 d0n't g0 thru0gh th4t g4t3. ^-^

Roodg's Text Box: oBVIOUSLY.

~~~

Roodg's Text Box: cRAP! wE NEED TO GO THRU THAT GATE.

E. E. Lynn's Text Box: Uh, n0! \/\/3 d0n't h4v3 t|/\/\3 4 th4t.

Roodg's Text Box: bUT THE pOSH wELSH tRIBESMAN ARE GOING 2 EAT THEM!

The All Seeing Eye Dog and the Nine Circles of Hellcat were tied up and about to be thrown into a comically large cooking pot.

E. E. Lynn's Text Box: N0p3. Th3y \/\/|ll r3sp4\/\/n s|nc3 th3y r p3ts.

Roodg's Text Box: bUT, WE NEED TO SAVE THEM!

E. E. Lynn's Text Box: \/\/hy?

Roodg's Text Box: bECAUSE THEY BELONG 2 De'vini and In'ferni WHO ARE AWOL. iF THEY RESPAWN THEN THE TWINS WILL BE ABLE TO ATTACK THINGS WITHOUT USING SPELLS & WILL BE MORE POWERFUL.

Cinnamon's Text Box: Roodg has a point.

E. E. Lynn's Text Box: F|n3. x-x. \/\/3 \/\/|ll \/\/4lk 4ll teh \/\/4y ar0und 4g4|n s0 teh p3ts c4n f4ll into teh l4\/4 4nd d|3 4ny\/\/4y.

Cinnamon's Text Box: No, that is silly. You don't need me to use the

Golden Tin Whistle tomorrow. Let me handle this.

Cinnamon left the party.

E. E. Lynn's Text Box: G00d |d34. \/\/3 \/\/|ll p|ck u up t0/\/\0rr0\/\/ |n S4\/\/3s0/\/\3 styl3.

Roodg's Text Box: iN sAWESOME STYLE?

Cinnamon's Text Box: Okay Posh Welsh Tribesman, cut it out already and stop cooking the dog and cat.

E. E. Lynn's Text Box: Y3p! S4\/\/3s0/\/\3 styl3.'

Cynddylan Bongam's Text Box: I don't think we can do that.

Maelmadog Chwith's Text Box: Not even a little bit I am afraid my good bean.

Roodg's Text Box: wHAT DOES THAT MEAN?

Cinnamon's Text Box: Oh come on, don't throw me in the pot. I know I don't taste good.

E. E. Lynn's Text Box: Y0u \/\/|ll s33! |t |s g0ing to b3 0ff teh sh|zz3l 4 r|zz3l!

Cynddylan Bongam's Text Box: Someone be a right bit of okay and fetch me the *Seasoning Handbook for Sacrifices* and find out what goes with Cinnamon.

Maelmadog Chwith's Text Box: Oh. I have that my good chap. I know sugar is jolly with it most certainly, but let me look it up.

Roodg's Text Box: nEAT!

Cinnamon's Text Box: Oh, for the love of Charlie! **Command H!**

Cynddylan Bongam and Maelmadog Chwith's Simultaneous Text Boxes: Yes master. We obey.

◈ Chapter 27 ◈

CYCLE 5
GROUP VOWELS,
BACK-UPS

The Secret Council Group Full of Mystical All-Knowing and Mysterious Members, also known as S.C.G.O.M.A.K.A.M.M. by some (but not many), had convened at their temporary headquarters, a gleaming magenta tower. Besides the tower and the lovely rosebushes outside, set to magenta, everything else in the area was stark white and empty.

> Administrator Allen's Text Box: Absolutely Not! Never! That is something that is not happening!

Allen, who was set to orange robes and had a Wi-Fi symbol on his chest bought for the low price of only total game destruction, was steadfast in his important decision. No matter what the other Administrators said, he would not budge.

> Administrator Ivy's Text Box: Fine. We will get eggrolls instead of spring rolls with the order. Maker you can be so difficult sometimes!

Ivy, the Administrator with hair showing from under the hood of her cyan USB robe, finally relented. She would suffer with the indignity of eggrolls with lunch.

> Administrator Yvonne's Text Box: We could get both.

Yvonne, the Administrator without hair showing from under the hood of her green robe, which had kickass firebird holding a cigar while surfing down a volcano, would not relent. She would not suffer with the indignity of eggrolls with lunch.

> Administrator Ethelred's Text Box: That is a great idea! We should

> order... wait... where did I put the coupon?

Ethelred the ever forgetful, who was not red as one would suspect but yellow, found the menus on his lap where he left them and suffered the headshakes of the others. His Ethernet symbol was glowing brighter than he wanted.

> Administrator Umple's Text Box: No, we can't okay. For the love of Charlie we can't make substitutions and still get to use this coupon!

Umple was as crotchety, violet, and volume symbol as ever. If this event was happening at his secret fortress, he would want the other Administrators to get off his lawn.

> Administrator Owen's Text Box: Enough already, I'll pay the extra two bucks. Stop arguing! I have important news. News that will change everything!

Owen was the same colour as his secret magenta fortress. The symbol on his robes was what he wanted the most, and it was neither spring nor eggrolls. He craved power. He waited until Ethelred was off of the phone ordering and then dramatically revealed his news that he had hidden under a magenta sheet. A phallic-shaped bronze machine, which had been altered with a variety of tubes, wires, and flavours of bubblegum. A gasp of alarm rung out from the others.

> Administrator Owen's Text Box: Behold! *The Device*!

> Administrator Allen's Text Box: No! Never! Impossible!

> Administrator Yvonne's Text Box: You found *The Device*? The most important item in the *Tales of Gentalia Series of Novelettes*? The machine of unlimited power?!

> Administrator Owen's Text Box: Yep! Hidden in a cloud. Now we will use it!

> Administrator Umple's Text Box: You can't intend for us to use that thing. It is strictly forbidden!

> Administrator Owen's Text Box: Yes, by us. The only reason that it is forbidden is because we forbade it in the first place.

> Administrator Umple's Text Box: Right, I forgot.

> Administrator Yvonne's Text Box: Let's use *The Device*! It is a great plan.

> Administrator Allen's Text Box: Yes and quickly! Right now! Before

the food gets here!

Administrator Ivy's Text Box: Then we should destroy it so no one else can use it.

Administrator Ethelred's Text Box: Then we should eat lunch.

The Administrator's used the *Diabolical Laugh Animation* in sync.

◈ Chapter 28 ◈

CYCLE 5: EVENING ΛNDEIS, FRIENDS WITHOUT BENEFITS

ow that Λndeıs had Angelic Wings, skeletal polygons, and an upside-down letter 'V' he was set. He knew exactly where he was going to go. With wings he could skip using the exceedingly long Stairway to the Clouds and fly to The Castle in the Sky. There he would go back and visit his old friend and first Optional Boss encountered, The Dryad.

While Λndeıs soared, he reminisced about his first experience with The Dryad. It was so tender, so loving, so unlike the rest of the encounters. He almost changed his *Blush Shade*, but remembered that it didn't really matter what he was set at since he still lacked any colour on his body and even if he could change it a visor covered his cheeks.

He landed at The Dryad's Grove, essentially skipping all of the puzzles, challenges, monsters, catchy Mr. Max song, and trouble of his last trip here. Λndeıs had decided, he should have looked into getting some *Angelic Wings* a long time ago. They were pretty badass.

The Castle in the Sky was trashed, but it had always been trashed so Λndeıs didn't pay much attention to the destruction everywhere. This place had a long time to get used to it. But when Λndeıs stepped inside of The Dryad's Grove he wasn't ready for what he saw. Destruction. This place had been spared the destruction of the outside, or at least it had been for a time. Now it was a complete mess, there was no plant life that hadn't been burnt with either fire or acid, no stone that hadn't been unturned, and a charred pile of long burnt out ashes in the corner.

Λndeıs felt a bit nauseated, he knew that the pile of ashes contained the burnt remains of The Dryad and his tree servants, including Eugene the Treant. A part of that was intuition, another big part was the sign made out of Eugene's face that had 'Burn for being a part of my death, fuckers' carved into it with a knife. Breaker had been here and killed them all. This trip down memory lane was a big let down.

After a solemn moment of using the *Campfire Making Animation* to create a fire to burn the face away, and then scattering it and the other ashes into the wind with his wings, Λndeıs lifted off and thought about what to do next. Looking from up here now, Λndeıs knew that this place was indeed much more destroyed than it had been the first time. There wouldn't have been any place that he could have used to walk here. Even the portal to The Plague of Shadow's lair had been ripped asunder. At least NPC Narbenock and The Plague of Shadow had escaped, Λndeıs had already seen them standing in the Starting City Whose Name No Longer Mattered Because it Was Destroyed ready to help new avatars join this fun experience.

Λndeıs looked closer at the portal to The Plague of Shadow's lair. He could see through it now that it was gaping open but saw something that he had forgotten about until now. Inside the portal, in the distance, there had been an exact duplicate of the entire The Castle in the Sky. Yes, it was completely black and covered in dramatic lighting effects, but it was an exact duplicate. More importantly, it was completely unscathed.

If someone had been lazy, they might had cut and pasted The Castle in the Sky from this one. If they had been really lazy and made that area second, which was possible, they might have not deleted anything there to save time. There might be a complete secondary version of this level hidden as a piece of scenery over there and that could mean a complete secondary version of The Dryad. He might not need to open his list and look for another Optional Boss after all.

He flew through the portal, avoiding the juicy sides as best as he could, and headed towards the distant scenery. When full-fledged pieces of geometry came into view Λndeıs was hopeful. When little tiny specs of monsters came into view he was excited. He had been right; once again laziness had saved the day. Everything was in grayscale, and glowing with an eerie light, but it was not nearly as damaged as the other version, and *Caution Step*'s song *The Plague of Shadow* was in the background. Sure it started playing in reverse when he got closer, but even backward that song made this place automatically qualify as better.

He landed, after getting turned around a few times, again skipping all of the puzzles and difficulty normally associated with the area. He gave his wings a stretch while nibbling on enough food for ten men. Λndeıs adjusted his *Knight Armour*, weapons, wings, and package for the most dramatic entrance possible and stepped inside evorG s'dayrD ehT.

It was as Λndeıs had remembered it, besides all the glowing and loss of colour. Plants of every shape and kind covered the walls, creating the feeling of an endless jungle. Tall trees lined the left wall, ready to be made into servants if requested, and vines covered the ceiling. Something was different, it took him a few rounds to place it, but everything was backward. This place had been mirrored.

Vines from the nearest tree grabbed Andeıs firmly and hoisted him up in the air. He recognized this face, even if it was mirrored, this was the Treant Eugene. The vines began to tighten but Andeıs had expected that.

> Andeıs' Text Box: It's okay Eugene, it is me. Is The Dryad here? I need to talk to him.

The vines continued to tighten, more and more joined the fray and soon without realizing it Andeıs had been put into the *Bound More More Status*. He had the Constitution to get out of it this time, but was amazed when he failed the check. He was stuck.

> Andeıs' Text Box: Eugene?

> Nega-Eugene's Text Box: Uuurg?

> Andeıs' Text Box: Nega-Eugene?

> The Nega-Dryad's Text Box: Alright Nega-Eugene. That isn't enough. It is him. Squeeze harder.

> Nega-Eugene's Text Box: Uuurg!

> Andeıs' Text Box: Oh doughnuts!

The vines tightened and Andeıs was forcibly squeezed and raised higher in the air.

> The Nega-Dryad's Text Box: To arms everyone. It isn't Breaker.

A gang of tree monsters perked up happily. They took their next turn to uproot themselves out of the ground and leave the scenery. By the time Andeıs was hanging upside down all of the trees were ready for battle.

> The Nega-Dryad's Text Box: But the question must be asked. Who isn't it?

From behind the legs of the monster tree Nega-Eugene, stepped a slim figure. The Nega-Dryad's looked almost identical to the regular The Dryad. He was slightly shorter than Andeıs ✓. His skin was a highly polished and varnished mahogany ✓ (but it was black mahogany). His body had been expertly carved and sculpted by a master craftsman ✓. He wasn't wearing clothing ✓. He really didn't need to be ✓. Vines and leaves crawled over his body ✓. Willowy branches and thin leaves were hanging from his head like dreadlocks ✓ (but they were purple). Another small patch of the leafy hair hid the creature's privates from view ✓.

The Nega-Dryad stopped in front of Andeıs.

> The Nega-Dryad's Text Box: It is some sort of dangerous sexy angel. I'll admit I am not a fan of the wardrobe choice. Who are you and why

> are you here?

> Andeıs' Text Box: My name is Andeıs. I was here a long time ago and I beat Breaker t—

> The Nega-Dryad's Interruption Text Box: You beat Breaker?

> Andeıs' Text Box: Yes, I beat him. My party and I came here to challenge the Plague of Shadow but defeated it. Not before he did, but it was a tie sort of.

The Nega-Dryad performed a *Blind Rage Animation*.

> The Nega-Dryad's Text Box: Of course, and you knew how to kill Breaker. That bastard did not come here to find his revenge on this place after his defeat. It is your fault that he didn't destroy everything!

> Andeıs' Text Box: No, it is his fault. He did it? Look, I've had most of this conversation already and I was wonder—

> The Nega-Dryad's Interruption Text Box: You are not getting away with it that easy! This is your fault and you are going to be punished for what you did. Get him Nega-Eugene!

Despite Nega-Eugene's repeated attempts, Andeıs' head would not crack underfoot. Considerable damage had been done, certainly, but the dangling elf was still barely conscious. During Nega-Eugene's smoke break, Andeıs tried to appeal to The Nega-Dryad.

> Andeıs' Text Box: I don't understand. The Dryad was so kind and nice. You are beating the *Double Danishes* out of me. What is the deal?

> The Nega-Dryad's Text Box: I may look like The Dryad, but I think you will find that we are nothing alike. We have much different, how shall I say this, alignments, tastes, and dispositions.

> Andeıs' Text Box: That is awful. So because your skin is grayscale, your aura is glowly, and you have a Nega in your name you are evil? How wrong is that? I might have to complain.

The Nega-Dryad used the *Comical Laughter Animation*.

> The Nega-Dryad's Text Box: Of course not. Evil because of one's skin colour, level of glow, or title. That would be stupid and highly illogical. I would complain as well quite frankly. No, I am how I am because I am mirrored, plain and simple. Things in mirrors or that have been

mirrored are always opposites. It is the hard cold truth of coding.

Anders' Text Box: So you are only evil because when they built this area, they mirrored it?

The Nega-Dryad's Text Box: I am only opposite because of that. I am the opposite, not evil. Now, what do you remember about this The Dryad encounter of yours?

The Nega-Dryad tilted its head playfully. With a simple flick of his wooden hand, the Optional used his control of vegetation to make the vines of his servants rip Anders' *Knight Armour* away. Anders hung there in shock, left wearing only his wings. A single feather blew away gently in the breeze.

Anders' Text Box: It was hard, fast, and painful?

The Nega-Dryad's Text Box: I admire that you are sticking with the idea of opposites, but that isn't going to work. I know reverse me better than that. Try again.

Anders' Text Box: It was the most love filled encounter that I can remember. The entire thing was gentle, slow, and rewarding. Let me guess, this is going to be the opposite of that.

The Nega-Dryad's Text Box: Yes, it will be. You however forgot some important though. Would you like to see my list?

Other Important Opposite Facts List
1. It will be fast, hard, and ex—

Anders' Interruption Text Box: No, not really.

The Nega-Dryad's Text Box: What do you mean no?

Anders' Text Box: I don't want to hear it.

The Nega-Dryad's Text Box: But I worked really hard on it!

Anders' Text Box: I don't care. I realized that your opposite logic is completely flawed. See, if the opposite thing should be happening then the only thing that should happen right now is that we don't have sex. The Dryad and I had sex, so therefore The Opposite Dryad and I shouldn't.

The Nega-Dryad used the *Completely Baffled Animation*.

> The Nega-Dryad's Text Box: No, that isn't the opposite!

> Andeis' Text Box: Yes it is. End of debate.

The Nega-Dryad used the *Furious Pout Animation*. This caused Nega-Eugene to tighten his grip and Andeis to let out a pitiful 'urk'.

> The Nega-Dryad's Text Box: How dare you mock the good name of carefully planned out opposite situations! You will pay dearly for your outburst.

> Andeis' In Pain Text Box: How… could I not? You are… perverting them… You are… only going to… follow the opposites… that work out for what you… want… and ignore the rest! I was… tied up and nearly strangled… by Eugene last time. What is happening right now… isn't an opposite… it is the same.

> The Nega-Dryad's Text Box: That is it! It is time for him to learn his first lesson.

> Nega-Eugene's Text Box: Uuurg?

> The Nega-Dryad's Text Box: Get ready for some real pain unlike anything you've experienced before! Prep him.

> Andeis' In Pain Text Box: No… stop!

> The Nega-Dryad's Text Box: Okay!

The vines of Nega-Eugene relented and a dumbfounded Andeis was placed carefully back on the ground. The dramatic background music faded like the vicious zeal in the Nega-Dryad's eyes.

> Andeis' Text Box: What? What happened?

> The Nega-Dryad's Text Box: You told us to stop, so we stopped. That's how it works.

> Andeis' Text Box: That isn't how it works. I know from lots of experience that isn't how it works.

> The Nega-Dryad's Text Box: That is our programming, if we get told to stop, we stop.

> Andeis' Text Box: No way. I've must have told monsters to stop a

dozen times.

The Nega-Dryad's Text Box: Evidently not. You can double check if you wish. If you find any references to monsters fused with Avatars being told to stop, that doesn't count, because that was the Avatar in control, not us.

Andeis doubled checked everything and he couldn't believe it. Barring that one instance with a fused monster (that needed to be mentioned or it would be called out eventually) no one had ever told a monster to stop.

Andeis' Text Box: I don't believe it. All this time, all anyone needed to do was say stop?

The Nega-Dryad's Text Box: Of course. That's the safe word. We are only programmed to be dominant, not to rape, unless told otherwise. We are monsters, not monsters.

Andeis' Text Box: Somebody probably should have mentioned that at some point!

The Nega-Dryad's Text Box: Remember, we were not meant to be available to the general public. Our programming dictates that we be aggressive and sexual unless told otherwise.

Andeis' Text Box: Are you serious?

The Nega-Dryad's Text Box: You can triple check if you wish.

Further researched proved that any monster that was told to obey did so. They became as docile as lambs and as easy to control as a joystick with two buttons.

Andeis' Text Box: Son of a biscuit!

The Nega-Dryad used the *Shrug Animation.*

The Nega-Dryad's Text Box: Sorry.

Andeis use the *Wicked Grin Animation.*

Andeis' Text Box: That means that I can tell you to do whatever I want, and you will have to do it!

The Nega-Dryad's Text Box: Eep!

Andeis' Text Box: I command you to drop this mirror opposite nonsense and do something only a Nega-Something can do!

> The Nega-Dryad's Text Box: Sure. I think I've got something that will work!

The Nega-Dryad jumped into the soil and used *Nega-Plant*. A beautiful purple flower grew from the ground until it was the size of a fully grown Landcat. The flower blossomed with a sweet scent to reveal the transformed version of the Nega-Dryad. He was now an elf Night Ranger, male, with a *#2 (average) Body Style, #6 Hairstyle (Light Blond)*, a scar on his cheek, protagonist green eyes, and a perky bubble butt of holding.

> Anders' Text Box: Hey there, you big monster you!

> Anders' Text Box: You are me! From the previous books!

> Anders' Text Box: Exactly! That is something that only a Nega-Something can do. Flaming Pit, it is exactly what all Nega-Somethings do!

Anders used the *Wink Animation* directed at Anders. He positioned himself on the now open flower bed, perky butt in the air, and looked back coyly.

Anders attempted a *Blush Shade* change, but he still lacked all colour. What did have colour (and lots of it) was the perky butt of himself, from previous books. Despite himself, Anders started to grow hard. He watched himself, looking at himself. Watching himself watching himself was a mind trip but not compared to watching himself fingering himself, or being watched by himelf as he stroked himself.

> Anders' Text Box: Hey Anders. Go fudge yourself!

This was a once in a playthrough opportunity (twice if you count Serdna) and Anders decided to go for it. There again would be no penetration of Anders this encounter, but there would be penetration of Anders. He stepped forward, placed his hands on that firm, cushy, and familiar backside, lined up, and pushed into the famous elfhole enjoyed the world over.

> Anders' Text Box: Holy Maker! I am way bigger than I thought I was before.

> Anders' Text Box: Holy Maker! I am way tighter than I thought I was going to be!

Anders took his time and pushed slowly all the way inside. He knew that his new member was pretty close to the maximum size that his old butt could take without activating *Stretch More*. Anders winced. He was nearly at his limit, he was sure to activate *Stretch More*. Anders put a stop to it, he knew his own butt far better than that. Things were about to get interesting.

Anders' thrusts were slow, yet precise, carefully executed so that he could give every tight delicious length unit of the elfbutt before him intense feelings of appreciation. A tingle of pleasure shot into his cock and Anders knew he had succeeded. Like clockwork the self-lubricating, magical ass became slicker and more accommodating due to the natural slime lubricants. Anders bucked backwards against Anders and sighed, thankful he had held off.

Their union fit exactly, and every thrust hit every note perfect. Anders went against his programming and got aggressive. After one particularly hard thrusting session he broke the union and pushed Anders onto the flower bed. Anders could have complained, but didn't, as he quite liked the look of himself, straddling himself, as he bounced up and down on himself. He was pretty hot when he took charge, so he decided to take charge. He tightly gripped his past waist and thrust hard with his present hips.

> Anders' Text Box: It is hot when you take charge!

> Anders' Text Box: I was thinking that!

Anders broke the union with a wet pop. He deftly double jumped backward and landed on a miscoloured pixel that only he could possibly have seen. He used the *Challenge Animation*.

> Anders' Text Box: Well then, take charge!

Not a single round was wasted before the challenge was accepted. Anders flew up on angelic glitter wings and tackled his opponent. They tumbled in the air and landed on the ceiling. Anders was taken off guard by the speed of it all, and could not stop the penetrative thrust of his opponent. Anders pushed in hard, again and again, as Anders writhed in pleasure, stomach against the ceiling.

> Anders' Text Box: I told you it wou—

> Anders' Interruption Text Box: Shut up and take my cock Elfboy!

> Anders' Text Box: ♥!

Anders blitzed the hot elfhole with an onslaught of powerful strikes. Each hit brought forth a shower of tingles from his opponent. The pleasure was becoming too much, Anders could no longer hold back. With one final foray he went in as far as he could and started to shoot his seed deep within himself. As was his custom, the feeling of hot seed gushing into him pushed Anders over the edge, and he shot out his only squirt of seed against the roof, planting a little purple flower into the ceiling.

Sweat still dripping from himself (both of himselves), Anders brought the pair to the ground.

> Anders' Text Box: That was lovely!

> Anders' Text Box: There isn't anything else like it in the entire world!

> Anders' Text Box: I know! That's why I am keeping you. Nega-Eugene,

throw him in the dungeon!

Anders' Text Box: What?

Nega-Eugene's Text Box: Uuurg!

One swift hit from Nega-Eugene against his startled opponent was all it took to knock him out. Anders woke up some time later to an Insta-Wiki Entry Screen.

Creature Name: The Nega-Dryad
Class: Nega-Humanoid (Plant)
Level: 50
Special Attacks: Nega-Snap, Nega-Plant, Nega-Vine Whip, Nega-Ivy Constrict, Nega-Command
Drops: Nega-Nothing
First Player Encounter Notes: Nega-Jerk! – Anders

Game Explanation Text Box: Polygons absorbed from Nega-Dryad 16.6%. Polygon absorption complete, thank you for using Polytech© brand Polygons in your reconstruction process and please report any cases of Flickering Head Syndrome to a Polytech© representative.

The cell that held Anders was made of purple flower petals.

Anders' Text Box: Hey, my name is back! I missed you so much name.

A fractal of polygons should have flown at the avatar with a spirited background song, but instead a mass of paint, textures and colour rushed at the avatar. His eyes were too dazed to see it but Anders knew that his colour had finally come back.

Anders' Text Box: …colour! I missed you too.

Game Explanation Text Box: Special trait absorbed from Nega-Dryad, Neganess.

Nega-Anders' Text Box: Neganess? My name!

Nega-Anders passed out again, from the Nega-Shock.

♦ Chapter 29 ♦
CYCLE 5
GROUP B, LOVER AND HATER

Hippolyta's Text Box: We definitely have enough Poffles now. I can't even count them anymore.

Mr. Max's Text Box: I had 318 *Creature Cages* and the materials to make 580 more. They are all full now and there are more Poffles were hanging out near the cages for fun.

Zal Finn III's Text Box: No! We can't kill them yet. Just... um... cause we need to eat?

Hippolyta's Text Box: True. I have been interested in this super special lunch that was promised.

Zal Finn swallowed hard as Max giddily ran inside to collect his super special lunch. He was proud of this meal and had worked on it for a long time considering it was food. It was going to be their Victory Over Poffles lunch. It was a fabulous spread that he could only bring out all at once due to the natural plate balancing abilities of giant muscles. Max was proud as the girls watched him in awe as he carried out the feast.

While the lunch was simply crackers, cheese, meats, and other foodstuffs to build little sandwiches with, it was the sheer number of options that was impressive. There was all three different kinds of cheese bricks carefully placed on a platter: *White Cheese*, *Yellow Cheese*, and *Beetle Cheese*, which would make a lovely base for the crackerwiches.

All varieties of *Bacon* filled another, including some that even Mr. Max had forgotten existed. Then there was *Roasted Landcat*, *Broiled Blasphemy*, and *Annoying Cow Steaks* for a hint of protein. For a sauce you could choose from *Undeadly Nightshade Butter*, *Wampahoofus Mustard*, or *Meganaise*. To top it all off was a generous amount of *Sahagin Spreadable Crackers*. While there was more than enough to feed an army, likely none of it would survive the meal.

> Zal Finn III's Text Box: You've outdone yourself Max. This is sweet. How long did it take you?

> Mr. Max's Text Box: I had to cook like ten times!

Zal Finn III used the *Impressed Whistle Animation*.

> Zal Finn III's Text Box: We should go and get Caela. I wouldn't want her to miss out on this spread.

> Mr. Max's Text Box: She's been busy all morning in her *Portie Tent Ultra+* fussing with the carpets in my room. She said she wasn't hungry then told me not to bother her again.

> Hippolyta's Text Box: How can she not be hungry? These little crackerwiches are amazing. I can't stop eating them. It is settled, there is something going on with her if she would rather have her face in a carpet than eat these… Damn! I wish I could think about it more. It is so loud in here.

> Zal Finn III's Text Box: But the Poffles all stopped making noises! Look at how polite the non-caged ones are being. They are even making crackerwiches for the caged ones… sure they are double dipping with the sauces, but still.

> Hippolyta's Text Box: Not here. Here. I have Keiko and Shyanne arguing about how to reassemble the computer they took apart looking for viruses on one side of me. Thankfully, the other side is right beside Trevor's room. It is a good thing that the headboard is obviously against the paper thin wall near my head or I wouldn't have the constant banging of it to remind me that the noises I am hearing are in fact two men having incredibly loud and gay sex. They never started their escape raft and wow does Jourdain has some lungs on him, I will tell you that much.

> Mr. Max's Text Box: Keiko? Shyanne? Trevor? Jourdain? Who are they?

> Hippolyta's Text Box: Sorry, it is so distracting I forgot to stay in

character. De'vini, In'ferni, Trev Terra, and Jorthan. I am trying to think about what is going on with Caela but all I can think about is which port was used for the DVD burner and how much harder it should be plowed.

Zal Finn III's Text Box: I am more concerned about what is going on with Gliint. What is he up to? Always running around everywhere and staying in *Stealth*. Constantly visiting Caela's room, standing next to De'vini and In'ferni for countless rounds and running around Onn in circles all night long. He was just here and he didn't even say hi. Ran into Caela's tent then left. Something unsweet is up with him.

Mr. Max and Hippolyta both used the *Jaw Drop Animation*.

Zal Finn III's Text Box: You know what else is weird? Yallundy is always with him, but last night when I saw them it was like he didn't even know. I guess that makes some sense because she was invisible, but still. It is weird.

Mr. Max and Hippolyta couldn't react. They were still stuck mid *Jaw Drop*, both had fragments of crackerwiches falling out of their mouths.

Zal Finn III's Text Box: What? Why is everyone looking at me? Was it because of how I ate a crackerwich made of only cheese and Meganaise? It is that isn't it?

Hippolyta's Text Box: How do you know all that about everyone?

Zal Finn III's Text Box: I got broken after I used Breaker's Auto-Locate code and it gave me Administrative avatar finding power. Don't you remember? See, it makes my eyes go all pink and sweet! I've been spying on some avatars and watching where they go since like forever.

Hippolyta's Text Box: What is Gliint doing right now? Where are the twins?

Zal Finn III used the *Shrug Animation*.

Zal Finn III's Text Box: Flaming Pits if I know. Basically it works like the Corner Radar but on my entire Micro-Mini Map. If I look for someone I can see their little arrow in their colour and a trail of where they have walked lately but not see them on camera or what they are doing. Gliint is already back in Onn and the twins are standing near Onn in a place I have never been.

Hippolyta's Text Box: Why didn't you speak up earlier? Couldn't you have done Group A's task instantly?

Zal Finn III's Text Box: I already did and was going to tell Palcath, but I kept getting distracted by... uh.

Mr. Max's Text Box: Her sweet melons? Yeah, me to! It is a good thing you girls are only Level 6 now. Hippolyta's boobs are almost flatter than Caela's and I can finally concentrate. It is how come I could make this lunch.

Hippolyta's Text Box: If you had not both provided this absolute delicious feast of food and were absolutely correct about my flatness Max, I would have slapped you with what is left of my Heaving Bosom.

Mr. Max's Text Box: Can you slap me anyway?

Zal Finn III's Text Box: Me too?

Hippolyta was surprised with an ambush of the *Puppy Dog Eyes Animation* by both avatars.

Hippolyta's Text Box: Somehow, I think it is more of a punishment for you both if I don't.

Zal Finn III and Mr. Max's Simultaneous Text Box: Aw, snap!

Hippolyta's Text Box: We need to think about this while eating more crackerwiches. In the mean time can you use those absolutely perfect eyes of yours to look for people we know Zal?

Zal changed to *Blush Shade #2*, and then began her search at her normal spying starting point.

Zal Finn III's Text Box: Lissa is in Onn.

Mr. Max's Text Box: Hmmm... Gliint is acting all strange. Look for him next.

Zal Finn III's Text Box: Gliint left Onn and went to the place where De'vini and In'ferni are. They moved at top speed to... somewhere else in Onn?

Hippolyta's Text Box: I wish I knew where but In'ferni's avatar has had a blindfold on for awhile now.

Zal Finn III's Text Box: Trev and Jorthan are still in the same place.

Hippolyta's Text Box: I could have told you that.

Mr. Max's Text Box: Wait! I figured it out!

Hippolyta's Text Box: What? You? How?

Mr. Max's Text Box: I know, right? Okay, Gliint is acting strange, so was De'vini. De'vini is locked out of her character right now. That must mean Gliint is too! Why didn't I think of that before? That explains all the strange emails he sent me through his fan site begging for help. Here I thought he was asking for help on the *Caution Step* album cover he was designing for me, but it was for real help. I better send him a note clarifying, give me a round.

Hippolyta's Text Box: He was sending you emails for help this whole time? Seriously? I'm going to have to not slap you again.

Zal Finn III's Text Box: Fourni is with Lissa and Palcath, so no surprise there. Gliint is with them again, Maker he is fast.

Mr. Max's Text Box: He is my biggest fan. He has been sending me twenty emails a day for I don't know how long. Oh, yeah, he replied... so he has been locked out of his avatar since way back in Chapter 5. He is... super pissed off.

Hippolyta's Text Box: I could imagine why!

Zal Finn III's Text Box: Good! Roodg isn't dead either! With E. E. Lynn no less. So someone else finally found her on that area covered with mist.

Mr. Max's Text Box: According to Gliint he has still been able to see what is going on, but can't act. He took some items away that samuri was searching through. One of them was a *Bell Charm* that he delivered to De'vini. He ruined Caela's PJs and made sure she put on that *Initiate's Jacket!* Oh good, I'm off the hook! He tried to fly to that island above Onn with Roodg's Carrot but couldn't so started to build a cake stairway there. He searched through a lot of rubble in Onn Coliseum but gave up looking after he rearranged Fourni's *Saddlebags*.

Hippolyta's Text Box: This is falling into place. Both Gliint and De'vini have been taken over.

Mr. Max's Text Box: That sounds like what happened in the Book Two climax to Anders!

Zal Finn III's Text Box: Still no Anders around, and only one green avatar arrow that is right beside me when I do a search for green.

Mr. Max's Text Box: There is only one avatar that I know that is capable of taking over avatars.

Hippolyta's Text Box: That douche Breaker? But he was eaten to death, we all saw it.

Zal Finn III's Text Box: I could never see Breaker because of his dummy accounts, too bad because it really would have saved us so much time if I could have said, 'Hey, Breaker is in Onn!' or something.

Mr. Max's Text Box: Wel—

Zal Finn III's Interruption Text Box: Holy fucking shitballs! Breaker is in Onn or something!

Mr. Max and Hippolyta's Simultaneous Text Boxes: What?

Zal Finn III's Text Box: I can see him! In Onn… oh wait, above Onn. He is on that island that floats above the world.

Mr. Max's Text Box: I thought you couldn't see him?

Zal Finn III's Text Box: I couldn't before, but there he is. Judging by that trail of his… he hasn't moved in weeks except for in the circle that island travels. Like not even breathing movement. Crap. De'vini, In'ferni, and a clear arrow… Who is clear? Are all circling about, likely on the *Parsnip*.

Mr. Max's Text Box: So Breaker isn't dead and he has been controlling Gliint and De'vini this entire time? How awful.

Hippolyta's Text Box: Possibly others we might not know about as well. Who else has been acting strange lately?

They thought on the situation for a few rounds, but were provided the answer when it spoke up.

Caëlahenãilenẃhei's Text Box: Oh Maxie-poo, can I see you privately in my tent for a moment? We need to talk.

Max spit out his crackerwich with such force that it knocked over the only remaining

Creature Cage that did not yet contain a Golden Poffle. It fell on a free Golden Poffle trapping it. Zal Finn crashed into the platter of assorted cheeses and sent food flying through the air, feeding dozens of caged Golden Poffles at once. Hippolyta dropped her ludicrously large crackerwich on the ground and had to fight a Golden Poffle for it, but she only managed to save half.

Mr. Max used the *Frantic Point Around Animation*.

> Mr. Max's Whisper Text Box: What do I do? What do I do?

> Hippolyta's Whisper Text Box: Be cautious and try to keep calm. Try to find out 'her' plan. We will be right outside listening.

> Zal Finn III's Whisper Text Box: Remember, if it is Breaker, he hates you more than anyone else and will likely try to kill you.

> Mr. Max's Whisper Text Box: That helps so much for keeping me calm, the threat of death. Thank you.

> Hippolyta's Whisper Text Box: Just go!

> Mr. Max's Whisper Text Box: Sure thing Caela! I'll be right there.

> Mr. Max's Text Box: I mean... Sure thing Caela! I'll be right there!

While Zal Finn, Hippolyta, and three curious Poffles set themselves up to spy inside, Mr. Max was busy taking a few cautious steps into the *Portie Tent Ultra+*. He knew that something had to be different, but nothing looked out of place in the sitting room.

> Caëlahenäilenẇhei's Text Box: Okay Max, this has gone on long enough. We both want you fucked and need to finally do this already. Come into your room and let's end this.

Max looked back but was only met with five *Go Ahead Animations*. He followed Caela into his room and was immediately suspicious of the much higher, lumpy, and loudly ticking carpet. Caela was already on his bed, hand under a pillow, and grin on her mouth (the mouth on her face). Max waited long enough for the girls to get closer before stepping forward.

> Caëlahenäilenẇhei's Text Box: Strip off some of that defense boosting Armour and step closer already. Into my embrace. I will be your fuck bitch.

Max saw the flash of steel under the pillow and he knew that Caela had something sharp in her hand. That was how he, pretending to be her, was going to do it. A quick stab in the back. He was much stronger than the Rocket Sorceress and since he knew about the hidden object he could 'mount' her and hold it down, preventing her from using it. That was a perfect plan, it would stop her, but he needed to play along to get closer.

Making a show of stripping off his *Spring Gear Armour*, Max stopped short of full nakedness by keeping on the *Pink Slime Jockstrap*. (He had liberated them from Anders' ashes. Yes, he had taken the underpants from the corpse of a dead guy, but they kept his giant package under control like nothing else could with their jelly expansive goodness and he technically was there for the encounter when Anders' sexy sister had found them, so these were part his. Besides, he looked good in pink.)

Taking a step towards the bed, Mr. Max did his *Flex Animation* for good measure, becoming full mast but in control and then got ready to make his move. He was going to have to mount this guy (who was controlling this girl) to save them all.

> Caëlahenãilenw̃hei's Box Text: Max stop! I'm possessed like De'vini and Glïint and am going to try to kill you! I have a knife in my hand, and the carpet is filled with explosives.

> Caëlahenãilenw̃hei's Text Box: What the fuck? How are you talking again?

> Mr. Max's Text Box: I know you are trying to kill me! We figured it out. I was going to take the knife away.

> Caëlahenãilenw̃hei's Box Text: It took you long enough! I've been blinking in Morris Code for cycles.

> Caëlahenãilenw̃hei's Text Box: How are you talking still? I'm in control of you skinny white 'c' word elf!

> Caëlahenãilenw̃hei's Box Text: You still haven't panned your camera down yet have you idiot?

> Caëlahenãilenw̃hei's Text Box: Why would I need to look down there... holy fuck you have a mouth where your vagina should be. Lady, you are messed up!

> Caëlahenãilenw̃hei's Box Text: Shut up you jerk! I am unique!

> Caëlahenãilenw̃hei's Text Box: No you shut up, cunt.

Caëlahenãilenw̃hei stopped all her movements, and then doubled over in a *Hilarious Laugh Animation*.

> Caëlahenãilenw̃hei's Text Box: Oh my Maker. I realized that the idiot that I have been calling a cunt this entire time... is a cunt. How is that possible? The cunt is actually a cunt. You can't make up stuff like that,

it is priceless!

Caëlahenâilenŵhei's Box Text: Quick, sit on the *Washing Machine Ultra+* or *Dryer+* now! I'm in control while he is distracted laughing. See, what happened is that he had Gliint set up a bunch of bombs under the carpet and they are going to go off in a matter of rounds. We don't have much time to act, and we will never get out of the tent in time. I did some calculations earlier and I know what to do. The explosion will destroy the *Portie Tent Ultra+*, for which I will never forgive Breaker, but at least we can survive thanks to the extra heat resistance from the *Dryer+*. It is —

Caëlahenâilenŵhei's Box Text: lucky that I have it. I first learned of the fire proof abilities of the *Washing Machine* and *Dryer Ultra+* combo set after my pajamas were ruined. I admit, I got a bit upset with that situation and tried to destroy them. I however am no Roodg Scenerybane and I did not have luck. What I did learn however will save us all right now, which is good, because this is likely the only group that knows what is going on. So, we should hurry up already and get on the aforementioned life saving devices before it is too late to do anything about it. Try to h—

Caëlahenâilenŵhei's Box Text: old onto something!

Caëlahenâilenŵhei's Box Text: Wait… Where are we?

Hippolyta's Text Box: Far, far away.

Mr. Max's Text Box: Yeah, I grabbed you when you started talking and shoved you right inside the *Dryer Ultra+*.

Zal Finn III's Text Box: Then the *Portie Tent Ultra+* exploded and we rocketed across the entire Spire G!

Mr. Max's Text Box: You should have seen it, it was pretty epic.

Caëlahenâilenŵhei's Text Box: It was badass! There was even fireworks and junk. Too bad you all lived through it.

Hippolyta's Text Box: Then Breaker took over your body again because he finished laughing.

Zal Finn III's Text Box: That part sucked. He summoned his *Magical Flying Parsnip Ultra+* and it showed up with a skeleton driving it! A frickin' skeleton with a clear map arrow! Where did he get that thing from?

Mr. Max's Text Box: Now you and the skeleton are getting ready to fly away to your secret lair and leave us here to die. Not me, but one of the girls.

Hippolyta's Text Box: Because it is almost nightfall and we have fallen to Level 3.

Caëlahenãilenŵhei's Text Box: They will never make it back to the Poffles in time and only have one *Elixir*. I left it for them even though I could have destroyed it. Who will live and who will die? I don't really care as long as one dies.

Caëlahenãilenŵhei's Box Text: Wow. All that happened? I really need to learn to Text Box while not looking at the keyboard.

Zal Finn III's Text Box: Maybe a little bit faster as well?

Caëlahenãilenŵhei's Text Box: And less.

Caëlahenãilenŵhei's Box Text: I have learned my lesson when it comes to talking too much. From now on I will be more careful when it comes to the subject of rambling on I assure you. This will be a life lesson that I will keep with me, close. I never want to forget what has transpired this cycle because… hey, now where are we?

Caëlahenãilenŵhei's Text Box: At my secret base, we flew away like forever ago you cootch breather.

◈ Chapter 30 ◈

CYCLE 5
GROUP A, THE
CAKELAMITY

Palcath's Text Box: I'm sorry Fourni, but I don't see it.

Fournimer's Text Box: but it is true! I know it was him. Anders is alive!

Draganders' Text Box: Chirp?

Palcath's Text Box: None of your story makes me think that you found Anders. First of all, you said this lad's name was ndeis, I will admit that is a little close, but that is the only part of the story that sounds remotely like Anders.

Lissa's Text Box: Yeah, listen to yourself. He was tall and muscular. He saved me from having sex with a woman by doing her hard in the lady parts while he swore like a Sailor Fish. His skin, eyes, and the wisp of hair that peaked out from under his visor was porcelain white and glittered. He was wearing white Plate Armour with gradient gray accents. He had a halo sword and magically sprouted angelic wings and flew away. What part of any of that sounds like Anders to you?

Palcath's Text Box: Anders' colour was green, he can't use Plate Armour since he wasn't a melee class, he didn't sparkle, he didn't swear, and most importantly the lad was as gay as a 3GP coin!

Lissa's Text Box: With that magical butt of his, he was obviously a bottom, maybe a sometimes switch hitter at best. He was certainly not the aggressive type of guy who rushed into a room to plow a girl, while they were on your back. They had sex on your back, while you were tied up no less. #RudeToCentaurs.

Fournimer's Text Box: I know it sounds silly, but it was him. I will prove it! don't worry I will, I have a plan!

Palcath's Text Box: Honestly, you have been a little bit intense for awhile now. Please can you tone it down, Fourni? You are starting to make me nervous.

Draganders' Text Box: Chirp?

Lissa's Text Box: I think you need to chill out.

Fournimer's Text Box: that is not what I need!

Palcath's Text Box: Look, hand me another *Grand FullCake* already before that lad Gliint gets back. Thanks to all of us working tirelessly through the night, not to mention that this new decorating work Margarine has been doing has increased the stability of these cakes by triple, and Fourni can walk up here now to help, we are almost at the floating island.

Lissa's Text Box: This new decorating is amazing by the way. The sprinkles are beautiful, the icing work is spectacular, and the frosting is the right colour... I could go on and on about them. I mean, I've taken screenshots of them. I am going to make a necklace inspired by them because they are that nice. #ThisCakeIsNotALie.

It was true, the cakes were pretty amazing, but Fournimer didn't care about the cake (he did care a little, they were that amazing). What Fournimer cared about most was his missing elf hole. He meant to think love not hole. This pent up centaur juice was getting to him more and more. Everything he looked at was becoming increasingly arousing, which made the cake that much more amazing. Even his companions were starting to have a special glow about them.

That thought made Fournimer throw up a little in his mouth. Lissa was pretty certainly and Draganders had his subtle charms, but Palcath? That was sick! This desire within was strong if it would even for a round make him consider Palcath. Lissa on the other hoof...

Fournimer's Text Box: Lis, can I ask you a favour?

Lissa's Text Box: Sure Fourni, what is it?

Fournimer's Text Box: uh… there is so much and it hurts and I was wondering, as a friend of course, if you could maybe help me rub —

Draganders' Interruption Text Box: Quick! We got back and Gliint is coming this way chirp!

Palcath's Text Box: Flaming Pit, lass! We only need like 6 more cakes until we can jump up there Yallundy.

Lissa's Text Box: If only we could *Double Jump* we could make it. Stack that cake dwarf! Stack it with your mad cake skills!

Gliint's Yelling Text Box: What the fuck are you three doing? There is no way in the Flaming Pits that I am going to let you idiots get up there. Ha, Flaming Pits! I made myself laugh again.

Fournimer's Text Box: I know how to stop him!

Gliint used his super speed and nearly flew up the spiral cakeway but Fournimer was ready. He was going to save the day, he would stop Gliint. He got his *Blue Bolas* out and aimed at the gnome missile. Gliint dashed by, and Fournimer turned and unleashed his special new attack, promptly missing Gliint completely. The *Bolas* did not stop flying and instead hit Lissa, who had managed to catch Gliint through her own much better idea of using her hands. Lissa was forced to let go, fell onto the cake, sexy like, and was completely helpless and bound. Gliint however, was now free and deftly *Double Jumped* off of Palcath's face and onto the floating island.

Gliint's Text Box: Ha ha losers! I made it up here and you didn't!

Palcath's Text Box: Like Flaming Pit we will not make it up there lad, we only need to stack three more cakes!

Gliint's Text Box: Hahaha! Flaming Pit, were does he come up with that shtick? That was such a great joke and he doesn't even know! Yeah, I almost forgot…

Gliint used the **POINT ANIMATION** directed at the base of the cake structure. The sexy animation made Palcath and Lissa quiver slightly, but it made Fournimer's blue balls ache to the point that he almost passed out. Stupid sexy gnome!

There were bombs at the base of the tower. Lots of bombs. Lots of bombs that were exploding. The cake spiral began to collapse. Gliint was right; they were not going to make it and instead would explode.

Lissa bit Fournimer's leg and simultaneously kicked Palcath in the shin. Fournimer reared up as Palcath jumped into the air. The pair collided midair and the resulting lift of the centaur buck shot Palcath into the air far enough for him to grab the edge of the floating island.

> Palcath's Text Box: Good thinking, lass!

Lissa could not respond because she was both plummeting to Onn below and had a mouth full of centaur hair. Palcath effortlessly swung up to the island.

> Palcath's Text Box: I get my joke now, lad. It was pretty good.

> Gliint's Text Box: Really? Why don't you people give up already?

> Palcath's Text Box: I think you need to give it up lad. We have you outnumbered!

> Gliint's Text Box: We? You don't really get the concept of math do you? You are the only one in your party that made it up here.

> Palcath's Text Box: My math is never wrong! Except that one time when it was wrong, lad!

> Gliint's Text Box: I think you will find it is wrong right now, for you see not only are you the only idiot that made it up here, but there is also…

Gliint ran towards the side of the island and jumped off. Palcath was stunned until Gliint rose into view dramatically. He was standing on the front of a *Parsnip* being flown by a skeleton. Riding on the back was De'vini, with an evil look on her face, and In'ferni who was blindfolded and tied up. Standing on the foliage to complete the drama was Caela, who was wearing absolutely no hint of pants. Gliint used this moment of extreme dramatic importance and activated the **Dummy Account Protocol**. Thousands of misshapen figures in every size and shape appeared around Palcath and began to close in. Avatars, Quest Fairies, NPCs, and even monsters. Some complete, but most not.

> Gliint's Text Box: I think you will find that it is you who is outnumbered.

> Palcath's Text Box: Aw… here.

~~~

> Lissa's Text Box: Seriously Fournimer. What the fuck?

Fournimer started to reply, he was going to defend his idea and explain that it was all an accident, but then he looked at Lissa. As she was, all sexy tied up and covered in frosting, face in a stack of cake, and ass up in the air barely concealed by her skirt. He had never seen anything lovelier, a simple light breeze and he would be able to see up her skirt. When a light breeze caressed his skin, Fournimer felt his horse cock fill to beyond full capacity and his balls began to throb with need.

He needed a hole, he needed it bad.

> Lissa's Text Box: Whatever. At least Palcath got up there so we still have a chance. #SafetyWord. Now can you please untie me?

> Fournimer's Text Box: so heart shaped and… lovely…

> Lissa's Text Box: What?

> Fournimer's Text Box: a little… just a taste.

> Lissa's Text Box: Fourni? What is wrong with you? Untie your stupid *Bolas* already!

Fournimer started to approach the helpless woman with a possessed look in his eyes. His *Centaur Virgin Detector* (which was something he learned he possessed this round) beeped, Lissa wasn't a virgin in her womanly hole, but she was in her back entrance. That knowledge made Fournimer start to leak. This would be it then, no more pressure bottled up inside. It was what he needed! This is what centaurs did after all, mythologically. She had agreed hadn't she? Of course she did. She probably wanted this. Right in the butt. They had always had sort of a sexual tension thing going on.

> Draganders' Text Box: CHIRP! Chirp chirp chirp!

Draganders bit Fournimer in the ear harder than ever before. Fournimer's eyes cleared and he was lifted from the sexual fog. He couldn't believe what he was about to do to one of his best friends. It was horrible and he hated himself for it. He felt sick, violently sick. He couldn't stay here anymore, what if he did it again and he couldn't get snapped out of it? He needed to leave. He galloped off with Draganders frantically flying after him.

> Lissa's Text Box: Hello? Still tied up and covered in cake here.

> Lissa's Text Box: … Fourni? … Where are you?

> Lissa's Text Box: Seriously? He left me here covered in cake without even untying me? #SoFuckedUp.

◊ **Chapter 31** ◊

CYCLE 6: MORNING NEGA-ANDERS, FRIENDS WITH BENEFITS

Nega-Anders awoke and looked around. He rubbed the dreams of piles of fallen frosting out of his mind. At least this time he awoke of his own accord, even if it was impossibly early in the cycle. The Nega-Dryad had demanded his presence a total of five times during the night. Nega-Anders had dismissed all possible follow up encounters, but the Nega-Dryad was persistent. What part of 'once in a playthrough opportunity' didn't he understand?

Nega-Anders didn't want another encounter, not even a little. Everything else, even the things that had wanted to rape him to death had come around eventually, but not in this mirror universe. The constant offers of sexual gratification with the finest bottoms in all of Gentalia was getting to be too much. What a horrible, soul crushing place the inside of a mirror was.

Despite all of his efforts to smuggle out an *Optional Flower*, he had been unsuccessful. There were dozens of them now littering The Nega-Dryad's Grove as a testament to his pent up desire, but they were always out of reach. Nega-Anders wanted nothing but to leave this mirror world. It was like he needed to recap things that had emotionally scarred him during his playthrough but he didn't have an outlet.

Nega-Anders used the *Eureka! Animation.*

> Nega-Anders' Text Box: That is it Nega-Dryad! If I could access my Player Pager you would be on my list! You know what? I'm going to put it on there as soon as I can, so consider yourself on it bucko!

Anders' List (From Memory):

1. Scenic Pillar Meanies
2. All the Glade Jerks
3. Status Effects that Affected Me
4. Constrict Bars that Needed Melee Attacks
5. Traps… sort of
6. (s) Gear… That One Could Come Off, it was Cool Now…
7. All Bugs
8. Hybrid NPC / Monsters… Maybe
9. Jumping Puzzle Blocks Still Suck
10. The Explanation Text Box, so not helpful
11. Breaker
12. All of Onn
13. Hair-Dryers that Belong to Kray
14. That Guy who wasn't Relevant to Any Quests
15. Kray
16. Dragons that I did not Beat at Staring Contests or Give Birth to
17. Breaker Again
18. The Administrators
19. Being Mistaken for a Total Top
20. Nega-Bullies from Mirror Universes

He reached into his somehow there inventory and pulled out some food. He didn't even take notice of what it was, he really no longer cared. He could hardly nibble at it. He was hungry but the thought of eating was making him annoyed. He wrapped it up in the *Napkin* that was holding it and froze.

Another *Napkin* from the paper product stalker? That was what he needed to feel worse. Curiosity got the best of him and he gingerly opened the note and got smacked in the face with a cartoon heart that exploded right after impact. Inside was writing that he recognized from the last note.

> *I know it was you that save me from The Avenger Anders. I will prove it!*

This made sense. The notes had been sent by Fournimer who must be holding his *Ultra-Pack*. That would explain the random attack hearts; they were his *Wonder Kisses* and Fournimer had sealed his notes with a kiss to be romantic. These were not scary at all, they were absolutely charming. The bite marks and drool on them had to be from Draganders, which made them better. That made Nega-Anders forlorn. The horse of his dreams was desperate to find him, but he couldn't do anything about it. He needed to keep this secret.

There was nothing Fourni could do anyway to get here. Centaurs couldn't fly, even with mini-dragons holding onto their butts. If things progressed to Nega-Anders being stuck here until the world ended tomorrow, he would write Fourni back. At least it would be something to look forward to after all the forced awkward dinner conversation with the Nega-Dryad.

> Giganticore Rib Bow+'s Text Box: Wow, aren't you a little miss mopey pants.

> Primary Circle Sword+'s Text Box: I'll say. This cell is so full of 'feel sorry for yourselves' and 'my life is all suckies' that I can barely see across.

> Nega-Anders' Text Box: Huh? My weapons can talk?

> Giganticore Rib Bow+'s Text Box: Sure we can, we are magic. Now hurry up and break out of here!

> Primary Circle Sword+'s Text Box: Yes, we have more important things to do than sit here and cry.

> Nega-Anders' Text Box: I'm in prison. What am I supposed to do, walk out?

> Giganticore Rib Bow+'s Text Box: You know, for an ultimate optional badass, you are pretty thick.

> Primary Circle Sword+'s Text Box: Not just in your big butt.

Nega-Anders changed to *Nega-Blush Shade #4*. For the first time since being a pixel, he changed colours, he guessed at least. It was pretty dark in here and not because of all the mope.

> Giganticore Rib Bow+'s Text Box: That is exactly what you should do! It is a video game prison, those can't hold shit.

> Primary Circle Sword+'s Text Box: You have ultimate optional boss powers. Your stats are off the charts. Punch a hole in the wall and walk out of here!

A simple test punch proved his weapons' theory. He punched a hole clear through the wall and revealed an all too easy way out. He had never thought about destroying part of the area to get out. He felt foolish now.

> Nega-Anders' Text Box: I can't believe that I didn't think of that. Now let's punch a hole through that other wall and go get the last *Optional Flower*. This is amazing! I feel so energized. Ready to take on the world!

Giganticore Rib Bow+'s Text Box: Perfect! We shall do that! Right after you energize yourself properly.

Primary Circle Sword+'s Text Box: You didn't get enough sleep back there to really heal. If it wasn't still the dead of night, I could probably still see the emotional scars.

Nega-Anders' Text Box: I guess we can wait until morning to come back.

Giganticore Rib Bow+'s Text Box: Come, I know a place that would be a perfect place to rest.

Primary Circle Sword+'s Text Box: Follow me!

Pulled forward by his enchanted, seemingly now intelligent weapons, Nega-Anders was forced to either fly or plummet. They flew at breakneck speed, out of the mirrored area, through the squishy portal, and back into the regular destroyed Castle in the Sky. They flew towards one of the only intact areas, a tall tower, and landed with a bit of a thump.

Primary Circle Sword+'s Text Box: This place is perfect. It is right beside the teleporter back to the starting area, there is a fluffy bed inside that used to belong to some NPC who died, and the monsters are easy pickings.

Giganticore Rib Bow+'s Text Box: We only have a little time to rest, and then we need to go! Important things to do!

Saving the entire game was important, but Nega-Anders had to admit he was tired. Some comfortable rest in a real bed would do him wonders. At least by then the sun would have come up for him to see properly. He stepped into the tower through the missing *Left Handed Door*.

The inside of the tower was completely unscathed. Breaker must have either not noticed its plush interior, or had a strong liking for grandiose tower-themed libraries. The bedroom would be in the top of the tower, that much was obvious, and Nega-Anders took a mighty step towards the direction of the stairwell. He was taken aback when from the inside of the stairwell, flitted a glowing ball of green light. It was a Quest Fairy.

Nega-Anders' Text Box: A Green Quest Fairy? No way! Abby?

Primary Circle Sword+'s Text Box: Pfft! No, don't be silly. That is a generic Pixie monster.

> Giganticore Rib Bow+'s Text Box: They share the same model as those annoying Quest Fairies, except these have butterfly wings.

Lazy developers had struck again, this was a generic monster. It did begin to follow him up the staircase, as did many others that noticed him. By the time he was at the midway landing/fruit table display, he had twenty of the little creatures floating above his head.

> Nega-Anders' Text Box: Why do they keep following me?

> Primary Circle Sword+'s Text Box: I think they are misfiled under monster. They are probably supposed to be scenery because they don't have any attacks. You can —

> Giganticore Rib Bow+'s Text Box: get the whole tower of them to follow you then wipe them all out with a single area attack. Not worth any Experience Points mind you, but funny.

He really didn't want to hurt the misfiled creatures, but by the time he had made it up to the bedroom of the tower there were six and a half rainbows of Pixies following him. His weapons were placed into a handy weapon rack (despite their desire to kill the floating parade following them), and they faded off into a deep slumber.

Though the comfortable bed was missing the one thing that made a bed comfortable, the colour green, but it did look inviting. Nega-Anders was bushed and climbed onto the surface. The sheets didn't open, but it beat the stuffing out of his previous quarters. With heavy eyelids closing, and quite a few curious eyes watching him, Nega-Anders drifted into a dreamless sleep.

~~~

He woke up with a start. Frantically struggling against bonds that he now knew held him tight. There was no escaping them and gradually the adrenaline wore off to the point that Nega-Anders could look around calmly. There was no boss here, so whatever had him *Bound Most* had left the area. That didn't make sense, why didn't it do anything to him after tying him down to the bed. Why would it leave him here?

The answer had to be somewhere, and Nega-Anders surveyed the situation more closely. His weapons were still snoring quietly in the weapon rack; they had nothing to do with this. Perhaps the bindings themselves would hold a solution, and he looked closer at them. Thin threads had pinned him down to the mattress, tied to the quilt buttons. Hundreds of them, all holding him down fast. Little, thin, braided, and in a variety of colours.

> Nega-Anders' Text Box: Wait a round, are those ropes?

They were ropes, and they were keeping him from moving even a length unit. As he watched a final little rope flew up over his chest, and was caught by something. Crooking his head to the side, Nega-Anders saw a Pixie grab the line and tie it to another button. Now that he looked around the room, no longer blind to unimportant monsters he noticed all manner of Pixies watching his every move. There was an entire army of them, and during his slumber they had positively Gullivered him!

Each Pixie was no bigger than his hand, but working together they had managed to restrain him. Nega-Anders wondered in a panic what the little monsters could want.

A round of cheering noises like happy little bells was heard from the army of multi-coloured soldiers. Now that the giant was under control, the Pixies began to celebrate. Celebrating, it turned out, was grabbing the nearest Pixie which you fancied and planting a big kiss on them while your bodies writhed about excitedly. The captured giant really hadn't seen that coming, which was unusual this late in the series.

Nega-Anders pondered this turn of events for a moment. These were not bosses, they were normal monsters. Normal monsters simply did not do sexy things, everyone knew that. They didn't have enough polygons to contain the Coding or the processing power to get creatively sexy with. Perhaps though, with so many of the same type, in the same place, at the same time they had begun to develop sort of a group consciousness. Nega-Anders knew where he had seen this exact thing before, with beetles. Individually, the monsters were nothing, but together all working in unison they had become a swarm. A hivemind of naughty thoughts, a swarm of sex.

That is what was happening now, and Nega-Anders watched in awe as the writhing Pixie orgy continued to break out all over his chest and stomach. Little six length unit tall humanoids with butterfly wings were rolling all over his body, blissfully dealing with each other's newfound sexuality. Originally, besides the different colours, they all shared the same model. Now that they became charged with sexual energy, they were different. They all kept the same model, a thinner, male model with lithe movements and pointed ears, but they were now all sporting different haircuts. It was enough to at least try and tell them apart.

A shy yellow Pixie with a #7 Hairstyle, the one with a lot of bangs, missed out on the opportunity to grab a close by red Pixie when a pair of blue Pixies grabbed the rest to make a blue and red kissing sandwich. Blushing too hard to join in, the Yellow Pixie decided instead to make out with something else to make up for lost opportunities and it chose Nega-Anders' left Nega-Nipple.

The tiniest of tongues began to sweetly play all over the gigantic mouthful of Nega-Nipple. An errant Purple Pixie backed up and hit the Yellow Pixie over, causing it to nearly swallow the Nega-Nipple. The little Yellow Pixie's mouth could barely contain the massive nub, but it didn't look like the little guy was going to give up easily. After a few practice attempts, the Yellow Pixie got into a good rhythm, bobbing his little head up and down. Bangs constantly getting in the way, and free hand constantly moving hair aside, the Yellow Pixie was doing its absolute best to fellate the nipple.

This little Yellow Pixie had discovered oral sex, and now all of the Pixies could do it. The kissing orgy shifted to a blowjob party. Every Pixie was now deep into the newly discovered sexual practice of licking dick. There was only a single Pixie that didn't have its mouth on a little hard Pixie member, and its tiny glowing dick in another, and that was the Yellow Pixie, who had decided to not change from its original target.

The erotic display combined with the gentle sucking motions caused fifteen things to happen, in the following obvious order:

1. Nega-Anders used the *Gasp Animation*.
2. The Yellow Pixie got encouraged and started to fellate that Nega-Nipple for all it was worth.
3. Nega-Anders used the *Mmmph! Animation*.
4. The Yellow Pixie brushed his bangs to the side, to help give the giant a better look at the action.
5. Nega-Anders became excited, and his Nega-Nipple engorged.
6. The Yellow Pixie could no longer handle the bigger Nega-Nipple orally, and it choked and sputtered a bit.
7. Nega-Anders used the *Shudder Animation*. So big was the giant in comparison to the little creatures that many fell over during their kissing and gyrating displays. The Yellow Pixie toppled over head first and landed with a cute thump, eyes completely covered in bangs.
8. Nega-Anders watched expectedly as the little yellow creature tried to stand up, but slipped on some saliva.
9. The Yellow Pixie fell over again, this time he landed square on the Nega-Nipple and in a feat thought to be impossible by proctologists everywhere; the Nega-Nipple had a Nega-Nipple-Slip and entered the little creature anally.
10. Nega-Anders blinked.
11. The Yellow Pixie changed to *Blush Shade #Pixie* and tried to get up, but by doing so he felt the exquisite pleasure that only the removal of a giant nipple from a rectum can provide. The Pixie wanted more, and it began to bounce heartily on the Nega-Nipple, annoying bangs constantly getting in the way.
12. The Pixie blowjob party watched the scene intently, for now they knew about anal sex. The Nega-Nipple was clearly a bad influence. All manner of Pixies claimed a fresh virgin hole and plowed in deep. They now knew how to fuck.
13. Nega-Anders used a *Strangely Happy Grin Animation*. His faith in the Game was restored by 98%. No longer was he in a bad mood about the Nega-Dryad. There was a Pixie butt orgy happening on his chest. That was more important than one crumblicker.
14. The Yellow Pixie used the *Tinkle Animation*, which cause a bell like moan. It was exceedingly sexy.
15. Nega-Anders' Nega-Cock twitched.

A full rainbow compliment of Pixies took notice of the giant's giant beginning to rumble from below and flitted over to investigate. They now understood what this was, a cock like their own. After a Blue Pixie, with a *#23 Hairstyle* (exceptionally long and curly) attempted to hoist up the big slowly hardening member, it accidently discovered masturbation for the entire Pixie collective. Every cock that was exposed was eagerly grabbed and tugged upon, and the Nega-Cock was no exception. Seven little sets of hands encouraged the captive cock to fully come to life.

Gently blowing a pair of handjob swapping Purple Pixies out of his field of vision, Nega-Anders watched on. He could see his cock grow higher and harder with each beat of his heart. Wider, thicker, straighter, and higher it grew as it reached its maximum capacity, all while the happy encouragement of the rainbow brigade incited intense feelings of need with their erotic display. The Nega-elf wanted his cock to be full, his desire had reached its peak, and with a mighty flex he caused the last few pulses to leap ahead and finish the job.

The little naked rainbow started to have a twinkly bell sound debate. Nega-Anders didn't have a clue as to what they were talking about, but he did have a hunch it was about the pillar of cock, standing nearly twice as tall as themselves. Perhaps they were deciding what in the map to do with it.

It was the Blue Pixie with the long curly hair that took the initiative. He began to lead the others in a round of what he had discovered: masturbation. Each of the little arms wrapped as tight as they could around the sturdy Nega-Cock. Jacking off the big member as best as they could only caused Nega-Anders to smile sweetly. Yes, it certainly felt great, but their sheer amount of determination was so enduring. They were tying their hardest to make their captive experience everything that they had learned about, but rounds of jacking off a Nega-Cock twice as tall as you are can quickly wear out even the hardiest of fey creatures.

Panting is what gave the Yellow Pixie with the annoying bangs his idea. With the help of his wings he gave Nega-Anders a big lemon-scented slurp all the way up his shaft to the tip. Licking was easier work than masturbation for the diminutive creatures and they all followed suit. Soon the Nega-Cock was dripping with the assorted scents of Pixie saliva. The captive was enjoying this particular idea thoroughly, and showed his appreciation by releasing a big dribble of his own scented fluid.

Closest to the tip, a Red Pixie watched intently as the gush of Nega-Pre squirted out of the giant. After greedily swallowing up a few mouthfuls, the Red Pixie with the *#1 Hairstyle* (the buzz cut) noticed something. The slit that the fluid had come out of looked much like something else the Pixies had recently learned to use. Nega-Anders was taken by surprise when a tiny red member was shoved into his big slit. The wings helped balance the little red blur as it pumped inside with vigor, and soon every one of the compliment was taking a turn on the new kind of thing to penetrate.

An innocent looking Green Pixie came up last to the slit. Nega-Anders could tell that this little fellow was more of the being a slit type, than the using a slit type. The

#6 Hairstyle (a style close to Nega-Anders' Nega-Heart) accented his cute little face with the pointed ears. This little fellow looked nothing like Nega-Anders would have if he were six length units tall and a Pixie, he was green with the right hairstyle. Still, the little guy was precious. Sitting down on the big member, the Green Pixie began to rub his impossibly tiny hole all over the dripping Nega-Cock. Its legs were splayed out at funny angles, but it kept trying its hardest, bobbing up and down on the member thicker than its own body. With Nega-Anders' big member sticking right into the splayed legs of a little green elfish creature he had come full circle in his encounter experiences. He was now experiencing exactly what the Frost Gigas had experienced during that encounter so long ago, and he was giving the experience to a little green elfish creature that was moaning like an elfboy in heat. It was such a strange turn around, and it was also strangely exciting.

Nega-Anders yearned to be moaning like that Green Pixie. Everything had mistook him for a total top lately, and he still had a new elfhole waiting to be broken in.

It was the Orange Pixie's turn now to think of something to try out on the big member, but the Green Pixie simply refused to be moved from its pedestal. Necessity had caused the Orange Pixie to abandon his original plan and to think up a new one. He ran a hand through his *#11 Hairstyle* (half shaved, half longer and swept to one side) and thought. The idea came to him like a bolt of lightning, mostly because it was a bolt of lightning. He used *Pixie Lightning Bolt* and directed it at the meat pillar. A jolt of electricity ran through Nega-Anders' body. Fortunately, it did not have enough power to overcome the Optional Boss Statistics and caused no damage, but it did cause a pleasurable little wave to hit Nega-Anders everywhere. Soon, all the Pixies with described haircuts (and the ones with described haircuts yet to come) were casting this spell on the big Nega-Cock, and Nega-Anders was moaning with over stimulation.

A Purple Pixie, with a *#5 Hairstyle* (at that crucial stage when it could be called either medium hair or short hair) was at a loss for what to try next. He flitted around to all of the other little scenes happening on Nega-Anders' chest and stomach and asked for advice, but none of the humping masses had any useful suggestions. The Purple Pixie flew up to Nega-Anders' face and started to ring out with assorted bell noises. Presumably, it was attempting to ask Nega-Anders for advice, but he couldn't understand a single ring of it. As the Purple Pixie was listing off some suggestions (Nega-Anders guessed this by the hand gestures). He interrupted it by giving it a light and deliberate lick from its inner calf up to the shoulder blade with one swift action. Only stunned for a round before succumbing to the idea, the Purple Pixie was getting long passionate licks from the giant captive. It could only be the object of envy for so long, and within a few rounds every Pixie was taking turns getting long sensuous licks over their entire bodies. Even the Green Pixie joined in, but it only wanted to get licked in one place that tasted like lime.

There was only one important Pixie left to go, a Pink Pixie with a *#7 Hairstyle* (known by others as the non angst-filled emo hair). Nega-Anders was a little upset that it was not either violet or indigo, but that was the proper rainbow, not a Pixie Rainbow. Pixie Rainbows always include pink. The Pink Pixie could only think of one thing, and it acted on impulse to do that. It flew around Nega-Anders with great speed, zapping off any quilt buttons it could find. Ropes snapped away, they released the tied up body of the giant. Some of the Pixies gasped as their tight grasp on the prisoner was severed, but Nega-Anders wanted to earn their trust and waited patiently for every rope to be removed by them. Once he was free he cautiously sat up, and reached up to the Pink Pixie.

Little pink feet landed upon his hand, and Nega-Anders brought the Pink Pixie closer. Originally his intent had been to discuss some options with the creature, but once he opened his mouth to Text Box the Pixie had a great idea. It started to furiously beat its little pink member and Nega-Anders promptly forgot what his idea had been. When three other Pixies joined the Pink Pixie upon the perch and joined in aimed squarely at Nega-Anders' tongue, the genital giant decided that this was a great plan and grabbed his own member to participate.

The tiniest of squirts came from the Pink Pixie, which tasted of peaches. Exhausted, but still happy to help, the Pink Pixie motioned for others to come up and join. Soon there was no more room upon Nega-Anders' hand as it was completely covered in small fey creatures jerking off into the maw of their once captive giant. Each little gush was accented by a cute little tinkle and a strangely fruity taste. Resisting the urge to lick his lips, as he wanted to keep all of it until the last moment on his tongue, Nega-Anders started to beat his big Nega-Cock with inspired vigor, and with the assistance of already gushed Pixies.

Each little scene on his hand was inspiring. There was fucking, blowjobs, handjobs, groups, and singles of every colour. Each little shot was purposefully shot into the giant, and Nega-Anders was certain he saw at least six various haircuts repeat but did not complain. When the shy little Green Pixie, with Nega-Anders' haircut, showed up and shyly began to jerk off Nega-Anders watched. The Green Pixie grimaced and shot his little tinkle driblets and Nega-Anders closed his mouth to savour the fruity taste of all of the captors. With that taste of the rainbow, the rest of the pixies reached critical mass.

The orgy burst into flames thanks to all of the stick rubbing. Nega-Anders was thankful that he was close. He came out of necessity, showering all of the flaming Pixies with his Nega-Spunk. The fire was out through the power of jizz.

The Pixies rolled in the life-saving nectar, licked it up, flung it in the air, and swallowed every thick droplet. Nega-Anders had lost his breath. He could not react fast enough to stop the little captors from flitting away in unison and caring their reward: a small purple flower.

It didn't make sense the Pixies were not an Optional Boss. Before Nega-Anders could think about it at length, his weaponry rustled awake.

Giganticore Rib Bow+'s Text Box: Much better!

Primary Circle Sword+'s Text Box: I see you defeated all those stupid Pixies, good job.

Nega-Anders' Text Box: I did.

Giganticore Rib Bow+'s Text Box: Whatever, details. Don't care.

Primary Circle Sword+'s Text Box: Okay, time to go! We have places to be.

Nega-Anders' Text Box: Yes, we need to go pick up one of those purple flowers!

Giganticore Rib Bow+'s Text Box: I already told you, we don't have time for —

Primary Circle Sword+'s Text Box: your silly things. We have more important things to do.

Nega-Anders' Text Box: But there is nothing more important than the *Optional Flowers* for saving the world.

Giganticore Rib Bow+'s Text Box: Yeah, yeah we all heard the bunny.

Primary Circle Sword+'s Text Box: There is something much more important, trust me.

Nega-Anders' Text Box: What could possibly be more important?

Giganticore Rib Bow+'s Text Box: You are right of course, there isn't. I didn't want to alarm you is all. See that Nega-Dryad has mirror stats. There isn't anyth—

Primary Circle Sword+'s Text Box: ing you can do against a backwards 8 and win. We should go while we can.

Nega-Anders' Text Box: Maybe I could—

Giganticore Rib Bow+ and Primary Circle Sword+'s Simultaneous Interruption Text Boxes: NO! You can't win. I... uh... found a different Optional Boss for you. We should go there.

Nega-Anders' Text Box: Where is there exactly?

Giganticore Rib Bow+ and Primary Circle Sword+'s Simultaneous Text Boxes: You don't want to ruin the dramatic reveal now do you? Let's go!

Despite the feelings that Nega-Anders was feeling right now, which included but were not limited to Nega-Confusion, Nega-Curiosity, and Nega-Suspicion, he didn't want to be the one responsible for ruining any kind of dramatic reveal. He left the library tower, and stepped into the daylight for the first time since becoming Nega.

Giganticore Rib Bow+ and Primary Circle Sword+'s Simultaneous Text Boxes: Wow, I got to say, I am really digging the colour choice.

◈ **Chapter 32** ◈

CYCLE 6
GROUP R, OFF THE
SHIZZEL FOR RIZZEL

Roodg's Text Box: i GET IT! bLOWING THE *gOLDEN tIN wHISTLE* OPENS UP THIS SECRET DUNGEON.

E. E. Lynn's Text Box: N0p3. Fl|pp|ng th|s l3\/3r d|d. Y0u bl0\/\/|t 4t teh 3ndn3ss.

Roodg's Text Box: tHEN WHY DID I BLOW IT NOW?

E. E. Lynn's Text Box: | \/\/4nt3d t0 t3st y0ur lung c4p4c|ty & u suuuuuuuuuck3d.

Roodg's Text Box: iT ISN'T FAIR! i HAVE REALLY SKINNY LUNGS! wHY? iS THERE A VINE SWINGING PUZZLE OVER WATER INSIDE OR SOMETHING?

Roodg used the *Shudder at the Thought Animation*. E. E. Lynn responded with a *Kawaii Kitty Girl Animation*, which for some reason was a standard animation included in the game.

E. E. Lynn's Text Box: 2 s33 h0\/\/ l0ng u c4n l|ck v4g b3f0r3 c0/\/\|ng up 2 br34th3. ^-^

By simply not responding to that statement and walking into the dungeon, Roodg ended that particular conversation. Roodg had tried to sleep all night, but did not get any (unlike E. E. Lynn who did get some, but not sleep). Everything with this girl was sex. She had never stopped talking about it or doing it all night long, not even for a round. During her orgy with the Posh Welsh Tribal Chief and his pet Basilisk she had tried to carry on a conversation with Roodg, who was in the other room, about the lost art of handjobs. After her skinny dip in the ocean and love fest with the Krakalackin', she had lectured Roodg about the proper insertion techniques of tentacles. Even during her visit to the Secret Sex Room of Naughty Delights (which she had dragged an almost-sleeping Roodg to), she made them up the stakes and throw some high level monsters into the Sex Pit. Not many survived that bloodbath besides E. E. Lynn.

Roodg had decided something this morning. Well, two things. One: E. E. Lynn was completely insane, but that was already public knowledge. Two: Getting off of this The Mist Covered Island You Knew About But Couldn't Land on Because of the Mist was a good thing to do. Sooner rather than later. If there was something in this dungeon that could make that dream of escaping happen Roodg would do it. Keeping your head down (or in Roodg's case, between one and three heads down) and advancing through the dungeon would help finish this area faster.

Getting off this island and meeting up with sane avatars was something Roodg was looking forward to. E. E. Lynn had followed into this dungeon, The Magical Misting Station, with a record number of hands down her skirt, three. She had picked up one hand, including most of the arm, from the remains of an unfortunate NPC named Sexgrippa. While Sexgrippa did have several spare arms, the fact still remained that E. E. Lynn was walking around with a severed limb down the front of her skirt that was still mostly fresh and moving.

Roodg wanted to leave this area behind, or at least E. E. Lynn behind. Roodg appreciated the eccentric, it was pretty much a calling card for the night elf, but E. E. Lynn was not eccentric, she was an entire secret bonus level of crazy.

This dungeon didn't look at all like a normal dungeon. It was tiled in wonderful mosaic representations of important Isle of Islana locations. This place had a high art budget, so it was clearly important. Judging by all the train tracks here and the motif of trains around the entire place, plus the fact that it was a station, Roodg believed that what they had come for was a train. That would make travel difficult, due to the lack of train tracks anywhere else except inside this location.

> E. E. Lynn's Text Box: B3tch4 \/\/0nd3r|n' \/\/h4t th|s |s 4ll 4b0ut, huh?

Roodg had to admit, E. E. Lynn was right. Curiosity for this area would warrant a reply.

> Roodg's Text Box: yEP! i DON'T KNOW HOW ANYONE WOULD FIND THIS PLACE OR KNOW WHAT TO BRING.

E. E. Lynn's Text Box: Th|s |s p4rt 0f 4 qu3st l|n3 c4ll3d Th3 C|rcl3 0f |sl4n4 |sl4nds. P4rt f|\/3 0f s|><. U sk|pped 0\/3r s0/\/\3 0f teh |sl4nds.

Roodg's Text Box: i DIDN'T. Jorthan the Male Troll Monk SOLVED THE PUZZLE ON dESSERTED iSLAND.

E. E. Lynn's Text Box: | \/\/0nd3r h0\/\/ h3 d|d th4t \/\/|th0ut teh *D3cod3r R|ng* th4t |s 0n |sl4nd Du /\/\0rt3?

Roodg's Text Box: hE WAS STUCK THERE A LONG TIME, BESIDES IT WASN'T MUCH OF A PUZZLE, IT WAS WRITTEN IN pIG lATIN.

E. E. Lynn's Text Box: But P|g L4t|n |s h4rd!

Roodg's Text Box: yES, IF YOU ARE fRENCH cANADIAN LIKE Jorthan. oTHERWISE NOT SO MUCH!

E. E. Lynn's Text Box: \/\/3 s0 sh0uld d0 st3p 6 r|ght aft3r th|s!

Roodg's Text Box: wAIT, tHE cIRCLE OF iSLANA iSLANDS MEANS THAT WITH iSLAND dU mORTE, dESSERTED iSLAND AND HERE… THE NEXT ISLAND IN THE CIRCLE IS THAT IS THE FLOATING ONE IN THE SKY ABOVE oNN!

E. E. Lynn's Text Box: Y3p! Th4t |s teh /\/\0st b4d4ss pl4c3 in teh \/\/h0l3 g4/\/\3. Th4t |s \/\/hy th3r3 |s—

Roodg's Interruption Text Box: i ALREADY KNOW WHAT YOU ARE GOING TO SAY. 'THAT IS WHYZORS THERE IS TEH HUGE BOSS GUARDING THIS WHATEVER IT IS WE CAME HERE FOR!'.

E. E. Lynn's Text Box: N0, but th4t \/\/4s cl0s3. Teh b0ss |sn't gu4rd|ng 4nyth|ng. \/\/h4t \/\/3 c4/\/\3 f0r |s teh b0ss!

They were standing on a bridge covered in railway ties. E. E. Lynn pointed far below where they were standing. At first all Roodg saw was a glimmer off a far distant surface. Whatever it was, it was moving.

Roodg's Text Box: iS THAT THE TRAIN?

E. E. Lynn's Text Box: D0n't b3 stup|d. Th|s Isn't Tr4|nv|ll3.

Roodg's Text Box: tRAINVILLE?

E. E. Lynn's Text Box: Duh. Teh c|ty 0f l|v|ng tr4|ns fr0/\/\ teh /\/\4|n st0ryl|n3!

Roodg's Text Box: i SKIPPED THAT ONE.

E. E. Lynn's Text Box: Y0ur l0ss. C0/\/\/\/\4nd3r Tr4|n |s hungzorz!

Shapes began to form in the darkness as Roodg closely surveyed the scene. What was it bashing around on the tracks, in a set pattern like that? It took until they got right up to the objects and a bright light from the ceiling shone on them for the objects to become visible. All of them were moving on determined paths, happily crashing into spike traps, getting chopped in half by spinning blades, and roasted by triple sized ancient Welshmen figurines breathing out all kinds of magical attacks (mostly fire).

Roodg's Text Box: aRE YOU KIDDING ME?

E. E. Lynn's Text Box: \/\/h4t?

Roodg's Text Box: tHIS IS THE MINECART LEVEL?

E. E. Lynn's Text Box: 3><c|t3d?

If Roodg was going to be honest, it wasn't something to be excited about. Even less so when E. E. Lynn spurted out some random directions and jumped into a cart at full speed. Roodg didn't even get a chance to write down half of them, and unlike Mr. Max's directions these did not come with a memorable song to facilitate remembrance. This was dangerous. Likely it would be game-ending.

Roodg got into the mine cart and used a *Take a Deep Breath Animation*. A few rounds of indecision later, Roodg came to a startling realization.

Roodg's Text Box: nOW THAT i THINK ABOUT IT... i CAN'T DIE HERE. THERE WOULD BE ABSOLUTELY NO PLOT SIGNIFICANCE TO IT IF i DID. iF i WAS GOING TO DIE, i WOULD HAVE DIED AT THE vINE sWINGING pUZZLE. fLAMING pIT, i WOULDN'T HAVE EVEN LANDED HERE ON THIS ISLAND IF i WAS GOING TO DIE BEFORE SOME KIND OF EPIC SHOWDOWN. wHY AM i EVEN WORRIED RIGHT NOW?

E. E. Lynn's Text Box: G0!

To answer Roodg's question E. E. Lynn pushed the mine cart with an impressive force for such a small cat and she jumped into the cart as it took off careening down the path. The mine cart took off at warp speed through impossible to navigate paths, break-neck turns, and mind breaking logic (why would mine cart tracks split into paths that end in shear drops?)

>Left< >Left< >Right<

> Roodg's Text Box: hOW DID YOU >Up< GET BACK TO >Hit the Seven Targets< THE TOP?

> E. E. Lynn's Text Box: >Right< T00k \/\/r0ng turn. >Left< R|ght h3r3, \/\/3nt r|ght.

> Roodg's Text Box: iNTO THE BED >Insert the Rabbinate Statue of a Woman With a Jewel Encrusted Harp< OF SPIKES?

> E. E. Lynn's Text Box: Y3p! U c4n st|ll >Down to Shaft 6< s33 teh bl00d!

Having no time to look at the accident scene, due to the need to complete a series of well timed mine cart jumps, all Roodg saw was a flash of blood and what was either the corpse of a catgirl, or an erotic statue of a llama.

The mine cart and occupants were completely hidden by rocks for a few rounds, which was actually a cleverly hidden loading screen, and the occupants reached their destination. Roodg had never been so happy to see a bottom. Now they were at the heart of the mine and lair of the dreaded—

> Roodg's Interruption Text Box: iT IS A BUNCH OF DICKS? wE CAME ALL THIS WAY FOR A ROOM FULL OF GIANT DICKS? aRE YOU KIDDING ME WITH THIS?

> E. E. Lynn's Text Box: \/\/0\/\/! | d|dn't n0t|c3 b4. Teh L4r\/4 d0 l00k l|k3 g|4nt d|cks! 4/\/\4z3b4lls! L0L @ Ch4rl|3!

> Roodg's Text Box: lARVA? Charlie? aMAZEBALLS? dID YOU DIE?

> E. E. Lynn's Text Box: Duh Ch4rl|3, teh guy \/\/|th r3pr3ss3d h0/\/\0s3><u4l t3nd4nc|3s! | n33d 2 t3ll h|/\/\ 4b0ut teh d|ck! N0, th3s3 r teh l4r\/4. \/\/3 r|d3 th3/\/\ |n 4 s33d 34t|ng /\/\|n|g4/\/\3 2 s33 \/\/h0 g3ts 2 cOntr0lz0rs t3h 4dult!

> Roodg's Text Box: yOU MEAN THE GREEN SEEDS THAT LOOK LIKE ANUSES AND THE RED VAGINA ONES?

> E. E. Lynn's Text Box: H4! Th3y d0. H|l4r|0us! \/\/h03\/3r 34ts /\/\0r3 g3ts t0 3\/0l\/3 |nt0 teh... 4ctu4lly | d0n't kn0\/\/ \/\/h4t th3y turn int0.

> Roodg's Text Box: sO... WHAT YOU ARE SAYING IS THAT WE NEED TO HAVE A GIANT DICK RIDING CONTEST TO PLOW THROUGH THE MOST ANUSES AND PUSSIES TO DETERMINE WHO GETS TO CONTROL THE LIKELY OMEGA PENIS THAT ONE OF THESE LARVA WILL GROW INTO?

> E. E. Lynn's Text Box: Y3p!

Without missing a beat, Roodg executed a mighty regulation *Jump* onto a nearby larva penis—a long skinny charcoal specimen that both matched the avatar's skin colour and body style.

> Roodg's Text Box: yOU ARE so GOING TO LOSE!

As if to reply, the catgirl hoisted herself up onto the most lewd looking larva in the entire area. A knobby red specimen covered in veins, it was constantly throbbing, the veins twice fold. Roodg thought that perhaps the kitty was right; this Charlie fellow might secretly be a pervert.

Giant numbers appeared above their heads in the form of 2:00.

> Countdown Clock's Text Box: Three. Two. One. Go!

The buzzer rang and the pair was off like a Shlot Flasher. The pair meaning Roodg and the slim charcoal larva penis. They were banging out anus and pussy seeds like nobody's business. With each seed they collected the larva got a little longer. They were completely oblivious to the fact that E. E. Lynn's attempt to pick the most sexual mount had backfired. The catgirl was trapped under a giant throbbing red larva that could do nothing but lie there and throb. Despite her cries for help that she couldn't believe this was happening again there was nothing she could do to even start the minigame.

When the buzzer rang out the score was an impressive 154 seeds for Roodg, all collected through seed slamming skill, versus an equally impressive 1 seed for E. E. Lynn, collected when a seed materialized right beside her mount and was accidentally collected it during an errant throb.

> Countdown Clock's Text Box: The winner of the Seed Slamming Minigame is Roodg with 154 points! Congratulations for setting a new all-time record beating the previous score of 'Error 78BSS: No Previous High Scores Found.'! Enjoy your prize!

E. E. Lynn finally managed to get out from under her restrictive mount-member to watch Roodg's already now impressively sized penile larva start to glow. It turned a bright, impossible to look at white, then flew up into the air and began to rotate as things that are transforming always do. Roodg was still riding it, and knew that transformation sequences had high budgets and were flashy, but did not hurt at all, due to having already experience one. The larva started to grow a pair of legs. It grew more pairs of legs down its long body, and even more. Finally, after the fiftieth pair of legs grew, the white light exploded and revealed the Gigantic Hover Centipede (charcoal gray body colour with red trim).

> Roodg's Text Box: sAWESOME!

> Text Box: This Gigantic Hover Centipede will allow you to travel anywhere in the game world, even places you have never gone.

> Roodg's Text Box: sAWESOME! oKAY, GET ON E. E. Lynn. i KNOW WHERE WE NEED TO GO FIRST.

> E. E. Lynn's Text Box: KK!

> Text Box: Please take a moment to register your *Gigantic Hover Centipede* by giving it a name.

> Roodg's Text Box: hMMM...

~~~

> Roodg's Text Box: oKAY BOYS GET ON!

> Roodg's Text Box: ... uH? ... bOYS?

> Roodg's Text Box: oH NO! aRE THEY DEAD? cURSED? pOSSESSED?

> E. E. Lynn's Text Box: H/\/\/\/\/\/\...

E. E. Lynn used the *Poke Someone in the Eye Dual Animation* with both Trev Terra and Jorthan the Male Troll Monk. Amazingly, she choose to be the pokee and not the poker.

> E. E. Lynn's Text Box: N4h. Th3y l00k AFK.

> Cinnamon's Text Box: We don't have time for people to be away from keyboard. Grab them and sit their asses down.

The All Seeing Eye Dog and Nine Circles of Hellcat shifted in their seats. They were getting antsy and were ready to hover out of here. Something startled them and they perked their ears up and ran between the two groups of avatars. They began to snarl at Trev Terra and Jorthan, much to Roodg, Cinnamon, and E. E. Lynn's confusion.

> Trev Terra's Text Box: Come on, do you really hate us that much?

Jorthan the Male Troll Monk's Text Box: Yeah, you are our frickin' abilities. Without us you wouldn't even exist you ungrateful jerks.

Trev Terra's Text Box: I know right? They are being completely unreasonable here.

Jorthan the Male Troll Monk's Text Box: I don't even care anymore honestly. Regardless though, I was right.

Trev Terra's Text Box: I know you were. There totally was voices coming from over here.

Jorthan the Male Troll Monk's Text Box: I know and it is Roodg! Roodg isn't dead!

Trev Terra's Text Box: That is super exciting! We should kiss in celebration!

Jorthan the Male Troll Monk's Text Box: Uh… but.

Trev Terra's Text Box: Right… man bits. Icky.

Roodg was too confused to use the *Confused Animation*.

Roodg's Text Box: uH. wHAT?

Jorthan the Male Troll Monk's Text Box: Sorry. Trev and Jorthan are still 'celebrating' but I think they are almost done.

Trev Terra's Text Box: Yeah, I think so too. The screaming is pretty much over.

Jorthan the Male Troll Monk's Text Box: We got back from getting sandwiches and heard voices so we came over here to investigate. Well, sandwiches and tacos.

Trev Terra's Text Box: Our screens suck. I'm blindfolded, tied up, and gagged.

Jorthan the Male Troll Monk's Text Box: Yeah, and I'm completely locked out of my keyboard right now. All I can do is stare at other avatars sitting in chairs that don't move. Lame.

Roodg's Text Box: lESBITWINS! i FOUND US ALL A WAY OFF OF THIS CRAPHOLE OF AN EXPANSION! wE NEED TO COLLECT EVERYONE ASAP!

Trev Terra's Text Box: We will sit the boys down then go tell them to freshen up.

Jorthan the Male Troll Monk's Text Box: Do us a favour. Call off our own guard dogs and cats first would you?

Trev Terra's Text Box: Wait. What was that Janey? I can't hear you will all that taco in your mouth.

Jorthan the Male Troll Monk's Text Box: It was who to pick up next. Got it.

E. E. Lynn's Text Box: 0k4y, but 4ft3r th4t | n33d 2 g3t 2 0nn.

◈ **Chapter 33** ◈

CYCLE 6
GROUP B, LEVEL 1

Hippolyta's Text Box: Stop Max. Here is a good spot I think.

Mr. Max's Text Box: No... but... If we—

Zal Finn III's Interruption Text Box: No, please stop.

Mr. Max's Text Box: But, but...

Mr. Max used the *Sigh Animation*. He knew they were right. They were still an entire forest away from the Golden Poffles and the girls had hit Level 2. There was no way they could make it there in time. They were going to fade away into nothingness and there was nothing he could do to stop it. Worst of all, this was all his fault. Breaker had done this to try and kill him and now these innocent lesbians were going to pay the price for his earlier deeds of ignoring others to Level himself. He placed the girls on the ground, and sat down, feeling horrible.

They all sat there in silence for some rounds, each thinking about different things. Content to rest for a moment. When they heard the Backwards Short Trumpet Song that signalled Level 1, they all snapped out of the relaxation trance.

Zal Finn III's Text Box: I guess this is it huh? Max, it has been sweet. Tell everyone else goodbye for me.

> Hippolyta's Text Box: Dare I say even say it… Max, It was eventually nice to play with you.

Max couldn't reply, he tried but his Text Box was full of tears.

> Zal Finn III's Text Box: Hippolyta, it was sweetdiculous. Look up Zal Finn IV?

> Hippolyta's Text Box: It was wonderful to meet you Zal, you are a great girl. That is why I want you to have this.

Hippolyta reached into her nonexistent cleavage and pulled out an item that she had hidden. By using the *Hand Something to Someone Else Dual Animation* she passed it to Zal Finn. Looking inside, Zal saw the one *Elixir* that they had managed to find. The item that could break this curse and save someone.

> Zal Finn III's Text Box: No, you t—

> Hippolyta's Interruption Text Box: Don't even start. It is yours and I want you to have it. Just so you don't try anything…

Using a flurry of random Animations, special attacks, *Blush Shade* # changes, and blinks Hippolyta quickly drained the rest of her Level 1 experience points. Had the situation not been so emotionally heart-wrenching the display would have been off the charts hilarious instead of a grandiose gesture. Before Zal could say anything, Hippolyta fell backwards, resting on a scenic column. She stopped breathing as her once *Heaving Bosom* finally turned concave.

Fighting through tears of her own, Zal Finn uncorked the *Elixir* and drank down the green liquid. This finally removed the cursed *Spring Gauntlets (s)* from her hands and they fell to the ground and crumbled into black pixels. Zal Finn was now Level 1.08, it wasn't much but she was alive.

Mr. Max took Zal Finn's hand, and they sat in silence together, again lost in thought.

> Zal Finn III's Text Box: I already miss her.

> Mr. Max's Text Box: She really was one of a kind. Truly the elf with the shelf.

> Zal Finn III's Text Box: I can't believe she sacrificed herself to save me. That was so… sweet.

> Mr. Max's Text Box: She was sweet. Also, she had the biggest rack I've ever seen. It was amazing.

> Zal Finn III's Text Box: I know! It was sweet. I look at her there and it is like I can still see them rotating away in all their glory.

> Mr. Max's Text Box: I wish she hit me with them one last time… but you are right, I can still imagine them bouncing away.

The avatars closed their eyes and held hands, and shared a moment thinking about Hippolyta's wonderful massive rack (and how nice she was as a person). After what they deemed to be an appropriate amount of time to wait there in mourning, which turned out to be 37 rounds, they both slowly stood up and started to walk away. A short correct direction trumpet song played.

> Mr. Max's Text Box: You got to Level 2 by standing up and starting to walk away from an emotional scene? I forgot how easy it was to Level up so early on!

> Zal Finn III's Text Box: Huh? No I didn't. I'm still Level 1.

> Mr. Max's Text Box: It wasn't me. I don't have Levels anymore!

Mr. Max and Zal Finn turned around and both used the *Gasp in Alarm Animation*. Hippolyta's body had taken in a huge breath, but that was not nearly as alarming as what happened next. Hippolyta's concave chest exploded outward, her breasts started to expand at an alarming rate. Within two rounds they had gone through every cup size that existed, to her original introduced *Heaving Bosom size* (a size that all had thought to be impossible) to even larger. The force of the sudden growth caused them to push the sides of the *Peek-A-Boo Leotard* and spring free with impressive force. They began to rotate at an unheard of level of jiggle.

> Mr. Max and Zal Finn III's Simultaneous Text Boxes: Gha-lu-lugga-ah…

With an impossible litheness for someone with breasts that were bigger than *MelonMelons* (the biggest of all video game Melons) Hippolyta used the *Kip-Up Animation* and was on her feet.

> Hippolyta's Text Box: That's right! I demand that you ogle my breasts! Wooooooooooooo!!!!

The others were more than happy to comply. In fact, getting them to stop complying was the difficult part. Hippolyta needed to stand still for several rounds and try to stop her bigger breasts from moving, but even the wind was providing enough force to keep them jiggly when they were out of her uniform. It took the Amazon fight elf many rounds to finally squeeze them into her *Peek-A-Boo Leotard*. During the ordeal that was putting her breasts back into her top she managed to boobslap Mr. Max six times and Zal Finn twice. She even managed to hit herself once, which caused her to fall over and set the one free that she had managed to get inside. Even though it took the better part of the morning to do so, Hippolyta did not care. She loved her giant bouncing *Spellbinding* rack of pure feminine glory.

Zal Finn III's Text Box: Wow… how long was I out?

Mr. Max's Text Box: How much health did I lose and why do I feel like I loved every moment of it?

Zal Finn III's Text Box: Hippolyta? How are you alive?

Hippolyta's Text Box: Normally, I would say it was because I am the ultimate goddess of all womanhood and I am immune to death by traps devised by male pigs… but honestly, I have no idea why I didn't die. Happy about it though.

Mr. Max's Text Box: Your boobs… are huge!

Hippolyta's Text Box: They are amazing, right?

Zal Finn gave them a good looking over before replying.

Zal Finn III's Text Box: Beyond amazing.

Mr. Max's Text Box: Wait a round here… Okay… I think I got it. As you Leveled down your boobs got smaller right? Remember when they were little rotating *PitCherries*? Now they are massive swinging love *MelonMelons*!

Hippolyta's Text Box: If I wasn't so happy about being alive and with my giant Goddess breasts I would have gotten upset with you for saying that and smacked you with them.

Mr. Max's Text Box: You still can if you want, they are amazing. But no, what I mean is Godessette that you must have… what Level are you now?

Hippolyta's Text Box: Level… ✪ ✪?

Mr. Max's Text Box: It all makes sense now! When you Levelled down past Level 1 logically you should have gone down to Level 0 and died. That is real world logic, not Game logic. See, the Programmers did not Program a Level 0, why would they? There would never be a reason for any Avatar to become it. When your experience points dropped to zero it became a number that the Game didn't recognize as a number!

Zal Finn III's Text Box: I get it! Sweet! So when she became Level 0 she didn't have experience points anymore.

Mr. Max's Text Box: Exactly and when the Game saw an experience point total that wasn't a number it applied the only thing that it knew as not having a number. Level ✪ ✪! Congrats on being number two to reach maximum Level Hippolyta!

Hippolyta's Text Box: Thank you Max! I feel so powerful it is ridiculous.

Mr. Max's Text Box: I always feel like that. It is pretty great, huh?

Hippolyta had to agree. It felt great.

Contest Announcement Text Box: Congratulations to Hippolyta, the second avatar to reach Level ✪ ✪! Enjoy your prize! Hurry everyone! There is only one more prize to be won for reaching maximum Level.

Zal Finn III's Text Box: Oh sweet! What did you get?

Hippolyta's Text Box: I don't think I want it.

Mr. Max's Text Box: How could you not want a one of a kind *Caution Step* lunch box? It has been filled with all of their albums, including the latest Album *Out of Service: Use the Stairs*? It has been autographed by the entire band and comes with a *Trip Hazard* thermos, an *Ashler Waldenmyer* fruit caddy, and most importantly a *Gunner M. Jefferies* sandwich cozy, for all your sandwich needs!

Hippolyta's Text Box: Meh... I generally eat tacos.

Zal Finn III's Text Box: No way. I want that. I am so jealous.

Hippolyta's Text Box: Wait. How did you know what I won?

Mr. Max's Text Box: I won first place and it was the real painted artwork for *Out of Service: Use the Stairs*. The lunchbox seemed like the logical second place reward.

Hippolyta's Text Box: Hmmm... I am not really a rock band kind of girl.

Mr. Max's Text Box: Are you sure? It is pretty awesome.

Hippolyta's Text Box: Maybe I will give mine to Gliint... He is quite the little fan and has had a bad experience lately as he isn't evil.

Mr. Max's Text Box: I think I heard him yelling from here with excitement. Are you sure you don't like *Caution Step*?

Hippolyta's Text Box: Yes. I am positive.

Mr. Max's (Wonderful) Singing Text Box: ♪♫ And then she tore my heart away with her purple nail tipped fists. Now she keeps it on display on a shelf up high in her room. ♪♫

Zal Finn III's (Average) Singing Text Box: ♪♫ In a gilded box she made herself, it sits and beats away. I know my friend was out of line, but it was more my fault than his. ♪♫

Mr. Max and Zal Finn III's Simultaneous (That join together to be pretty decent) Singing Text Boxes: ♪♫ I never should have got involved with the girl with purple hair. Now I spend my days without a heart because… ♪♫

Mr. Max and Zal Finn both used the *Excited Look Animation*. Hippolyta used the *Barely Able to Keep From Bursting Out Singing Animation*.

Hippolyta's (Bad) Singing Text Box: ♪♫ … because Lizzy you're such a bitch!

Hippolyta used the *Kickass Air Guitar Rift Animation*.

Mr. Max's Text Box: I knew it!

Hippolyta's Text Box: Fine, okay. I like *Caution Step*. I didn't at first but De'vini and In'ferni make out to it all the time and that shit is stupid catchy.

Zal Finn III's Text Box: I'm sweet jealous now. You have ultimate badass stats like Mr. Max, your sex power is fully charged, and you are going to get some limited edition swag in the mail. That is such a far stretch from where we were this morning. You are super powerful and amazing and I…

Zal Finn III's Text Box: am…

Zal Finn III's Text Box: FUCK!

Hippolyta's Text Box: I'm sorry Zal. I didn't know. I was trying to sacrifice myself for you! Honest.

Zal Finn III's Text Box: I know and it was fucking amazing! You are so fucking wonderful it makes me sick with appreciation. But I am still furious. I could have been Level ✪ ✪ and commanded every NPC in the world to join in my global orgy with my ultimate badass sex power!

Plus I would have gotten swag! Now I am Level 1 and can't even do the *Training Two-Step*. I am so pissed off! To top it off now you are leaving me here while you get to fly on Roodg's *Gigantic Hover Centipede* with Max to go to Onn to fight Breaker!

Hippolyta's Text Box: Sorry. It would be dangerous for a Level 1. I don't want you to get hurt!

Zal Finn III's Text Box: But leaving me here of all places? With all the Poffles?

Mr. Max's Text Box: Exactly! You can start to kill them all with that Level 1 *Basic Box Cutter* and get massive amounts of experience. You will probably get to like Level 90 at least.

Roodg's Text Box: Carrot Jr. AND I WILL PICK YOU UP WHEN YOU ARE DONE. gROUP cHAT ABOUT SCENTED CANDLES WHEN YOU ARE READY TO GO!

Hippolyta's Text Box: Carrot Jr.?

Roodg's Text Box: i GOT TO NAME IT! sEE RIGHT THERE, HER NAMETAG SAYS IT.

Hippolyta's Text Box: So, you got to name the *Gigantic Hover Centipede* and you called her Carrot Jr.?

Roodg's Text Box: yES!

Mr. Max's Text Box: Wonderful!

Roodg's Text Box: i KNOW!

Hippolyta's Text Box: See you soon Zal!

Carrot Jr. grew a few segments to allow Mr. Max and Hippolyta to come aboard and hovered off towards the city of Onn, leaving an upset Level 1 Zal Finn III behind.

Dressed in the only Level 1 gear that anyone could find (a *Brown Cardboard Box* that would certainly not help her stand out), and wielding a not-dangerous *Basic Box Cutter* Zal Finn turned towards the piles of caged Golden Poffles. The first one would be the hardest, a few hundred stabs at least, but Mr. Max had assured her that killing one would get her to Level 17 and then she could use some dance moves to help speed things up. Zal Finn approached the closest cage, rose up her *Basic Box Cutter*, and aimed it at the cute little ball of golden puff. The first one would be the hardest.

Zal Finn III's Text Box: Die!

Golden Poffle # 742 used the *Cute Gwowl Animation*.

◈ Chapter 34 ◈
CYCLE 6
GROUP F, MR. GRUMPY HOOVES

Hiding far from Lissa in the back corner of *Onn*, Fournimer scratched the chin of his adopted dragon, who chirped happily at the attention. Once Fournimer had finally snapped out of his mad lust for his friend's lovely heart shaped ass and gone back to free her, she was already untied and using the *Fuming Animation*. Fournimer knew that she would have been none too pleased with his actions, but was uncertain if she knew that he had been approaching her with inappropriate intentions in mind.

Fournimer was upset at himself for how he acted, and now that his sexual lust was under control he really didn't know what to do. Even getting close to Lissa again to see if she was alright had caused his loins to stir and he had decided that it would be best if he stayed away completely until he could get some much needed relief.

> Fournimer's Text Box: stupid centaurs!

Fournimer used the *Sigh Animation*. He still didn't know why centaurs were even a race in this Game. They couldn't do so many things like normal non-horsed avatars. Thinking about it made Fournimer get madder. To top it off, the two reasons he had changed into a centaur in the first place, Max and Anders, were mysteriously straight now, or maybe not. Max certainly was, but Anders was only possibly straight and not answering any of Fourni's kiss sealed letters, which was a complete other reason to get mad.

> Fournimer's Text Box: stupid Anders!

Fournimer used the *Pout Animation*. He was so annoyed with Anders right now. Why was he hiding himself from everyone? That angel had to be Anders, the scar was a dead giveaway, but why wouldn't he at least tell the guy that was head over hoofs for him that he was alive? Fournimer could keep a secret (actually he couldn't, but that wasn't the point). One more try Fourni thought, one more try and then it might be time to give up hope. One more letter to Anders and he would move on. The centaur reached for his pen and paper but remembered that he couldn't reach them without help because they were in his *Saddle Bags*.

> Fournimer's Text Box: stupid *Saddle Bags*!

Fournimer used the *Facepalm Animation*. He couldn't write Anders without some assistance and Draganders didn't understand the desperate need that Fournimer had for taking out a *Napkin* to write on. At least Fournimer knew where to find more. Taking a step over the dead Spiderboy, who was even less relevant to any quests now that he was dead, Fournimer accidentally hit his now low hanging blue balls with his own hoof causing jolts of pain to go through his entire system.

> Fournimer's Text Box: stupid balls!

Fournimer used the *Wince Animation*. He was angry with his balls right now. They hurt to even think about. He stood there trying to stop from crying and regaining his composure. By the time he could walk again, he had completely forgotten where he was going. His mind was still fuzzy and concentrating on anything was difficult. He decided to walk randomly, but every street in this accursed Onn lead back to either the main square or the castle. The main square contained an upset Lissa and the castle would only piss him off more now that his perfect throne hole had been destroyed.

> Fournimer's Text Box: stupid Onn!

Fournimer used the *Fuming Animation*. Onn was stupid. He had already spent way too much time frustrated here and all this additional cake frustration time was not helping to paint Onn in a better light. Then Fournimer remembered that not every street in Onn led to the main square or the castle. Thanks to Mr. Max and samuri there was one path that led to a toppled tower and a destroyed multi-family home. The rubble had blocked the way through, so it was the only street in town that didn't go to the same place. Fournimer turned quickly in that direction without thinking and hit the scenic pole that was out of place (because Roodg had bent it) face first. Once the random hearts and fireworks cleared out of his vision from the kiss he accidentally gave the pole (which had also leveled it up into a *Scenic Pole+*) he only got madder.

> Fournimer's Text Box: stupid kisses!

Fournimer used the *Temper Tantrum Animation*. He had the worst sex ability in his entire group of friends, that even included the Lesbitwins power which required them to be glued together to function and Zal Finn's, which forced her to look like a generic

NPC. What a ridiculous power he had. Start Rat *Wonder Kisses*. The hearts were cute and all, but compared to the ability to make people orgasm by using animations or a bubble butt that held all your stuff, they were laughable. He had almost leveled it up to maximum, but none of the additions were anything better. Fournimer was getting ready to get mad at something different (he wasn't sure what yet) when he heard voices coming from inside the rubble of the little house. He tried to stop breathing as best as he could and missed his old Night Ranger *Stealth* ability.

> White Quest Fairy's Text Box: urder.

> Gray Quest Fairy's Text Box: That isn't good enough. We need to find him! He is the most important one!

> Other-Blue Quest Fairy's Text Box: Hey woman, stay groovy, man. We like tried, but… he rather kind of, well, he jumped away I mean. Out of the way.

> No-Colour Quest Fairy's Text Box: Yah well, I don't think that is good enough.

> Other-Purple and Other-Orange Quest Fairy's Simultaneous Text Boxes: Don't blame us. That is rude. We didn't even know that we couldn't fly! Yeah, who knew? We can only hover. So odd.

> Purple Quest Fairy's Text Box: That is #SoScrewedUp! How are we going to get up there?

> Macintosh's Text Box: It is okay pals and gals. He was the most important one, but we don't need to get him first. We can always adjust our plan.

> Blue Quest Fairy's Text Box: I still don't know about this Mac. I am still pretty torn.

> Orange Quest Fairy's Text Box: Maybe we should have another vote, framers and framerettes!

> Macintosh's Text Box: Can it pals and gals! We already voted three times. This is going to happen.

> Other-Yellow Quest Fairy's Text Box: Personellement, je ne peux pas attendre le jour où je dégusterai le sang de mes ennemis. Un rêve qui deviendra réalité!

Despite the fact that he had no idea what in the Flaming Pit any of these Fairies were talking about, Fournimer listened with intense interest. If he could sneak a little bit closer he would be able to see inside the building. He only moved when the Text Boxes chimed in, to help cover his hoof clicks.

Green Quest Fairy's Text Box: My scouting indicates that there are three other avatars in Onn right now. Why don't we go for one of them? Two are men and totally have it coming. I say we get one of them first.

Fournimer's Internal Text Box: there are three avatars in Onn? He and Lissa only made two. who was the third?

Macintosh's Text Box: Good point, gal, but I think to bring the snake out of hiding a better bet would be to go after target number two on our list. She has it coming!

Fournimer's Internal Text Box: the only she in Onn is Lissa, but what does target number two on their list mean?

White Quest Fairy's Text Box: Yes, and obviously what will happen after is that the head of the snake, that obsessive lad spewing idiot, will come back for vengeance. We can get target number one quickly and remove him right away, the rest of the snake will surely fall without a head to rely on. We will have smooth sailing for the rest.

Fournimer's Internal Text Box: there is only one obsessive lad spewing idiot. that is Dwarfman without a doubt. why is he target number one?

Macintosh's Text Box: Exactly, pal. I like that plan and heck if we need to warm up on target #11 or #14 on the way so be it.

Fournimer's Internal Text Box: what? #11 or #14. one of those is me. why am I so low on this list?

Gray Quest Fairy's Text Box: Sweet vengeance will be ours.

Fournimer's Internal Text Box: vengeance?

Brown Quest Fairy's Text Box: Woot! *Cheer* This is going to be good!

Other-Yellow Quest Fairy's Text Box: Je vais danser dans leurs cages thoraciques et utiliser leurs organes vitaux comme chapeau.

Fournimer had reached the window and could finally look inside. The Quest Fairies were getting ready for war, or at least they were applying *Wartime Facepaint*.

> Macintosh's Text Box: Alright pals and gals. What do you say? Is it time to go teach that purple haired bitch a lesson? Are we all ready to go kill our first avatar?

Fournimer nearly spat out his *Hard Leaf Gum*. Kill their first avatar? Holy fucking shitballs Palcath had been right! The Quest Fairies had been planning to kill everyone like he said. He had to go warn target #2 that little balls of deadly light were coming for her head. He turned around quicker than he probably should have to be stealthy and the corner of his *Pick Javelin* hit the window frame. It did not make a noise, but a cascade of little sparkles courtesy of his Extra Weapon Effects Code flooded into the secret headquarters of the Quest Fairies, alerting every single one of them to his presence.

> Fournimer's Yelling Text Box: STUPID GLITTER!

Fournimer was off like a shot of glitter, running at full speed while Draganders flew behind him, chirping happily and completely oblivious to the peril. Fournimer didn't know where he was running, but seeing as how two rainbows worth of malicious framing devices where chasing him down and calling for his death, he didn't really care which way he went.

> Purple Quest Fairy's Text Box: That is #SoScrewedUp, #14 heard everything! We need to stop him!

That only made things worse. Fournimer was #14 on the kill list? He was so unimportant that he was the last target on the list! (Fournimer still wasn't good with math. There were 15 known targets.)

> Fournimer's Text Box: stupid fucking Quest Fairies!

Since every road in *Onn* lead to the same two places it was only inevitable that he would run past Lissa at some point. He got his Text Box ready by running around the castle a few time and headed for the town square. He sprinted past a startled Lissa and yelled at her. Then he pushed her into the fountain on the way by, to hide her from the rampaging mob of Quest Fairies.

> Fournimer's Yelling Text Box: Lis! you fucking need to run! Palcath was right! the Quest Fairies are going to kill us all and you are target #2! hide and tell everyone else!

Fournimer didn't know where to go now it would only take so many runs through Onn until the Quest Fairies remembered that to catch him they would only need to stand still. There was no another way to go, except out of Onn. Fournimer ran towards the town gate. That was odd. Where was NPC Greeta? She was always there in her little booth blocking... that hidden doorway?

Fournimer ran towards the doorway hidden behind the most annoying NPC in all of Onn. No one would ever look there, what an absolutely perfect place for him to hide. Fournimer wrenched open the door and was thankful that it was not a scenic one. He hurried Draganders inside and ducked in after. He shut the door tightly and remained still, hoping no Quest Fairies had seen where he went.

It took a few rounds for his eyes to adjust to the darkness. What was this place that was so secretly hidden in plain sight? It certainly was a lot bigger than he had expected it to be. It was absolutely massive and now that he could see a bit more it felt familiar.

Something clicked beside him, joining him in the space. It was a familiar presence, clopping along with a blur of rainbow features, a belt pouch that jingled constantly with the sound of silver coins, and with the impressive ability to make someone who was not a virgin explode if they mounted it. It had a *Blue Cat Keycard* that it relinquished with only a little slut shaming.

> Fournimer's Internal Text Box: stupid fucking unicorn!

The unicorn gave a hearty smile, and continued silently with Fournimer down the poorly lit path. Everything here was covered in pictures of cats.

> Fournimer's Text Box: oh fuck me. stupid Chad!

Chapter 35

CYCLE 6
GROUP L, FUMING
ON FUMES

Lissa was furious. After spending the entire night tied up with her face full of cake, she was not impressed. The only thing she wasn't mad about was the fact that when she woke up this morning she was untied, as the laws of sleeping means you recover from regular status effects. But that was literally the only thing.

She had been doing all of the anger themed Animations since finishing her delicious breakfast of even more cake. She had already done the *Fuming Animation, Glare Animation, OMMWTF Animation, Head Chop Animation, Scream to the Heavens Animation, Eyebrows Furrowed and Face Twitch Animation, Furious Animation,* and the *Understanding Why the Centaur was so Nervous Before About Jumping Animation* (that last one was used by mistake) and she was still looking for more to help vent her anger. She found the perfect one right near the end of the list.

Lissa used the *Vent Anger Animation,* but even that didn't help. She was mad at everyone. She was mad at Fournimer for ruining her plan to catch Gliint, and leaving her there all night in a pile of cake. She was mad at Gliint for being a little douche, and destroying the tower of cake. But who she was the maddest at was Palcath.

> Lissa's Text Box: #SoFuckedUp! How could that lad have not found a way to get me up there yet? #SoFuckedUp! That idiot has bundles of *Bundles of Rope*, why doesn't he tie them together and drop one end down? #BrainlessDwarfLad is#SoFuckedUp! Going up there to have a dramatic battle in a secret unexplored area and completely forgetting to bring the #FemaleLead! #SoFuckedUp!

Lissa stamped through Onn, randomly punching, hashtagging, and kicking various scenic objects. When she bitch-slapped the corpse of a dead unfortunate NPC guard she caught a glimpse of herself in the shiny side of his shield. She was covered head to toe in cake and icing, her hair was standing in every direction possible and was covered in sprinkles, and the words *'Happy Birthday Chad'* where scrawled across her face backward in pink icing. Lissa used the *Burst Out Laughing Animation*. She looked too ridiculous for her to stay mad.

Lissa felt better and her anger subsided after laughing at herself. She even took a few screenshots (that she would never share with anyone else) to remember how #StupidlyCakeCovered she was.

It was time to calm down and get cleaned up. Thankfully, yesterday a washing machine had fallen from the sky and crushed a small statue of the King of Onn. There was no dryer in sight so her clothes would need to hang dry, which would mean she would be naked for a bit, but she had a good idea where to spend her time. After setting the washer to Ultra-fast her clothes were clean in five rounds and she used them to badly cover herself up while sprinting to the town fountain.

Her old forgotten *Maces* and *Shieldlets* were enchanted with a casting of *Fire Edge* and tossed into the water. The water reached the right temperature after seven items were inserted. She turned on the songs she liked the most that she had unlocked in the Sound Test Menu (taking great care to omit any and all songs by *Caution Step*). After dropping in an *Essence of Absolute Bubble* and using *Whirlmace Strike* on the water to give it a good mix, Lissa stepped right into exactly what she needed; a hot and relaxing bubble bath. She didn't give a fuck if it was cliché for a girl to like bubble baths, she needed this right now.

Cycles of stress (and countless weight units of icing), melted away as Lissa relaxed in the large and luxurious fountain. It was absolute bliss and she was upset when her clothing appeared dry and her mana points were too drained to reheat the water any longer.

Finally relaxed and clean Lissa stepped out of the fountain, dried off as best as she could with a half used *Double Danish* and put her equipment back on. Her hair was purpler now and she was no longer smudged with dirt. She would have to remember to do this more often, but not in this fountain. It was now absolutely filthy and pink with dirt and icing. It was a lost cause.

> Lissa's Text Box: That is SO much better. #MeltAwayTheStress.

Lissa used the *Relaxed Stretch Animation* and turned around in time to see a blurred out mass of horse rushing towards her.

> Lissa's Text Box: Fourni?

> Fournimer's Text Box: Lis! you fuck—

Lissa didn't hear the rest of the Text Box as it was interrupted by Fournimer pushing her ass first into the filthy fountain. She came up furious five rounds later spitting out cake and dirt. She was ready to smack the bitch out of Horsimer.

> Lissa's Text Box: Seriously, you Jive Turkey. Why the fuck did… where did you go?

Fournimer was nowhere to be seen.

> Lissa's Text Box: That is #SoFuckedUp!

Now she was so angry that not even the nicest bath in the entire Expansion (The Dire Hot Springs of Shuckels K'hila) would be able to cheer her up. She was wet, dirty, and miserable. Palcath had now slipped down her list of the avatars she was most upset with. It only took her three rounds to dry herself off (due to the intense heat that her anger was producing) and now her *Fashionista Bodice (s)* had orange icing across it that read *'Congratulations! Your face melted off'*. Lissa tried to clean the icing off the delicate lace fabric but stopped when she saw what was walking towards her.

It was cake. An entire pillar of cake to be exact, stacked eleven high. She couldn't see who was carrying it, but it was likely NPC Margarine given the pink apron. No, it was too skinny to be her. Maybe it was Greeta, Illiandro, or that other one who no one remembered. Regardless of who it was they used the *Hand Something to Someone Else Dual Animation* and passed Lissa twelve items. Lissa casually threw the eleven cakes into the Onn Sewer Access Manhole and looked at the other item. It was a note.

Hi there hun. We finished up the last of your order and we really hope you like it. Please see the attached for a summary.

Grand FullCakes x1,468 at 7,250 GP
Subtotal - 10,643,000 GP
Rush Fee + 25% - 2,660,750 GP
Orange Icing Levy (9GP per cake) - 13,212 GP
Luxury Tax + 12% - 1,277,160 GP
Islana Expansion Tax + 10% - 1,064,300 GP
Less Down Payment - -500GP
Grand Total - 15,607,922 GP
Please sign if you agree upon the estimated price -
Palcath Ironburrow, son of Gloni and Defender of the Dwarven clans

Payment due upon completion of order from either Palcath or Lissandra Collinswood.
Thank you for choosing NPC Margarine's Bakery Shoppe, hun. We hope to be able to cater to your future events.

Fournimer was bumped from top anger spot.

> Lissa's Text Box: 15,607,922 GP!? #SoFuckedUp. If that dwarf thinks that I am going to pay for that he is completely off his dwarf ass. Billable to either Palcath or Lissa. What a complete load! If you think that I am going to cough up the GP to pay that samuri you are completely out of your mind.

> samuri's Text Box: …

samuri used the *Headshake Animation*.

> Lissa's Text Box: Wait a turn. samuri?! What the Flaming Pit are you doing dressed in a pink apron and delivering cake?

> samuri's Text Box: …

samuri used the *Proudly Display Apron Animation*.

> Lissa's Text Box: You can't be serious. You are working there now?

> samuri's Text Box: …

samuri used the *Nod Animation*.

> Lissa's Text Box: What the chunk happened to you? Half of your hair is cut off and your eye is missing completely. The rosette eye patch is #Brilliant!

> samuri's Text Box: !!!

samuri used the *I Suddenly Remembered That I Forgot To Tell Everyone Critical Plot Information Because I Got Too Distracted Decorating Cakes With Sprinkles Animation*, bringing the global world count on that Animation up to an amazing total of seven.

> Lissa's Text Box: Wha—

> Mr. Max's Interruption Text Box: We are here adventurers and adventurettes… and Roodg!

> Roodg's Text Box: i LOVE YOUR SHIRT Lissa! aND i FOUND E. E. Lynn FOR YOU!

> E. E. Lynn's Text Box: F|n4lly \/\/3 h3r3. | g0t sh|ts 2 d0 b|tch3s. L4t3r!

> Lissa's Text Box: Yes, but she ran off!

> Roodg's Text Box: tHAT SUCKS!

Lissa's Text Box: What in the Flaming Pit are you driving Roodg?

Roodg's Text Box: Carrot Jr.! i CAN GO ANYWHERE IN THE GAME NOW! sHE IS SO sAWESOME!

Lissa's Text Box: Anywhere?

Roodg's Text Box: yEP! wHY?

Lissa's Text Box: Take me to that floating island and do it now! I have something to deliver to a certain in trouble dwarf!

samuri's Text Box: ...

Lissa's Text Box: Do it now!

Roodg's Text Box: bUT WE HAVE IM—

Lissa's Interruption Text Box: NOW!

Mr. Max's Text Box: We better listen to her. We don't want to get on her bad side.

Roodg's Text Box: gOOD THINKING.

Lissa hopped onto Carrot Jr., who grew another segment, and impatiently waited for the agonizingly slow *Gigantic Hover Centipede Take Off Animation* to complete.

Macintosh's Whisper Text Box: Quick pals and gals. Now is our chance during that agonizingly slow *Gigantic Hover Centipede Take Off Animation*! Jump on.

~~~

Lissa's Text Box: Of course!

Lissa was not pleased. The icing on her bodice was going to stain. This amazing top was going to be stained forever and of course the icing had to be orange. Lissa's least favorite things were all orange and annoying. Speaking of which.

Mr. Max's Text Box: I had to tell you adventurette that bodice looks amazing now. I really like how you picked the best colour of all for the writing. Orange!

Lissa's Text Box: What are you still doing here? Carrot Jr. already left with everyone! I was supposed to be here to do this alone!

Mr. Max's Text Box: I know you said that, but I had something important to tell you so I stayed behind!

Lissa's Text Box: Fine. What did you desperately need to tell me?

Mr. Max's Text Box: I did tell you! Didn't I? I love that orange writing on your bodice. No wait, it was that Cinnamon told me on the flight that my fellow dancing chef friend got accepted to cooking school, I'm so proud! No that was from my cameo. Was there more for this game? I forget.

Lissa's Text Box: #Unbelievable!

Mr. Max's Text Box: What is this place? It isn't like I expected at all for a floating island in the sky.

Lissa's Text Box: I forgot to look!

It was all on fire. That was something to take note of. There was something different about the fire, something a shade off that Lissa couldn't place. The colour of the fire was a bit off, but it was more than that. What was more alarming was that the fire was Level ✪ ✪. Heck, now that Lissa looked around everything around here was not only Level ✪ ✪ but also named and on fire. *The Burning Trees of Brimstone*, the *Lakes of the Abyss*, the *Infernal Milking Dairy*, the *Pandemonium Netherfield*, *Purgatory's Blade of Grass*, and even *The Scenic Clouds of Valhalla*.

Lissa's Text Box: Where in the Flaming Pit are we?

Mr. Max's Text Box: I don't know adventurette but it is all epic. All of it.

Chapter 36

CYCLE 6
GROUP E (THE E
STANDS FOR EVIL)

The first thing Palcath thought when his vision finally cleared and he had awokenfrom his passed out state was, why were chapters always starting with people having blurred vision waking up from near comas? It was an epidemic. Palcath decided to shake things up by making this blurry wake-up different by being completely tied up and immobile. He had also been unique by having himself nearly beaten to death last night by cows when he turned away from Gliint's army and ran. Palcath was good like that, always willing to make things a little more interesting.

He didn't feel bruised this morning. Since he had not slept in a proper position to recover, someone must have healed him with either magic or a potion. Perhaps it was one of the other avatars sitting in the chairs around the circular table in this ornately decorated room made completely of glass.

None of the other avatars were moving, sitting there with blank expressions on their faces. Everyone who had been riding on the *Parsnip* was here. De'vini, who had likely healed him. In'ferni, who was blindfolded and now Palcath could see also had Caela's old *Full Ball-Gag* in her mouth (but how De'vini wasn't ball-gagged while attached to her at the lips was anybody's guess). Caela was in the next chair, possibly still not wearing pants as Palcath couldn't see under the table. There was also a skeleton, although Palcath had no idea why a monster with a bad red wig was here. Finally, Gliint sat at the head of the table. It was a round table and technically didn't have a head, but that chair was much larger than the others.

Gliint sprung to life with a smug look on his face. It was the *Too Dark Shades* that really set the look off. Palcath had never been a fan of them.

> Gliint's text Box: Finally awake, you insufferable busy-body?

> Palcath's Text Box: Awake, yes. Busy-body, yes. Insufferable, no. I think I have a certain charm about me, lad.

> Gliint's Text Box: Hmmm... I'm not so sure. Anyway, you will do.

> Palcath's Text Box: I will do? Do for what, lad?

> Gliint's Text Box: I was afraid we were going to have to keep our plans secret until tomorrow.

Gliint stopped moving, Caela started to move.

> Caëlahenãilenẃhei's Text Box: Yes, but now we have you. We can talk and talk and talk. That is what we can do. Talk a lot. That is what I do. Talk far too long for my text boxes. You know what. That is long enough to get my point across. I talk too much.

> Palcath's Text Box: So you lad and lasses are going to monologue... as a group? Oh sweet Maker why?

Now De'vini was the one who was moving, and Caela had frozen completely.

> De'vini's Text Box: Like why not for sure? Because our plan is that good or whatever!

In'ferni used the *Mmmfferr Murrm Mmmmff Animation.*

This continued; each person that was talking would be the only one who would move, besides In'ferni who was always feebly struggling against her bonds.

> Gliint's Text Box: It is pretty good. I'll admit.

> Palcath's Text Box: I am interested in it, lad, but first I would like some explanations.

> Gliint's Text Box: I will indulge that I suppose. I really have nothing else to do this cycle so shoot. What do you got?

> Palcath's Text Box: I can understand why someone might go evil, but three of you going evil all at once? That doesn't make any sense, lad.

> Yallundy's Whisper Text Box: Yeah Palcath, ask him that!

Palcath now knew who had healed him over the night. Yallundy was ghosting here, stuck because of Gliint's presence.

Gliint's Text Box: They saw the light and joined me in my holy quest from the Maker to cleanse the world of the plight that has ruined it. That plight, of course being Mr. Max.

Palcath's Text Box: What? That doesn't make a lick of sense, lad. You are Mr. Max's biggest fan! Why would you hate him?

Gliint's Text Box: How could anyone like that insuf—

Caëlahenâilenŵhei's Interruption Box Text: Oh for the love of the Maker Palcath, are you that dense? That isn't Gliint talking. That isn't me or De'vini talking! We have—

Caëlahenâilenŵhei's Interruption Text Box: Stop ruining my moment you big cunt!

De'vini's Text Box: I knew I should have used that *Full Ball-Gag* on your cunt instead of on that half character. She wouldn't have ruined my moment like that.

In'ferni used the *Mmmfferr Murrm Mmmmff Animation.*

Gliint's Text Box: Shut up!

Palcath's Text Box: You lasses and lad are under someone else's control? That makes sense.

Yallundy's Whisper Text Box: It hasn't been Gliint? Thank goodness!

Caëlahenâilenŵhei's Box Text: Your math is wrong again, Palcath.

Palcath's Text Box: No lass it isn't, my math has hardly ever been wrong… wait… what math? I didn't do any math.

Caëlahenâilenŵhei's Box Text: Sure you did and it is. Lad is single, you cannot count. There are two controlled lads here.

The skeleton turned to Palcath and began to talk. Palcath would have jumped out of his chair if he wasn't already tied down.

Kray's Text Box: No, he is like so right. His math is fine. I'm like not under control, kay. I'm watching.

Palcath's Text Box: Kray?! No way. What happened lad you are —

Kray's Interruption Text Box: Super impossibly skinny now? I know, kay.

Palcath's Text Box: No lad, what I mean is look at you. Your flesh—

Kray's Interruption Text Box: Was keeping me super fat, kay. Now I am the skinniest ever! Plus I have this jelly Armour. Now I can take any cock I want. I am the best elf.

Palcath's Text Box: Take the cock in where, lad? You are —

Kray's Interruption Text Box: The best, I know, kay.

Yallundy's Whisper Text Box: Ignore him.

Gliint's Text Box: Shut up! This is my big reveal scene and I will not put up with it!

Caëlahenâilenŵhei's Box Text: No it isn't. We already know you are Breaker. That happened Chapters ago.

Palcath's Text Box: It's Breaker?

Gliint's Text Box: Only you did! They didn't. You ruined it for everyone.

In'ferni used the *Mmmfferr Murrm Mmmmff Animation*.

Gliint's Text Box: What? This isn't working! Everyone is getting all muddled up!

A glowing ball of black light used the *Descend Dramatically to the Ground Animation*. The *Full Ball-Gag* and blindfold disappeared from In'ferni. Gliint, De'vini, and Caëlahenâilenŵhei all used the *Sneeze Animation*. Kray did not, as he wasn't being controlled, only watching.

Breaker's Text Box: Okay. This is important. Who already knew it was me? Show of hands!

Kray used the *Raise Your Hand Animation*.

Caëlahenâilenŵhei's Text Box: The rest of us are tied up idiot. But I knew it was you.

Breaker's Text Box: Thank you miss bossy boots. I already knew you did.

Palcath's Text Box: I didn't, lad.

Yallundy's Whisper Text Box: Me either.

Breaker's Text Box: I knew that already. Thanks for the input.

Kray's Text Box: I knew it was you as soon as you took control of me, kay. It felt like the last time. I didn't care. Look at how hot you made me. I am like so skinny now. Thanks! Will you be my best man?

Breaker's Text Box: No! Also you raised your hand. I knew that as well! I want to hear from other people!

Gliint's Text Box: Finally! *Cheer* I have been controlled so long! I can finally do things again. I totally knew it was you because my eyes were the only thing I could move! Like Anders before. *Wamp, wamp, wamp*

Breaker's Text Box: I suspected you might be suspicious.

In'ferni and De'vini's Simultaneous Text Boxes: I knew it was you. Yeah, so did I. We are in the same room as someone who was there for the first reveal.

Breaker's Text Box: Wonderful... Just wonderful.

In'ferni and De'vini's Simultaneous Text Boxes: Yeah, sorry. Your reveal sucks. They finished telling everyone about you FYI. It turns out that the only avatars who didn't already know where the ones in Onn! Well, one did. True.

Palcath's Text Box: I feel so out of the loop now. I was one of the only lads that didn't know.

Breaker's Text Box: How aggravating! My first big reveal and nearly everyone already knew!

Palcath's Text Box: First big reveal, lad?

Breaker used the *Smirk Animation*, even though he was a ball of light.

Breaker's Text Box: Caught that did you? Yes, my first reveal. I have three others. Let's go through them together shall we!

With a Glowing Out of His Light and a Dramatic Movement of his Ball Animation, Breaker opened up the drapes, revealing the glass windows looking out on his gigantic army of dead avatars, NPCs, monsters, bosses, and Quest Fairies.

Breaker's Text Box: Behold my unstoppable army!

In'ferni and De'vini's Simultaneous Text Boxes: Even your ball gets its own Animation? That is pretty badass. Yep!

Caëlahenãilenẃhei's Text Box: Seriously? I'll try to be nice here. Breaker, you already revealed them to Palcath. Even worse we were all PART of that reveal since we were all in your army. The only one who didn't see that was In'ferni, but she would have seen it on De'vini's screen.

In'ferni and De'vini's Simultaneous Text Boxes: Yeah, I totally saw that. It was pretty dramatic. I guess you had to be there! Like us. Zing!

Kray's Text Box: I totally rocked flying that *Parsnip*, kay.

Breaker's Text Box: Right. Sorry, late night planning your deaths.

Gliint's Text Box: *Nod* Thanks for reminding us to tell everyone else about that.

Breaker used the *Facepalm Animation* (sans face).

Breaker's Text Box: Fuck!

Kray's Text Box: Sorry, spoken for, kay.

Breaker's Text Box: You know what? That is better. Now they know that my giant army of death is coming for them and they will not be able to find anywhere to hide.

In'ferni and De'vini's Simultaneous Text Boxes: Except the fact that Roodg found Carrot Jr. True, now they can all go hide anywhere. Yeah, even places none of us have been. That works out well for them.

Breaker used the *Irritated Animation*.

In'ferni and De'vini's Simultaneous Text Boxes: Wait. Never mind. They told us to tell you they are going to wait for your army instead of running and you are free to try and kill them all. That works out for you right? Yeah, then they will not be hidden!

Caëlahenãilenẃhei's Text Box: So far these reveals are not working out so good for you.

Breaker's Text Box: That is okay, I am saving the best one for last!

With a Glowing Out of His Light and a Dramatic Movement of his Ball Animation Breaker flipped a switch in the room and revealed… half of himself, the upper half to be exact. Wires, sci-fi tubing, and coloured gels were affixed to the avatar's model 3 (of 5) body in every which way.

Palcath's Text Box: I don't get it, lad. How is that the best one? It is part of your dead avatar and it is the boring half-dragon one. We already knew about you, that wasn't much of a reveal.

Breaker's Text Box: I don't recall saying this was the last one. This is a lead up to the last one, again thank you for your input. You see way back when you idiots were trying to get out of Onn, I found a wonderful *The Device* lying out in the middle of a cloud. It created a duplicate of my avatar.

Gliint's Text Box: *Confused* So you used it and ate half of yourself in boredom while waiting for us to finish Onn?

Breaker's Text Box: No, but I should have, you idiots took that fucking long. I experimented on it and learned countless things about the Code. About how to manipulate avatars and bend the Game to my every whim. Good times. I wish that before that gay pride dragon ate me, I made another clone because this one is shit all useful now. It really is a conversation piece.

Palcath's Text Box: I was meaning to ask that, lad. You were eaten, how are you still here?

Breaker's Text Box: I wouldn't tell you idiots normally, but it really does paint me in a good light so I am going to. I have linked myself into various dummy accounts, as I think you all know by now, if not read the dwarf's notes that I am sure he has far too many of.

Palcath's Text Box: I do indeed lad. I don't think that it is an exce—

Breaker's Interruption Text Box: Anyway, thanks to the knowledge of the Code that I gained by dissecting my own screaming body, I learned how to place backups within these dummy accounts. As long as one of them is active I simply cannot be destroyed. I have quite a few by the way.

Palcath's Text Box: I get it now. Your body was up here and you needed to bring the others. That is why you agreed to help make the cake tower, lad, because the *Carrot* turned *Parsnip* couldn't bring them up here to get back because none of the avatars you possessed had been here before.

Breaker's Text Box: Precisely. Slow clap, good job. I needed to bring someone up here. Not that it ended up mattering anyway. Things can be funny like that sometimes since he found his own way to get here.

Gliint's Text Box: That is great and all, *Still confused* but why are you a ball of light right now? That isn't scary, all-mighty, or anything really except perhaps framing device like.

Breaker's Text Box: That was my fault. I made myself auto-update. So when that little bitchboy friend of yours used his dragon to eat me, I got stuck as the ball of light and really couldn't do anything.

Caëlahenãilenŵhei's Text Box: That is sure a menacing form for you.

Breaker's Text Box: Silence!

Caëlahenãilenŵhei's Box Text: I think we both know that I am incapable of that.

Breaker and Caëlahenãilenŵhei used the *Agree Dual Animation*.

Breaker's Text Box: Actually C word, being the ball of light was fortuitous. It isn't a ball of light, it is a return sphere. It returns something, such as a summoned dragon, back to a host which then absorbs it. That is how I got stuck up here alone, returning to that useless husk over there. However, I control this sphere and with a little bit of work I can absorb into anything I want. Of course, I will not be getting absorbed, oh no. I was smart enough to prevent that little possibility when I re-coded this. I will absorb them. And I happen to have the perfect specimen.

Kray's Text Box: He is good at that, kay. Evil would be the talent portion on his beauty contest application.

Palcath used the *Gasp and Point While You Open Your Mouth and Cross Your Eyes With a Sudden Realization Animation*.

Palcath's Text Box: That is why you kidnapped me, lad? I am going to become your new host body? I knew that people sort of looked up to me and all, but I didn't suspect that much. I am sort of svelte and—

Breaker's Interruption Text Box: It isn't you, you dwarf self-centred blowhard.

Palcath's Text Box: Why did you bring me here, lad?

Breaker's Text Box: I didn't bring you here! You walked here by yourself and sat down before you passed out, from what I could only assume was self importance. If you recall I didn't even want you up here in the first place.

Yallundy's Whisper Text Box: I walked you here.

Palcath's Text Box: I am relieved but a little let down, lad.

Breaker's Text Box: No no no, who I do have to take over will be more than a surprise to all of you. The most important reveal of them all.

Caëlahenãilenŵhei's Text Box: It is going to be something we all know about already isn't it? Like how your virus didn't work and in fact made people gain Levels in the end. Am I right?

Breaker's Text Box: What? It did. Shit. That isn't it. I clearly said who. This reveal is a who.

Caëlahenãilenŵhei's Text Box: Thought I would cover my bases.

Kray's Text Box: My turn to guess. I totally got this. It is Sami-guy isn't it?

Breaker's Text Box: Who is that?

Palcath's Text Box: samuri. He means samuri. warrier changed his name way back when, didn't you notice, lad?

Breaker's Text Box: That idiot? I hate to tell you, but he is dead.

In'ferni and De'vini's Simultaneous Text Boxes: samuri? Yeah, he isn't dead Breaker. He was in Onn, making cakes the whole time. He is fine.

Breaker's Text Box: What?! But I saw him get buried!

Caëlahenãilenŵhei's Text Box: I think I am going to rest my case here. Your reveals suck.

Breaker's Text Box: Shut up already! They do not because this one IS fucking amazing! No more guesses allowed, but feel free to speculate after they get down here! That will please me.

With a Glowing Out of His Light and a Dramatic Movement of his Ball Animation Breaker motioned to the ceiling which opened up in a cut scene. The cut scene was supposed to be used to reveal an important switch puzzle, but Breaker had heavily modified it.

Descending dramatically to the ground by using a *Descend Dramatically to the Ground Animation* floated an angel. It was likely an angel with evil intent due to his dark and mostly black colour palette. Anyone who had any concept of Nega-Universes recognized this as a Nega-Angel and therefore evil. He was tall, muscular, and armed to the teeth. Badass black sparkly Armour (with badass rainbow accents), a bow taller than him by three times, and a halo that could double as a sword were a few of his impressive assets.

> Breaker's Text Box: He is bigger... He is badder... He is Negaer... He is...

Breaker used the *Pause for Dramatic Effect Animation.*

> Caëlahenãilenẁhei's Text Box: Okay, this one is more interesting. Who could that one be? I will have to put some thought into it.

> Gliint's Text Box: *Shrug* They don't look familiar at all.

> Yallundy's Whisper Text Box: They... feel familiar?

> Kray's Text Box: I don't know who that is, kay. They look all muscular, but look closer. He is super chubby.

> In'ferni and De'vini's Simultaneous Text Boxes: Who is that? They do look badass. Yeah, super badass.

> Palcath's Text Box: No way. I know who that is!

> Breaker's Text Box: What? You are going to ruin my last reveal? How?

> Palcath's Text Box: Because I know who it is! It is ndeis, the angel Fournimer found hidden in Onn. One of the two. The boy angel that saved him from the girl one.

> Breaker's Text Box: Never mind, carry on. Thought you had figured it out. My mistake.

> Palcath's Text Box: Can you believe that silly lad was convinced that it was Anders in disguise. Unable to contact anyone because of some mysterious reason.

> Gliint's Text Box: *Nod* Like a secret quest?

> Palcath's Text Box: Exactly lad. Like something saved him from death for a higher purpose.

> Breaker's Text Box: Or maybe some bunny took advantage of the fact

that something else saved him from death for a higher purpose? Not that it didn't work out expertly.

Caëlahenãilenŵhei's Text Box: That would make a much better reveal that whatever it really is. Even I would have to concede that Breaker's reveals were stupendous, instead of stupid, if that was the case. Unfortunately, Anders is dead. We all saw him get killed by the Admins.

In'ferni and De'vini's Simultaneous Text Boxes: Unless something amazing happened. Yep, like divine intervention or a glitch.

Breaker's Text Box: Or maybe he was fast enough to log out and save his skin?

Caëlahenãilenŵhei's Text Box: Doubtful. The timing for that would have to been immaculate. The reflexes required to dodge the lightning with a logout would have been near impossible and Anders wasn't even aware it was going to happen.

Breaker's Text Box: What if someone had been watching it unfold from the sidelines? Someone that could do it for him and still secretly control him?

Palcath's Text Box: They would still have needed lightning fast reflexes. I doubt anyone could have been that amazing and stopped that from happening. Besides, we saw his polygons disintegrate. No, we need to accept the fact that he is gone.

Breaker's Text Box: Funny thing about that, and don't get upset when I tell you this because cross my heart I really really mean it when I say this…

With a Stretching Out of His Bow and a Dramatic Jiggle of his Butt Animation the Nega-Angel flipped up the helmet's visor, earning a *Gasp Animation* from everyone in the room. His eyes were frantically moving but he was under the complete control of Breaker.

Breaker's Text Box: I am that fucking amazing!

Nega-Anders' Text Box: Sup bitches?

Chapter 37

CYCLE 6 GROUP F, HORSELESSLY LOST

Things sure had worked out great for Chad. Fournimer was convinced that even though the Fickle Fortune Wheel of Fate had been spun, it had not been spun 'randomly' as the flying cat guaranteed. Not only had Fournimer accidentally started the last of the flying cat's quests, he had spun Escort: Chad the Flying Feline of Fortune to Location: Out of the Expansion. Normally that would have been a dream spin, but since there wasn't a way to leave the Expansion (to his knowledge) Fournimer was likely going to be stuck with the flying monstrosity until his last breath.

Chad the Flying Feline of Fortune's Text Box: I was sort of thinking that mew would have gotten some... relief.... before coming back to rescue me.

Fournimer's Text Box: don't you think I tried to?

Draganders' Text Box: Chirp!

Chad the Flying Feline of Fortune's Text Box: They look purrfectly painful.

Fournimer's Text Box: they are painful! I think that you should help me with them. it is mostly your fault.

Chad the Flying Feline of Fortune's Text Box: First of all, I don't spin that way. Secondly, tiny little cat parts, big giant horse parts. Thirdly...

Chad the Flying Feline of Fortune used the *Retractable Claws Animation*.

Fournimer's Text Box: points taken.

Chad the Flying Feline of Fortune's Text Box: Meow let's focus on getting out of the Expansion before the entire thing gets destroyed tonight. Follow me to the secret exit of my lair.

While he was relatively sure that he could have found the secret exit himself (it was marked with a flashing neon sign), Fournimer knew that following his escort up the ladder would be more difficult. It was not an easy task but it was eventually accomplished by Draganders carrying Fournimer's horse butt, and with a reluctant Chad who had to help hold some of Fournimer's newly gained ball weight. Fournimer was in more pain, he had dragon claw marks all over his rump and kitty claw marks all over his balls. At least he was out of The Art Gallery of Cute Kittehs.

They were at the port in area, which would have made this escort quest especially easy to complete under normal circumstances. A shadow slowly crept over them. That little floating island that Palcath had made it on was slowly approaching Onn again.

Chad the Flying Feline of Fortune's Text Box: Fiddle faddle. Mew were right, this Portal is completely destroyed. We will never get out of here that way.

Fournimer's Text Box: told you. we should go back to Onn. Lis is there if she is still alive.

Chad the Flying Feline of Fortune's Text Box: We shouldn't have taken the ladder exit. Too bad we can't go back inside. I guess we have to walk.

Only resisting the temptation to *White Mule Kick* Chad in the side of the head, Fournimer turned towards the city of Onn, for the umpteenth time. Draganders happily walked behind, only resisting the urge to use Chad like a bite-sized, flying chew toy, but for completely different reasons.

They walked towards the city in the distance uneventfully for an entire seven steps. From the sky fell a mass, it landed hard on the ground accompanied by a horrid bone breaking thud. No one wanted to get closer, but curiosity finally got the better of Fournimer. He used his *Deviated Septum* to turn the mass over so they could get a better look.

Fournimer's Text Box: it's a lady. a f-ed up looking dead lady with no eyes. ugh, and I kinda touched it.

Hellsfight's Text Box: Uuuurrrrr-ggghhhhh-bl-lur-spurl!

Hellsfight used the *Get Up, But in an All F-ed Up Way Animation*. If she had eyes, she would have been looking right at them.

Fournimer and Chad the Flying Feline of Fortune both used the *Gasp in Alarm Animation*. Draganders did not. He had sort of seen it coming.

Another avatar body fell to the ground, a messed up monster followed, another avatar fell, and then about four more things of incomprehensible origin. Group F looked up and the sky was dark with falling corpses. The mounds of dead meat filled their view. The only other thing that Fournimer caught a glimpse of was a *Parsnip*.

> Hellsfight's Text Box: All pain!

Hellsfight attempted to grab Fournimer but he managed to kick her away. Wasting no time, the centaur, the dragon, and the cat started to flee for their lives. Onn was their destination, even if the island that all the corpses were falling from was slowly drifting in that direction. At least there were a few places still standing in Onn to shelter you from rain of all varieties, Water (Light), Water (Heavy), Water (Frozen), Corpse (Newly Discovered), Acid (Scenic), Acid (Damaging) and Carp (Heavy).

While valiantly fleeing Draganders stopped in his tracks and started to chirp excitedly. Fournimer's attempts to lure the rainbow dragon away from the horde of approaching monsters were not working, but he was not going to leave the last piece of Anders behind, no matter what.

> Fournimer's Text Box: what are you doing? we need to get out of here!

> Draganders' Text Box: Chirp!

> Chad the Flying Feline of Fortune's Text Box: I had a feline he would say that.

Fournimer tried everything he knew to get the dragon to move, but nothing worked. Draganders was as *Steadfast* as his father's boots had been, circling the random spot on the road with determination. It was a useful ability compared to Fournimer's *Light Gigas Pant's* ability of… Fournimer honestly couldn't even remember what they did. It must have been something particularly spectacular. He had never even remembered to use it.

> Fournimer's Text Box: come on! the giant army of death is coming.

> Draganders' Text Box: Chirp!

> Chad the Flying Feline of Fortune's Text Box: Why is he staying purrt there?

> Fournimer's Text Box: I don't know, maybe he found some *Dragon Candy*?

Draganders sat on the ground, looked directly in front of himself, and went cross-eyed staring at the air above his nose.

> Draganders' Text Box: CHIRP!

It was when Fournimer had used his *Light Gigas Pants* to improve all of his stats with *Improve* to increase his Strength for stubborn dragon pushing that he saw it. A thin wisp of a white was hanging in the air above Draganders' nose. It was miraculous that the dragon had seen it as it was only 0.25pt line thickness and only two length units long. Getting a closer look at the line, Fournimer noticed that it was two lines, joined together at the ends. It was radiating a little bit of heat and a soft white light was emanating from between the two segments.

The bottom join of the lines was accumulating a drop of something. Fournimer experimentally touched it, forgetting for now all the lessons everyone else had ever learned about touching mysterious objects, and the drip was moist. It smelled lovely and tasted sweet. Fournimer went in for another drop and the stimulation sent the white lines shivering, opening up. After a few prods with his finger, the white lines had stretched open, as if they were inviting Fournimer openly.

Fournimer tossed Draganders the last piece of *Dragon Bacon*, patted his little dragon head affectionately, and approached the tight pair of mysterious white lip lines with a *Grin Animation*.

> Fournimer's Text Box: oh my Maker. good dragon! good! such a good dragon!

> Chad the Flying Feline of Fortune's Text Box: Are mew serious? Right meow? There is an entire army over the ridge and you are going to get your rocks off in a mysterious hole?

> Fournimer's Text Box: shut up, this will only take a few rounds and they are shambling. my *Centaur Virgin Detector* says that this is a mostly virgin hole and I will take any sloppy seconds I can get.

Wasting not even a round Fournimer inserted himself into the floating hole. He didn't care that Chad was watching, he didn't care that an army was over the rise, he didn't even care that Draganders was still staring cross-eyed at the hole as the centaur cock slid inside. It was warm, it was moist, and it was tight. It was perfect and Fournimer began to thrust with a desperate need.

> Access Portal's Text Box: *Spare Key Type - Centaur Cock* accepted. Welcome back!

The wonderful tightness of the hole relaxed and Fournimer screamed out in a mad sex rage. Not only was he going to be unfulfilled, he also had to ponder who in their right mind would make a centaur cock work as their spare key?

The lines had expanded and now they all could easily fit through, even Fournimer which was a first for him. Inside was white, nothing else could be seen. Draganders chirped happily and jumped through without hesitation.

> Fournimer's Text Box: where does it go?

The army of corpses crested the rise and shambled closer.

> Chad the Flying Feline of Fortune's Text Box: Not here?

> Fournimer's Text Box: sold.

Chad and Fournimer walked through the portal and it closed up tightly and permanently. Wherever they were the approaching army would not be able to follow them.

> Fournimer's Text Box: where are we?

> Draganders' Text Box: Chirp!

> Chad the Flying Feline of Fortune's Text Box: No way! Impurrible. How did we get here? This is some amazing luck and that is coming from me, the Flying Feline of Fortune!

> Fournimer's Text Box: luck? me? you must be wrong.

> Chad the Flying Feline of Fortune's Text Box: No, it is beyond lucky! We are not in the Expansion anymurr. We are safe from the reset meow! More importantly that also means...

Fournimer heard the Quest Complete sound effect chime. He had accidentally completed the quest that he had accidentally started. Chad was no longer in the Expansion and his huge Fickle Fortune Wheel of Fate popped into existence in the stark white area.

> Chad the Flying Feline of Fortune's Text Box: Good luck on your spins. I hope you purrlion something nice!

> Fournimer's Text Box: oh Flaming Pits no. I am not spinning that.

> Chad the Flying Feline of Fortune's Text Box: So mew are opting for the party spin? That is a good idea. Then you both will share the reward.

> Draganders' Text Box: Chirp!

Draganders stepped forward and spun the Fickle Fortune Wheel of Fate with enough force for it to continue to rotate through the following dialogue.

> Fournimer's Text Box: no way. I am not accepting that.

Chad the Flying Feline of Fortune's Text Box: Sorry, but he agreed. It is going to happen meow.

Fournimer's Text Box: he said chirp! that is all he ever says!

Chad the Flying Feline of Fortune's Text Box: That was his yes chirp. I could tell, couldn't mew?

Fournimer's Text Box: no I could not. it was a chirp. undo it. stop it!

Chad the Flying Feline of Fortune's Text Box: Sorry. He selected yes for both of you. I don't have any control over it. Mew are going to have to accept your fate. Whatever it may be.

Coming to a painfully slow ticking halt the Fickle Fortune Wheel of Fate finally came to a stop, nestled between *Encounter - Horrible Tentacle Rape* and *Item - Commonly Rare Empty Bottle*.

Chad the Flying Feline of Fortune's Text Box: That a purrfectly good one I bet!

Dragander's' Text Box: Chirp!

Fournimer's Text Box: why? what is it? what does *Mystery Ability - Unlock Hidden Potential* do?

Chad the Flying Feline of Fortune's Text Box: I have no idea, but I bet we are about tuna find out.

Chapter 38

CYCLE 7
GROUP E, THE
ONNSLAUGHT OF ONN

Caëlahenãilenŵhei's Text Box: Well, this is just lovely isn't it? Marching off as the figureheads of a gigantic army that is going to siege the least inspiring named town in history. A town that is going to be defended by our friends and we are going to be helpless as we are controlled in an attempt to kill every single one of them in horrible ways. If we win our friends are going to be dead and then we will be turned on each other no doubt. If we lose we will likewise be killed, except by our friends instead of by each other or by Breaker when he wants to get kinky later at hi—

Caëlahenãilenŵhei's Text Box: s leisure.

In'ferni and De'vini's Simultaneous Text Boxes: I know, it is pretty hopeless. Muffble murrm mummble. I agree, at least we are together. Mnnsble murrg mu? Almost in Onn. Murrghumleble. I love you to.

Gliint took a big swig of *Full Mana Potion* and wiped his lips clean of the blue residue.

Gliint's Text Box: *Sigh* I wish we were not marching with that undead horde down-wind of us. They have a unique odor. Not what I expected zom—

Caëlahenãilenŵhei's Interruption Text Box: They are not that!

Gliint's Text Box: *Nod* I am pretty sure they are.

Caëlahenãilenŵhei's Text Box: While they are technically undead they are not being reanimated by magic, science, or a virus of any kind. It also is not contagious as Kray proved when he got bit in the femur.

Gliint's Text Box: How does that prove anything? *Confused* Kray doesn't have any flesh anymore! It might be contagious.

Kray's Text Box: I am still mad about that, kay. He was so fat that zom—

Caëlahenãilenŵhei's Interruption Text Box: They are not that! They are being controlled by an external source and not using their own motor skills. They show no desire to consume flesh, so therefore they are not that. I will call them Breaker's Spawns. We are technically under the same effect but I would call us Breaker's Thralls as we are still alive. I would also consent to calling them Revenants, that is probably the closest term. I refuse to be part of any book series that contains something so overused as... those.

Gliint's Text Box: *Headshake* I still don't get it though.

Caëlahenãilenŵhei's Text Box: A Revenant is the corpse or spirit of the dead returning to the world of the living through unnatural means, most often under the control of a master. Would you prefer Wraith?

Gliint's Text Box: Not that. *Eyeroll* I mean that there are thousands of them, plus us. How in the map is Breaker controlling all of us at once?

Kray's Text Box: He's not controlling me, kay. I'm coming to collect Sami-guy for our meeting with the caterer. Do you think Minotaurs will go for the vegetarian option?

In'ferni and De'vini's Simultaneous Text Boxes: That is a good question Kray. Mummg mummf murble? That is a better one Gliint. Mee mnow mright? You win babe, that was the best one. Mff! How many computer monitors do you think he has?

Caëlahenãilenŵhei's Text Box: I doubt he has that many. What he likely has done—

Caëlahenâilenẇhei's used the *Sneeze Animation.*

> Caëlahenâilenẇhei's Box Text: is programmed most of the dummies to auto-attack.

> Caëlahenâilenẇhei's Text Box: That is exactly what I did little miss C. I have more than enough monitors and accounts to control all of you individually. I also programmed the dummies to attack most anything but you idiots and each other. As an added bonus some of them are going to target certain avatars, to really make an emotional sting. Name changed warrier is in for some fun times. Thanks for telling me he was exhumed while I was taking a spying break and getting a sandwich!

> Kray's Text Box: Not this again, kay. It is confusing. Can't you be Breaker?

> Caëlahenâilenẇhei's Text Box: Sorry, can't. I'm still stuck up here.

> Caëlahenâilenẇhei's Box Text: If you programmed the dummies I guess that explains the group of four that went straight off in the wrong direction. Honestly, what I would have done—

> Caëlahenâilenẇhei's Interruption Text Box: Fuck. Why did I randomly choose to invade the one avatar that can still talk back when I block their Text Box abilities?

> Caëlahenâilenẇhei's Box Text: I would think that was obvious for someone like you. What I would have done is—

> Caëlahenâilenẇhei's Interruption Text Box: Good idea! Thanks C word!

Caëlahenâilenẇhei reached over to Kray's *Backpack* and rummaged around. Finally she pulled out one of the many wedding product samples that Kray had been bugging him with for cycles now. The *Jumbo Sandalwood Scented Candle* was unceremoniously jammed up Caela's mouthgina, silencing her. She had been candle hacked.

> Kray's Text Box: Thank you so much Breaker! Now I know which scent of candle to pick, kay. Not Sandalwood cause it will smell like a dirty mouthgina now.

> Caëlahenâilenẇhei's Text Box: You hear that? It is nothing. It is silence. It is the sound of you finally shutting up you cootch breather!

> Caëlahenâilenẇhei's Box Text: Mmmfmble murrsh!

Caëlahenãilenẁhei's Text Box: I love it. Finally it is quiet. I got other things to do. I will control all you idiots later!

Caëlahenãilenẁhei's used the *Sneeze Animation*. Released from the control of Breaker she tried to take the scented candle out of her nether regions but it wouldn't budge.

Caëlahenãilenẁhei's Text Box: Bloody Flaming Pit! I can't get it out of there. The candle was way too big and now it's stuck in my teeth.

Kray's Text Box: That's fine, kay. You can keep it. I don't need it anymore. I picked *Vanilla Chip Cookie Scent*.

Caëlahenãilenẁhei's Text Box: Perfect. I will treasure it always. Now I am stuck with two items I don't want.

In'ferni's and De'vini's Simultaneous Text Boxes: Mmmfu muugg mulee? Oh, good point. Mmmhmm. What do you mean two items?

Caëlahenãilenẁhei's Text Box: Two items. Obviously I mean the candle and the *Initiate's Jacket*.

Gliint's Text Box: Don't be so harsh on that jacket. *Avert eyes* It is basically the only thing keeping your outfit even a little bit modest.

Caëlahenãilenẁhei's Text Box: Alas, Breaker never bothered to equip my pants back on me, I can't help that. The jacket is how Breaker is controlling me.

Gliint's Text Box: *Eyes wide but are still averted* Really? That is how he is doing it, with items?

Gliint took another sip of his potion and wiped off more traces of blue.

Caëlahenãilenẁhei's Text Box: Really? Wasn't that part obvious? All of the dummy account Revenants are wearing his tainted items. I went under his control as soon as I started wearing this cursed pajama top, that you forced me to wear by destroying the others thank you. De'vini's necklace has a giant black skull on it. I think that would be a hint. Kray is somehow wearing the Anderses Only Slime Gear and Anders likely still had on whatever Breaker used to control him the first time. Also, you have been constantly drinking potions of every variety like they are going out of style-

Caëlahenãilenẁhei's Text Box: drinky!

Yallundy's Text Box: So that is how he is doing it!

Gliint, Caëlahenãilenŵhei, Kray, In'ferni, and De'vini's Simultaneous Mixed Up Text Boxes: *Gasp* Yallundy, where are you?! I was wondering how long it would take for you to say something. Who is that again, kay? Mmmble? Is she invisible or something?

Yallundy's Whisper Text Box: Crap. I didn't want to talk out loud. I'm in your *Backpack* Gliint, remember? You put me in there! It doesn't matter right now. Don't talk about me again in case Breaker is paying attention. I need to go tell everyone else in Onn about this so we can stop it.

Gliint's Yelling Text Box: *Joy!* That is most fortunate!

De'vini used the *Sneeze Animation*.

De'vini's Text Box: What is?

Gliint's Text Box: *Eye twitch* That it isn't raining? I hate Carp.

De'vini's Text Box: Good point, I hate getting soaked with fish. Time to get into your battalions and start this fucking war!

~~~

Trev Terra's Text Box: This isn't going to work, well I guess it might, but it is sort of unlikely, well what I mean is... gosh. We are pretty boned.

Jorthan the Male Troll Monk's Text Box: Mon petit lutin amour, she is not so bad. Leaving we can always do.

Hippolyta's Text Box: Exactly, so buck up kiddo. If we need to leave we can easily jump on Carrot Jr. once Roodg gets back from picking up a fully leveled Zal Finn. It isn't hopeless, I am level ✪ ✪ now. I can kick some serious jackass ass if required.

samuri's Text Box: ...

The All Seeing Eye Dog and Nine Circles of Hellcat ate their face treats from their long lost friend happily. They had missed him so much more than they had ever missed their masters.

NPC Margarine's Text Box: True. We are here to stand by you no matter what happens. This is the last stand, hun.

NPC Greeta's Text Box: Welcome to Onn!

NPC Galapas' Text Box: Illiandro will be back soon with the entire Coliseum. That will help even things out a small amount. Better than nothing I guess.

Hippolyta's Text Box: Who are you again?

NPC Galapas used the *Sigh Animation.*

Yallundy's Text Box: There is no time for me to explain why I need to explain this so listen.

Everyone stopped their getting ready to die preparations and listened to the ghost that had shown up in the centre of town.

Yallundy's Text Box: First, important news. Both Anders and Kray are alive.

samuri's Text Box: …

samuri used the *Extremely Conflicted as to if I Should be Happy or Mortified Animation.*

Yallundy's Text Box: Planning time! Breaker is controlling everyone with his broken items. We need to find a way to destroy the items to free everyone! They formed into battalions and are getting ready to attack us, so we need to find the person we know the most about and help them. Breaker also programmed some dead avatars to target certain people, so be wary.

Yallundy's Text Box: Skeletal Kray is leading the huge army of dead avatars. Destroy the *Slime Armour* set to free him. Most of the dead avatars have gray target beacons, so they are coming for you samuri.

samuri's Text Box: …

samuri used the *Nod Animation.* The Nine Circles of Hellcat and the All Seeing Eye Dog brushed up against his leg to show their support. Then someone else chimed in, which startled samuri.

NPC Margarine's Text Box: We will help you, hun. That is likely the strongest army and you will need all the support you can get! You helped us decorate all that cake so we will help you decorate all those corpses!

NPC Galapas' Text Box: You lack any weapons, so I would be glad to lend you my spear. Well, I can't lend it you really, it is attached to my

> hand, but you know what I mean.

> NPC Illiandro's Text Box: My Coliseum friends and I will help you unlock secret areas in their heads!

> NPC Greeta's Text Box: Welcome to Onn!

> samuri's Text Box: ...

samuri used the *Smile Animation*.

> Yallundy's Text Box: De'vini is being controlled by her necklace. In'ferni is not being controlled but is tied up. They have an Optional Boss with them... half of one at least.

> Jorthan the Male Troll Monk's Text Box: They are being our team! We should help them.

> Trev Terra's Text Box: I agree... yes, rather. We need to do that.

> Hippolyta's Text Box: I will use every weight unit of breast flesh I possess to release the Lesbitwins! On this I swear.

> Yallundy's Text Box: Caela is being controlled by her jacket and has a legion of dead Quest Fairies with her. She is flying the *Turnip*. I think that Fourni, Lissa, Palcath, and Roodg can handle her, because I am pretty sure for my plan against Gliint and the monsters to work I will only need Mr. Max and Zal Finn.

> samuri's Text Box: ???

samuri used the *Shrug Animation*.

> NPC Margarine's Text Box: Sorry floating hun, but none of those avatars are here. The dwarf, human, and half-elf all went up to the island and I doubt will be back soon. The night elf is off picking up the NPC girl you all hang out with.

> Yallundy's Text Box: What? Shoot! I will have to think up a different way to deal with Gliint. Can you please tell Roodg and Zal Finn what to do when they get here?

Yallundy vanished as quickly as she had appeared. As Carrot Jr. was descending from the sky a loud clear guitar rift could be heard ringing throughout the world. It was a well produced non-official background music called *The Onnslaught of Onn*. It was on in Onn.

Roodg's Text Box: i'M BACK!

NPC Greeta's Text Box: Welcome to Onn!

samuri's Text Box: ...

samuri used the *Wave Animation*.

NPC Margarine's Text Box: There you are, hun. Where is that NPC you went to pick up?

Roodg's Text Box: i DUNNO. sHE WASN'T THERE. wHAT IS GOING ON? wHERE DID EVERYONE GO?

NPC Margarine's Text Box: That is simple, hun. We are defending Onn in groups. Your group is all missing besides you, but you are in charge of going and fighting Cal... Caell... that impossible to remember the name of one. She is above the skys on a *Turnip*.

Roodg's Text Box: gOT IT!

Roodg and Carrot Jr. were off to their battle like a night elf riding a gigantic hovering centipede. The NPCs tried to Text Box but were too late to catch the speedy centipede.

NPC Margarine's Text Box: No wait, hun. We didn't tell you about her jacket!

NPC Greeta's Text Box: Welcome to Onn...

◊ **Chapter 39** ◊

CYCLE 7
THE BATTLE OF
CAUTION STEP

> Mr. Max's Text Box: I keep forgetting. I was supposed to tell you something else.

> Lissa's Text Box: I know that meathead! You keep saying that and then you get distracted and run off to kill something instead...

Lissa used the *Heartfelt Sigh Animation*. Mr. Max hadn't even bothered to listen to her reply. He was already distracted attempting to chop up a Marauder Cow. The big idiot was so excited that things were not falling in one hit that he had nearly regressed to his old pre-Level ✪ ✪ state. Lissa almost complained, but the experience points here were unlike anything she had ever experienced before. She watched and healed him on occasion. She was already up 21 Levels, hitting 93 when this last cow let out her *Death Moo*, and he had only managed to chop up seventeen assorted cows thus far.

> Mr. Max's Text Box: I wish I knew about this place before I spent so long Leveling up adventurette. Look at your Levels go!

> Lissa's Text Box: I am not going to lie, that part is sawesome. What I want to know is... seriously? Again?

> Mr. Max's Text Box: Must Level up! Must Level up whoever you are!

It became clear to Lissa. Mr. Max had reverted to his old self, but for completely unselfish reasons. He was Flaming Pit bent on Leveling her up. She may as well enjoy the ride!

> Mr. Max's Text Box: Must kill all the cows. Must win you the third place amazing prize!

> Lissa's Text Box: Wait, there is a prize? I forgot about that.

> Mr. Max's Text Box: Of course there is a prize fellow adventurer. Didn't you read the contests? Go look on the websi—

> Lissa's Interruption Text Box: No time for that now! I want a prize. Hark! There is a cow. #BeholdThatBovine!

Killing the assorted demonic cows went much faster now that Lissa was truly helping. She put her dislike of orange to the side (for now) to focus on healing, buffing, and supporting Mr. Max. He was a sight to behold when he was experience point lusting, his game skills were evident and every move was perfectly calculated. Lissa did not want to admit this, but she had to conceal the fact that her nipples had gotten a little aroused with her excitement. Thankfully, the orange icing covered it up nicely.

A final Maddest Cow fell to the combined strike of an *Eight Handed Sword* and an *Ultimatium Mace* and Lissa heard the final trumpet music song that signalled Level ✪ ✪ . Both avatars were drenched in sweat, and were both hot and bothered. Working together had done something different to them. They had far more chemistry together than Lissa had imagined. She was concealing her *Blush Shade* now as well as her nipples. Mr. Max could never hope to conceal his excitement.

> Text Box: Congratulations to Lissa, the third avatar to reach Level ✪ ✪! Enjoy your prize! Sorry everyone, there are no more prizes to be won by reaching maximum Level. Thanks for trying!

> Lissa's Text Box: I did it!

> Mr. Max's Text Box: Good job Lissa!

Now that the experience hunting was over, Mr. Max had reverted back to his new self. He could remember who she was.

> Mr. Max's Text Box: I bet you are going to love it! Do you drink tea? If so, you can drink it in style now!

> Lissa's Text Box: Sometimes... wait, how do you know it is for tea?

> Mr. Max's Text Box: The *Caution Step* painting and the *Caution Step* lunchbox are gone. Logic dictates that it is going to be the *Caution Step* tea service set.

Lissa's Text Box: Are you fucking serious?

Mr. Max's Text Box: I am! It is so exciting right?

Lissa's Text Box: I got the email… Fuck. It is a *Caution Step* tea service set.

Mr. Max's Text Box: All the album covers are the teacups. The pot is—

Lissa's Interruption Text Box: Are you #KingOfTheMeatheads? I know you are forgetful, but damn. How can you forget that I hate them so much?

Mr. Max's Text Box: Are you sure you hate them?

Lissa used the *Furious Animation*.

Lissa's Text Box: Of course I am sure! With every fiber of my eternal soul!

Mr. Max's Text Box: Piffle, you are like Hippolyta I bet. Now let me … *clears throat* ♪♫That girl with the pur—

Lissa's Interruption Text Box: Don't you dare utter another word of that song. If you do I will rip your heart out of your chest and show it to you as it slowly stops beating before your eyes. #NoJoke.

Mr. Max's Text Box: See! You do like them! That ripping out your heart bit is a line in the song!

Lissa's Text Box: Of course it is a line in the song because I was the one who sa—

Mr. Max's Interruption Text Box: So you do like them!

Lissa was at the breaking point. She was so angry that she somehow broke into the Standard Animations database and altered one. Forever it would now be hers and hers alone. Lissa used the *Furious Flex Animation*. Mr. Max would never be able to use his favorite Animation again. He had been perma-locked out.

Lissa's Text Box: Are you serious? You are #SoFuckedUp. How could you say that?! That is #SoFuckedUp! Don't you remember me talking about *Caution Step*? You are #SoFuckedUp! Don't you remember my entire story about them? That is #SuperBeyondSoFuckedUp. Fuck!

Mr. Max's Text Box: I don't remember that at all. I'm sorry. Really.

Lissa's Text Box: Don't think you are getting away with it that easy! I am looking it up right here on the Battle Logs... I will show you that you are a complete and total introduction ruining moron, you wait. Oh, how I will show you. How red will your face go? An as of yet unlocked *Blush Shade* I bet. I think *#9* was being saved for something special and this must be the time! You will unlock it. See right here... oh.

Mr. Max's Text Box: Oh?

Lissa's Text Box: You were getting a sandwich there... but there were other times, let me go and... you were gone there. Don't think that you can get off that easy because I said... shit... then there was that other time when... crap... you know what?

Mr. Max's Text Box: What?

Lissa settled down, a tad.

Lissa's Text Box: You were right.

Mr. Max's Text Box: No way! Really? Me?

Lissa's Text Box: Yes, I looked and every single time something about *Caution Step* happened around me. You were never there. I'm sorry.

Mr. Max's Text Box: That is okay Lissa. I'm sorry too. I figured I would have remembered a story about *Caution Step*! Will you tell me what it is?

Lissa's Text Box: I might as well, everyone else already knows. Okay, so you know that song *Equ—*

Lissa was interrupted by a loud and well played guitar rift. The background music shifted to The *Onnslaught of Onn*.

Lissa's Text Box: What the here?

Mr. Max's Text Box: Ha! Love it! Because of where we are.

Lissa's Text Box: What is with this sudden angry music?

Mr. Max's Text Box: I don't know but it sure is catchy. The production value is amazing and I am digging the instrumentals!

Lissa's Text Box: It sounds familiar.

Mr. Max's Text Box: You're right. It does sound familiar. Wait... who is that party coming over the Hill of Endless Suffering? How did they get in here, the Expansion is locked? Wait, Lissa do I know these people and am forgetting they are supposed to be here? I do that sometimes.

Lissa's Text Box: No Max, you don't know them. Strangely though, I do.

Chapter 40

CYCLE 7
THE BATTLE OF
UNHOLY MATRIMONY

Brenna Jay fell apart in two equal halves. This caused the stitching holding the dead avatar together to separate, causing Brenna Jay to fall apart in four unequal quarters. NPC Margarine was more deadly wielding a knife in a block of cake than samuri had expected. samuri was grateful, Brenna Jay had a flashing gray beacon glued to his face and had been coming directly at the weaponless avatar, but now him, and his ill gotten *Light Gigas Pants*. were gone.

> NPC Margarine's Text Box: Don't worry, hun. I got this one!

samuri did not reply, not even with a '…' in fear of opening up the Bakery Shoppe menu. Margarine would know that he was thankful.

There were many corpses here with flashing gray beacons, samuri didn't have to count. He already knew the number without a pause, there were 119. Every avatar that samuri had chopped in half for Breaker was headed straight for him. There were also about a thousand that he didn't have any part in killing, but he still felt responsible for their deaths. It was true Breaker had killed them, but samuri was responsible for allowing Breaker to get so powerful and every walking Revenant here weighed heavily on gray shoulders.

Cheekera, the overly friendly night elf who once had a serious case of the 'Not being able to shut the fuck ups' as Breaker had put it, approached samuri. She was brandishing her broken *Three Handed Sword*, courtesy of Breaker of course, and nothing else. She took a swipe at samuri but he deftly dodged out of the way, throwing her off her balance. NPC Greeta took advantage of the slip in Cheekera's guard and chopped off the night elf's head along the already provided seam. This was already the ninth avatar to fall to the might of Greeta's *Welcome to Onn Sign* and she showed no further signs of stopping now. Cheekera's headless corpse kept coming, and Greeta jumped on it, bashing every part of the Revenant into a fine paste.

NPC Greeta's Text Box: WELCOME! TO! ONN!

Wabbino was coming next, with his *Emerald Chain Armour* and the *Orichalcum Daggers* he had been given by Breaker. His only crime had been being a Backstabber, but he had been burned to a crisp shortly after equipping the 'present'. While technically not samuri's fault, there was still a gray flashing beacon on this avatar. Perhaps samuri did need to count the beacons after all if Breaker had put them on anyone who had died while samuri was around. Not even getting a chance to attempt to attack, Wabbino was taken down by the All Seeing Eye Dog and Nine Circles of Hellcat. They had jumped the avatar and ripped the dwarf apart to devour. This time his only crime had been to smell particularly delicious.

A swath of corpses that samuri did not recognize came next, they were handled by NPC Illiandro with his fabulously confusing weapon sized *Coliseum Keysword* and a swath of Coliseum Boss monsters that samuri did not recognize.

Jee Co Nah Rah had been approaching since the start of the encounter due to the fact that he was as large as the Frost Gigas, but he was here now. His *Comfortable Sandals* gave him the size of a giant. He had already crushed a few incidental Revenants on his way and thus far had proven himself a lot more useful than while alive. samuri backed up, everyone he knew about that was helping here was indisposed in other combats. Jee Co Nah Rah took a big step forward, his floppy exposed dick swaying with the motion as he attempted to stomp on samuri with his left sandal. samuri used the *Wince Animation* and prepared for the worst, but NPC Galapas stepped forward and held out his *Generic Guard Spear*. This stopped the behemoth long enough for samuri to get out of the way and for Galapas to start stabbing at the giant gnome's eyes. samuri was thankful for the intervene but was embarrassed that he had completely forgotten about Galapas.

samuri recognized the group of adventurers coming up next. Samantha, Piping, Mary, and (the now able to go into *Stealth* even though he was a Warrior) Frillo. samuri was weaponless, but these guys were still low level and he might be able to do something about them without help.

Piping was exceptionally easy to eliminate. He took one slash with his *Mad Daggers* and opened up a portal to the GameFrame. A paper cut out of a bunny hand grabbed him and dragged him into the portal with a blip. Screams of paper cut induced death followed. Samantha had never taken a gift from Breaker and was samuri's next target. With a single *White Wolf Kick* he smacked the helpful right off of her face and the *Fritzing Gloves* right off of her hands (that Breaker must have equipped on her corpse for spite). Mary would be more of a challenge due to her Auto Locating *Loko's Helmet*, unfortunately for her Frillo did not possess such an item and he broke from his hazy wispy confusing stealth mode and stabbed her through the forehead instead of his intended target.

Only Frillo and his *The Glum Ring* were left. samuri dodged a slash from *Stang* and countered with a kick from his *Bushido Beach Sandals (s)*. The pain was unbearable, samuri was sure he had broken his pinky toe. As he used the *Ouch I Broke my Toe Animation* he also remembered that the original ability of *The Glum Ring* before it had been altered by Breaker had been damage reduction. samuri was not going to be able to kick himself out of this one. Frillo disappeared again into his wispy world.

There had to be something samuri could do, he was not going to let himself get beaten by an unimportant Level 4 character.

> samuri's Text Box: …

samuri used the *Grand Idea Animation*. He did have something on him, and while it wasn't deadly in any sense of the word, at least it would stick to Frillo so samuri could avoid him until someone else could help. Dual wielding his newly acquired *Multicoloured Icing Dispenser* in one hand and the *Shaker of Unlimited Sprinkles* in the other samuri turned to where he thought his target was. samuri used the Warrior attack with the biggest range, *The Sword of Fate*, but in his hands it became *The Sprinkles of Fate*. samuri opened his mouth in shock after what happened, his giant tongue spilling out on the ground.

> samuri's Text Box: Hothly Phuck!

Frillo was on the ground, still half in stealth mode, dead. The Sprinkles that had not blasted through Frillo's ribcage like *Gratling Gun* bullets were embedded in his skull. Icing had cut right through the little avatar, completely severing his right arm and left butt cheek. The hand with *The Glum Ring* continued to crawl towards samuri and he sprayed thick pink icing at it in terror. It wasn't until *The Glum Ring* was destroyed by the icy glaszs of gray doom that the pieces of Frillo stopped crawling towards samuri.

samuri used the *Grand Idea Animation* again. He had learned somehting. He was PVP broken, not his sword. Anything he wielded would become a dangerous PVP attacking machine, even if it was sprinkles.

Two of the highest Level corpses cut their way through the mess of unimportant ones before them. These ones were different. They were almost fully decked out in equipment. One was only missing his *Wind Gigas Helmet*, the other only missing her *Fire Gigas Necklace*. They had the biggest gray beacons flashing and one looked right at samuri with his dead eyes (the other also looked right at samuri, but she didn't have eyes).

> Grandiger's Text Box: You! You killed us! This is all your fault. We would still be alive if it wasn't for you!

> Hellsfight's Text Box: You killed!

samuri was dreading this moment, but now it was even worse. His old party before meeting Breaker, and also first kills to 'help' on Breaker's 'holy mission from the Maker' were here confronting him. It was his now ex-best friends, Grandiger and Hellsfight. They taunted him as they took swings, attempting to snuff out the leader of *guild collecter*. samuri deflected blows with masterful cake decorating as he tried to defend his honour, or what little he had left.

> samuri's Text Box: No, Breakther trickthed usth all!

> Grandiger's Text Box: Did he now? Really? You were the one who chopped us apart, not him. You can't blame him for your mistakes.

> Hellsfight's Text Box: Your fault!

samuri was having a hard time fighting back, they were right. It was his fault, this was all his fault.

> samuri's Text Box: I changeth my wayths! You havth no ideath howth haard it wath to noth cutth Kray in halfth!

> Grandiger's Text Box: You deserve to die you snide little useless lackey! You deserve this fate!

> Hellsfight's Text Box: Deserve death!

samuri backed up and hit a wall, he could no longer retreat. A slash from one of Grandiger's *Diamond Hammers* nipped off a piece of samuri's ear (somehow) and blood gushed over the avatar's face. They were right, he did deserve this. samuri got ready to accept his fate. He would die to cleanse his soul, to be at peace. He had avoided this comeuppance for far too long.

> NPC Margarine's Text Box: No, hun, don't listen. They are programmed to say that!

> samuri's Text Box: Huth? Buth i killth them!

> NPC Margarine's Text Box: Welcome to my Bakery Shoppe, hun. How can I help you today?

samuri closed the Bakery Shoppe menu.

> NPC Margarine's Text Box: Sorry, hun, but take it from me, the master of being stuck in a programming loop, they are not saying that, it isn't really them. Try talking to them again!

> samuri's Text Box: ...

Grandiger's Text Box: You! You killed us! This is all your fault. We would still be alive if it wasn't for you!

Hellsfight's Text Box: You killed!

NPC Margarine's Text Box: See, hun! I knew it! They already said that. The most dialog anyone would ever bother to write for an unimportant NPC is three lines.

NPC Greeta's Text Box: Welcome to Onn!

NPC Margarine's Text Box: Sometimes even less. They are not who you killed, they are programmed shells. It doesn't matter what you did in the past if you are trying to make it better now. What you really need to do is apologize for what you have done and try to make it up to the people you hurt, hun. After you chop up their corpses.

She was right. samuri had been doing this all wrong. With a *Grim Resolve Animation*, samuri got up off the ground, and faced the corpses of his old friends. He set his *Shaker of Unlimited Sprinkles* on *Skull Sprinkles* and changed his *Multicoloured Icing Dispenser* to *Blood Red*. With a use of *Sprink-a-pult* and of *Rage of the Icing Gods* samuri decorated their corpses to death. He was a boss of cake. He told NPC Greeta to thank NPC Margarine for him.

samuri took a round to finally hit send on the two long overdue apology letters to the actual Grandiger and Hellsfight in his email inbox that he had been too scared to send. He hoped that they would read them.

Kray's Text Box: Oh my Maker! That is the best decorating I have ever seen, kay! I changed my mind, you are going to make our wedding cake now Sami-guy, not that ultra chubby butter NPC!

The NPCs of Onn, lead by an upset and somewhat chubby NPC Margarine, approached Kray with the intent to kill. samuri reminded them that this was Kray, and despite the fact that he did look pretty dead as a walking skeleton, he was still a living avatar and they needed to try and save him.

samuri's Text Box: Okath Breakther! Timeth fort youth to dieth! Leth Krayth go!

Kray's Text Box: What are you rambling on about Sami-guy? Breaker isn't controlling me. I am totally helping him because he is so nice, kay. I mean look at how skinny he made me, it is amazing right? Plus he showed me how to use this special jelly Armour so I am the best gay elf now!

> samuri's Text Box: …

samuri used the *Shocked Animation*. Kray was helping Breaker, on purpose? He almost deserved to be cut in half, almost. The problem still remained, even if Kray wasn't being controlled by Breaker right now, Breaker could at any moment take over Kray. More troubling was the fact that the *Slime Armour* that Kray was wearing was one of Breaker's dummy accounts; if it was allowed to live then Breaker would not be able to be truly defeated.

They needed to get that Armour off of Kray without killing him. If samuri still had his *Katana-Nata* he could have expertly cut it off, but these sprinkles were far too random and this icing was far too deadly. He asked if anyone had any ideas, and everyone did.

NPC lliandro and Galapas both charged at Kray and attempted to yank off the pieces of Armour, but they wouldn't budge because the *Slime Armour* was too slick.

> Kray's Text Box: Oh hi. It's okay, kay. You don't need to do that. I'm not going to get a tux, so you don't need to fit me for one. I am going to wear this.

Various Coliseum monsters tried next, they used every weapon at their disposal to try to pry off the Armour, but their weapons wouldn't stay in critical pry off areas due to the slippery coating of the Armour.

> Kray's Text Box: You don't need to let this outfit out. In fact you need to take it in a little, kay. It used to belong to a real chub.

NPC Margarine and Greeta jumped into the mix, they tried to beat the Armour off with their knife in a block of cake and *Welcome to Onn* sign respectively.

> Kray's Text Box: Thank you, pounding that Armour in is making me look even skinnier. It is good you are here. I wanted to talk to you both, kay. Sorry Chubby Butter Lady, but Sami-guy insists on making our cake now so you are fired. Greeta, I was wondering if you would be our wedding greeter.

NPC Margarine and Greeta beat harder to release their respective frustrations with the skeleton, but to no avail. The All Seeing Eye Dog and Nine Circles of Hellcat jumped in, attempting to gnaw off either Kray's boots or ankles. They didn't really care which, they wanted bones to play with. Their bites only slid off the Armour.

> Kray's Text Box: You silly pets! I know you love me more than Sami-guy but come on, kay. This is a little embarrassing.

samuri was flustered. None of this was working. There had to be a way to get Kray's Armour off.

> samuri's Text Box: …

samuri used the *Grand Idea Animation*, but this time he was not happy about the plan he had come up with. He knew of one sure fire way to get Kray out of his Armour. It would work without a shadow of a doubt, but it would be horrible.

Walking up to Kray he shooed everyone else to the side. He cupped his hand and used the *Whisper Something to Someone Else Dual Animation*.

> Kray's Text Box: OMM! Kay, right now?

samuri used the *Whisper Something to Someone Else Dual Animation* again and changed his *Blush Setting* to #6.

> Kray's Text Box: What? No way, kay! I thought you wanted to save that for our wedding night!

samuri used the *Whisper Something to Someone Else Dual Animation* again and changed his *Blush Setting* to #7.

> Kray's Text Box: That Sami-guy is a good point, kay.

samuri used the *Whisper Something to Someone Else Dual Animation* again and changed his *Blush Setting* to #8.

> Kray's Text Box: Of course, kay! Right now! Right now! For the love of the Maker let's do it right now!

samuri used the *Whisper Something to Someone Else Dual Animation* again and changed his *Blush Setting* to #9. To do so he needed to invent *Blush Shade #9*, but now anyone who was embarrassed as samuri was could use it, but it would take an epic amount of embarrassment to do so.

> Kray's Text Box: Good point, kay!

Kray started to rip off his Armour, but this was the *Slime Armour*. As soon as it sensed the sexy situation it automatically disappeared into the *Pink Slime Jock-Strap*. More precisely, it would have, if Kray had the *Pink Slime Jock-Strap* on. Instead it only attempted to do so, collided with itself midair, and exploded in a flurry of black pixels. The *Slime Armour* was destroyed and the already free Kray was forever free of Breaker's control. Kray did not notice, he was far too busy prostrating himself against some corpses while wiggling his naked skeletal butt in the air.

> Kray's Text Box: Kay, I'm ready to try that amazing tongue out Sami-Guy!

samuri couldn't say anything. He was too busy looking for the non-existent *Blush Shade #10*.

> Arcade Unicorn's Text Box: He will do no such thing you filthy skeleslut!

> Kray's Text Box: What, kay?

From through the crowd of remaining corpses (that had been polite enough to wait for Kray's thing to be over) charged a blood splattered Unicorn. He ducked his head between the legs of a shambling corpse and caused it to fling up onto his rainbow backside. Once the shambling slut was perched upon the back of the unicorn it was slut shamed to the highest degree, exploding into a fine mist of trampy guts.

> Arcade Unicorn's Text Box: There is still a battle to fight and a thousand corpses to destroy! I saw the shining light of the purest, most virginal soul ever gleaming in the distance and I had to come help. I am forever at your service.

The Arcade Unicorn bent his neck down in admiration for the purest of the pure.

> Kray's Text Box: About time, kay!

Kray approached the unicorn but even the act of stepping toward it caused the skeleton to burst into flames. It didn't hurt him, but he was leery of approaching closer.

> Arcade Unicorn's Text Box: Not you, you flaming hussy. This vision of virginal beauty!

samuri, pure as newly dusted snow, mounted the unicorn. An angelic harp plucked the air around the pairing. The unicorn bit his quivering bottom lip when a rainbow shot out of his horn and vaporized a nearby corpse.

> Arcade Unicorn's Text Box: Holy Maker, this feels so pure! Ride me like I'm your dirty fuck bitch you sweet ass virgin!

samuri raised his icing into the sky. Before him lay an army of darkness, behind him was an army of light (and also Kray).

> samuri's Text Box: Onthe morth intoth theth breathch, dearth friendths! Toth battlth!

They were rallied in the fight to end all fights. It was on in Onn.

> NPC Greeta's Text Box: Welcome to motherfucking Onn bitches!

◈ **Chapter 41** ◈

CYCLE 7
THE BATTLE OF
INTERRUPTIONS

Lissa could barely believe it, but it was happening. Marching over the Hill of Endless Suffering was a group of avatars that she knew. All were human and mostly equipped with epic high Level gear.

Quoona was in the lead, which was not at all a surprise. The Night Ranger had always scouted ahead diligently looking for traps and other dangers. Her long, impossibly coloured red hair was for the first time blending in with the scenery due to the impossibly coloured fire that burned here. She had been decked out with Armour and weapons that were really on fire, unlike everything else here which was for show. She was only missing a pair of pants to show the fact that she had been brutalized by Bridge Ogres. Her belly button was adorned with a flashing purple homing beacon.

O'Sklorm was next in line, as short and wiry as ever. Shaggy blue hair topped the head of the Magic Mage. He was covered in head to toe in shards of ice. Despite the fact that he was most definitely dead, he was shivering. He was missing his pants to emphasize how crotchless he had become in his last moments with the Flamalith. He had a new pretend penis, a flashing purple homing beacon was placed right where his old one used to be.

Nerchiner came next, even though Lissa had seen him before O'Sklorm and Quoona due to his large height and frame. The Warrior proudly wielded a *Truestrike Doublesword* and his Armour had been laced with fragments of rock and assorted cheap gems. He was missing pants, as well as legs due to his explosive encounter with The Titan. He did not have any problems moving around, despite his lack of parts. His purple homing beacon was hovering where his midsection should have been.

Finally, neon yellow hair came over the hill and Lissa's heart sank. Vendimm, the leader of the group. His *Hammerspider Hammer*, *Citrine Shield*, and *Golden Plate* caused the flames of the area to glisten and dance off their reflective surfaces. The Defender was humming a tune to himself that only he could fully hear and was only missing the flesh on 58% of his body. The rest had been consumed by the Feaster. What flesh remained was sparking with electrical energy. A purple homing beacon completed his look, attached directly onto what was left of his pancreas.

> Mr. Max's Text Box: I remember them!

> Lissa's Text Box: What? Seriously?'

> Mr. Max's Text Box: Yep! You told us the story of how they where your first group, how they all died, and how they ruined your avatar by blaming you for them cheating and you got blacklisted and broken. Wasn't there one more of them?

> Lissa's Text Box: You… remember that?

> Mr. Max's Text Box: Of course I do! You told me that way back when we both got introduced at almost the same time. I eventually remembered everything you have ever said!

Mr. Max tried to use the *Flex Animation* but it was locked to him, it instead turned into the *Perplex Animation* and he only looked foolish.

> Lissa's Text Box: You remembered this random fact about me but you completely forgot my name and everything about me for how many cycles? That is #So…Fucking…Nice.

Lissa was too stunned to be mean. She never thought she would have lived long enough to see that happen. She did not have time to dwell on what it meant, to be nice to Mr. Max? The party of her former allies that had been approaching had stopped in a line facing her. They stayed like that, motionless, blinking purple, and oozing. On second thought, maybe she did have some time.

> Mr. Max's Text Box: Why are they standing there? Why are they blinking purple? Why don't any of them have on pants?

> Lissa's Text Box: I don't know. It's weird. What are they even doing here? Should we do something?

Mr. Max used the *Shrug Animation*.

> Macintosh's Text Box: I know what you can do #2 gal and #3 pal…

> Lissa's Text Box: Huh? Who the fuck is Macintosh?

Mr. Max used the *Shrug Animation*.

Macintosh revealed himself. He had been hiding behind a part of Vendimm's remaining liver. The ball of light had a wicked smirk on his face and his hands behind his back.

> Macintosh's Text Box: ... You can both d—

> Lissa's Interruption Text Box: A Yellow Quest Fairy? Who is that?

> Purple Quest Fairy's Text Box: Seriously? You don't know who that is? You are #SoScre—

> Lissa's Interruption Text Box: No I don't know who that is. I don't know who you are either.

A Purple Quest Fairy, with a mean expression appeared from behind Nerchiner's husky frame. It also had both hands behind its back.

> Orange Quest Fairy's Text Box: Don't be so hard on her framers. Max, we never properly introduced. I am—

> Mr. Max's Interruption Text Box: Who are you and why do you know my name?

An Orange Quest Fairy came out of hiding from Quoona's gaping void, it hadn't been the cleanest hiding spot, but it had worked. He had changed his mind and had both hands behind his back.

> Macintosh's Text Box: I see you changed your vote F—

> Mr. Max's Interruption Text Box: They were voting?

> Macintosh's Text Box: As I was saying... before I got so rudely interrupted, it is time for yo—

> Lissa's Interruption Text Box: I wonder what about?

> Macintosh's Text Box: I am going to tell you gal. We are here to—

> Mr. Max's Interruption Text Box: I don't know, maybe we should ask them.

> Macintosh's Text Box: ...

> Lissa and Mr. Max's Simultaneous Text Boxes: Well? What were you three voting on?

> White Quest Fairy's Text Box: I am afraid your math is wrong. There are a few more than three of us here and—

> Lissa's Interruption Text Box: Who is that one now?

Mr. Max used the *Shrug Animation* as the White Quest Fairy flew out of O'Sklorm's sleeve, his hands behind his back.

> Gray Quest Fairy's Text Box: You both will pay for what you did to Abby and Tyreese! Your blo—

> Mr. Max's Interruption Text Box: Who and who?

The Gray Quest Fairy flew out from behind a scenic Pile of Burning Souls Damned for All Eternity, hands behind his back. Mr. Max and Lissa performed the *Who are Abby and Tyreese Dual Animation*.

> Pink Quest Fairy's Text Box: You don't remember Abby and Tyreese? How unswe—

> Lissa's Interruption Text Box: How many are there?

The Pink Quest Fairy was in *Vendimm's Golden Boot (r)*, he was now holding his hands behind his back.

> Other-Blue Quest Fairy's Text Box: They knew who you were man. Like be all with the ebb and flow of the universe. Be like all, not square man. I didn't think that I wanted to resort to being a square, but to remove a square rather, one must sometimes be a square man. I thin—

> Mr. Max's Interruption Text Box: The Other-Blue Quest Fairy? Where is the blue one?

The Other-Blue Quest Fairy had been hiding behind Macintosh the entire time. She was now holding her hands behind her back.

> Blue Quest Fairy's Text Box: I am rig—

> Lissa's Interruption Text Box: There they are!

The Blue Quest Fairy was also behind Macintosh, but she did not have her hands behind her back.

> Mr. Max's Text Box: Why is there a second blue one? That is stupid. We only need one blue one. Whoever you are, go hide again and stop making this more complicated!

The Blue Quest Fairy followed suit and now had her arms behind her back.

> Other-Purple and Other-Orange Fairy's Simultaneous Text Boxes:

> You can have the same colour as someone else and still be important! Yeah. Don't be all mean like that. Ye—

> Lissa's Interruption Text Box: We already have a purple and an orange one in this conversation! We definitely don't need two oranges here!

> Mr. Max's Text Box: Or two purples!

The twins joined the arms behind back club.

> Other-Yellow Quest Fairy's Text Box: J'adore. Tous les deux, vous avez tout essayé pour nous faire changer le vote et vous laisser vivre, mais bientôt vous serez morts et nous serons heureux de jouer au ping-pong avec vos yeux.

The Other-Yellow Quest Fairy had not been interrupted, but her arms were behind her back. Both Lissa and Mr. Max used the *Shrug Animation*.

> No-Colour Quest Fairy's Text Box: Yeah well, I think we should do all that. Ping-pong i—

> Mr. Max's Interruption Text Box: I love ping-pong!

The No-Colour Quest Fairy had no colour at all, however that was possible, and both hands behind his back.

> Brown Quest Fairy's Text Box: Great idea! *Confused* Maybe. Does anyone speak Fren—

> Lissa's Interruption Text Box: They keep on coming, don't they?

The Brown Quest Fairy was not an inspired colour for a ball of light, but it did set off his hands behind his back nicely.

> Constantly-Colour-Changing Quest Fairy's Text Box: I totally call… whatever position in ping-pong that is a sexual innue—

> Lissa's Interruption Text Box: Look at that one flashing!

> Mr. Max's Text Box: Blinky-blinky!

The Constantly Colour Changing Guest Fairy joined the group, now voting yes. Nathaniel signaled this by putting both hands behind his back.

A Green Quest Fairy floated out from behind an abandoned *Infernal Milking Machine*. Her hands were behind her back with extreme prejudice.

> Mr. Max's Text Box: Hey it's Abby! Hooray, she is alive!

> Green Quest Fairy's Text Box: I am not Abby! Abby is dead you

forgetful pig of—

Mr. Max's Interruption Text Box: No, I'm pretty sure you are Abby.

The Green Quest Fairy used the *Eyebrows Furrowed and Face Twitch Animation*.

Macintosh's Text Box: That is everyone and amazingly now all of us pals and gals are on the same page. Now if you will be so kind as to direc—

O'Sklorm's Sleeve's Interruption Text Box: We are not all on the same page!

Everyone who was floating with their hands behind their back let out a gasp. Coming out from O'Sklorm's sleeve came the Red Quest Fairy.

Mr. Max and Lissa's Simultaneous Text Box: Herbert!

Macintosh's Text Box: Why the fuck do you know who she is and not any of us pal and gal?

Lissa's Text Box: Because that is her name? Obviously, we are going to know who Herbert is.

Mr. Max used the *Shrug Animation*.

Macintosh's Text Box: Unbelievable! You lot are completely unbelievable. I have even less respect for you now. Okay pals and gals it is time to teach them a —

Herbert's Interruption Text Box: No! Macintosh this is wrong! We can't do this.

Macintosh's Text Box: Okay, I tried to be nice with you gal, but you can't keep interrupting… If you interrupt me one more time I thi—

Herbert's Interruption Text Box: I don't care if I need to keep on interrupting. I will not let you do this.

Macintosh's Text Box: Fine, then your fate is sealed with theirs Pe—

Herbert's Interruption Text Box: My name is Herbert!

Macintosh's Text Box: Fine. Whatever. Herbert. Then your fate is sealed w—

Lissa's Interruption Text Box: What fate? What is going on?

> Macintosh's Text Box: If you would let me finish gal I will tell you, you—

> Mr. Max's Interruption Text Box: I can't wait to find out what it is!

> Macintosh's Text Box: …

> Lissa and Mr. Max's Simultaneous Text Boxes: Go on, tell us.

Macintosh and a rainbow assortment of other Quest Fairies did the *Dramatic Reveal Animation*. Behind their backs all this time had been scavenged pieces of the PVP broken *Katana-Nata*. Each little piece gleamed with a sickly light.

> Herbert's Text Box: They are going to kill us now!

> Mr. Max's Text Box: No way. Palcath was right! They were up to something.

> Lissa's Text Box: That is #SoFuckedUp!

> Macintosh's Text Box: Now don't look so surprised dear avatar pal and gal. We will try to make it quick, because unlike you we are compasiona—

Macintosh was then interrupted. A hammer had hit him from behind and knocked him to the ground. Before the little yellow Fairy could react a *Golden Boot* stepped on him, crushing in his yellow skull. He was dead. Dead Dead.

> Vendimm's Text Box: Shut up and die you annoying little shit!

> Mr. Max's Text Box: Lissa, I remember what I was supposed to tell you!

◈ Chapter 42 ◈
CYCLE 7
THE BATTLE OF
TWINCEST

De'vini burst into the Onn Castle Courtyard riding her custom steed; half of the Legendary 13 Headed Hydra. While it was now officially called the Legendary 6.5 Headed Hydra, the fact still remained that this was half of what used to be an Optional Boss and it would still be powerful. Unlike the Hydra from Gentalia, this Hydra had once owned 12 regular heads and only one head downstairs.

In'ferni was bound tightly and gagged with the *Full Ball-Gag*. She was riding the less glamorous side of the Legendary 6.5 Headed Hydra and her legs were entangled in half of some putrid internal hydra organs including a head spawn sac, and a lernaean gland. The only thing holding the Hydra up on her side was one of its heads, acting as a make-shift leg which pushed up from the ground to keep it steady.

Given the math, with one head being used as a leg, and the one half-head being the creature's split down the middle penis, there was still five useable heads here. Each was big enough to devour an avatar in one bite, and there were only three avatars facing it. That was 1.6 (continuous) heads each.

Each of the five usable heads bellowed out and made a display of shooting their breath weapons up in the air all at once. There was a cloud of green which would induce *Poison*, a spray of purple to cause *Blind*, a spritz of yellow to cause *Confuse*, a mist of orange to cause *Sleep*, and a splash of blue to cause *Silence*. The head that was a leg tried to squirt red, but it didn't work.

> Hippolyta's Text Box: Crap! It is the annoying Status Effect causing boss in this game. I can't cure any of that kind, only buff us to have a

lesser chance of it working.

Jorthan the Male Troll Monk's Text Box: Then be doing that perhaps?

Hippolyta's Text Box: I wasn't planning on it, but I guess since you asked nicely.

Trev Terra's Text Box: Please… he is trying to… well, we are helping here… right?

Hippolyta's Text Box: You see I—

De'vini's Interruption Text Box: Silence! I don't have all day to destroy you less important chumps. So stand there like that in a big clump so I can breathe you to Status Effect death!

Jorthan the Male Troll Monk's Text Box: Good point he has. Spreading out!

Beautiful colours of breath attacks coated the area they had once been standing in, however everyone had taken the advice and spread out, getting completely missed.

Hippolyta's Text Box: Thanks for the warning idiot.

De'vini's Text Box: Bloody Flaming Pit! No matter, the heads biting is a spread attack, which will hit you in your little hiding places!

Trev Terra's Text Box: Regroup! Well, I mean if you want to not get eaten that is… well, yes. Go to the middle.

The Hydra heads chomped out but missed everyone because they had followed the advice again and had gotten into a clump.

Hippolyta's Text Box: Thanks again, idiot!

De'vini used the *Furious Animation*. Alternating turns of avatars being in clumps and being spread out happened, as they tried to figure out what to do.

Hippolyta's Text Box: This isn't working. All we are doing is running. That male chauvinist Hydra will figure out what to do eventually. We need a plan!

In'ferni used the *Mmmfferr Murrm Mmmmff Animation*. The Hydra's left most head exhaled and Trev Terra's hair was grazed by purple and succumbed to the Blind Status Effect.

Trev Terra's Text Box: In'ferni has a plan! That is rather great!

Hippolyta's Text Box: No it isn't. She is bound and gagged. We can't get that *Full Ball-Gag* off since none of us have a Sexcessory to exchange it for!

Hippolyta was hit right in the *Amazon Leaf Skirt (s)* with a spritz of yellow from the next Hydra attack. It was now Confused and thought it was a pair of *Flan Flops (s)* but was otherwise unchanged.

Jorthan the Male Troll Monk's Text Box: I am wishing we know what her plan was being. I am completely loss.

Jorthan's right *Big Knuckle Duster* was splashed with blue. It was now forever under the Silenced Status Effect and would never talk again.

De'vini's Text Box: It doesn't flippin' matter! Soon I will hit something non-hilarious with a Status Effect and you will be snatched up by a head of this thing and chewed to bits!

In'ferni used the *Mmmfferr Murrm Mmmmff Animation.*

De'vini's Text Box: Shut up!

In'ferni used the *Mmmfferr Murrm Mmmmff Animation.*

Hippolyta's Text Box: It sounds like she has a pretty good plan.

Trev Terra's Text Box: I wish we could… well, I wish that we could find out… I wonder what?

Jorthan the Male Troll Monk's Text Box: I am also bewilderment!

De'vini's Text Box: It doesn't matter what it is, it wouldn't work anyways!

Trev Terra's Text Box: Are you sure? I mean what if it does. It might you know… well, maybe it will… it could. Why not? It is possible. She might have the best plan ever after all, well, rather… she could?

De'vini's Text Box: What?

Hippolyta's Text Box: He is saying, why not put your gold coins where your combined mouth is? If you are so sure that her plan isn't going to work why don't you let her say what it is?

De'vini's Text Box: No. I don't have time for that.

Jorthan the Male Troll Monk's Text Box: Ba-kawk!

De'vini's Text Box: What?

Jorthan the Male Troll Monk's Text Box: That is what the chicken says. You know, the Cockly-Doodly-Doo?

De'vini would not stand for being called a chicken, and certainly not a French chicken! *With a Stretching Out of Her Wings and a Dramatic Adjustment of her Halo Animation* De'vini snapped her fingers and released In'ferni from her bindings and *Full Ball-Gag*.

De'vini's Text Box: What is this amazing plan of yours?

In'ferni's Text Box: This!

In'ferni flapped her demon wings once and the pair began to hover above the Hydra mount, she executed the *Kiss Passionately Dual Animation*. Breaker was suddenly experiencing what it was like to be passionately kissed by your lesbian lover who happened to be already attached to your lips. The sensation hit him like a real life brick, but In'ferni did not stop. She executed her signature set of Dual Animations, the order of which was guaranteed to make the actual De'vini melt with pleasure. De'vini started to flap her wings after a *Loving Fondle Dual Animation*. De'vini started to smile after an *Inappropriate Grope Dual Animation*. De'vini started to breathe heavier after a *Hard Spanking Dual Animation*. De'vini started to kiss back after the *Nipple Twist Dual Animation*. Finally, what the demonian had been waiting for, after the *Sudden Finger Insertion While Rubbing the Nub Dual Animation* De'vini closed her eyes and moaned.

De'vini was completely unaware that during this long list of ever increasing Dual Animations, the Legendary 6.5 Headed Hydra had become the Dead 0.5 Headed Hydra. Hippolyta had mesmerized each head to keep it from moving, Jorthan had used his gigantic fists to hold it down, and Trev Terra had cast *Fire Edge* on his *Felling Axe* and chopped off each one. No heads would ever grow back, due to the fire damage sealing up the wounds. This team knew their fantasy monster weaknesses well and even how to work quickly together.

The black pixels of the dissolving Hydra hitting De'vini is what finally got her out of the lesbian experience trance. Unfortunately, the *Bell Charm* had a hard clasp to undo and In'ferni had only managed to unhook one of the four clasps during the make-out session.

In'ferni's Text Box: Stupid clasps! Why wasn't it a bra? I can get those clasps off in no time.

De'vini's Text Box: Don't think you can win this with some stupid lesbianism!

Hippolyta used the *Eyebrows Furrowed and Face Twitch Animation*.

Hippolyta's Text Box: STUPID LESBIANISM?

In'ferni's Text Box: Now you've done it.

Hippolyta's Text Box: You male chauvinist pig! You sorry excuse for a man controlling a woman! You asked for this! Witness the power of my amazing Level ✪ ✪ breasts! Ogle them you bastard!

Hippolyta used the *Dramatic Reveal Animation* to expose her amazing Level ✪ ✪ breasts. She started to rotate them manually; it took longer than usual due to their increased size and amazingness.

De'vini's Text Box: Whoa there lady. Calm yo tits! I don't see how SHOWING me your breasts is a symbol of feminism. If anything it is the opposite of feminism you idiot! Why showing me them only proves th… Gha-lu-lugga-ah…?

Hippolyta's Text Box: This is how!

Hippolyta smacked De'vini hard with her breasts. It snapped her out of the Spellbound Status, but also snapped one more piece of the clasp.

De'vini's Text Box: Seriously? Did you smack me with your tit? Are you fucking kidding me?

Hippolyta's Text Box: Girl power at its strongest, pig!

De'vini's Text Box: No matter. I still have control of her and two pieces of that complicated clasp!

De'vini used the *Rue The Day Animation*, followed by the *Beg Pardon Animation*.

De'vini's Text Box: What are you two doing?

Jorthan the Male Troll Monk's Text Box: What is it looking like? We are fucking.

Trev Terra's Text Box: Fuck, your ass feels so good baby!

De'vini stood there, confused.

De'vini's Text Box: Since when are gay elves tops?

Jorthan the Male Troll Monk's Text Box: He is always been one.

Trev Terra's Text Box: Damn baby, you are rather tight. It has been so long, well, rather long. Saving it up for you.

De'vini's Text Box: It is lovely that he saved himself for your big troll ass, but I am going to kill you now.

> Jorthan the Male Troll Monk's Text Box: Not be saving it for me, he is nicer than that!

> Trev Terra's Text Box: Well, I have been saving it up for you Breaker!

> De'vini's Text Box: What?

Trev's thrusts quickened. He had been saving for the longest he could remember, and it was amazing that he had lasted through the conversation. Jorthan had been helping things along with his *Fisting Fists* (but only the *Prodding Pinky*). Trev pulled out of his lover and with one final thrust on top of trollish backside released his pent up torrent. The first blast (and many others) hit the twins right over to the ground and the force broke free another clasp of the complicated Accessory.

> De'vini's Text Box: I changed my mind. Tit lady was better. I can't believe you shot me with your jizz you wacko!

> In'ferni's Text Box: Never have I been happier to be covered in spunk!

> De'vini's Text Box: You people are fucking crazy. I am going to go grab another mount to deal with this nonsense. You will rue the day that you messed with Breaker. Trust me on this.

With a Stretching Out of Her Wings and a Dramatic Adjustment of her Halo Animation, De'vini flapped her wings and took off into the sky, exactly one move unit high. De'vini's head snapped back and she fell to the ground, unable to leave without In'ferni. The violent shaking dislodged the final piece of the clasp and the *Bell Charm* fell to the ground with a tinkle.

> In'ferni's Text Box: We are still attached at the face you stupid jackass. You can't take off without me.

> *Bell Charm's* Text Box: Fuck, I forgot.

> De'vini's Text Box: Please allow me the honour!

> In'ferni's Text Box: No, let me help!

> De'vini's Text Box: Of course!

De'vini and In'ferni used the *Trinket Stomp Dual Animation. The Bell Charm* shattered into a million and seven different pieces of black mist. It was forever destroyed and De'vini forever freed from Breaker's control.

> In'ferni and De'vini's Simultaneous Text Boxes: That is so much better! I know, so much. Maker I missed this. I missed this more! That is sweet. Kiss me? Nope! What do you mean nope? Because I can do

> one better! What do you mean?

In'ferni used the *Sudden Finger Insertion While Rubbing the Nub Dual Animation* on De'vini.

> De'vini's Text Box: ♥!

The twins were busy making up for lost time.

> Hippolyta's Text Box: That worked out way better than our original plan. We should have planned on him being a stupid jerk.

> Jorthan the Male Troll Monk's Text Box: I enjoy when Breaker, he fall to the ground after forget he was attached and he fell in the lutin juice.

> Trev Terra's Text Box: I can't believe he forgot we were in the same room, and well, rather In'ferni could, well, she told us her plan.

> Hippolyta's Text Box: Exactly. A stupid jerk.

Chapter 43

❖   ❖

CYCLE 7
THE BATTLE OF
LOOKING FOR GROUP

> Gray Quest Fairy's Text Box: They killed Macintosh! They must die!

> Vendimm's Text Box: Right on! Kill them!

The Quest Fairies rushed towards Lissa and Mr. Max, brandishing their mini *Katana-Natas*. They were bravely stopped by Herbert who got in the way regardless of the danger.

> Herbert's Text Box: No they didn't! That random guy did!

> Vendimm's Text Box: You're right. I did. It was amazing, right in his dramatic speech and everything.

> Mr. Max's Text Box: No, he didn't.

> Lissa, Vendimm, Herbert, and every other Quest Fairy's Simultaneous Text Boxes: Huh?

> Mr. Max's Text Box: He isn't controlling himself. That is Breaker in disguise. Breaker isn't dead, that is what I forgot to tell you Lissa!

> Lissa's Text Box: What the fuck? Breaker isn't dead and you 'forgot' to

> tell me this? That is #SoFuckedUp!

The Quest Fairies were also in complete shock. Their biggest foe, killer of their friends, their leader, and their race was still alive.

> Vendimm's Text Box: What? The stupid purple girl and all the Quest Fairies didn't know about that yet? Son of a bitch! I totally could have used some mind games on her with these avatars that she used to know and I totally ruined the opportunity! I was looking forward to watching her and her stupid name die, but if I had known that I could have also fucked with her as well... I am so pissed off now.

> Lissa's Text Box: Well too bad, we are going to kick all four of your pantsless butts!

> Vendimm's Text Box: That was sort of tied up to the back-up plan. Good luck, getting to the back-up plan. I don't want to pull any punches, but damn do I want to see the back-up plan.

Vendimm, Quoona, O'Sklorm, and Nerchiner raised their weapons high and prepared to attack. Most of the Quest Fairies had started to play ping-pong, but were slapped out of it by Herbert when she reminded them that who they should really be killing was Breaker and his minions. That perked them up, as they all really wanted to kill something.

Nerchiner was the first to approach. The mob of angry Quest Fairies rose up their blades and met his challenge. Taking advantage of the fact that Nerchiner was mostly hollow inside and had a huge access point in his abdomen to reach his vital areas, the Quest Fairies had started to make quick and messy work of the green haired Warrior.

> Nerchiner's Text Box: Don't be counting me out yet boyos. We were all made extra special to help deal with that purple haired bitch over yonder. Watch this. (:

> Lissa's Text Box: Maker how I hated those backwards smilies of his.

A regulation swirling vortex formed within Nerchiner's empty abdomen. Rocks and gems of every description left his Armour and joined in, changing the regulation swirling vortex into an unregulated swirling vortex of gem terror. Worthless crystals, gems, and caught Quest Fairies alike swirled about until finally it exploded outwards sending everything flying.

> Mr. Max's Text Box: Don't worry littl—

> Nerchiner's Interruption Text Box: No! No interfering! We are doing this one at a time to avoid confusion, boyo. (: You will get your chance to die soon if it pleases you, but right now it is their turn.

> Mr. Max's Text Box: Fair enough.

Battered and bruised the Quest Fairies regrouped to have a quick meeting on how to handle this threat. It was during this meeting that they noticed that they were hovering safely above Nerchiner and were out of his range completely due to both his sword and vortex being short ranged attacks. They positioned themselves carefully and dropped their *Katana-Nata Daggers* with deadly precision. Nerchiner was now missing his arm. Without two arms his sword was useless and the vortex animation took too long to catch them off guard. Slicing off pieces of Nerchiner thinner than prosciutto the Quest Fairies gathered for a final assault and cleaved his head off of his shoulders. The green haired goliath slumped over.

> Nerchiner's Text Box: Well played boyos.): I am dead.)X

> O'Sklorm's Text Box: F**k you b****h! Time to f*****g die. Eat s**t named Red Quest Fairy a****t!

> Lissa's Text Box: I forgot about his stupid self censoring…

O'Sklorm cast *Fireball* at Herbert, but missed due to Herbert's small size and the spell flew off into the distance, exploding on a passing Harem Cow, killing her. He cast *Icicle Explosion* and *Whirlwind Extra*, completely missing the tiny Herbert yet again, the spells collided midair and killed another unfortunate Harem Cow. He cast *Nuclear Fire Grenade*, *Impossible Earthspike*, and *Demi Less* on other Harem Cows, also by mistake.

> O'Sklorm's Text Box: You f*****g impossible to hit little s**t! Stop bobbing up and down while you f*****g hover you s**t eating b****h!

Herbert, who did not own a piece of the broken *Katana-Nata* due to ethical reasons, floated there, randomly bobbing, and accidentally dodging expertly.

> Herbert's Text Box: Never! I am sawesome at this!

> O'Sklorm's Text Box: That is it b***h! Eat this s**t you c**k s*****g p***y s*****r!

O'Sklorm activated his *Amazing Blue Icicle Barrage of Deathness* (that he had named himself). Hundreds of shards of ice, and a single accidental ice cube, flew directly at Herbert. One of them was bound to hit. It turned out to be the ice cube, and as Herbert flew backwards on the harmless ice cube she eventually came to rest in the middle of a group of now dead Specially Selected Harem Cows. She turned to the only living monster left in The Circle 8 Milking Field and *Shrug Animationed*.

> Herbert's Text Box: Can you believe the nerve of that guy Optional Boss of The Flaming Pit, The Bull King? How many of your harem did he kill?

> The Bull King's Text Box: All of them.

> Herbert's Text Box: Do teach him a lesson!

> The Bull King's Text Box: Good idea.

Riding on the shoulder of The Bull King, Herbert only watched as O'Sklorm was savagely burned by the *Male Cow's Milk Barrage*. That was the name of the attack, but in reality O'Sklorm was burnt to a crisp by the angry bull's ejaculate. O'Sklorm fell over, crispy and defeated.

> O'Sklorm's Text Box: B***h!

> Herbert's Text Box: Asterisk! Star! Exclamation Point! Swirly thing right back at you, asshole!

> Quoona's Text Box: i think it is going to be like my turn next because i said so mr max has no ranged attacks at all and i am pro with mine so i am going to choose him as my target it is a great plan and i like thought it up all by myself which is amazing i really like my plan also i like horses and my bffs last weekend was a total blast i met so many new bffs that i will remember forever and ever like whatevs their names were i shoot at you now

Mr. Max nearly got hit with Quoona's arrow. He had been trying hard to read what she was saying, but without any punctuation, capital letters, or hint of sentence structure it was next to impossible.

> Lissa's Text Box: Right... I forgot about her whole herness.

> Mr. Max's Text Box: Why did you even hang out with these people?!

Mr. Max attempted to target Quoona, but she had impolitely been sneaking onto a *Powdered Creamer Filled Silo of Torment* during the other combats, which was unsportsmanlike of her. Deciding to even the odds Mr. Max forgot about Quoona for a bit and instead started to chop at the *Powdered Creamer Filled Silo of Torment*.

> Quoona's Text Box: hey you down there what are you doing i mean well there is no reason to attack the silo because you are too unjumpy to get up here that isnt going to solve anything you suck by the way oh also i had such a good breakfast today it was amazing with like fruit in it and stuff you know what i mean for like true hey this isnt fair i cannot aim at you when you are so close to that silo move away so i can like hit you

> Mr. Max's Text Box: No thanks!

Mr. Max continued to hack away at the *Powdered Creamer Filled Silo of Torment's* supports and soon he had carved one of the five pentagon support beams away completely. He went to the next leg and hacked it away, then the third, and the fourth. Quoona rambled on the entire time, with no comma, periods, or thoughts to stop her. When the last leg was gone and the silo fell to the ground in a heap of dust, Max finally spoke up.

> Mr. Max's Text Box: Come on already, don't you have something fiery you can do? Wasn't that your special power since you were the one on fire? Do it already, my arms are getting sore.

> Quoona's Text Box: oh right i forgot sorry my mistake okay here comes my wicked fire spell of big old fires that i like totally named myself or whatever

Quoona started to activate her poorly named ability, it caused the creamer dust from the *Powdered Creamer Filled Silo of Torment* to violently explode, sending Quoona rocketing into the sky. When she finally came down, she was close to death and burnt worse than O'Sklorm. Mr. Max chopped through Quoona, ending her reign of terror on the grammar community for good.

> Quoona's Text Box: i am all dead and stuff that like so sucks or something i think i have a hangnail gross i touched a bug it is so icky i like hate bugs

> Vendimm's Text Box: That last one was kinda my fault. I forgot all about creamsplosives.

> Lissa's Text Box: Just you and me then huh 'Vendimm'?

> Vendimm's Text Box: Nah, where is the f—

> Vendimm, and Quoona's Simultaneous Text Boxes: —un in that? Not whe—

> Vendimm, Quoona, and O'Sklorm's Simultaneous Text Boxes: —n I can do something a—

> Vendimm, Quoona, O'Sklorm's, and Nerchiner's Simultaneous Text Boxes: —s fun as this!

The defeated avatars stood up as best as they could, it was troublesome to watch and slightly unnerving.

> Lissa's Text Box: That is cheating! Your back-up plan was to do this all along wasn't it you jerk! #LameSauce.

Vendimm, Quoona, O'Sklorm's, and Nerchiner's Simultaneous Text Boxes: No, good try, points for effort. A+!

Lissa's Text Box: What was the back-up plan then?

Vendimm, Quoona, O'Sklorm's, and Nerchiner's Simultaneous Text Boxes: Yes, I suppose I can tell you that, now that you all did such a good job killing these pathetic nobodies for me. Guess what...

Vendimm, Quoona, O'Sklorm's, and Nerchiner began to tick ever so quietly. They opened up their Armour pieces and showed the world that they were completely stuffed to the brim with explosives of all varieties except for Creamsplosives.

Lissa's Text Box: #Fuck.

Vendimm, Quoona, O'Sklorm's, and Nerchiner's Simultaneous Text Boxes: Boom!

Chapter 44

CYCLE 7
THE BATTLE OF ZING!

There he was, smug as ever and knocking back a *Full Stamina Potion* like it was *Infernal Milk* from the back of the refrigerator that expired at midnight. It had took Yallundy longer to find Gliint that she had thought it would, considering he was leading an entire army of dead and corrupted monsters. They had been hidden, travelling through Onn Forest. They had started near the Airship area and were trying to sneak into Onn. Thanks to her vantage point, Yallundy knew why, they were coming this way to take samuri's group by surprise. Gliint was yelling at various monster groups to stop being so stupid.

Onn Forest was a shadow of what it once was. A giant line of trees had been carved out through the middle by Jorthan's huge fists and the rest was covered in spider web graffiti calling Anders an asshole in various ways. The huge wreckage of the S.S. PlotDevice was still on fire in a corner of the area. It must have had a lot of fuel to still be burning.

A stray Golden Gribblet had fallen into webs near the airship that said *'Elfboy is an Elfpussy'* and Yallundy quietly possessed it and forced it to commit a silent suicide. While initially she had only did this to prevent any survivors from keeping Breaker alive it did give her an excellent idea.

Breaker had never been stuck in Onn Forest and his army was randomly teleporting every which way attempting to get to the carved out Jorthan path which was tantalizingly close but may as well have been length leagues away. They would find the way eventually with so many things trying.

Yallundy, however, had been stuck in Onn Forest before and could use that to her advantage. She began to subtly move pieces of scenery to lure a group of Gruffer Goats into the warp that would move them directly into the fire of the S.S. PlotDevice. She casually switched the locations of the *Safe Travel Arrow Fruit* and sent an entire regiment of Heat Pigs tumbling down a cliff, forever disappearing in a mass twinkly grave of light points. She set up a trap for a group of Black Window Spiders using the offensive webffiti and forced them to widow themselves. She even possessed a Frosty Flork, which was walking in the middle of a group of lesser Florks, allowing her to cause some serious *Flork Carnage.*

She was forced to stop when the monsters started to get wise to her ways. They all met back at the airship, except that one group of Jack Jumper Honey-pots that 'accidentally' killed themselves with the 'accidental' toppling of Onn Mountain. While the jig was up now, Yallundy was still proud of herself for killing nearly half of the entire monster army all by herself.

Gliint was standing in the middle of the army, furiously pointing at the ground. It was a challenge to whatever was killing his troops in the forest. Yallundy replied by toppling over a scenic statue of Airshippa, the Goddess of Airships, and killing all of the corrupted Manic Mackerel and all but one of the Lunatic Herrings.

> Gliint's Text Box: That is enough. Show yourself!

Yallundy replied by startling a Nukamander. Since all the varieties of Salamander exploded when scared, it set off a chain reaction. All of the other Nukamanders became startled and exploded, which in turn scared the Freezamanders and Shockamanders. This scared the Terramanders and Flaramanders, whose explosions scared the Firamanders. By the end of the chain reaction only a single Fizzlemander remained, mostly because it had fizzled when it tried to explode.

Gliint took a big swig of *Medium Health Potion.*

> Gliint's Text Box: This is your last warning.

Yallundy used her last warning to yank hard on a Displacer Fox's tail. It yelped and teleported itself, and fifty-six of its closest neighbours, into the heart of the sun itself. Yallundy was delighted to see the small puffs of smoke even from here.

> Gliint's Text Box: That does it. I warned you.

Gliint took out his *Gratling Gun*, pointed it at his own head, and cocked the hammer. Yallundy panicked and materialized.

> Yallundy's Text Box: No, don't hurt him!

Gliint nearly fell over.

> Gliint's Text Box: You? Seriously? Where are the others?

> Yallundy's Text Box: I am the only one here, Breaker.

Gliint's Text Box: That is impossible.

Gliint took a nonchalant sip of his potion.

Yallundy's Text Box: It isn't. I am the only one here.

Gliint's Text Box: Nope, that is impossible for many reasons. Soothers cannot attack or use stealth so you couldn't have done this. I need to stress this next one the most. You are timid as a poorly dressed mouse and couldn't possibly be behind all of the senseless wreckage that has happened to my army.

Yallundy's Text Box: It is possible for many reasons. First of all, your broken coding was faulty and it didn't kill me but turned me into a ghost. Secondly, Wind Elementals can certainly attack and use stealth. Finally, and I need to stress this the most, I gained self confidence and became as brave as a well dressed mouse and I am behind the senseless wreckage that happened to your army.

Yallundy accentuated her point by using *Supreme Shock* on a nearby Direphant, causing it to have a heart attack and die prematurely at a young age. Yallundy used the *Smirk Animation*.

Gliint took a big swig of *Furniture Polish+* and spat it out. He took a bigger swig of *Mana Potion+*.

Gliint's Text Box: Colour me impressed, I guess. It doesn't matter because I control Gliint. You don't want him to be hurt because you love him, but I don't really give a fuck. So no matter what you will not be able to do anything about it.

Yallundy's Text Box: Funny how things work out sometimes isn't it?

Gliint's Text Box: What do you mean?

Yallundy's Text Box: For instance…

Yallundy disappeared and Gliint began to pan his camera angle around wildly in an attempt to find her. So wildly in fact that he knocked loose his *Too Dark Shades*. Yallundy appeared behind Gliint and with a simple touch possessed him as well. One of Gliint's irises changed from the controlled black state of Breaker to the controlled violet state of Yallundy.

Yallundy's Text Box: …You are not the only one that can possess Gliint.

Gliint's Black Eye Side's Text Box: How in the map did you do that?

Gliint's Violet Eye Side's Text Box: You killed me and turned me into a ghost and allowed me to take over the only monster in existence that could possess things. I really should thank you because you gave me the powers and stats of a raid boss while you are only...

Gliint's Black Eye Side's Text Box: I am only what?

Gliint's Violet Side used the *Bitchslap Dual Animation* on Gliint's Black Eye Side. That side was now a bit worse for wear and possessed a legitimate black eye.

Gliint's Violet Eye Side's Text Box: You are only Gliint.

Gliint's Black Eye Side's Text Box: Need I remind you that Gliint is the fastest avatar in the entire game? I am controlling his every action.

Gliint's Black Eye Side attempted to shoot Gliint's Violet Eye Side with his *Gratling Gun* but the shot was expertly deflected.

Gliint's Violet Eye Side's Text Box: I am the Wind Elemental. Wind is the element tied to Agility! Why do you possibly think that the fastest avatar in the world could be faster than the fastest monster in the world? Interesting side note: I am also on the side that has the *Blast Bombs*.

The *Blast Bomb* exploded and Gliint's Black Eye Side's now was blackened with explosive residue, his *#3 Gnomehawk* would now forever be two-toned black and dark brown, thankfully it was wicked cool.

Gliint's Black Eye Side's Text Box: I still control all these monsters! I can make them turn on Gliint any time I want. Like right now!

Gliint's Violet Eye Side's responded by leaping up into the air and flying.

Gliint's Black Eye Side's Text Box: You can fucking fly too?

Gliint's Violet Eye Side's Text Box: Wonderful how I picked off all the flying monsters already isn't it?

Gliint's Black Eye Side's tried to sneak a sip of *Mana Potion+*, but the bottle was slapped away by Gliint's Violet Eye Side.

Gliint's Violet Eye Side's Text Box: Oh no you don't! I know that is how you are controlling Gliint!

Gliint's Black Eye Side's Text Box: Big deal. I don't need to keep drinking, it lasts forever.

Gliint's Violet Eye Side's Text Box: Strange how you are sweating when

> you say that. No, I know that it runs out after 15.7 rounds.

> Gliint's Black Eye Side's Text Box: How could you possibly know that?

> Gliint's Violet Eye Side's Text Box: Two reasons. One - that is how long Potions residual recovery effects last. Two - I have been spying on you for this entire fucking book, dumbass.

This started a slapping Gliint match. Each side tried to knock the crap out of the other side of Gliint. Gunshots, Bombs, a round where the Black Eye Side got a sip of potions was quickly followed by a round where Gliint's inventory was dumped into a spider-web by Gliint's Violet Eye Side (which included the lifeless body of Yallundy). The Black Eye Side's started to take pot-shots at Yallundy's corpse, which distracted her, further allowing another swig of Potion several rounds later and the retrieval of another *Mana Potion+* from the nearby spider-web.

It came down to both sides of Gliint, holding the *Mana Potion+* in each hand. One side was desperately attempting to make Gliint drink, the other side was desperately attempting to prevent that from happening. It was a desperate struggle, but there was still much liquid in the *Mana Potion+* and even the scarce drops that would find Gliint's tongue were making Breaker's control last that much longer.

> Gliint's Black Eye Side's Text Box: Give up! You will never win!

The Violet Eye Side of Gliint got ready to Text Box the obvious reply of 'Never!' but then it occurred to her, that was an excellent idea. The Violet Eye Side let go, both of the vial and of Gliint. The *Mana Potion+* sprung up with all of the Black Eye Side's strength, shattering on Gliint's face. This both destroyed the remains of the *Mana Potion+* and broke Gliint's nose. Gliint fell to the ground, far away from reach of any of the Potions trapped in the spider-web.

> Gliint's Text Box: You bitch! That is it! I am going to bomb the fuck out of this guy, but first...

Gliint got ready to perform his Breaker Animation, Gliint Style.

> Yallundy's Text Box: No! You're in Gliint right now. Your custom animations take forever. Don't you have any idea what a sexy animation that long will do to—

> Gliint's Text Box: Oh shut up, what could a stupid animation possibly do?

Yallundy flew away as far as she possibly could before Gliint picked up his shades and used the WITH A RAISE OF HIS EYEBROW AND A DRAMATIC MOVEMENT OF HIS SUNGLASSES ANIMATION. It was the ultimate in sexy. Too ultimate.

When the smoke from the resulting sexy nuclear explosion settled, all the black puddle of gross stuff Gliint had coughed up could do was stare at his once massive monster army. Half of which had been killed by the timid and poor excuse for a troll Yallundy, the other half by himself after he had caused them all to explode with the most violent group death orgasm ever experienced in the Island of Islana.

Gliint lifted his own foot for the first time in a long while and crushed the puddle of black sick with an aggressive step. It exploded into smaller puddles of black sick and vanished, forever freeing Gliint from Breaker's control.

Gliint's Text Box: *Smug smile* Asshole!

Yallundy flew down from the sky and tackled Gliint with slightly more force than he thought was necessary given how badly he had been beaten up by himself. He was still glad to see her and looked up into her eyes. They were crazed and glossed over. Gliint was startled by her wild expression and he started to feel wetness seeping through the front of his *Slick Pants (s)*. He became worried when he realized that the wetness was coming from Yallundy. Had she been hurt in the explosion or by Breaker? If she had Gliint was going to make sure to personally *Bitchslap Animation* his corpse.

Yallundy tore off *Gliint's Slick Pants (s)* with animalistic intensity, setting both his *Mega Strap-On* and his less mega manhood free. It was then when Gliint knew that the wetness was coming from Yallundy's elemental lady parts. She was gushing out sexual fluids at an unfathomable rate.

Yallundy's Text Box: Fuck! Now! Me!

She had only made it far enough away from the pleasurexplosion to avoid being killed, but she was now wild with sexual rage. Gliint couldn't have stopped her if he wanted to.

Gliint's Text Box: Yes!

Gliint really didn't have a say in what happened. Yallundy was much bigger than him and was in control. She lowered herself onto his dual members and started to bounce up and down with urgency. She needed these cocks, and every bounce was another fantasy fulfilled. She smiled a wicked smile and enjoyed every single movement while on top of her smaller lover. Gliint was enjoying himself, but was doing everything he could to not animate and cause this experience to end prematurely.

Yallundy looked into Gliint's now properly brown eyes and her eyes unglazed. Her intense need for this to happen due to the sexy animation had subsided. She did not subside in what she was doing, instead she doubled her efforts. This was something she wanted to happen regardless, but was happy that at least now she could try something she had only dreamed about.

Yallundy's Text Box: Gliint, I'm glad you are finally safe! Now… um… I'm going to try something. Is that okay?

> Gliint's Text Box: I'm glad that you rescued me! *Smile* Do whatever the Flaming Pit you want with me big beautiful lady!

Yallundy used the *Shy Smile Animation*. She activated her special sex power of *Empathy*. Now everything she was feeling Gliint could feel and everything Gliint felt she likewise did. Glint could feel his vagina getting penetrated by himself and Yallundy could feel her penis thrusting inside. It doubled the pleasure of the experience and Gliint nearly lost himself in the moment but stopped his climax when Yallundy froze her movements.

> Yallundy's Text Box: No, not yet. There is more.

> Gliint's Text Box: More? *Grin* How could it possibly get better?

Equipping herself, Yallundy turned into her avatar. Gliint was confused at first but when Yallundy went into ghost form he was even more confused. As she flipped them around Gliint stayed motionless, terrified of animating himself. When Yallundy left her body and possessed half of him, he understood. Now Yallundy and Gliint were busy fucking Yallundy together. Every thrust they each felt at three times the intensity.

> Gliint's Text Box: Holy fuck Yallundy. *wince* I can't keep this up.

> Yallundy's Text Box: I know. Me either, but hold off as long as you can! When you are ready to shoot use an Animation.

> Gliint's Text Box: But my Animations are sexy dangerous! *Gasp* Didn't you see what happened?

> Yallundy's Text Box: Please? Use the smallest one you can find! I've been dreaming of this moment.

Gliint and Yallundy continued to plow into Yallundy. Both were drenched in sweat and at the absolute limit. Gliint wouldn't even dare blink, convinced that little bit of Animation would set him off. On the next of Yallundy's thrusts into herself Gliint empathetically felt what it was like to make a vagina pulse with the full pleasure of a double penetration orgasm and he lost it.

> Yallundy's Text Box: Yes, Gliint do it!

Gliint used the **SHH ANIMATION** with extreme happiness.

Chapter 45

CYCLE 7
THE BATTLE OF THE
FINAL GLADE

Lissa's Text Box: We are alive? #HolidayMiracle?

Vendimm's Severed Head's Text Box: It isn't even near any holidays loser!

With a hearty *Boot Stomp Animation*, Lissa crushed the head of Vendimm along with the last tatters of the *Diamond Helmet* that was keeping him alive.

Lissa's Text Box: I wasn't talking to you, asshole.

Lissa looked at Mr. Max expectantly, she executed a *Well... Animation* but the hint was missed.

Lissa's Text Box: I was talking to you Max.

Mr. Max's Text Box: Right! Sorry, but I don't know why either.

Herbert's Text Box: He had his eyes closed and was waving his hands all around like a little girl.

Mr. Max's Text Box: I wouldn't really say it was 'like a little girl'.

Herbert's Text Box: True, Lissa was being a lot less girly about it.

Lissa used a *Smug Animation*, Mr. Max did not.

> Herbert's Text Box: What happened is that they saved you.

Making a motion to the horizon, Herbert and the avatars watched as the other Quest Fairies came into view, only slightly charred and worse for wear.

> Orange Quest Fairy's Text Box: Hi there adventure and adventurette! We saved you!

> Purple Quest Fairy's Text Box: I can't believe we jumped in front of the explosion like that. We are #SoScrewedUp!

> Brown Quest Fairy's Text Box: *Gasp!* We are?

> White Quest Fairy's Text Box: No we are not. I simply cannot believe that you didn't remember that Quest Fairies are completely immune to area damage. It is to protect us from avatar attacks. Heck, we are immune to all damage because we are only framing devices. Monster attacks don't kill us, other avatars don't kill us, and terrain damage doesn't hurt. The only exception apparently seems to be broken asshole PVP attacks that specifically target us. Since those were not *Chemist Bombs* that had been broken for PVP but were *Bomber Bombillo Bombs* none of us were in any danger a—

> White Quest Fairy's Text Box: t all.

> Brown Quest Fairy's Text Box: *Gasp!* We weren't?

The White Quest Fairy looked at all the other Fairies and was met with blank stares.

> White Quest Fairy's Text Box: Apparently, they all forgot that part and jumped in to shield you without knowing they wouldn't get hurt. I guess we are screwed up!

> Lissa's Text Box: Wow, thanks! We owe you all an apology.

> Mr. Max's Text Box: Yeah, we really mistreated you guys. Can you ever forgive us? Will you come back to us and be our framing devices again?

> Lissa's Text Box: What do you say? Friends?

Mr. Max and Lissa both used a *Handshake Dual Animation* directed at the Orange and Purple Quest Fairies respectively.

> Other-Purple and Other-Orange Fairy's Simultaneous Text Box: Um, we are not your Quest Fairies. The ones over there are your Quest

Fairies. That is kind of embarrassing. Boy are your faces red. Yeah, it totally makes me want to make out. Me too! Nice.

Purple Quest Fairy's Text Box: Talking to the wrong Quest Fairies. You two are #SoSccrewedUp.

Orange Quest Fairy's Text Box: Needless to say, the answer is no. But still adventurer and adventurette, apology accepted.

Green Quest Fairy's Text Box: Tender loving moment successfully averted. Shall we continue on?

The party floated forward, continuing towards the Tall Gleaming Tower of Supreme Importance. It was a good sixty-eight and a half stories taller than anything else in the area and would be a likely spot to search.

Lissa's Whisper Text Box: Why didn't you tell me they weren't our Fairies Meathead?

Mr. Max's Whisper Text Box: You put your hand out first. I was following your lead.

The path to the Tall Gleaming Tower of Supreme Importance was absolutely teaming with resistance, monsters, and things that had been named in an equally badass fashion. Thankfully, when you have a near double rainbow of tiny impossible to hurt framing devices which are armed with impossible to deflect PVP weapon fragments and are thirsting for revenge, the normal challenge rating of the area decreases somewhat. They reached their destination in what would have been a record-breaking time, had anyone ever been here before to set a legitimate record in the first place.

The Tall Gleaming Tower of Supreme Importance stood before them, and from this closer vantage point it looked even taller—half a storey at least. A huge open courtyard sprawled out before the stairway to the tower, lined with lush purple trees and hedges. Six gigantic topiaries of the Titans filled the areas not already filled with the six gigantic marble statues of the Elementals. Huge fountains flowed freely everywhere, shooting out what looked to be water. In the centre of the circular area were two life sized statues made of distilled magic. One was of the Plague of Shadow being ridden by Narbenock; the other was of Fred being ridden by The Dragon Rider. Narbenock and Viviane (the Dragon Rider was named Vivian) were side by side, length units away from completing the *Fist Bump Dual Animation*.

Mr. Max started to take a step forward, into the area but was stopped by Lissa's hand.

Lissa's Text Box: Wait… something isn't right. Doesn't this feel familiar to you?

> Mr. Max's Text Box: Not really, I think they only time you ever touched me was to hit me.

> Lissa's Text Box: This place is odd.

> Mr. Max's Text Box: I'll say. There isn't anything here at all that is cow themed. It's all off.

> Lissa's Text Box: That is the stupidest thing you have… wait… that is genius! There isn't anything at all here cow themed. This is something special.

> Mr. Max's Text Box: Now that you mention it Lissa, I think you are right. Something is here.

Lissa changed the status of her hand from restfully placed to sudden smack of realization. Mr. Max only winced a little.

> Lissa's Text Box: I got it! It is huge as fuck but this is a gigantic glade! There is going to be a boss here I know it.

> Mr. Max's Text Box: If only there was some way we had of knowing what it was.

Herbert used the *Clear Throat Animation*.

> Lissa's Text Box: Right! We have them.

Herbert started to talk, Mr. Max wanted to interrupt but both he, and Lissa, kept his mouth shut.

> Herbert's Text Box: This is the Glade of Supreme Finality. It is the only place that stands between the player and the sixty-nine floors of pure no-monster-guarded epic treasure that inside the Tall Gleaming Tower of Supreme Importance. The guardian of the glade, The Lost God Glackronix, the Guardian of the Glade is the supreme challenge for players, requiring not 100 avatars like normal raid bosses, but 1000 to be present for him to spawn. My notes indicate that even 1000 avatars would not be enough to slay the beast, he is that strong.

> Herbert's Text Box: This area hasn't been made live yet. He can't spawn. It was going to be saved until interest in the game started to dwindle, and then it would be 'unlocked' for free to bring players back. It is good he is still locked because even if there were 1000 avatars here, the test data for the boss indicates that he would take cycles and cycles to defeat. A real epic play experience.

Max nearly exploded he was keeping back his excitement for so long.

> Mr Max's Text Box: The Lost God Glackronix? *THE* The Lost God Glackronix? I can't believe it! He is rumoured to be the second hardest raid boss ever designed, and the hardest raid boss that it is possible to kill! And we are here, right next to his glade?! I saw a leaked screenshot of him, it was blurry and impossible to make out anything, but I think he is a mix of Flork and Dragon! His song is great! To be here, it is amazing! ♫♫

> Lissa's Text Box: You are legitimately geeking out right now aren't you?

> Mr. Max's Text Box: Yes and I don't care. This is so cool!

> Lissa's Text Box: You heard the Fairy. It doesn't matter because he can't spawn. Let's go and hack down that doorway over there down, get sixty-nine floors of treasure, and then I can deliver this Makerdamn bill to Palcath. That coward of a lad has to be hiding in there, and he is going to be in so much trouble when I find him. #DwarfSpanking.

> Mr. Max's Text Box: Breaker is probably in there as well, unless he is hiding somewhere stupid again like under Onn.

> Lissa's Text Box: Of course he is in there this time. It is a huge phallic tower to compensate for his tiny manhood.

Lissa took a single step forward and a Loudspeaker spoke up.

> Loudspeaker's Text Box: Hello there dumbass and stupid!

> Mr. Max's Text Box: That is Breaker's voice!

> Lissa's Text Box: How dare you call us that! I am not stupid!

> Mr. Max's Text Box: And I am not a dumbass!

> Loudspeaker's Text Box: Ha! Did you prove my point? I gave you enough time to reply, but I am on a Loudspeaker you idiots. I can't hear you from here.

Lissa and Mr. Max both performed a *Facepalm Animation*.

> Loudspeaker's Text Box: Anyway, I wanted to say that you are fucked. Could you imagine me of all people having a giant fortress like this and not having a guard dog? What kind of piss poor planning would that be? I gave my spare key to this little boss I happened to find lying

> around in the code. It is stunning what you can accomplish when you have hundreds of cycles to waste while waiting for incompetent idiots to get through one stupid area. Well, kiss kiss! Have fun dying!

In the far off distance Narbenock and Viviane completed their *Fistbump Dual Animation* and a long clear chime rung through the area. The sky parted with a high-animation-budget cut scene (complete with a laser light show.) The guard dog arrived. It was absolutely stupid-massive and it barely fit into the gigantic area. It was so big that it had to crouch to avoid hitting its head on the sun. It was The Lost God Glackronix, the Guardian of the Glade, *The* The Lost God Glackronix, the Guardian of the Glade. He let out a roar that was also the first wicked note to his theme song, *Double Shafted Opening* by *Caution Step*.

Lissa let out two *Skin Crawl Animations*. One, because The Lost God was exactly what Mr. Max had theorized it to be and the Armoured giant was a bipedal mix of Flork and Dragon. It was something truly stomach churning. Another, because of hearing *Caution Step*, which was possibly even more stomach churning. Alternately, Mr. Max was jamming out to the music and taking screenshots.

> Lissa's Text Box: Fuck. We are fucked. What are we going to do?

> Mr. Max's Text Box: The weak point is on his chest. If that dies he dies with it.

> Lissa's Text Box: How do you know that?

> Mr. Max's Text Box: Well, two reasons. One, it has a giant obvious flashing red orb in its chest and two, in the theme song right… now… it says that is the weak point.

> Lissa's Text Box: I don't really see how that helps us, we are not thousands of avatars and we don't have cycles and cycles to waste #HeartSmacking a lost God.

> Mr. Max's Text Box: We couldn't reach the heart unless we hit all those glowy balls on the feet and destroy them first. Then the ones of the shins, then the knees, the thighs, the belly button, then the arm ones so it falls over, then that one on the head so it rears up and we can hit the chest once. Then he stands up again and we do it again. Seriously? Are you even listening to the song?

> Lissa's Text Box: Wait a round, all that so we can hit the chest once?

> Mr. Max's Text Box: Yes, and you have to do it twenty times!

Lissa's Text Box: That is it? Twenty times?

Mr. Max's Text Box: Now I know you are not listening to the song. His chest only has twenty hit points, but an impossible amount of defense so that every attack only deals one point of damage. It is his foundation that makes him strong, not his heart. The worshipers never loved his cruel, cruel cheating heart. That is pretty much the entire ninth verse!

Lissa's Text Box: If we can hit the heart twenty times we can win!

Mr. Max's Text Box: It is like talking to a brick wall. Yes. That is how we win, but we need to kill the other balls first, that is the challenging part.

Lissa's Text Box: Why do we need to do that? If you say 'because the song tells us we have to' I will hurt you. There has to be a way to hit up there without knocking him over first.

Mr. Max's Text Box: He is so tall that it would be out of range for even a Night Ranger (Ranged specialty) to hit that final sphere even when he was knocked over. I am sure that the programmers thought of that.

Herbert's Text Box: We can only float, not fly. Sorry, we could never get all the way up there. Even if we could, a single hit makes him teleport and puts him into defensive mode, which would start the entire process over!

Lissa's Text Box: Unless… *think Lissa think* We need to somehow get up there and hit him twenty times at once. I think if we did something to cheat our way up there, like use the stair glitch, we could make it! That is the first part of this plan! Quick, we need to try dropping things to see if we can step on them, or if it was a onetime thing with cake.

Mr. Max's Text Box: You can stack *Creature Cages*, but I am all out of those.

Lissa's Text Box: There has to be more items!

Mr. Max's Text Box: We need to hurry and look before it finishes charging that huge first attack of his!

Lissa's Text Box: I think we still have some time. He is only at 3%.

They tested every item they had. There was a good supply of stackable items, but there wasn't going to be enough to do it twenty times over. They had enough to do this once.

> Mr. Max's Text Box: This is hopeless. How are we going to pull this off and hit all those balls?

Herbert used the *Eureka! Animation.*

> Herbert's Text Box: That's it! You gave me the best idea!

~~~

Palcath watched on with a lump in his throat. Many things had been happening while he had been tied up with one of his spare *Bundles of Rope.* Breaker's command centre, a heavily altered array of monitors that originally was to function as the Ultimate Moments of the Raid Boss Replay Screen, had slowly been losing monitors. From what Palcath could see all but four of the screens had blacked out. The others had faded as soon as Breaker had lost control over his general or army. The only screens left were Caela's, the dead Quest Fairies, that big thing rampaging outside, and one more that Palcath couldn't see because it was blocked by the command centre chair, but was still giving off light.

It made Palcath so proud of his followers, because even without him to lead them they had all been experiencing wonderful victories. He really had taught everyone else well.

Breaker, the little ball of light, had been so distracted attempting to deal with Palcath's followers that he had not had enough time to complete his permanent body meld procedure with Nega-Anders. There was all sorts of strange looking alien crap hanging from the Nega-Angel, and eventually Breaker would own him forever, but the progress bar was only at 46%.

Now, outside this glass tower, a determined Lissa was hugging onto Mr. Max's legs as he rode her piggyback. The big guy was throwing out all manner of crap for Lissa to jump on which was being properly aligned by a frantic ball of red light. This stairway of random drop items, mostly *Flork Skulls, Extra Yellow Puzzle Blocks,* and *Suspicious Wooden Stacking Platforms*, was being built at an alarming rate. Had Palcath and Lissa used this method of climbing, they would have reached this floating island in only a fraction of a cycle. This raid boss was tall, but he wasn't nearly as tall as a floating island in the sky, or maybe he was, it was hard to judge from here.

The lump in Palcath's throat grew bigger. Not only was Lissa coming here specifically to rescue him, she was doing it while using his cake stacking plan! The lump in Palcath's throat was made entirely of self-satisfaction.

The best part was Breaker was so busy reconfiguring his window displays to make them properly self-centred, that the ball of light didn't seem to notice anything going on. The stacking duo jumped right behind his display, turned the corner with a well placed *U-Pipe Junction*. They approached the blinking chest heart of The Lost God Glackronix, the Guardian of the Glade, and Breaker didn't see a thing.

They were going to leap out and attack his chest, stack some more, and repeat the process a total of twenty times to defeat the raid boss. Hopefully, they would finish before Nega-Anders was lost. Palcath watched on in interest as the group stacked past the blinking chest and kept going towards the head. That was foolish. Attacking the head would only make The Lost God Glackronix, the Guardian of the Glade fall to his knees (Palcath had also done some research on the raid boss).

When the trio of Lissa, Mr. Max, and Herbert (Palcath was surprised to see that the Quest Fairy had been so useful at stacking) reached the eye level of the raid boss they put down a final platform. The largest item in the game, a *Meditative Zen Garden with Sand*, was now the stage. Palcath's eyes widened when Lissa ripped open her *Fashonista Bodice (s)* and gave The Lost God Glackronix, the Guardian of the Glade an eyeful of her half-elf titties. Mr. Max released himself and gave a few meaty pumps in a show of good faith. It was Herbert, who turned around and gave her ass a good spank that did it. The Lost God had a fetish for the tiniest of tiny creatures and after a good show of Fairy spanking he had grown forth a mighty erection capable of crushing humanity.

With the combined attacks of Lissa's *Ultimatium Mace*, Mr. Max's *Eight Handed Sword*, and Herbert's dropkicking, the trio jumped off the platform and went for the weak spot. They did not go for the chest, but fell towards the biggest cock in existence. It had three flashing weak points (his cock and each ball). The trio each hit one weak point causing The Lost God Glackronix, the Guardian of the Glade to climax in massive waves of ultimate spunk. The 'second most difficult Raid Boss in all gaming history', (according to the leaked article with the blurry screenshots that Palcath had read) had been defeated while still only at 13% charge for his first attack because three things had touched his junk. Talk about sensitive.

The force with which the spunk-explosion hit the tower caused Breaker's #4 monitor to shatter, sending fragments everywhere. This was unfortunate because it alerted him to the death of his guard dog. It was also fortunate because it disguised the sounds of trumpets. Yes, Breaker knew that his guard dog had been defeated, but he did not know that because Palcath had been so close to the defeat of the Raid Boss and had been describing it, the game had decided Palcath had qualified as participating in the battle.

Palcath had a major jump in Levels and was now at Level 96. That, as it happens, was exactly enough of a boost in his Constitution score to make him a bit more sturdy. Enough of a boost that the *Bundles of Rope* could no longer hope to contain his massive sturdiness and they snapped apart like they were a mere *Heap of Rope*.

Palcath had to contain a *Smirk Animation*. His new sturdiness was not only attractive to all the ladies it had also set him free. As a great bonus he also gained his last racial ability: *Dwarf ex Machina*. Now that Breaker was distracted with trying to catch the giant centipede in the sky that had shown up, it was the time for Palcath to act.

Chapter 46

CYCLE 7
THE BATTLE OF
THE BOXES

Roodg's Text Box: aWFUL LOT OF EXPLOSIONS TODAY…

From high up in the clouds, surveying the different battles of Onn, Roodg had heard slightly more explosions than normal for a given cycle. There had been avatar bomb explosions, monster bomb explosions, status effect cloud explosions, milk silo explosions, orgasmic gnome/troll explosions, unicorn slut explosions, demonic bull explosions, raid boss explosions, and even 'cursed item has been destroyed forever' explosions. All in all, there were a lot of different sound clips for explosions.

Another new explosion type and an accompanying sound effect happened right beside Roodg's pointed left ear. A *Blizzard Explosion*. There was only one avatar in the game capable of casting that spell because there was only one player of the least popular class in the game. The explosion smoke revealed a pantsless Rocket Sorceress with a scented candle shoved up her lower mouth (which Roodg thought was an interesting touch) piloting a flying *Parsnip*.

Roodg's Text Box: yOU MISSED.

Caëlahenäilenẇhei's Text Box: Only because your stupid retro insect is moving all fucked up. I've calculated the move trajectory of the 'random' animation cycle. I will not miss next time.

Despite her cockiness, the *Magnitude 16* missed as well. She shrugged it off as only a miss because of the unsteadiness of her flying *Parsnip*. Roodg agreed with that one, it had been next to impossible to hit anything with an earth based spell while riding on *Carrot Sr.* due to the wind resistance.

> Caëlahenãilenẃhei's Text Box: Didn't you unlock any vehicles that hover non-fucked up?

> Roodg's Text Box: iN THE FUTURE i WILL STRIVE TO ONLY WIN VEHICLES THAT CONFORM TO THE HIGH STANDARDS OF THE MAIN VILLAIN. yOU HAVE MY WORD.

> Caëlahenãilenẃhei's Text Box: Well, at least this battle will be good target practice. You see despite all my other back-up plans that I really didn't care about failing, controlling this skinny little elf cunt was actually my main back-up plan from the start. She doesn't even need to be PVP broken to kill all of you other idiots, as I am sure you know all too well with your own area magic attacks little Magic Mage. With all of her obsessive compulsive resource management, she has enough horded *Mana Potions* stockpiled to burn the entire world to smoking cinders five times —

> Caëlahenãilenẃhei's Text Box: over!

Caëlahenãilenẃhei used the *Mortified Expression Animation*.

> Caëlahenãilenẃhei's Text Box: Sweet Maker! I am controlling her and now I have started to talk so much I break into the next Text Box! I need to stop acting like that mouthy little cunt.

> Caëlahenãilenẃhei's Box Text: Mmmble! Mmmrf, Murrf!

> Caëlahenãilenẃhei's Text Box: Shut up you mouthy little cunt!

> Roodg's Text Box: yOU CAN'T JUST BURN THE WORLD!

> Caëlahenãilenẃhei's Text Box: Oh, but I can. Observe.

With a Dramatic Toss Back of Her Long Hair and a Flick of Her Wick Animation, Caela cast *Momentous Firefall*. Comets of fire fell from the sky and crashed into a portion of Onn Forest; trees, scenic wildlife, grass, directional arrows, and graffiti spider webs were bathed in a fiery explosion that shook the area. The smoke cleared and revealed the entire area looked exactly the same as it had before.

> Roodg's Text Box: nO, i LITERALLY MEANT THAT YOU CAN'T JUST BURN THE WORLD. i TRIED THAT ALREADY.

> iT DOESN'T WORK. yOU HAVE TO GET MORE CREATIVE WITH YOUR SPELLS!

> Caëlahenãilenŵhei's Text Box: Wow. I really don't care. All that matters is that I don't have to get creative to kill you with my magic.

> Roodg's Text Box: i WOULDN'T BE SO SURE ABOUT THAT.

Caela was sure about it and she tossed over an *Acid Barrow* followed by a *Devil's Whisper*, both deftly dodged by Roodg and Carrot Jr. She furiously followed up with a *Blizzard Explosion* and was criticised by a dodging Roodg as had already used that spell this battle. Spell after spell followed, but aiming at a randomly moving centipede that was being controlled by an avatar who was nearly as random was an exercise in frustration. Even the big area-attacks didn't seem to singe either of her targets.

The light elf didn't care. She had a bigger mana pool than anyone else in the game (excluding avatars who had broken mana pools). She started to cast every spell at her disposal as fast as possible. She was entering them so fast that the spells did not have time to go off. They were building up in the action queue and the next would go off as soon as her turn came again as she chased the night elf on the centipede.

> Roodg's Text Box: fINALLY YOU PICKED THE ONE i WAS WAITING FOR YOU TO CAST!

Caela stopped dead in her flight tracks. Excluding the queued up spells that would go off every round and her hands doing casting spell motions, she was motionless.

> Caëlahenãilenŵhei's Text Box: What are you talking about, idiot? Why were you waiting for me to cast a *Lightning Toad* specific spell when I have cast more than enough of them for you to get hit with.

> Roodg's Text Box: sILLY, i WAS WAITING FOR THE *The Light Fisting of the Heavens* SPELL THAT i COULD USE TO DEFEAT YOU WITH.

> Caëlahenãilenŵhei's Text Box: What in the Flaming Pit *Pit Flames* are you talking about? That is stupid. There is no such thing.

Despite Caela's tough front, the beads of sweat on her brow said otherwise. She was not so secretly trying to cancel her queued moves, but without success.

> Roodg's Text Box: oF COURSE THERE IS. wHAT DID i TELL *Mudpie Earthspike* YOU ABOUT BEING CREATIVE WITH YOUR SPELLS?

The ticking down of abilities continued and Caela did her best to target Roodg. She was ecstatic when her next spell, *Blazing Onions*, hit. She was happy when *Gutterous*

Windwrath struck Roodg right in the chest. She was a bit confused when *Tornado Technical* directly hit Roodg who was charging right at her. She was concerned when *Hellatious Ice Crystals* should have ripped her target apart but did nothing as Roodg leaped off the flying centipede at her. She was plain confused when the *Earth Version 2* did nothing to stop Roodg who landed on top of her and grabbed on.

> Roodg's Text Box: hERE IT COMES. iT IS THE NEXT ONE.

> Caëlahenãilenŵhei's Text Box: That is like the lamest and weakest spell in the game! I did it by accident. What could *Magic Fizzle* possibly do?

> Roodg's Text Box: wATCH!

When casting *Magic Fizzle*, Caela purposely aimed completely off target, to stop any funny business that Roodg was planning.

> Roodg's Text Box: sEE THE THING ABOUT *mAGIC fIZZLE* IS…

The arc of fizzle lightning stopped in its path.

> Roodg's Text Box: THAT IT ALWAYS HITS, NO MATTER WHAT.

The arc turned around and started to come towards the pair.

> Roodg's Text Box: iT IS A LOW DAMAGE AREA ATTACK.

The arc hit Roodg, and by extension also Caela.

> Caëlahenãilenŵhei's Text Box: So what? I am immune to my own magic spells.

> Roodg's Text Box: i AM IMMUNE TO YOUR MAGIC SPELLS TOO!

The lightning sparked on, covering the pair in dangerous looking fizzles.

> Caëlahenãilenŵhei's Text Box: What? How?

> Roodg's Text Box: bECAUSE i AM sAWESOME AND HAVE A *hEART OF eVERYTHING* i GOT FROM A MYSTERIOUS NUTCASE THAT MAKES ME IMMUNE TO ALL ELEMENTS!

> Caëlahenãilenŵhei's Text Box: You dirty cheater!

> Roodg's Text Box: lIKE YOU CAN TALK!

The lightning stopped, fizzling out of existence. Neither avatar was damaged.

> Caëlahenãilenŵhei's Text Box: Crap, you are immune to my spells! I didn't bother to PVP break this stupid cunt so I can't even smack you to death with this moronic secondary book weapon.

> Roodg's Text Box: nOPE AND i AM NOT GOING TO CAST SPELLS BACK EITHER.

> Caëlahenãilenẇhei's Text Box: What was the point of all of this nonsense? If we were both immune to the stupid spell in the first place, why did you jump on me to hit us with it?

> Roodg's Text Box: bECAUSE i WASN'T AIMING FOR US.

Caëlahenãilenẇhei use the *Confused Animation*. She honestly didn't know where this was going.

> Roodg's Text Box: nOW MY REAL PLAN BEGINS!

One pair of Caela's lips were sealed, she had no idea what to say. The other pair of Caela's lips had plenty to say, and were no longer sealed.

> Caëlahenãilenẇhei's Box Text: Roodg was aiming for the candle you blowhard. No one but Roodg could possibly know that candles can only be properly melted with fizzling lightning attacks.

> Caëlahenãilenẇhei's Text Box: Fuck not you again!

> Roodg's Text Box: pERFECT! nOW STEP TWO OF MY PLAN. qUICK Caëlahenãilenẇhei TELL ME WHAT TO DO TO SAVE YOU!

Caela's box had started to type in the plan that she of course already knew, but she was taking too long to type, as usual.

> Caëlahenãilenẇhei's Text Box: Your plan is to wait for her to type? Horrible plan. My plan. 1. Kick you in the balls/cootch/both. 2. Steal centipede. 3. Kill two avatars in other areas who are not immune to my spells and are pissing me off.

She was true to her word. Steps one and two were already executed before Roodg could even act. Despite the pain of a double crotch kick, Roodg started to chase down *Centipede* Carrot Jr. with the more manoeuvrable *Parsnip* Carrot Sr.

They had flown to the island that was floating above Onn and chased each other through the crumbling remains of The Lost God Glackronix, the Guardian of the Glade. Roodg swooped in just in time to save Mr. Max, Lissa, and a whole flock of Quest Fairies from falling into *Caela's Eternally Dark Deathward* thanks to having more seats on the broken *Parsnip* than the default *Carrot* setting. All were so shocked to be suddenly rescued from the danger which had suddenly occurred, that they sat there, on the Parsnip, with *Shocked Animations* on their faces.

Finally, Caela's Box began to talk. Caela tried to stop her by shoving her hand inside, but only forced herself to painfully bite her own finger.

> Caëlahenâilenŵhei's Box Text: Didn't anyone tell you what was going on Roodg? We specifically sent word through Yallundy to tell everyone what to do to stop us. I mean seriously, what was the point of us risking our best spy like that if no one even bothered to listen to our plan! I sure hope that everyone else has more sense than that and actually found out what to do to stop us. Otherwise we are seriously in trouble! I mean come on, all of our characters are riding on this, even the world. I am far too powerful to leave in the dirty hands of Breaker, and you should smarte—

> Caëlahenâilenŵhei's Box Text: n up!

> Caëlahenâilenŵhei's Text Box: What? She took that long to type and she didn't even type her plan? All she did was scold you? That is hilarious! What an idiot.

Caëlahenâilenŵhei couldn't contain herself, it was too hilarious. She had to use the *Burst Out Laughing Animation* at the pathetic moron. When she opened her eyes, she was no longer looking through *Prince-nez Glasses* but instead through the buttons of the *Initiate's Jacket*. During the time Breaker had been laughing and out of control, the real Caela had stripped off the controlling jacket.

> Initiate Jacket's Text Box: Wait, what just happened?

> Caëlahenâilenŵhei's Text Box: My perfect plan of tricking you into laughing at me for being an 'idiot' worked. You lose control when you get distracted. Now Roodg, use your scenery destroying powers to delete this clothing monstrosity!

> Roodg's Text Box: wITH PLEASURE!

Roodg had been trying to destroy wearable equipment since the start of the game, but the cycles of research had not been wasted. You had to treat it like laundry. First, you had to get it in the Soaked Status, and heat it as hot as possible but dry it double fast with an *Absorbing Cloth*. If it got hot and dry enough at the same time, it would shrink completely out of existence (like real laundry). *Orbital Firestrike*, the hottest spell in the Magic Mage arsenal was more than hot enough to do the trick, and while there were no *Absorbing Cloths* on hand, Roodg had a spare *Double Danish* that would likely work.

The fire magic/danish combo finished its animation and the cum-stained, much maligned, bane of Anders' low Level existence, the *Initiate's Jacket* was destroyed forever. Caela was now free from Breaker's control, exhausted, drained of mana, and completely naked.

Roodg's Text Box: i'M SO GLAD YOU ARE SAFE! wE NEED TO TALK SO MUCH!

Caëlahenãilenŵhei's Text Box: No. There is no time for talking right now.

Everyone but Caela used the *Shocked Animation*.

Caëlahenãilenŵhei's Text Box: Someone needs to go collect everyone so we can get out of here before the world explodes, and I have access to the Parsnip. You three need to race up that tower and go save him before it is too late!

Lissa's Text Box: Save him? What has that dwarf gotten himself into? #SaveThePrince? He is in even more trouble now! Come on!

Mr. Max's Text Box: Check!

Roodg's Text Box: nEAT! aND AFTER WE GET BACK WE GET TO TRY OUT THAT *mOUTHGINA* Caëlahenãilenŵhei!

Caëlahenãilenŵhei changed to *Blush Shade #9*, thankful for the new shade. Lissa, Roodg, Mr. Max, and a throng of Quest Fairies ran off and had ported into the Tower before Caela could reply with information that would have been useful for any of the three people who didn't know it yet.

Caëlahenãilenŵhei's Text Box: Dwarf? I wasn't talking about Palcath. Don't you three know?! I was talking about saving Anders.

◈ **Chapter 47** ◈

CYCLE 7
THE BATTLE OF
DWARFMAN

Sneaking was not easy when you are a melee classed avatar in heavy Armour. After one step Palcath had removed everything but his prized *Wind Gigas Helmet*, *Last Boss Shield*, and the pair of *Striped Heart Boxers* that he had been given as a gift from the Bleeding Heart. Attempting to be silent was slightly easier while naked. Fortunately for Palcath, Breaker was too distracted by his remaining monitors to notice a dwarf tripping over a chair and cursing while in his 'special dwarf stealth mode'.

Palcath unplugged the first of the strange alien tubes from Nega-Anders' unconscious form and the Nega-elf woke up with a silent gasp. Even after Palcath had pulled out three more tubes the progress bar did not slow down. A quick spot of math in his head and Palcath had calculated that The Ultimate Machine of Absorbing Avatars Forever That I Built After Learning About Stuff From The Device (which Breaker had obviously named himself) wasn't as accurate as Palcath would have liked. The 68% could in reality be anywhere from 59%-77%. That was reason enough to hurry or possibly slow down, and Palcath unplugged as fast as he could.

> Breaker's Text Box: Bah, I don't have time for this nonsense. My good back-up plan was candle hacked. You know what? I am just going to let this last unimportant idiot follow the programming and the other unimportant idiot army auto-target whatever they seen next and be done with it.

Breaker minimized the remaining monitors and opened his custom security camera windows. He decided that watching avatars try to navigate his special tower filled with treasure chests, each rigged with a different elaborate trap, would be far more entertaining that watching useless Quest Fairies flitter about killing his enemies with glitter.

> Breaker's Text Box: What? Why aren't they opening up any chests?

As soon as his Nega-arm was free, Nega-Anders began to frantically help Palcath un-plug. By the time the glowing ball that was Breaker started to yell at the security footage, Nega-Anders was unplugged from the waist up. He had slumped down against the back of the machine and both he and Palcath were working on his legs.

> Breaker's Text Box: They are already on floor 26?! How? They haven't opened a single chest? That is madness! Who can resist the new colour of epic chests?

Palcath perked up. There was an entire new colour of chest? He wondered what colour it could possibly be. It couldn't be red, blue, gold, or that ridiculous side-quest-starting green chest. If it was orange, or purple then Lissa and Max would have stopped to argue. Maybe it was platinum, that seemed the logical choice to be more important than gold.

> Breaker's Text Box: Crap. They will be here in no time now. I better step this up or my new skin suit will not be ready in time.

Pressing the big red button, Breaker put The Ultimate Machine of Absorbing Avatars Forever That I Built After Learning About Stuff From The Device into Top Priority Mode. All but one of his security cameras shut down and all of his impressive computing power was transferred to the device. Dozens of new avatar connectors shot out of the machine. Only a few new ones had hit Nega-Anders, but Palcath was troubled by two things.

Most troubling was that this new progress bar did not work with the math. The numbers of new mechanical tendrils in Nega-Anders and the progress of the bars did not line up. Palcath did some quick numbers in his head and figured it out. Breaker had been lazy when designing this. The progress bar had only for show all along. It was made to follow along with a preset timeline, which explained why it had filled to 100% with Nega-Anders no longer attached to it. There had never been a way to tell how much of the progress was done.

Less troubling was the suction device now stuck in Palcath's arm, feeding lines of sickly black code into him. It was stuck in his sturdiness, far more stuck than the ones that had been stuck in the beefiness that was Nega-Anders. Nega-Anders was now helping Palcath get out of the machine, returning the favour. Palcath made a mental note to get his priorities in better order.

As Palcath unsuccessfully attempted to remove the offending device from his body, Breaker was getting ready for his big moment. *With a Glowing Out of His Light and a*

Dramatic Movement of his Ball Animation, Breaker was as badass as possible for the arrival of Lissa, Mr. Max, and Roodg.

> Breaker's Text Box: How nice of you all to come and join me.

> Lissa's Text Box: Can it fuckbutt! We don't have time for your stupid games.

> Breaker's Text Box: How your words wound me so.

Lissa had spoken and spotted the now even sturdier dwarf. He was pulling on some odd alien thing in his arm. He had almost escaped from that whatever it was, and she understood what to do thanks to the helpful progress bars. She was going to have to pretend that she did have time for these stupid games.

> Lissa's Text Box: #ToughTitties! We got here to foil your plan and no matter how clever it is, it isn't going to work!

> Breaker's Text Box: I beg to differ because it is a clever plan. The best part is that every single one of you annoying fucks that stopped me the first time is going to be here to witness it, and then die to it.

> Roodg's Text Box: Fournimer ISN'T HERE.

> Breaker's Text Box: I said the ones that were annoying in your original party. That centaur is all right, I quite like his scarf. Very dramatic.

> Mr. Max's Text Box: We are here to end your plans, get ready to fight.

Mr. Max's statement was met with an *Elbow in the Ribs Animation* by both Roodg and Lissa.

> Lissa's Whisper Text Box: Quiet!

> Breaker's Text Box: Fine, if a fight is what you want, a fight you shall ha—

> Roodg's Interruption Text Box: wAIT!

Watching on with impatience, Breaker gave a motion that suggested Roodg should explain why he should wait. At least that is what Roodg decided that the bobbing of his light ball meant.

> Roodg's Text Box: uM… yOUR PLAN INVOLVES THAT THING THERE WITH THE TUBES RIGHT? iT IS sAWESOME LOOKING. i NEED TO KNOW WHAT IT DOES BEFORE i DIE OR i WILL NEVER BE ABLE TO LIVE WITH MYSELF.

Breaker wasted no time explaining his machine in great detail as he was quite proud of it. The method of construction and materials used were discussed, the full progress bar was explained in great detail, the elaborate naming process was revealed, the way that he had found a The Device that had belonged to someone called the Mistress and used that as a template, how the tubes of code were fully rationalized, and even the purpose of the machine was eventually divulged. Breaker knew so much about his machine that he didn't even need to look at it while explaining.

> Breaker's Text Box: So, in conclusion, this machine is going to allow me to take over the most powerful avatar ever permanently. With his body I will rule the old map like the Maker, except that I will find the Maker and kill him first. With this body I will be the new God!

Breaker made a motion of light towards his machine, showing Palcath attached to it. Nega-Anders was hidden behind the sturdy.

> Mr. Max's Text Box: What, him? I hate to break it to you Breaker, but he isn't that powerful of a class or even at max Level.

> Breaker's Text Box: He is the perfect vessel for my vengeance!

> Roodg's Text Box: wHY?

> Breaker's Text Box: Is your creepy one visible eye blind or something? He is the ultimate avatar and I will own him forever!

> Lissa's Text Box: No!

> Breaker's Text Box: No?

Lissa used the *Dramatic Adventure Pose Animation.*

> Lissa's Text Box: No!

> Breaker's Text Box: Umm… sorry, but yes.

> Lissa's Text Box: I said no! #PayAttention.

> Breaker's Text Box: Yes, I heard.

> Lissa's Text Box: You can't have him!

> Breaker's Text Box: I am pretty sure I already do have him.

> Lissa's Text Box: I said no! You can't have him! You can't have him! No!

> Breaker's Text Box: Okay, you are kind of freaking me out here.

> Lissa's Text Box: You can't have him! I will not let you! You can't have him! You just can't!

Lissa used the *Determined and Steadfast Animation*.

Breaker really didn't know what was going on with Lissa. She had a wild competitive look in her eyes and he was almost too scared to reply. Almost.

> Breaker's Shaken Text Box: Why… not?

> Lissa's Text Box: Because Palcath is mine!

> Breaker's Text Box: Huh? Who?

Lissa rushed forward and struck at Breaker's Ball with her *Ultimatium Mace*. She deftly deflected his *Ball Blast* and leapt across the room. She ripped out the suction device in Palcath's arm with a mighty show of competitive power. He fell into her arms, weak from his capture, and she executed a forceful *Kiss Passionately Dual Animation* on the stunned dwarf as she lifted him up off the ground into and her arms. She had successfully saved the dwarf in distress that had been locked away in a tower by the evil villain. Regardless of recent sexual tension with other party members, she had chosen Palcath.

> Palcath's Text Box: Your plan was good Breaker, lad. I was the best avatar to take over.

> Breaker's Text Box: But—

> Roodg's Interruption Text Box: omm! lOOK! bEHIND Palcath! iT IS Anders! hE IS ALIVE? nO WAY!

> Mr. Max's Text Box: Wow I had no idea! Look at how cool he looks now. So much Optional Boss power is coming from him you can almost taste it.

> Roodg's Text Box: nEAT! Breaker yOUR PLAN SHOULD HAVE BEEN TO TAKE OVER Anders. lOOK AT HOW BADASS HE IS.

> Breaker's Text Box: What? You three idiots didn't know Anders was still alive? Fuck! Another dramatic reveal wasted. I guess that cunt elf was right, I am bad at this. Because you are all stupid I will explain it again. That idiot dwarf was—

> Palcath's Interruption Text Box: Was the perfect main plan for sure. Nega-Anders was a great back-up plan Breaker.

Breaker's Text Box: No you see, Nega-Anders, he—

Nega-Anders' Interruption Text Box: He is free now from your machine, he was not fully converted over to be absorbed by you forever, he has been secretly charging an arrow for some time now, and he is not under your control!

An arrow zinged through the air and struck Breaker's Ball. With the PVP broken ability of the *Giganticore Rib Bow+* it pierced through the ball and caused severe damage. Breaker's Ball flashed three times and faded away, it was forever dead.

Roodg's Text Box: yEAH! tHAT SHUT HIM UP! aRROW TO THE BALL!

Mr. Max's Text Box: Great job teammates!

Lissa's Text Box: That was a bit anti-climatic, but fuck it. He is dead and we won!

Palcath's Text Box: I get to be a prize!

Herbert's Text Box: But we didn't even get to do anything!

Nega-Anders' Text Box: You were only right on three counts.

Everyone Else's Simultaneous Text Boxes: ?

Nega-Anders' Text Box: Nega-Anders' last statement, go back and read it again. You see, he was only right on three counts. Sure he got free from my machine. Sure he had not been fully converted over so I cannot absorb him forever. Sure he had even been secretly charging an arrow while he was hidden behind the stupid dwarf in underpants. But the one he was wrong with is important. He is under my control.

Nega-Anders' took to the sky on his angelic wings, his eyes moved around wildly in their sockets. He nocked another arrow and got ready to do a serious proper final climax battle with his enemies.

Roodg's Text Box: cRAP.

◈ Chapter 48 ◈
CYCLE 7
THE BATTLE OF
NUMERO UNO

Zal Finn III's Text Box: Thanks Vivian and Fred for the ride!

Dragon Rider Vivian's Text Box: No problem. It is the least we could do for you telling us that the world is about to be destroyed. Are you sure you don't want to fly around with me for a bit and collect some NPCs and monsters to teleport out of the Expansion?

Fred's Text Box: Frrrruuuuuuuggghh?

After politely refusing so that she could hunt through Onn for her friends, Zal Finn III thought about how much easier this whole escaping the world endeavour could have been had they originally asked the Dragon Rider for help. Vivian, who was also known by anyone who followed the story of the expansion as 'The One Who Could Transverse Both Time and Space to Meet Their Goals' could teleport back to the main map at will due to her climactic final battle that involved Fred and The Plague of Shadow merging into the Dragon Mount of Shadow. Even if it was a bit of a *Slap in the Face Animation*, at least Vivian could get them all out of here after she finished collecting the few remaining residents of The Island of Islana.

Activating her *Auto-Locate Eyes*, Zal Finn III surveyed the area. Who would be a good avatar to collect first? Lissa was still up on that floating island with Breaker, Max,

Roodg, Palcath, and some rainbow arrow, so she was out. Hippolyta was with her entire original party and they were headed towards samuri, that colourless arrow, and a bunch of NPCs. They were just over the rise. She didn't need her eyes to see them, they were finishing up a battle with a huge army of diseased avatars and monsters, and Zal Finn was in no shape to join them. While Zal was scanning for Caela, she joined the battle, carpet bombing monsters from atop the flying *Parsnip*.

That only left Fournimer, who did not appear to be in the Expansion (which Zal Finn thought was suspicious), and Glünt and Yallundy, who were in Onn Forest. Onn Forest was by no means anyone's favourite place, but at least you could avoid all but one of the monsters if you knew the right route (and you could avoid that one too if you could *Double Jump*).

Stealthily avoiding the main battle as she skirted around the outside of Onn, Zal Finn made a nice discovery. Onn Forest was even easier to navigate now that it was mostly a giant smoking crater. Stepping over the shattered husk of what was probably that first Golden Gribblet, and giving it a *White Wolf Kick* for good measure, she *Double Jumped* past some lewd webbing and towards what used to be Spire H, the Airship Docking Mini-Spire.

Her third *Double Jump* gave her a view of an unnoticed series of high platforms. Normally, it would have been hidden by camera angles and the lush vegetation, but it was now visible due to the destruction. Normally Zal Finn would have just avoided the jumping puzzle entirely, but nestled on the top of it was a golden chest. It was a never before discovered golden chest, and six easy *Double Jumps* away (as opposed to the nineteen difficult single *Jumps* it would take nearly everyone else). It would barely set her back any time, especially if she jumped off the top after getting the chest. In fact, she decided, it would save her time.

As she made the final leap Zal Finn was intercepted in mid-air by a pink blur. It grabbed her neck tightly for just a fraction of a round before it threw her down hard on jumping puzzle platform #13. It landed beside her and stared down.

Zal Finn III was choking and sputtering, trying to recover from the near crushing of her windpipe. Her vision slowly returned in a mass of fuzzy and mostly pink balls, and as her attacker came into focus she was more initially confused than alarmed.

> Zal Finn III's Text Box: What? How is that possible… it's…

There she was in all her glory. A Warrior dressed in full-plate, with pink accent colours, and wielding a simple *Two Handed Sword*. Someone had taken great care to either fix her torso, or jam all the pieces back into the Armour. Her hairstyle was *#15* and set to an unselectable bubblegum pink, her features were carefully selected and unique, *Body Type #4 (curvy)* with *+3 tall*, *#12 eyes* (the ones with the sexy lashes), full pouty *#17 Lips* with bright pink lipstick, and even the *#4 Button Nose*. There was nothing at all on this avatar that was set to the default *#10* besides the default #10 flashing pink beacon on the tiara that Zal Finn III had never seen before.

Zal Finn III's Text Box: … it's me?

Zal Finn I's Text Box: I know, it is swell right? Wait, that isn't it… What do I say all the time again… something like swell. I remember now. I think. It was sweet, right?

Zal Finn III didn't even know what to say, she was legitimately speechless.

Zal Finn I's Text Box: Finally! I got in a dramatic reveal that was dramatic. What is even better is that you are even more generic than you were before dressed in that starting Armour and gear. I couldn't have planned that better myself.

Zal Finn III's Text Box: Breaker! You unsweet bastard, this is all your fault! You drained all of my Levels away with your stupid virus!

Zal Finn I's Text Box: All of them? That is even better! I didn't even notice, thanks for the tip. You are a Level 1? Ha! I didn't even bother spending the time to Level up this Zal Finn I, because fighting you really wasn't all that important, I just wanted to rub in how generic and boring you are now compared to your old body.

Zal Finn III's Text Box: I forgot about that! You made me all generic with your stupid Codes!

Zal Finn I's Text Box: No, the Dopple Doubleganger Boss did that if you will recall, but it was sort of my fault, so I will take all the credit. Thanks!

Zal Finn III's Text Box: I am going to make you pay for all the unsweet things you did to me… myself!

Zal Finn I's Text Box: I doubt it, this better version of you is better. It is Level 19, PVP broken, has a bunch of sword abilities, outrageous pink hair, and has a much bigger vagina. You are Level 1, have a *Basic Box Cutter* as a weapon, are wearing a *Brown Cardboard Box*, have no abilities to speak of, and as far as I can tell a normal everyday generic vagina. This isn't a fair fight in the slightest, I love it!

Zal Finn III's Text Box: Still… I'll do something, you'll see!

Zal Finn I's Text Box: A pity really, but I will not see anything. It is a shame because this was becoming a fun back and forth with your expressive wit and unwillingness to sacrifice your sweetness, but I need

> to leave to do other more important things. As I said before, all this was to make you feel bad about how much of a loser you are. I am not going to even bother to stick around and find out what happens. You are that unimportant.

> Zal Finn III's Text Box: But...

> Zal Finn I's Text Box: I know, you are not even important enough to watch one sword attack slice you in half. Think about that for a bit. It is unsweet of me to not just do it myself, I know. Toodles!

Zal Finn I used the *Sneeze Animation* and was switched to Auto-Attack mode. She brought her *Two Handed Sword* down hard and nearly cleaved Zal Finn III apart. She barely managed to get out of the way in time, saved only by her higher than normal Level 1 starting Dexterity, ability to *Double Jump*, and bonuses due to higher Roman Numerals. Puzzle platform #13 was not as lucky and succumbed to its wounds, dying a painful but quick death. Zal Finn I had fallen down to platform #8, but she was already back on her feet and jumping towards Zal Finn III who was now sprawled all over platform #11.

> Zal Finn I's Text Box: Sweet.

The crazed Warrior Zal Finn used the standard Warrior air attack combo. Zal Finn I executed three horizontal slashes and one final more powerful vertical slash. Zal Finn III was happy to know about the flaws of that move from past experience. Attacking Start Rats with it proved ineffective, as they were too short to hit with the horizontal slashes. She avoided the first three slashes by playing rat and simply not standing up, and the fourth by using a *Dodge Roll*. While this did save her life, it also caused her to fall towards the ground, stopping short by accidentally ledge grabbing platform #2.

> Zal Finn I's Text Box: Sweet?

The tattered remains of platform #11 that Zal Finn I had been standing on gave way, and the pink Warrior fell to the ground, madly slashing at anything in her path. By the time that her airborne combos (which slowed your fall speed significantly if you could keep them up) had finished Zal Finn I was on the ground, Zal Finn III had jumped up to platform #4, and platforms #3, #5, #9, and #16, were severed from the beanstalk platform tower.

> Zal Finn I's Text Box: Sweet!

Charging at the Dancing Ninja Assassin with the help of a *Double Handed Sword Slash*, Zal Finn I managed to take the front folding flap off of the *Brown Cardboard Box*. This move stunned Zal Finn III as her ordinary cleavage was now visible, it pleased Zal Finn I as it had hit, and it flat out destroyed platforms #7 and #8.

> Zal Finn I's Text Box: SWEET!

Sword-a-pult was the free move that Zal Finn I executed on the stunned Zal Finn III. This original Zal Finn was not programmed to auto-attack by someone that had ever been a Warrior, Zal Finn III noted as she flew up in the air undamaged by the attack. That move had only helped Zal Finn III to grab onto platform #12 on her way down. In fact, seeing things from the air gave Zal Finn III an idea.

> Zal Finn III's Text Box: Smooth move there me! Thanks for the help.

> Zal Finn I's Text Box: SWEET!?

> Zal Finn III's Text Box: Whatever you do next, please don't use *Returning Swordarang*.

Choosing to avoid the request because that is what Breaker would have wanted, Zal Finn I used *Returning Swordarang*. The *Two Handed Sword* flew through the air and devastated platform #12, which Zal Finn had already *Double Jumped* from. As the sword returned it eliminated platform #2 from existence as well. A few more aggressive sword returns were executed and platforms #4, #14, and #15 had been carefully trimmed by Zal Finn III's moving target technique.

> Zal Finn III's Text Box: Whatever you do, don't use *Hurt of the Triad* next. It will finish me for sure.

> Zal Finn I's Enraged Text Box: SWEET!!!

Again ignoring the advice of herself, Zal Finn I used *Hurt of the Triad* next. Her *Two Handed Sword* split into full sized thirds and they shot upwards, destroying platforms #6, #10, and #17 as Zal Finn III watched from platform #18.

> Zal Finn III's Text Box: Ha! You just destroyed all the platforms that you needed to jump up and get me! Now I'm safe up here and completely out of range of your *Returning Swordarangs*.

> Zal Finn I's Furious Text Box: SWEEEEET!!!

The pink Warrior was so upset by this turn of events that she steamed and stamped all across the ground as the Dancing Ninja Assassin watched on amused. This would never do, she had to finish her job for Breaker, and she was the most important minion in his army (if only by the merit of the fact all of the other ones had been destroyed by this point). She did the only thing she could do, she invented a brand new move for Warriors. It would now be gained by every Level 19 Warrior, but no one would ever be stupid enough to use it more than once after getting it.

Zal Finn I used *Unreturning Swordarang*. Zal Finn III used the *Wince Animation*. The *Two Handed Sword* cut Zal Finn III's box completely in half as it flew by her, destroying platform #18, and vanished forever in a twinkle of light. The Ninja was grateful that it was the *Brown Cardboard Box* that got destroyed and that she had only been cut slightly on her hip.

She started to fall, but used the second half of a *Double Jump* to get to platform #19 thankful that the rules didn't mind that her first jump had been out of her skin. This platform was crowded with a golden chest. There was not room to move. Zal Finn III watched as the remains of her box fell gently to the ground at Zal Finn I's feet. Yes, she was stuck up here, but at least her former Warrior self had destroyed her weapon and couldn't do anything else to put her in danger.

She was going to need to signal for help. Maybe she could get Caela's attention from here if she tried. Standing up, Zal Finn III was alarmed to feel wet on her side. She was covered in blood it was dripping down her legs. She nearly passed out, the cut on her hip must have been worse that she thought… but it wasn't? It was fine, only a little scratch, it wasn't even bleeding.

Confused, Zal Finn looked around for the source of the blood. It was the air beside her hip. That lead to more confusion as she poked the air around her and her hip mounted *Basic Box Cutter*. The cutter was only hanging on by a thread, the invisible area around it that had kept it floating beside her hip thanks to video game weapon equipment equipping logic. Scabbards were not things, so weapons hung in the air, and that air was what was bleeding. She tried to move her weapon to her hand by attacking with it, but that was all it took for the *Basic Box Cutter* to slip off the invisible air of her hip and fall to the earth. It hit Zal Finn I square in the forehead, but it didn't do any damage as it was not a PVP broken weapon, at least not yet.

> Zal Finn I's Victorious Text Box: SWEEEEEEEEET!!!

> Zal Finn III's Text Box: Unsweet.

There was no way that Zal Finn I was going to use *Unreturning Swordarang* again, she had learned her lesson. What she could do was stand on platform #1 and hack at the base structure of the beanstalk to make the entire thing collapse. The progress was faster than either had expected, likely as Zal Finn I was wielding the weapon in two hands, which everyone knows makes for much more effective box cutting.

The top #19 platform was shaking violently with each expert cut. Zal Finn III had been forced to hug the golden chest to keep from falling. Chests were solid and would not go anywhere without a fight, much like Zal Finn III at this moment.

Zal Finn I had gone near mad with box cutting power, to the point of foaming at the mouth. She was going to topple this stalk, and she was going to prove her worth to her master. She would show him. She was important!

> Zal Finn I's Guttural Text Box: SWEEEEEEEEEEEET!!!!!

With one last slash the beanstalk cracked. Zal Finn III squeezed the golden chest so hard that once it had been freed of platform #19's existence, it popped out of her arms and flew up high into the air.

> Zal Finn III's Text Box: Holy fucking shitballs!

Zal Finn III fell hard to the ground, while the pink Warrior version of Zal Finn got her *Basic Box Cutter* ready to finish the deed.

> Zal Finn I's Primal Text Box: SWEEEEEEEEEEEEEEEEETEST!!!

> Zal Finn III's Text Box: Come on, I say more than sweet!

With a *Wild Look in Her Eyes Animation*, Zal Finn I raised the weapon in the air, wound up, and started to come forward for a final strike. She was unceremoniously interrupted when a golden chest fell from the sky and hit her in the back of the head. The force was so intense that it knocked her to the ground, crushed her skull and the *Tremendous Tiara* that Breaker had been using to establish control, and even popped the pink hair right off her head.

Zal Finn III moved the pink hair from in front of her eyes, as it had landed backwards on her head, and looked at her formal self. It was dead, completely dead. Those chests didn't mess around. When they were on the ground, they damn well owned that bit of ground.

> Zal Finn III's Text Box: Sweet!

Zal Finn had done the impossible. She had encountered a much higher Level version of herself who was using a much stronger class, and who was capable of hurting her, and she won. She briefly considered wearing her old sweet pink hair as a wig, but decided against it and pocketed it instead. She rightly determined that wearing her old scalp as a flesh hat would be a little bit creepy (plus it was covered in blood).

> Zal Finn III's Text Box: This is so sweet! I'm not dead. Now I can ju—

> Abby's Interruption Text Box: Die a completely different but equally painful death?

Looking up Zal Finn saw them. There were thousands of colour-unassigned dead Quest Fairies moving together as a huge mass of black pixel sickness. In the lead, a few move units ahead of the disgusting mass were two colour assigned Quest Fairies acting as leaders of the monstrosity. There was a rainbow flashing one who had just interrupted. The fairy had a thick black spike through her head, making it a miracle that she could even have talked in the first place. Zal Finn had never remembered seeing a rainbow Quest Fairy. Beside her crawling on the ground, was a black one. He had been snapped in half at one point, which explained the slithering way it moved. This Quest Fairy Zal Finn did recognized. He had briefly belonged to Breaker.

> Zal Finn III's Text Box: Come on! This isn't fair. I totally won my big

> battle.

The large mass of sickness all began to speak in unison.

> Quafam's Text Box: Welcome to the Expansion, the Island of Islana!

> Zal Finn III's Text Box: Pardon?

> Abby's Text Box: Hey listen! It is your own cheddaring fault for being the closest thing to us when we were put into Auto Attack Mode. You will face the smashing power of the Quafam!

> Zal Finn III's Text Box: Sorry, the what?

> Abby's Text Box: The Quafam, It stands for the Quest Fairy United Amalgamation For the Advancement of Mega-Fists.

> Tyreese's Text Box: I named it myself!

> Quafam's Text Box: I am your personal guide and keeper of all things Quests.

Zal Finn III had little time to ponder that Quafam did not stand for that because the Quafam punched with a powerful M and jolted her out of her thought process. She rocketed across the tattered remains of Onn Forest, and hit a scenic palm tree. The palm tree had only survived the carnage in the area because it had been misplaced there by a designer, as the rest of the forest was evergreens, but Zal Finn was thankful it was there. It had saved her from falling over a ledge.

Looking down over said ledge, Zal Finn swallowed hard. There were crazy swirls and colours flowing at the bottom. If she fell there would be no twinkly light and instant respawn back up at the top of the ledge, perfectly fine except for a small amount of health loss. This was far worse. This was a deadly unbottomless pit.

Clutching the palm tree firmly, Zal Finn III used a *Worry Animation* as three horrible acts against the Maker came towards her. The giant mass of dead fairies, the floating fairy with a spike through her head, and the slithering fairy that had to drag himself across the bare earth. The Quafam was large enough to block all possible means of escape down the narrow path, and tall enough to stop any *Double Jumps*. She was trapped.

> Abby's Text Box: Nice save there you waffling NPC idiot, but you will still be stomped by the powerful foot of the Quafam!

> Quafam's Text Box: You can always depend on me!

Stepping closer towards Zal Finn, the Quafam stopped for a round and started to blink.

> Quafam's Text Box: The first available Quests are nearby.

> Zal Finn III's Text Box: What is going on?

> Abby's Text Box: They are initializing?

> Tyreese's Text Box: How could they do that? This is a stupid, worthless NPC?

> Quafam's Text Box: You may call me Quest Fairy—

The Quafam stopped blinking, each individual Fairy inside started to pop into an assigned colour. In a few loud rounds the Quafam had turned completely pink.

> Quafam's Text Box: Quafam, the NPC Crusher!

> Zal Finn III's Text Box: For the last time, I am not a bloody NPC!

> Tyreese's Text Box: Not yet, but soon you will be bloody after you get pounded up a bit. Get her!

> Quafam's Text Box: HEY LISTEN!

As the now pink monstrosity charged at her, Zal Finn clutched the palm tree and thought. Either she could clutch there and die, or she could stand up and fight. Zal Finn III unclenched the palm tree, got her *Basic Box Cutter* out, and adjusted her regulation sized cleavage. Maybe this would be for the best after all, the real avatars, who were not a miserable Level 1 and never mistaken for NPCs, would have an easier time killing this if she thinned them out at least a little bit. With a *Grim Resolve Animation,* Zal Finn got ready to die as she lifted her *Basic Box Cutter* and slashed madly at the charging pink Quafam.

Attacking was like trying to pluck out a single bee in a swarm. The Quafam had swallowed her up and now all she could see was masses of pink blurs. Individual Quest Fairies were coming up to her and painfully biting off little pieces of her flesh. She was pretty sure she had killed a few of them, but wasn't entirely sure. Her measly Hit Points were drained and Dire Status took control. She could not longer fight back. The swarm stopped, and she wasn't sure why.

> Abby's Text Box: What in the freshly greeted heavens is that?

> Tyreese's Text Box: Ignore it, it's just a worthless monster.

> Abby's Text Box: Why is it looking at me like that?

> Tyreese's Text Box: It can't look at you. It is a monster. We are immune to their attacks. The stupid thing isn't even a boss.

> Abby's Text Box: I guess you're right. I don't know why I wa—

Abby was interrupted by a chomp.

> Quafam's Text Box: Holy fucking Shitballs!

> Tyreese's Text Box: No fucking way. Did it just eat her?

> Quafam's Text Box: Oh my Breaker, fly for your lives!

> Tyreese's Text Box: But I can't fly! Oh fu—

With a Feeble Crawl Forward and a Dramatic Bloody Gurgle Animation, Tyresse was both interrupted, and consumed.

The mass that had been Quafam began to scatter every which way and Zal Finn III fell to the ground, no longer suspended within. She finally saw what had spooked the Quest Fairies. Tens of thousands of pink Quest Fairies were fleeing in terror from 1,856 Golden Poffles. The 1,856 Golden Poffles that Zal Finn did not have the heart to kill this morning and instead had set free.

The Poffles were munching up the fleeing Quest Fairies like flashing blue ghosts, and each one that was devoured acted like a colour changing power pellet to the Golden Poffles. Quest Fairies that tried to escape by hovering were shocked when some Poffles sprouted wings and chased them down. Zal Finn watched them eat with a strange fascination. The Golden Poffles had slowly shifted into Impossible Pink Poffles.

Only after the last straggling member of Quafam was consumed did a Pink Poffle, with a black pom pom tail, and rainbow coloured eyes, come up to Zal Finn. With a flick of the pom pom the Poffle had completely restored Zal Finn's health.

> Zal Finn III's Text Box: Wow! That was sweet. I didn't know you guys could fly!

> Pink Poffle #1,172's Text Box: We couldn't until we ate some Quest Fairies.

> Zal Finn III's Text Box: You can talk?

> Pink Poffle #1,172's Text Box: If enough regular monsters get together they can form a hivemind. There were so many of us together at once that I am now more intelligent than Optional Boss Elfbane.

> Zal Finn III's Text Box: Sweet!

> Pink Poffle #1,172's Text Box: We had only come here looking to thank you for not killing us earlier, and of course to beg for more crackerwiches, but then we saw what they were doing to you and we

> had to stop it. We didn't even know we could eat them until we tried.

> Zal Finn III's Text Box: Thank you! I guess it pays off to let cute things like you live, huh?

> Pink Poffle #1,172's Text Box: We couldn't just stand by and watch while our favourite NPC of all time was killed.

Zal Finn III used the *Heartfelt Sigh Animation.*

> Zal Finn III's Text Box: I'm not an NPC. I only look like one. It is a side effect of my power.

> Pink Poffle #1,172's Text Box: Serious?

Zal Finn III used the *Depressed Nod Animation.* The Poffles were shocked, they could barely believe that an real-life avatar had scarified so many potential Levels and had let them go. Here she had been feeding them, singing them to sleep, and settling arguments between them all out of the goodness of her real-life heart. She hadn't been the NPC in charge of maintaining Poffles, she had been nice to them. For real.

> Pink Poffle #1,172's Text Box: You are so (s)…

> Zal Finn III's Text Box: (S) as in sweet?

> Pink Poffle #1,172's Text Box: (S)as in sexy!

A wave of cute Pink Poffles all started to snuggle her at once. Zal Finn gleefully cuddled the cute balls of friendly fur back. There were so many that they could never hope to reach her at once, and they started to show love to everything else in the area as well. Love, it turned out, was using all of your monster special attacks in (s) as in sexy ways all over your now naked saviour. Zal Finn was taken off guard as she had never expected that she was important enough to have a sex scene in this book series.

Pom Pom Rub caused untold pleasure as the fluffy balls felt and sparked electrical energy all over Zal Finn's body. *Piffle Poffle* licked the choicest places, and the *Poffley Nubbins* were absolutely mind-shattering to feel rub up against the rest. *Wancake* became Zal's favourite move in a hurry. Her long neglected womanhood was tickled, teased, and shown the proper attention that it deserved. The Poffles were taking care of everything, back support, breast stimulation, poffley kisses, and even levitating the orgy of swarming monsters and Zal high into the air to provide better access. It was the ultimate in group sex for the ultimate group sex avatar.

> Zal Finn III's Text Box: Sweetdiculous! I am getting close.

> Pink Poffle #1,172's Text Box: Now! Do it!

1,856 Poffles all activated their last move, *Frenzy*, on the same round. 1,856 tongues went into overdrive and a blur of tantalizing pink pleasure spread over the entire area. Sparks of love bounced between the Pink Poffles, Zal Finn, and the environment. By the time the *Frenzy* session was over, nearly everything in the area had experienced multiple intense orgasms, and become pink because of them. The lucky palm tree, the remains of the beanstalk tower, the nearby golden chest, and even Zal herself. The colour she could change, her hair, was completely pink in the best way, looking like a sweet action sweetcake! Way better than that Coded in hair from before. This was real amazing Poffle soft hair.

Zal Finn went over and examined the pink chest carefully. It had been gold moments before. This was a special chest made just for her, a special chest much like she remembered hearing that Anders had received. Pink chests were the rarest, and she finally understood why her accent colour had been pink from the start of the book series, for this exact joke.

> Pink Poffle #1,172's Text Box: We turned that useless *Neverending Elixir* into something sweet. Just for you, as a proper thank you. It is for our favourite avatar ever!

Zal Finn III opened the pink chest and was surprised to find it empty.

> Zal Finn III's Text Box: I don't get it. What is it?

> Pink Poffle #1,172's Text Box: Wait for it.

She was bathed in a pink light and began to spin quickly in midair. This was one of those spinning transformation sequences with its own theme song she had heard so much about.

> Zal Finn III's Text Box: Sweetacular!

◈ Chapter 49 ◈
CYCLE 7
THE NEGA-BATTLE OF NEGA-CLIMAX

W*ith a Stretching Out of His Nega-Bow and a Dramatic Jiggle of his Nega-Butt Animation*, Nega-Anders unleashed a *Double Shot*. Each arrow expertly hit his intended target, which both slumped over, sputtered out a last breath, and died on the cold crystal floor. No avatars would be leaving this room, at least not through the recently deceased double entry doors.

> Roodg's Text Box: i WAS SCARED THERE FOR A ROUND, i THOUGHT IT WAS US!

> Nega-Anders' Text Box: Don't worry. All of you will be next!

> Mr. Max's Text Box: I don't know about that. There are like four of us here and a double rainbow of framing devices. We have two Level ✪ ✪s here to top it off. Sure that Nega-Dude is all angelic and Nega now, but he isn't even max Level.

> Lissa's Text Box: Yeah, jerk off! You are seriously out gunned here.

Nega-Anders used a *Bring It Animation*.

> Mr. Max's Text Box: I have an idea so crazy that it just might work. We should all work together to beat Nega-Anders!

Everyone knew that the idea was madness, but what other choice did they have? They decided, against their better judgement, to use team work. Mr. Max began to unleash his entire Stamina Bar with attack after furious attack. Lissa did something that shocked everyone; she cast supporting spells on Mr. Max to bolster him every way possible. The assortment of Quest Fairies rode on *Max's Eight Handed Sword* and with each attack added one of their own with their tiny little *Katana-Nata* blade fragments. Roodg cast a barrage of spells on various pieces of scenery, causing them to melt, fritz, topple, and splurge, which created a barrier of protection around the wildly swinging Max. Palcath assumed the defensive position and got ready to deflect any frontal attacks from Nega-Anders.

When the smoke settled, and the avatars caught their breath, they lost it again. Nega-Anders was there, flying exactly where he had been before, completely unscathed and grinning from ear to pointy Nega-ear.

> Nega-Anders' Text Box: That was all you assholes had? Pathetic.

> Mr. Max's Text Box: I don't understand fellow adventurers! We worked together, that always works with a plucky team of mix-matched heroes! His life bar didn't even jiggle!

> Nega-Anders' Text Box: Sure it did! Why don't you give me a scan with your Broken McEyesLad? I'm surprised you haven't already.

> Palcath's Text Box: I forgot Nega-lad.

As the dwarf did math, the Nega-elf watched on.

> Palcath's Text Box: What? His base statistics have passed through the impossible wall of 255! I can't even tell how high they go. Worst of all, we only did one point of damage to the Nega-lad!

> Nega-Anders' Text Box: See, I told you. You did hurt me. Good for you.

> Palcath's Text Box: How did your stats get so high Nega-lad?

> Nega-Anders' Text Box: It is simple really. This little harlot has been traipsing around all over creation and absorbing the polygons of optional whores. He took the stats from every single one of them, and as far as I can tell they layered upon each other through his different polygon structures.

> Roodg's Text Box: wHA?

> Nega-Anders' Text Box: It means I am Nega to the power of fuck!

> Palcath's Text Box: I still see a chink in your Armour, and I have a plan.

Okay, lads, lasses, and Ro—

Nega-Anders' Interruption Text Box: Wait, wait, wait. What are you doing?

Palcath's Text Box: I was going to try my plan to defeat you, Nega-Lad?

Nega-Anders' Text Box: And for some reason you think I am going to just float angelically here while you explain it, and then act it out?

Palcath's Text Box: I was kind of hoping, Nega-Lad.

Nega-Anders' Text Box: I like this idea. I have run through every scenario in my head, I have calculated the risks, and most importantly I have learned a lot from the past few chapters. Let's do this plan of yours, but make it interesting!

With a Stretching Out of His Nega-Bow and a Dramatic Jiggle of his Nega-Butt Animation, Nega-Anders used *Charge*. He held his attack for exactly 0.183 rounds and let an arrow fly. It hit Mr. Max square in the face and the big pile of beef slumped over.

Roodg used the *Dramatic Gasp Animation*.

Lissa's Text Box: What the fuck?

Palcath's Text Box: Sweet Maker!

Mr. Max's Text Box: What was that for?

Nega-Anders' Text Box: Besides the fact that I desperately hate you and it was really fun, that was about your idea.

Herbert's Text Box: His idea? What do you mea—

Nega-Anders' Interruption Text Box: Quiet, the adults are talking. I was talking about our new little game, and unfortunately Mr. Max already lost. His great idea of 'working together' didn't work. So, like any rational avatar controlling powers that surpass the Maker himself, I shot him in the face and into Dire Status.

Roodg's Text Box: wHY?

Nega-Anders' Text Box: Simple. His little idea failed and now he is out of the running for the Breaker's Badass Who Can Find a Way to do the Impossible Challenge!

Lissa's Text Box: You named that yourself didn't you?

Nega-Anders' Text Box: Yes, and right on the spot no less. No prep!

Mr. Max's Text Box: Why not just kill me Buddy?

Nega-Anders' Text Box: First of all, I'm not your buddy, or friend, or whatever. Secondly, where would the fun be in just killing you? You wouldn't get to watch all your stupid friends fail as well. When their plans fizzle, they will be shot into Dire status. When you all realize how pathetic you really are, I will line you up, and domino you to death with a single *White Wolf Kick*.

Palcath's Text Box: I don't know if I like being part of this little game, Nega-lad.

Nega-Anders' Text Box: Or I could kill you all now.

Palcath's Text Box: Okay, so my plan is this. When I scanned the Nega-lad, and secretly whispered to you all my findings, you will note that he has a serious weakness. His 'layers and layers' of statistics have left him with a high Fire Resistance score. However, since something optional along the way must have had a negative to Fire Resistance, now he has a huge penalty to fire damage. We are going to hit him with every fire thing we got!

Nega-Anders' Text Box: That seems logical. Have at it.

Before Palcath's *Anvil Smasher* came down hard on the Nega-Foe, it was boosted with every possible Fire Enchantment that could be found in the assorted packs, spell lists, and forgotten key plot items of everyone. Palcath's most damaging attack, *Hammer Festival*, was accompanied by an expertly timed *Orbital Firestrike*, and a *Whirlmace Strike*.

This time when the smoke cleared Nega-Anders was using the *Slow Clap Animation*. With a *Stretching Out of His Nega-Bow* and a *Dramatic Jiggle of his Nega-Butt Animation*, Nega-Anders used *Charge* on Palcath and knocked him down to a single Hit Point.

Palcath's Text Box: I don't get it. That totally should have worked but the Nega-lad only lost 1,470 Health.

Nega-Anders' Text Box: The Elemental Resistances work AFTER the base damage is calculated, and that is based off of my Wisdom score. Even with a Fire Resistance of -147,000%, when the damage started off at 1 measly health, it was only increased to 1,470. I'm surprised you didn't know that dwarf.

Palcath's Text Box: I did, Nega-lad, but I was hoping that it didn't.

Nega-Anders' Text Box: That seems sensible. Who is next?

Herbert's Text Box: We have been talking as a group ov—

Nega-Anders' Interruption Text Box: Nope, pass. Quest Fairies are not important enough to get a turn.

Herbert used the *Hmmph! Animation.*

Nega-Anders' Text Box: Who is really next?

Roodg's Text Box: pICK ME! i HAVE A PLAN AND AMAZINGLY IT ALSO INVOLVES MATH.

Nega-Anders' Text Box: Why is that amazing exactly?

Roodg's Text Box: bECAUSE i HATE MATH.

Nega-Anders' Text Box: Sure, why not. Proceed.

Roodg's Text Box: i NOTICED WHEN Palcath SENT ME YOUR STATS THAT ALL YOUR sTATISTICS ARE sAWESOME EXCEPT TWO. fIRE rESISTNACE DIDN'T WORK OUT, BUT YOUR lUCK SCORE IS ONLY ONE.

Mr. Max's Text Box: That is because Optional Bosses only have a 1 in Luck to prevent them from getting Critical Hits on masses of avatars at once and ruining a raid.

Palcath's Text Box: Of course, lad, and 1 to the power of anything is still one.

Nega-Anders' Text Box: Quiet both of you are dead to the game! We are listening to multi-crotch right now. I want to find out what not being able to do Critical Hits has to do with winning here.

Roodg's Text Box: iT DOESN'T HAVE ANYTHING TO DO WITH THAT.

Nega-Anders' Text Box: Well played.

Roodg's Text Box: LoL. bUT lUCK ALSO CHANGES YOUR ABILITY TO AVOID THE THREE USELESS SPELLS THAT NORMALLY HAVE NO CHANCE TO HIT.

Reaching deep into the section of normally unused spells, Roodg got ready to cast a spell that no Magic Mage would ever dare use. The spell that hardly ever hits, the spell that is based on math and therefore is naturally repelling, the advanced form of *Demi Less* that hits even less often than the original that hardly ever hit in the first place, the dreaded spell *Demi More*. Nega-Anders disappeared into the void, and popped back out with only a quarter of his hit points left.

It took Nega-Anders a round to compose himself. He had just lost 74,999,888 Hit Points in one fell swoop, so it was a needed break.

> Roodg's Text Box: hA!

> Nega-Anders' Text Box: Well colour me impressed. I certainly didn't expect anyone to do that much damage to me, let alone in one attack.

> Roodg's Text Box: tRUE. mY PLANS ARE STRANGELY THE BEST FOR SOME REASON.

> Nega-Anders' Text Box: Slight problem. Even if it was by far the best plan, I am still alive, I am immune to other Demi spells for the rest of the encounter, and you are in Dire Status.

> Roodg's Text Box: i AM?

With a Stretching Out of His Nega-Bow and a Dramatic Jiggle of his Nega-Butt Animation, Nega-Anders used *Charge*. Roodg was knocked flat onto the floor and into Dire Status.

> Nega-Anders' Text Box: Yep.

> Roodg's Text Box: cRAP.

> Nega-Anders' Text Box: There is only one of you left. What is your plan going to be? Your plan can't be to heal everyone so they get another chance. I'm not a Genie, I don't work like that.

Lissa used the *Heartfelt Sigh Animation*. She dropped her *Ultimatium Mace* on the ground and fell to her knees.

> Nega-Anders' Text Box: What is all this?

> Lissa's Text Box: What is the point? You are right Breaker. There isn't anything we could do to stop you even if we had a thousand tries. Even if we beat on you all day we could never off you. #AllIsLost.

> Nega-Anders' Text Box: I'm glad someone finally realized that.

> Lissa's Text Box: My idea was going to be just bitchslapping Breaker

> for fun.

> Roodg's Text Box: i LOVE THAT IDEA! dO IT!

> Lissa's Text Box: I think I have given up. I know it is #SoFuckedUp of me guys, but I have. This isn't fun anymore.

> Palcath's Text Box: But…

Lissa used a *Fall to Your Knees in Defeat Animation* followed by an *Accept Your Fate Animation.*

> Mr. Max's Text Box: You? You of all people are giving up?

> Nega-Anders' Text Box: This is too nice. I can't wait!

Nega-Anders' raised his bow, his eyes moved around frantically, and he aimed carefully.

> Lissa's Text Box: Wait!

Nega-Anders stopped aiming and lowered his bow.

> Nega-Anders' Text Box: What? Seriously?

> Lissa's Text Box: Why are your eyes going all crazy?

> Palcath's Text Box: That is sort of strange. Why is that?

> Roodg's Text Box: tHIS SEEMS LIKE A PLOT POINT. dID ANYONE SEE THIS BEFORE?

> Mr. Max's Text Box: Maybe. It feels like I should know something about this.

> Nega-Anders' Text Box: You should know about this, idiot! It happened to you with the cunt elf. It means that Regular-Anders is trying to get your attention!

> Lissa's Text Box: I changed my idea from bitchslap!

> Nega-Anders' Text Box: You can't do that! You gave up! I was going to kill you.

> Lissa's Text Box: I said I was only thinking of giving up! Check the log.

> Nega-Anders' Text Box: Fine. What is it? This amazing plan of yours?

Lissa's Text Box: I give my plan to uncontrolled Nega-Anders, because he looks like he has a plan.

Nega-Anders' Text Box: You can't do that!

Roodg's Text Box: i THINK SHE CAN. iT FITS YOUR RULES OF THE CONTEST EXACTLY. tECHNICALLY, HE SHOULD GET AN IDEA ANYWAY. sO YOU ARE STILL ONE UP IF Lissa USES HER'S HERE.

Nega-Anders' Text Box: Fine. Fine. It doesn't matter. He will not be able to do anything either. Make it quick. You only get your voice back.

Nega-Anders used the *Sneeze Animation*.

Nega-Anders' Text Box: Finally! Hot buttery rolls, that was horrid.

Primary Circle Sword+'s Text Box: Okay. Spit it out.

Nega-Anders' Text Box: Right, sorry. I am going to side with Lissa here. I am just going to give up as well...

This statement resulted in *Gasp Animations* all around.

Primary Circle Sword+'s Text Box: Perfect! Time to get to avatar slaying.

Nega-Anders' Text Box: ... providing...

Primary Circle Sword+'s: Providing? Providing what?

Nega-Anders' Text Box: Providing you answer a single question for me.

Primary Circle Sword+'s: What? That's stupid.

Nega-Anders' Text Box: You have to swear to answer it legitimately. Promise me.

Primary Circle Sword+'s Text Box: Fine, I promise. Just ask your dumb question so I can shoot your friend's faces off.

Nega-Anders' Text Box: Okay, my question is this: Why are you doing this?

Primary Circle Sword+'s Text Box: Huh? Why? That is a lame question. My answer: Cause. Time to die.

Nega-Anders' Text Box: No, answer the question!

> Primary Circle Sword+'s Text Box: What... What are you talking about?

> Nega-Anders' Text Box: You brownie well know what I am talking about. I want to know why. I want to know what your motivation was for killing thousands of avatars, monsters, and NPCs. I want to know why you decided to hate us all and ruin this game for everyone. I want to know why.

> Primary Circle Sword+'s Text Box: Because we are enemies!

> Nega-Anders' Text Box: That isn't a reason. That is a result. I want to know why!

> Primary Circle Sword+'s Text Box: ... I wanted to win... and...

> Nega-Anders' Text Box: You did win the Insta-Wiki Contest! What is the real reason? Tell us why!

> Primary Circle Sword+'s Text Box: I... and... I...

> Nega-Anders' Text Box: Tell us. Tell us why you needed to win this badly. Why you needed to take over other people's avatars to accomplish your goals. Why you needed to slaughter entire villages of NPCs. Why you needed to destroy whole sections of the map. Why you needed to break the game for everyone else playing it but yourself. Why you needed to do any of this. Just tell us that, and you can win. Fair and square.

Nega-Anders floated with limp wings, and slumped shoulders for uncounted rounds in total silence. His theme music had faded out, but the normal music of the area did not return, nor did the constant crackling of the Flaming Pitfires. No far away monsters made a peep, and no glass floorboard did creak. He floated there, face now obscured by visor, in silence.

For countless rounds Nega-Anders used the *Fall to Your Knees in Defeat Animation*. His visor popped up and revealed his face, it was soaked with tears. Lissa got up off the defeat floor, walked over to him, helped him up, and executed an *Understanding Hug Dual Animation*. Everyone else broke the rules of Dire Status and joined in. Nega-Anders started blubbering.

> Primary Circle Sword+'s Text Box: Nothing ever seems to turn out right for me. No matter what I do with my life, it always gets messed up.

Palcath's Text Box: Life can be tough, lad.

Primary Circle Sword+'s Text Box: I know, but I smile and pretend it doesn't bother me, even though it does!

Lissa's Text Box: I know what that can be like.

Primary Circle Sword+'s Text Box: Everyone I love rips my heart out and shows it to me!

Roodg's Text Box: tHAT DOESN'T SOUND GOOD!

Primary Circle Sword+'s Text Box: It isn't. Nothing ever works out for me!

Mr. Max's Text Box: You are not alone. I totally have a friend like that.

Primary Circle Sword+'s Text Box: But it gets worse! Of course it does. I try to have fun for once with a friend and get addicted to Heroine.

Herbert's Text Box: Heroine? Don't you mean heroin?

Primary Circle Sword+'s Text Box: No, I don't. It was a whole thing in a *Tale of Gentalia*. Then I get this game for free and it is pretty fun. Suddenly my problems don't seem that big anymore and I don't need as much Heroine. In fact there is this contest that you can win if you work really hard at it. I can work hard, I always work hard.

Nega-Anders' eyes were misty; he was getting close to an emotional breakthrough.

Primary Circle Sword+'s Text Box: I do work hard, but despite being in the top spot for an entire day, a guy shows up out of nowhere and starts to dominate. I could win if I find the Green Slimes, but they are missing. I write Codes to try and find monsters and don't even know they break people forever and get blamed for it in the WorldForums by some girl in a tower. I crash into some dwarf who isn't paying attention and drop my *Wallet*. Finally, I get electrocuted by a *Bucket* that someone somehow had charged up with Scenic Minnows!

Nobody said anything.

Primary Circle Sword+'s Text Box: I got mad. Winning was the only thing that was important. Being nice isn't important anymore. Being helpful isn't. Even rehab isn't important. Only this game and Heroine are important. So I use all my knowledge, and skills to destroy the virtual lives of people I've never even met. Now you ask me why, and

> I finally know the answer.

Nega-Anders used the *Emotional Breakthrough Animation*.

> Primary Circle Sword+'s Text Box: It is because I am garbage. I am human garbage.

> Nega-Anders' Text Box: That isn't true.

> Primary Circle Sword+'s Text Box: Yes it is. I'm garbage. Horrible disgusting garbage.

Lissa used a *Face Slap Dual Animation* and Nega-Anders was genuinely shocked.

> Lissa's Text Box: You are not garbage! You just need to smarten the fuck up and get your life back on track! Go back to rehab and get clean. Go back to rocking at whatever you were doing before this. Tell your loved ones how they made you feel. Straighten up, fly right, and get back to the real world!

> Primary Circle Sword+'s Text Box: Oh my Maker. You are... you are... right. I am... I am... I am so sorry.

So ashamed was Breaker that he relaxed the grip on Nega-Anders' *Primary Circle Sword+*, and *Giganticore Rib Bow+* in shock. His broken self had been fought, and it had been patched.

This was exactly what the Quest Fairies had been waiting for and they descended upon Nega-Anders' hands and attacked them madly with their tiny blades. Nega-Anders was taken so off guard that he dropped both weapons. The clang from them hitting the crystal floor was what broke the spell over the weapons and freed the real Nega-Anders. The actual Breaker gasped from across the room, having returned to his half-there experimented upon body.

> Breaker's Text Box: Ouch!

> Herbert's Text Box: Now! Strike now!

> Nega-Anders' Text Box: No wait!

It was too late. The Quest Fairies descended upon Breaker's avatar and used their devastating attacks to graphically tear him to shreds. Breaker's original half-dragon body was now dead.

Everyone stood motionless for a few rounds. The reign of Breaker was over. The eventual repent of Breaker was now meaningless as he had been torn to pieces. Hopefully, the player behind Breaker took the words to heart. While they could finally relax, they were uncertain of their feelings.

Palcath's Text Box: May I just say Nega-lad that was the absolute best plan I have ever seen, and I congratulate you fully on it.

Mr. Max's Text Box: I can't believe we won by 'Hugging it Out'.

Lissa's Text Box: It was the #BestPlanEver. How did you know he had so much bottled inside?

Nega-Anders' Text Box: I realized that he was so bad at being an antagonist that he couldn't be truly bad on the inside. Something had to have happened to him to turn him evil.

Roodg's Text Box: nEAT!

Nega-Anders' Text Box: It is too bad that he got cut to ribbons right after.

Herbert's Text Box: We can handle clean up here. You all get to the plot resolution! Have fun!

Roodg's Text Box: bYE FOR NOW Herbert! sTAY SAFE!

Chapter 50

◆ ◆

THE GAMEFRAME

Everyone cheered when Nega-Anders stepped off of Carrot Jr. and onto the stark white floor of Ni Hao Bunny©'s private section of the GameFrame. They were heroes that had saved the world from Breaker. Nearly every avatar that was still alive was here, but were lost in their own conversations.

Nega-Anders looked around for things he desperately wanted to cuddle in celebration but he noticed a distinct lack of centaurs or dragons.

> Nega-Anders' Text Box: Has anyone seen Fourni, or Draganders?

> Mr. Max's Text Box: Yeah, my Bro needs to be here for the final wrap up!

> Roodg's Text Box: hE ISN'T REPLYING TO CANDLE CHAT.

> Palcath's Text Box: Fourni isn't even answering his texts. We were hoping he was with that lad Chad.

> Chad the Flying Feline of Fortune's Text Box: I haven't seen either of them for some time meow I'm afraid.

> Nega-Anders' Text Box: Wait, I know! He has been writing me letters. We can check my pack and see where he is.

A flood of *Napkins* erupted from Nega-Anders' imaginary pack as soon as he opened the imaginary clasp. There were hundreds upon hundreds of them, and Nega-Anders was almost buried when they finally stopped exploding out. All of them had lip marks coving their surface. Some were so wet with kisses that they couldn't be opened. Sparks of hearts were shooting from the seams, and pluses were dripping down in large wet gobs.

Mr. Max used the *Impressed Whistle Animation*.

> Roodg's Text Box: hE'S BEEN BUSY!

> Lissa's Text Box: Be careful when opening them... they are a bit... moist.

> Palcath's Text Box: I'm not sure I even want to open them, lass.

Lissa wanted to take a break from the constant healing spells needed to get everyone back up to full health after the climax. She insisted they look through some messages.

> Mr. Max's Text Box: This one talks about the horrible containment. Do you think Bro is getting held against his will?

> Palcath's Text Box: This one talks about release. I guess the lad got out.

> Lissa's Text Box: Hmmm... This one is apologizing for so many messages.

> Roodg's Text Box: LoL. tHIS ONE JUST SAYS MOIST.

A single word was the most common, such as 'hot', 'full', 'dump', and 'leaking'. Finally, Nega-Anders found one with more writing on it, it looked a bit older, and he read it aloud.

> *dear Anders, your dragon will not stop chirping, it is making me so thick, why did you fly away from me when there was so much dripping? I really miss you and your perfectly shaped bubble butt. it was even nice when you were topping that skank. I am going to slide my big horse wiener into you and...*

> Nega-Anders' Text box: um... never mind what the rest of it says.

Nega-Anders changed to *Nega-Blush Shade #7* and pocketed the filthy letter to read later.

The air near the centre of the light glade opened up with a knife wound. Out stepped another cat Nega-Anders had never seen before, and this one was mostly school girl.

> E. E. Lynn's Text Box: F|n4lly. ^-^ \/\/h4t t00k u s0 l0ngz0rs N3g4-

hunk? \/\/3 \/\/3r3 \/\/4|t|ng 4 3v3r! kekeke.

Nega-Anders' Text Box: Huh? What did she say?

Cinnamon's Text Box: I'll handle this. You need to hurry your asses up and save the world!

Nega-Anders' Text Box: We just finished saving the world from Breaker's reign of terror. We don't have to worry about him anymore!

Cinnamon's Text Box: Not from him, from the Admins! You are the one who was collecting the *Optional Flowers*, right?

Nega-Anders' Text Box: Right... I forgot all about those guys.

Palcath's Text Box: I think we all did, lad.

E. E. Lynn's Text Box: kekeke! \/\/3ll g00d th|ng \/\/3 d|dn't!

Cinnamon's Text Box: Yes, we just finished locating them. The portals will be opening up to their realms now. You need to go distract them while Nega-Anders takes them out. Go along now. In pairs.

Six shimmering portals opened up, right on queue.

Mr. Max's Text Box: What are we waiting for fellow adventurers? You heard Cinnamon! We all need to split up and distract them! Everyone go in there and give it your best! Charge!

Mr. Max used the *Perplex Animation* and led the charge. In less than a round almost all of the avatars that hadn't been mentioned in this Chapter (and Roodg) had vanished into random portals.

Palcath's Text Box: Wait lads, lasses, and Roodgs. We needed to plan this out first before jumping into random portals.

Lissa's Text Box: Meh. I'm sure it will work out fine.

◈ Chapter 51 ◈

ADMINISTRATOR
WRAP UP!

~~~

In'ferni and De'vini's Simultaneous Text Boxes: Hey, where did everyone go? Into the portals I think, I wasn't paying attention. Who could with you here to kiss? Should we go into one? Nah, we are finally all alone! We don't need to wrap anything up anyway. Shut up and kiss me! Yep!

~~~

Administrator Umple's Text Box: You damn immoral kids! Go on, git! Take your interracial relationship and get off of my law—

A purple arrow silenced Umple with death.

Nega-Anders' Text Box: Shut up bigot!

Yallundy's Text Box: Can you believe he thought Gliint and I were the immoral couple?

Lissa's Text Box: Did he even read the rest of the books?

Gliint's Text Box: *Cheer!* I don't care about our races or our height differences Yallundy. You're the one I want!

Yallundy grabbed up Gliint in her big arms and kissed him deeply.

~~~

> Jorthan the Male Troll Monk's Text Box: This be working keep distracting with kisses.

> Trev Terra's Text Box: Sorry, she is making me a little nervous.

> Administrator Ivy's Text Box: Get it hard! Aw yeah, he's been a bad little elf. Get is so hard you dirty litt—

Ivy was dead after a blue arrow pierced her forehead.

> Nega-Anders' Text Box: Stop being a creeper!

> Palcath's Text Box: Agreed. Where to next and do you lads want to come?

> Jorthan the Male Troll Monk's Text Box: We will be doing that as soon as you be leaving!

Trev Terra used a *Smirk Animation* and Jorthan used one right back.

~~~

> Kray's Text Box: Kay, let's try out that tongue!

samuri used the *Blind Panic Animation*.

> samuri's Text Box: !!!

> Administrator Ethelred's Text Box: I did it! I finally found my stuff! Thanks for waiting, it was behind m—

Administrator Ethelred was interrupted by a yellow arrow.

> Nega-Anders' Text Box: Get your act together!

samuri used the *Please, Please, Please Offer to Take me With You Animation*, but the others had already gone.

~~~

Hippolyta and a one winged flying pink princess in a regal, yet revealing mini-dress, an impossibly cute pink hairstyle, a thin black tail with a pink pompom on the end, and completely unique facial features were on Yvonne's driveway. The Administrator herself was nowhere to be seen.

> Hippolyta's Text Box: I already liked you the way you were, but this is nice.

> Zal Finn IV The Pink Poffle Princess' Text Box: That is sweet of you.

Zal Finn IV and Hippolyta used the *Understanding Hug Dual Animation*. Zal Finn was lost for a time in the massive cleavage of Hippolyta.

> Administrator Yvonne's Text Box: Sorry I was late, I got caught in—

Yvonne was dead. A green arrow hit her right in the kickass firebird.

> Nega-Anders' Text Box: Show up! It is your job!

~~~

> Roodg's Text Box: wE NEED TO TALK!

> Administrator Allen's Text Box: About what? What do we need to talk about? What is—

Administrator Allen was interrupted by an orange arrow to the mouth.

> Nega-Anders' Text Box: Stop repeating yourself!

> Caëlahenäilenŵhei's Text Box: I know we do, and you even saved me from being controlled by Breaker in that epic showdown. Everything should line up, and it is true that I have feelings for you. Despite the Caps Lock you are one of the smartest, kindest, and friendliest avatars I know. It is more complicated than I can say. I am really sorry, but I don't even know where to begin. You are so nice and I don't want to hurt you, which is what I think will happen if I even start to explain. Please, just trust me on this one. I'm so sorry Roodg. Really.

> Roodg's Text Box: nOPE! nOT ACCEPTING THAT. wE WILL TALK MORE AFTER i GET BACK FROM THE LAST cHAPTER!

~~~

There was a giant flashing red button beside Owen.

> Administrator Owen's Text Box: Why did it have to be you? Just showing up here proves how much of a complete asshole you are.

> Mr. Max's Text Box: Why, what did I do?

> Administrator Owen's Text Box: Not you fathead. Him.

> Cinnamon's Text Box: Me? I am only here in the wrap up because E. E. Lynn was busy.

> Administrator Owen's Text Box: You know damn well what you've done. Secretly working with Eleanor this entire time! You need to be eliminated! Administrators of Gentalia I command you to assemble!

Administrator Owen executed a **Command D**. When none of the other Administrators assembled, Owen became worried.

> Administrator Owen's Text Box: Where is everyone! I command you to——

> Nega-Anders' Interruption Text Box: Stop being so bossy!

He took up his bow in his Nega-hand, nocked an arrow, drew it back in a charged style, aimed…

> Nega-Anders' Text Box: Strudel!

> Lissa's Text Box: What's wrong?

> Nega-Anders' Text Box: I forgot that I didn't get enough *Optional Flowers* for this. I'm one short!

> Administrator Owen's Text Box: Ha! I'm going to walk over to this mysterious flashing red button and hit it now.

Cinnamon's Text Box:: If I may interject for a round. Nega-Anders I need you to imagine something for me.

> Nega-Anders' Text Box: Sure.

> Nega-Anders' Text Box: Imagine an impossibly huge monster, taking you by surprise, throwing you to the ground, and shoving his throbbing cock up against your tight hole. You ache for it. The thick meat slids inside and hits you exactly where you need it to hit.

Nega-Anders changed to *Blush Shade #8*. Cinnamon snapped his fingers and Nega-Anders' codpiece opened, revealing a limp purple flower in a pool of Nega-fluid.

> Administrator Owen's Text Box: No wait, we can talk this over guys it is——

Owen was interrupted killed by a red arrow.

Mr. Max's Text Box: How did you know there would be a flower there Cinnamon?

Cinnamon's Text Box: Nega-Anders' polygons are completely made from Option Bosses. He is an Optional Boss right now and I hid Administrator killing power in their jizz.

Nega-Anders' Text Box: That explains so many things!

Nega-Anders reflected on the knowledge that he could have just spent a busy afternoon jerking it and completed his task cycles ago.

Administrator Owen's Text Box: Think you can get rid of us that easy, huh? You were wrong!

Stunned, avatars looked around to find all the Admins grinning and standing on Owen's porch. They were gathered near the mysterious flashing red button.

Lissa's Text Box: Dammit! Doesn't anybody stay dead? #InfiniteContinues.

Administrator Ethelred's Text Box: I found it! I finally found my coffee mug, and my duplicated clone backup that we made from The Device!

Administrator Ivy's Text Box: I can't believe you killed me like that, bitches. I was wrist deep!

Administrator Allen's Text Box: Killing us all off in a stupid wrap up! That is lame. Completely stupid. Utterly inexcusable!

Administrator Umple's Text Box: Yeah, darn kids today! We are not the forgotten villains that you think we are.

Administrator Yvonne's Text Box: I am also here!

Administrator Owen's Text Box: Now face our ultimate wrath! Administrator Force Assemble!

All six Administrators pressed the mysterious flashing red button at the same time, together.

◈ Chapter 52 ◈

SUPER CRAZY GIANT ROBO-MECHA ADMIN FORCE BONUS CLIMAX BATTLE GO!

There was no denying that it was cool, it was a giant robot, but it was piloted by the six Administrators. They were going to use it to bring destruction. They would stomp out the Expansion, and the rest of the game world while safe within the confines of their super cool robot.

> Nega-Anders' Text Box: Hey, no fair! We already had the climax!

> Roodg's Text Box: iF ANY BOOK SERIES WAS GOING TO HAVE MULTIPLE CLIMAXES, IT WAS THIS ONE!

> Palcath's Text Box: Maker! The stats on that thing makes Nega-Anders look like a Start Rat! What do we do?

> Lissa's Text Box: We hit the big flashing weak point in the chest, obviously. We just need to get close enough for Nega-Anders to shoot it!

> Nega-Anders' Text Box: I am out of Mana and flowers! I could never charge up enough to kill that!

> Cinnamon's Text Box: I have a plan! Get all of us up there and I'll do the rest.

Cinnamon started to mess around with some stray polygons, shaping an item from them.

> Mr. Max's Text Box: How do we get up there fellow adventurers?

> Nega-Anders' Text Box: What we need is a miracle. I don't think there are any of those left.

The stunned silence was interrupted by an ear piercing noise. So loud it was that everyone needed to cover their ears and couldn't quite hear what it had said.

> Lissa's Text Box: Cheat?

> Palcath's Text Box: Chiefs?

> Mr. Max's Text Box: Chick?

> Roodg's Text Box: cHUNK?

While everyone else had been contemplating the word that had been screamed at them, Nega-Anders knew what it was. He saw it coming from the distant horizon, a huge mass of claws, wings, fangs, and rainbows.

> Nega-Anders' Text Box: No, he said Chirp!

The rainbow dragon landed with a colossal ground shaking thud. He was gigantic, as big as The Plague of Shadow if not more. He nuzzled Nega-Anders' affectionately.

> Nega-Anders' Text Box: Draganders! Look at you! You got so huge!

> Draganders' Bellowing Text Box: CCCCHHHHIIIIRRRRPPPP!

> Nega-Anders' Text Box: I am so glad to see you! Did you find me because all that mental link dream stuff that was foreshadowed? Can you fly us up there to confront the super cool robot?

> Draganders' Bellowing Text Box: CCCCHHHHIIIIRRRRPPPP!

Lowering a wing, Draganders allowed them all to climb up and stand on his back. They all held on as Draganders took off and approached the giant robot that was using a giant digital sword to cut open various portals to key Expansion. Draganders tackled the robot and pushed it through one.

With the Administrator's Super Crazy Giant Robo-Mecha distracted by fighting a gargantuan rainbow dragon it was time to discuss the plan. Thankfully, there was plenty of time to talk while the battling robot and giant dragon crashed around the city of Onn, destroying well established landmarks.

> Palcath's Text Box: Cinnamon lad, what was your plan?

> Cinnamon's Text Box: Text Box: Nega-Anders is full of optional

polygons. He is just as good as a flower.

Lissa's Text Box: If you are suggesting we shoot our friend into the robot to kill it you are off your nut.

Cinnamon's Text Box:'s Text Box: I am suggesting almost that!

Palcath's Text Box: What, lad? I knew it! I knew you Fairies were up to something and evil!

Roodg's Text Box: wE ALREADY RESOLVED THAT BIT!

Cinnamon's Text Box: We need power. A lot of power. We something that is more powerful than a *Charge*.

Nega-Anders' Text Box: What is more powerful than a *Charge* though?

Cinnamon used a *Reveal Animation*. In a few rounds he had assembled a crossbow the size of a Tanker Tank.

Primary Circle Sword+'s Text Box: A *Charged Charge* of course! I will use my absorbing sub-routine to drain Nega-Anders Optional Polygons, and replace them with others I have stashed away. Your power will become an arrow that we will all *Charge* at once!

Nega-Anders' Text Box: That is a surprisingly great idea.

Nega-Anders aimed, drew back the crossbow, and allowed Cinnamon to prepare the plan. The crossbow became harder and harder to keep drawn as Optional Polygons vanished. Thankfully, his friends helped to steady the bow and keep it drawn. Once every Optional Polygon was converted into the arrow, Nega-Anders, and the rest of the party released the string. The *Arrow of Teamwork* pulsed with purple energy as it flew towards the Super Crazy Giant Robo-Mecha Admin Force, and when it struck true by hitting the flashing weak spot it paused for a round. It was almost as if it had taken a moment to say goodbye before unleashing the hidden explosives Cinnamon had hid inside.

Every piece of the Super Crazy Giant Robo-Mecha Admin Force flew into the distance, disappearing in a twinkle of light, save one. The magenta crotch plate that had been Owen's secret fortress fell to the middle of Onn. and the giant crotch would forever remain there as a testament to what had happened this cycle. #NeverForget.

Draganders had spent all of his full potential power and landed just in time to save everyone from plummeting to the ground when he transformed back into his normal size. He attacked Anders and nuzzled him hard.

Anders' Text Box: Aw little guy I missed you!

Palcath's Text Box: Hey lad, your name is back to normal.

Lissa's Text Box: Thank the Maker, all the Nega-this and Nega-that crap was getting Nega-annoying.

Mr. Max's Text Box: You're the Dragon Cultist! I knew it!

Cinnamon's Text Box: I'm glad that worked!

Roodg's Text Box: pLUS, YOU ARE ALL NAKED AGAIN!

Anders realized that he was indeed non-optional, had his normal stats, and was naked. He covered himself up as best as he could with Draganders and changed to *Blush Shade #3*.

Anders' Text Box: Naked again? Every time with this!

The sound of metal being pushed aside distracted everyone from looking at the naked elf. Coming out of the discarded magenta crotch was a badly beaten Administrator Owen. His robes had nearly burnt completely off and he was naked from the neck down. In his hands he held up a control that contained a single button.

Lissa's Text Box: Oh come on! Seriously?

Palcath's Text Box: The Adminilad has a single Hit Point left!

Anders' Text Box: Now what do we do?

Administrator Owen's Text Box: You die! Bwahahahahaha! I may not have been able to delete the world by stomping it, but I still can use this backup button that destroys it instantly! Yes, I'll die, but so will all of you!

Administrator Owen held up his device high in the air and got ready to press the button that would obliterate everything everywhere. He was grinning like a madman as his finger dramatically approached the button, but just before he hit it a loud noise broke into the area. It was so loud that everyone needed to shield their ears again.

~~~

So many. Hot. Wet.
So many. Choice!
Need. Need them. So many. Hot. Wet. Ready.
So many need it. So many want it. Give to the hot wet ready. Give all!
Take it. Take it wet hot ready.
You body covered thick hair. You hairy man on top animal below. Big animal.

Swollen need. Tied up blue fabric on neck. Release needed. Release! They need it. Find it. Take it.

Charge in! All surprise! Many wets here. Many readys. Scan them. Scan them!

> Administrator Owen's Text Box: The fuck is that?

Scan! Wet not ready. Not taken. Backup.

> Palcath's Text Box: No idea, lad.

Scan! Not wet. Not taken. Not best, lad.

> Cinnamon's Text Box: He is hung like an elephant!

Scan! Too tiny. Not b3stz0rs.

> Lissa's Text Box: Looks #FamiliarSomehow.

Scan! Wet. Half taken. Not #HalfBad.

> Mr. Max's Text Box: Do we attack?

Scan! Not wet. Not taken. Not best, bro.

> Roodg's Text Box: hE IS IN PAIN.

Scan! Wet. Wet. Wet. All Taken. Three wet?

> Anders' Text Box: Can we help him?

Scan! Wet. Taken. Remade? Remade virgin? Double Remade virgin! Plumptious! Booty off charts. Quivering need! Aching all book for it. Perfect. Perfect hole. Need to take!

Charge hole owner. Take hole. You own hole. Hole is for you.

> Beast Man's Text Box: HHHHOOOOLLLLEEEE!

~~~

The Beast Man charged forward and pushed Anders to the ground. He gave the startled elf not even a courtesy spit before he lined up his throbbing member with the elfhole.

> Beast Man's Text Box: HHHHOOOOLLLLEEEE?

> Lissa's Text Box: We need to stop it!

> Mr. Max's Text Box: Someone start the battle music!

> Anders' Text Box: No, wait. Don't hurt him!

> Palcath's Text Box: Why not, lad?

> Anders' Text Box: Don't you see? He hasn't entered me yet. He is asking nicely if he can use my hole. He is in pain. He needs help.

> Beast Man's Text Box: HHHHOOOOLLLLEEEE?

> Anders' Text Box: Yes. I will help you. Use my hole.

Within a fraction of a round the Beast Man had control. The pulsing tauric cock was fiercely jammed into Anders, who thanks to his butt of holding only let forth a *Fantastic Smile Animation*, taking the beast member like a pro (without even needing to warm up). The pair toppled onto Owen, pinning him under hot elf/beast man loving.

The Beast Man was getting something that he needed, a hot, wet hole, but Anders was doing more than helping, he was also helping himself. He had needed a giant throbbing monster cock inside him for so long now that he would have done anything to get it. He had been quivering for more impossible cock since Chapter 10.

He decided that he might have a fetish.

> Anders' Text Box: ♥!

> Mr. Max's Text Box: The Dragon Cultist is gay? Who knew?

It was evident by the look on Owen's face that not only was he displeased by this turn of events, he was being ignored again and could do nothing. It was evident by the look on the creature's face that not only was it pleased by this turn of events, but that it was downright euphoric.

> Cinnamon's Text Box: This is sexier than I thought it would be. Maybe I'll try out this vagina.

The Beast Man whinnied and thrust with an intense need against Anders' steadfast form. Every thrust was pure pleasure for the beast, and no one would dare approach to try and stop it because Anders had a constant look of pure monster-cock filled bliss on his face. The thrusting began, elf and beast were one, but as usual no one could keep their opinions to themselves.

> Palcath's Text Box: That angle is all wrong, Anders lad. My calculations indicate that if you rotated your hips by 12°s forward your pleasure zones would be hit with 2.6 times more accuracy.

Anders was doubtful at first, but when he rotated his hips as instructed the math totally checked out. No one knew math better than Palcath.

> Anders' Text Box: ♥♥!

> Beast Man's Text Box: MMMMAAAATTTTHHHH HHHHOOOOLLLLEEEE!

The Beast Man was wild. Foaming at the mouth. He was higher than the Castle in the Sky, the Flaming Pits, or any other floating island for that matter. Anders was not filing any complaints with an Administrator, despite there being one right under his hands, helping to hold him steady from the force of the man beast.

> Anders' Text Box: Please use me!

The beast listened; he kept pumping away into Anders with wilder and wilder thrusts. His face became twisted when he was hit from a barrage of pleasure tingles from the willing elfhole. The force of the thrusts caused Anders to tip forward towards Owen. Without thinking Anders used his new found power from his experiences with optional polygons; topping. He pushed into the shocked Owen hard and started to pump rapidly.

> Administrator Owen's Text Box: Are you fucking me?

> Lissa's Text Box: Looks like it.

> Mr. Max's Text Box: Now, I know the Dragon Cultist doesn't have a lot of experience with topping, but if he attacked more with his core and less with his butt he would be able to increase the power that his thrusts and the value of his experience.

Anders knew that no one knew the game mechanics of thrusting better than Max, and he tried the advice out. He was glad that he did.

> Anders' Text Box: ♥♥♥!

> Beast Man's Text Box: PPPPOOOWWWWEEEERRRR HHHHOOOOLLLLEEEE!

Now Anders' thrusts and the powerful thrusts of the Beast Man were in perfect timing, which causes motes of tingle pleasure through everyone in the sandwich, even the unimpressed Owen had started to pant after his nipples were flicked.

> Roodg's Text Box: i KNOW YOU ARE USED TO SPREADING YOURSELF WIDE Anders, BUT IF YOU BRING YOUR KNEES IN A BIT IT WILL HELP YOU TO GET SANDWICHED BETTER!

There was no one better (in the history of ever) at sandwiches than Roodg and Anders followed the advice without even a round of hesitation. Roodg was right! Bringing in his knees did allow him to both gain extra thrusting into Owen power, and increases his squeezing pleasure of the beast cock to new levels.

> Anders' Text Box: ♥♥♥♥!

> Beast Man's Text Box: BBBBRRRREEEEAAAADDDD HHHHOOOOLLLLEEEE!

Bread hole was right! Or at least with Anders' filthy pastry mouth it was right. He was getting bred by this massive stud with the enormous monster wang and he loved every round of it. He wanted his friends to watch, he wanted them to suggest more ways for him to do this. He bottomed his cock out into Owen with great force as he bottomed the Beast Man's thick member in his ass with the skill that could only come from three novels worth of experience.

> Lissa's Text Box: #ImpressiveButtwork.. If you really want to win this encounter you need to take this to the next level and think outside your comfort zones!

There was no one better at competition than Lissa and Anders desperately wanted to use the advice, but he didn't know how. It hit him like a giant monster dick pressing against his button. He always used his powers while thinking of bottoming, he had never once used his powers while thinking of topping. It was time to get versatile. Anders cast *Stretch More More* while thinking of his dick pounding into the sweet hole of the Administrator. The magic activated and Anders felt his topping tool stretch out to hit new levels of pleasure as he further stretched out the now gaping hole of Owen.

> Anders' Text Box: ♥♥♥♥♥!

> Beast Man's Text Box: CCCCOOOOMMMMFFFFYYYY HHHHOOOOLLLLEEEE!

Anders was at untold levels of pleasure. Five hearts was an unheard of bliss ranking, and he only wished that their missing teammate, Fournimer, was here to provide a suggestion to bring him to the mythical levels of pleasure that six hearts could bring.

> Beast Man's Text Box: HHHHOOOOLLLLEEEE FFFFIIIILLLLLLLLLL!

The Beast Man was getting close and Anders could feel the giant cock within him pulse with the start of what would be an absolute mess of an orgasm. The twitching and anticipation brought Anders to the limit break of pleasure (which was six).

> Anders' Text Box: ♥♥♥♥♥♥!

Everyone ducked for cover as best as they could as the Beast Man executed one final needful thrust into the hole. The creature's face first tensed up in extreme pain one instant, and then the next relaxed into complete and utter blissful relief. You could hear the pumping cum flooding out into the waiting elf.

> Beast Man's Text Box: **HOLE FILL BLISS**!

The Beast Man unlocked an ability, *Hopeful Kiss*. Apparently, the rhyme was close enough to count as it was slightly slurred. The Beast Man glowed for a round, and the ability activated. Surging through him the power of hope. Surging the power directly into Anders.

Hope felt pretty swell. Anders couldn't believe how horny the hope had made him. He was nearly blinded by orgasmic hope.

> Anders' Text Box: ♥♥♥♥♥♥♥!

> Administrator Owen's Text Box: Seven hearts? Seven! That isn't even possible. You need to stop before it is too late!

Owen was wrong. It was already too late to stop. The seven hearts exploded and Anders reached the final climax. The last remaining pixel from the original Anders, the tip of his nose, began to glow softly. Hope. Anders arched his back so ferociously when he orgasmed that the Beast Man slipped out, still pumping out fluids, and was thrust back, missing the elfhole and hitting a new target. Owen who had been perfectly opened by the skillful topping of 'seven hearts in the sheets' Anders.

> Administrator Owen's Text Box: Urk!

Owen did not fare as well with Beast Man cum as Anders had, the gushing filled him up after a few squirts and there was much more to come. Impossible to defeat Administrator Hit Points meant nothing if your body can no longer contain them, and thanks to the one final pixel of hope filled optional goodness, Owen's final hit point was shattered. His body expanded under the pressure so much that it burst as the last stream of mixed monster and elf juice shot into him. Owen cold only Splodgasm.

A misting shower of pent up tauric semen sprayed over the area, and it was combined with hope, elf spunk, and the magenta pixels of Administrator Owen. If you had not known what it was, it would have been exceptionally beautiful. Anders reached backed and was passionately kissed by his beastial lover, all as the pixels rained down from the Double Penetration Victory.

> Roodg's Text Box: bEST WAY TO LOSE YOUR LAST HIT POINT EVER! sAWESOME CALL BACK THE FIRST SEX JOKE IN THE BOOK SERIES!

> Palcath's Text Box: Great teamwork lads, lasses, and Roodgs!

> Mr. Max's Text Box: We do make a pretty good team fellow teammates!

> Lissa's Text Box: #WeAreTheSexChampions!

The Beast Man was finally sated, his eyes cleared from the mad rage, his penis and balls returned to their normal size, the hair covering his upper human body retracted, his scarf untangled, and his mating rut ended. He fell to the ground exhausted, full potential realized. Anders cuddled the fallen creature's side and cradled his sopping wet head in his arms.

> Anders' Text Box: Are you alright?

Fournimer's Text Box: Thanks to you I am now.

Anders' Text Box: ♥!

◊   Chapter 53   ◊
MEETING YOUR MAKER

N i Hao Bunny©'s Text Box: Great job everyone! I would like to thank you for what you did today!

samuri used the *Squee! Animation.*

samuri's Text Box: I loth youth stho mutch! Youth areth my heroth!

Lissa's Text Box: Why are we talking to Ni Hao Bunny©?

Anders' Text Box: I forgot to ask that before.

Palcath's Text Box: That bunny lass isn't even in this franchise!

Ni Hao Bunny©'s Text Box: What?! Son of a bitch! I am a bunny. I didn't even notice. Eleanor!

E. E. Lynn's Text Box: \/\/h4t?

Ni Hao Bunny© used the *Toe Tapping Animation.*

E. E. Lynn's Text Box: 0h scr3\/\/ u. Th4t's funny.

Ni Hao Bunny©'s Text Box: Come on.

E. E. Lynn's Text Box: F|n3.

After the *Traffic Cone+* that E. E. Lynn took out of her *Kitty Backpack* had been placed on Ni Hao Bunny©'s head a shining spinning transformation animation took place. The smoke settled and the bunny had changed into a tall slightly scruffily man dressed in stylized wizard robes. He grinned without even needing to use a *Grin Animation*.

> Palcath's Text Box: Sweet Maker it cannot be!

> Anders' Text Box: What? Who is that?

> Palcath's Text Box: It's the owner of *Tornado Tech Games*! It is the Maker!

The Maker chuckled slightly when a few avatars stumbled to their knees as a sign of respect.

> Charlie's Text Box: Now now, there is no need for that. I should be the one thanking you for stopping my corrupt staff, and giving me back the way to fix this game properly! I would like to especially thank you Anders for being such a great secret assassin.

> Anders' Text Box: It was no problem Charlie!

Palcath winced at the Maker being referred to as Charlie, but Charlie only smiled.

> Charlie's Text Box: I don't even know how to thank you all, but I am sure this will be a good start!

A *Golden Ticket* appeared in the sky next to each and every avatar, it was added to their play accounts.

> Anders' Text Box: What are those?

> Charlie's Text Box: They are special passes to get you into the greatest event of the year! Full access to everything, bonus prizes, full accommodations, airfare, meals, and everything else paid for.

> Palcath's Text Box: You can't mean it Maker, lad… these are…

> Charlie's Text Box: GameCon Deluxe VIP passes for all of you? Why yes, yes they are!

> Nearly Every Avatar's Simultaneous Text Box: Sawesome!

> Mr. Max's Text Box: Aw man, I already have one of those.

> Zal Finn IV's Text Box: Do you have something else?

◊ END PART THREE ◊

Roodg's Text Box: wAIT! wHAT ABOUT gAMEcON?!

◈ EPILOGUE ◈
OUR TIME AT GAMECON

The man gave his name to the black shirted GameCon employee working the entrance, "Matthew Anderson."

"I'm sorry," the girl with the official check in list replied, "I don't have a record of that name here."

Nervous, Matthew insisted, "But I have to be on there, I am supposed to have a GameCon Deluxe VIP pass!"

Darcy (the nametag she was wearing told Matthew her name was Darcy) shook her head sadly, "I'm sorry sir, but I don't have a record of an avatar named Matthew Anderson on my list."

Feeling slightly foolish for his mistake, Matthew sheepishly continued, "Try Anders Matthewson."

After apologizing for her mistake, and saying that she had kept on forgetting to tell people to use their avatar name, Darcy gave Matthew his special laminated name tag and labeled him as Anders. A similar nondescript man in a black GameCon shirt named Jay gave him a tote bag stuffed full of great deluxe goodies, a similar empty tote bag, and a pile of coupons that listed what he could go pick out to fill the empty bag with. Jay even directed him to the first place to collect. It was right near the entrance, and Anders already knew he had a tough decision ahead.

It took him a few minutes (and who knew how many rounds) to look over the choices. Many of them held special places in his heart, but he finally decided and pointed to the one he would take. Jessica handed him the box, and commented that no one else had bought, picked out, or even seemed to know about the existence of that one. Anders told Jessica that he was happy to be the first and he slid the Pink Slime Action Figure (Complete with Scenic Pillar Scenery Piece) into his tote bag.

Anders surveyed the massive world of GameCon. This place was gigantic and he didn't even know where to start. Some of the other gamers who were milling about were even in character. Anders had never even thought about trying to dress up as himself. It was a fun idea, even if he would have to be naked most of the time to do so.

He stopped briefly before delving into the Con when he heard Jessica, or Darcy, or Jay, or whatever her name was arguing with a handsome well-dressed man in a jacket who insisted that his name was Bernhard and that he should be allowed to enter. Anders reminded the unimportant gate-keeper that people had to use their avatar names to get inside. Bernhard appeared to be thankful, his jaw was wide open and he was staring at Anders. That made Anders feel great; random cute guys were stunned by his helpfulness.

Anders contemplated helping this Bernhard fellow further, but got distracted. There was a person leaning against a support pillar, reading a copy of *Advanced Literature Theory & the Development of Proper Plot Structure*. They were dressed in an oversized hoodie with the top up that obscured their face, a pair of faded skinny jeans, and oversized boots. A clump of dyed red hair hung from the hoodie, obscuring the face of whoever was inside. It was impossible to tell what was under all that hood. This could only be one avatar, and Anders went over to introduce himself.

He was finally going to find out the truth about this matter, but as he approached it was just as impossible to tell now as the first time he had seen the avatar. She was tall enough to be a short man, or a tall girl. He was thin enough that anything under those baggy clothes was hidden. They had noticed him approach and Anders tried one last ditch effort to solve this mystery.

"Hello, I'm Matthew," he slyly stated, putting his plan into action.

"Sam," the hooded figure replied. Anders was initially pleased with himself, but noticed the name Sam had solved absolutely nothing. The mystery of the gender of Roodg would remain, which was probably for the best. Anders wouldn't want to ruin the mystique.

Without warning the hooded figure hugged him, tightly enough for it to be friendly, but not tightly enough to reveal anything.

"I am so glad I ran into someone I know!" Roodg looked genially relieved. "I've been really nervous about this whole thing."

"You," Anders asked confused, "nervous? You are the last person who I ever thought would be nervous."

"Why would you say that?" Roodg asked with a slight head tilt.

As Anders talked, his hands moved around nervously, "You know, you always seem so confident and put together. I mean, you are always screaming in Caps Lock, how could anyone who does that be shy?"

Roodg blushed before answering, or at least Anders thought they did, it was hard to see a face under all that hood. "That? It isn't on purpose. I dropped my sandwich on my laptop in *Slime Pop! Saga* after my English Literature final. There was so much jam everywhere, and once I cleaned it up I couldn't turn Caps Lock off!"

Anders was genuinely shocked, "You're an English Literature student?"

Roodg was genuinely proud of the compliment of genuine shock. "Third year now, Anders!"

"Wait," Anders replied suspiciously, "how do you know I'm Anders? More secret plot sage knowledge?"

Laughing as they replied, Roodg also used a finger to bop him on the nose. "For starters it is on your name tag. Also, I have never seen anyone that looks so much like their avatar. Did you look in a mirror when you designed yourself? You could be twins, except you know, you're wearing clothes. It is an uncanny resemblance."

Anders laughed back, claimed that any resemblance was unintentional, and mentioned that he would be justified in saying the same thing about Roodg. They decided to join forces and explore GameCon together. Before long they had collected a Dark Gigas action figure for Roodg, a Night Ranger mouse pad, and Magic Mage place matt respectively.

They were leaving an area boasting authentic Gentalia cuisine, which they both decided to not try in case it did taste like appliances, when they heard their character names being called from across the buffet. An excited girl rushed towards them. She was wearing a top that was a little too small for her and it was pushing up her modest cleavage to higher levels. Her hair was black, but there were a few spots that had been coloured at one point. The colour had been washed vigorously out. Anders knew the colour that had been washed out was purple.

Sparkles were hanging from her neck. A necklace with a dragon hung in exactly the right place to make the dragon jump around excitedly on her breasts. Roodg grabbed it before the girl had a chance to say anything and admired it closely.

Roodg said a statement that in any other context would have seemed odd. "Wow! It looks just like your nipple piercings!"

"I know!" Lissa replied. "I made it myself."

Roodg and Anders both agreed that the necklace was great. When Lissa gave Roodg a spot on replica of a *Bigass Bitchslap Ring* and Anders a *Primary Circle Sword+* necklace, they both decided that the necklace was not only great, but exquisite.

Roodg was admiring the new ring and getting ready to bitchslap anyone who got in their way. "I just love this Lissa. Look how big and stupid it is! Just like the unreal thing."

"Thanks!" Lissa said with extra ounces of pride in her voice. You know who else liked them? Brenna Jay and his friends! I just sold a bunch of bracelets to them. Don't tell anyone about that."

Lissa showed off more of her designs for other important avatars, which both Anders and Roodg admitted were pretty. Before they pressed on she commenting on the fact that they both looked way too much like their Avatars (Anders especially, but with unpointy ears). They decided to leave the buffet tables and continue onward.

They all traded in a coupon for their favourite official Annals of Gentalia framed art prints with an unimportant employee named Amanda, but Anders got distracted when trying to put away the framed artwork showing the various angles of the standard male centaur avatar model. He ran right into another person who was equally distracted by something behind him. Anders fell over, but the stoic man dressed all in gray, except for a faded pink Ni Hao Bunny© backpack, did not. He silently helped Anders up, looking embarrassed about the entire thing, but noticed who he had picked up and hugged him tightly.

The tall, silent man, who was at least in his mid forties and just starting to show some salt and pepper in his hair and mustache, also hugged both Lissa, and Roodg. He handed everyone a small printed card and a box each, which he took out of his backpack. He had two stacks of such things, one that each of them received that said "It was a pleasure to adventure with you", and another much larger stack that said "I'm sorry I cut you in half."

One of the unnoticed-until-now friends of the tall man, (the man with a missing arm, not the girl with glasses that you wear after having cataract surgery) motioned behind them and let out a mad blurt of directions of where to go. The thin woman said, "Just Go!" As quickly as the silent trio had entered, they had fled, seemingly terrified of what was pursuing them.

Abruptly, what had been pursuing them appeared from behind a t-shirt stall run by unimportant GameCon employee Vanessa. It was wearing an outfit composed of such clashing colours that it was no wonder the one armed man had seen their pursuer so far away. There was no doubting who this was; the bitchy posture, flippy red hair, and pursed lips gave Kray away. Anders noted with interest that not only was Kray taller than he was, Kray was also quite a bit on the chubbier side.

Kray walked up to Anders, but before the much friendlier player of a gay elf could open his mouth to say an unenthusiastic hello, Kray had grabbed his face. He moved Anders' face in all directions, while making humming and hawing noises to himself. After about a minute of this awkward interaction Kray let go as suddenly as he had grabbed on, saying to himself something about how he knew he was much cuter and better than Anders and how he was glad to have proof of that fact. Kray stormed off in the direction his Sami-guy had fled before anyone could come to their senses to say something.

Anders broke the silence with what they were all thinking; "That was really weird."

Both Lissa and Roodg agreed that Anders was in fact, cuter than Kray before Roodg suddenly burst into laughter. Anders was initially hurt slightly by the outburst, but Roodg assured him, it wasn't because Kray was cuter.

"I just remembered where I have seen that symbol before!" Roodg finally managed to say through what had become tears.

Anders just shrugged, but Lissa had seen it as well. "You are referring to that triangle patch on samuri's backpack aren't you? I was wondering what it meant, it was so out of place amidst the pink."

Roodg agreed, and when pressed revealed the true meaning with a quick search of the real world InstaWiki, the internet. "That colour blind fool Kray has been barking up the wrong tree for who knows how long because samuri and his friends were all wearing the official symbol for, wait for it." Roodg turned the phone towards them.

Lissa and Anders nearly yelled at the same time, "Asexual pride!"

They all shared both a big laugh at Kray's expense, and a solemn moment for the pain that samuri must be feeling to constantly have to deal with Kray for this long. Then they remembered, presents. samuri had given them presents!

Inside the little gray boxes with their names on them were cupcakes. All hand decorated with beautiful icing work. They all had gotten little cute character Avatar icon cupcakes!

"Hashtag no way!" Lissa squeed with delight. "We need to take a picture with them!"

"Oh," Roodg replied, with a mouthful of cupcake.

They took a picture anyway, confident in the fact that Roodg's having a bit bite out of the side was more fitting to their character.

A big table of official Annals of Gentalia coffee mugs distracted them from what would have been their next task: finding samuri to give him another hug. While later they would feel poorly for forgetting about samuri, they would never feel poorly about how wonderful these coffee mugs were and how great of a selection there was. Anders didn't even drink coffee and he bought a second to go with his freebie one because they were that nice.

It was time to leave the stall, which was run by another nearly identical GameCon employee named Bethany. Roodg stopped them and grabbed onto someone who was entering Wall o' Mugs. A short boy with mousy hair that needed to be trimmed. The boy blushed bright red upon contact and Roodg laughed and slapped him hard on the back. The boy's companions formed up and hugs were given by all members except the tall woman, with short hair wearing a flannel shirt, who gave out handshakes instead.

Anders noted during this exchange that while Trev Terra looked a little like his avatar, he carried himself exactly like it; shy, nervous, and hunched over. Hippolyta looked and acted like a flat busted version of her Avatar, but she was at least a little warmer in person. Jorthan really didn't look much like a butt ugly troll, but he still had his natural charisma and friendliness to fall back on. The twins De'vini and In'ferni however, didn't look a thing alike. Anders had only known they were the twins because they were holding hands and wearing the same outfit, otherwise they were as opposite as two girls could possibly be (they were still cute together).

"Let's walk!" Roodg made a motion to Trev and he came over. From out of Roodg's pack came a mysterious package that Trev accepted before returning to his friends.

They said goodbye for now to Jorthan's party, but Lissa and Roodg were giggling.

When Anders asked why, he was informed about how Hippolyta had obviously been wearing a padded push-up bra due to her newfound love of having larger breasts. Anders hadn't noticed that himself of course, but he did think it was funny.

"So," Lissa asked casually, "what was in that mysterious package?"

Roodg confidently replied. "That was the manuscript for my novel, *The Sawsome Sincubus in the Lair of the Musky Minotaurs*. Trev agreed to beta read it and I know no one better at finding useless rathers, wells, and actuallys!"

"I need to read that!"

Everyone looked around for the source of the outburst and Anders was embarassed when he noticed that he was the one that had said it. He tried to change to *Blush Shade #6* but couldn't as this was the real world and *Blush Shades* were not usable here.

After taking far too long to pick out key chains (and admit that they all have devloped monster cock fetishes) the trio headed towards the ramp to the lower conference floor. Two steps into the walk down the gentle slope, the ramp started to shake and they all grabbed the railing to steady themselves. From the floor below burst a giant, running at full speed, and looking excited. Giant may have been a word, that was a little bit too mythical, but it certainly wasn't far off the mark. This guy was tall, at least 6'6", but he abruptly stopped in his tracks when he saw the three people clutching the railing. He was wearing a black *Caution Step* T-Shirt, and while it was an extra-large, on him it was a belly shirt, so he was wearing a much longer brown shirt underneath. He jumped in the air excitedly, causing the ramp to shake again, ran over to the group in two big steps, and crouched down to say hello.

Lissa was the first to figure it out, through her sly tactic of reading his name badge. "Flaming Pit, Gliint! You are fricking huge!"

Gliint only laughed before he started to talk about something that he was always excited about, *Caution Step*. "Oh! My! Maker! I can't believe it! Can you believe it? *Caution Step*?! All this time, it was *Caution Step*! Did you know they are finally back together and they are here of all places to perform a live concert for VIPs later? Songs that no one has heard yet and we get to be the first to hear them!? On their brand new album! Their brand new album that we all get copies of!" Gliint took out their new album extremely enthusiastically to show it off. "And they used it! They used my cover and want me to design for them from now on! Everything! This is so exciting. I need to go get my laptop to show them my other designs! Wow!"

Before anyone could attempt to reply, Gliint had bounded off towards the entrance.

Anders spoke first, "He was certainly animated."

"That was his character trait," Roodg reminded.

"I am so pissed off! I can't believe they are here!" Lissa added, nonsensically. When she noticed the others looking at her she realized she needed to clarify, "Not Gliint, he's great. I meant *Caution Step*. I'm mad that they are here."

Everyone agreed with how Lissa would be upset about that, even if Roodg and Anders were secretly excited about it (and the free album). They pressed onwards for three steps until they spotted another person running up the ramp who recognized them. She did not cause it to shake, it almost caused her to shake. She couldn't have been over four and a half feet tall, even with her platform shoes on. She was a little short of breath, but otherwise looked determined.

She approached Lissa and offered her immediate condolences, "I'm really sorry about Gliint. I'm sure he went on and on about *Caution Step*. I know how much you hate them, and how finding out would have been such a shock, but just so you know, I'm here for you anytime."

Lissa thanked Yallundy with a *Blue Lute* locket, and a hug. Finding out *Caution Step* was here had been a bit of a shock, but Lissa was going to be strong about this setback. Yallundy exchanged a few more pleasantries and then asked if they had seen which way her stomping goliath lover had run. Anders pointed the direction, while Roodg pointed out that after she found him he should carry her around for a change. He could manage it. Yallundy said goodbye and went to chase down Gliint with her significantly smaller (yet determined and now confident) strides.

Nondescript Christina and unimportant Lucas allowed entry down the ramp to the advanced area of GameCon to anyone with a manila paper badge or higher. Since they all had laminated VIP badges, passing here was no problem at all. The lower levels of GameCon, and the prizes that they held would soon be revealed.

When they had nearly reached the bottom of the ramp, Roodg got so excited that they literally jumped up and down while pointing to the bottom. The others asked what had been so exciting and Roodg yelled that the best laminated name tag ever had been spotted near the end of the ramp. So great in fact was this name tag that it couldn't even be contained on a single tag. It was on an impressive six name tags in total: Caëlahenãilenŵhei Oŏrendaliaęllyŕn Ņimĕlyandareaṁ.

Roodg ran up and hugged the shocked Caela, impressing everyone by pronouncing the entire name flawlessly. Caela admitted that nobody had been able to pronounce the entire thing before, not even the creator of the impossible mouthful of a name.

Smitten already with Caela, Roodg was already trying to discover the big secret that Caela had hidden away, unable to tell anyone. "What is this big secret that you were going to tell me at GameCon? I haven't been able to sleep. I've been so excited."

Caela was obviously perplexed, "I really thought that would be obvious Roodg. I am next to speechless that you are even asking."

"Why wouldn't I ask Caëlahenãilenŵhei? I really wanted to know!" Roodg was impossibly curious, and Caela was too stunned to talk.

"Wow, you did it Roodg. Caela is speechless!" Anders quipped.

Still not getting it Roodg asked again, "So, What is it? Tell me please!"

Lissa decided to fill in Roodg, "Look Roodg. In case you didn't notice, Caela is a man."

Roodg laughed, "Of course I noticed that, now what is the big secret?"

Caela smacked his face with his hand, "That is my big secret. I couldn't tell you that this entire time I was a guy in a dress."

"Why not?" Roodg asked, innocently enough.

"Because…" Caela stammered, "because if you knew that I was a guy you wouldn't like me anymore. I didn't mean to lie to anyone, but to be fair I didn't know that while playing this game as a female avatar the world would be sexually broken and I would have to live with my talking vagina the entire time, or that I would meet anyone that I had feelings for. How you must hate me, for keeping this truth from you."

Roodg laughed again, "Why would I hate you for that? Cocks rock remember?"

Caela looked relieved, but needed to make sure, "You're not mad?"

Roodg insisted that there was nothing to be mad about, and Caela calmed down.

The likely straight boy Caela had a sudden thought. "So… uh… I hate to ask, but what are you exactly?"

The reply from Roodg was obvious, "Duh. I'm Roodg."

"No," Caela replied, "I mean are you a girl or a boy? I need to know!"

Roodg slyly moved closer to Caela and gave him a kiss on the cheek. Roodg whispered into his ear, for Roodg was the straight whisperer. "Yes, I know that is what you meant. But if I told you, then all the fun will be ruined tonight when you try to find that out!"

Walking away with a smirk, Roodg noticed that Caela was blushing an intense shade of red, which was hard to noticeable through his freckles and red hair.

"I think you just broke the poor straight boy," Lissa said with a smirk. Roodg only grinned.

An unimportant gate guard by the name of Jenn let them through, and the trio went on their way until Lissa had a thought. Why do you think she… I mean he, was just standing there at the bottom of the ramp? That is a pretty odd place to stand when there are so many great things to loot.

Anders and Roodg shrugged, they had no idea, and it did seem weird.

"She wasn't," The unimportant GameCon employee named Jenn who had been following them unnoticed replied.

Lissa, Roodg, and Anders all jumped out of their skins. They had even gone as far as saying Holy fucking shitballs (Anders had fudged). They turned to the girl and noticed that she had two name badges. One was the GameCon badge that gave her full name of Jenn Ericks, and another laminated one on the other side of her GameCon shirt.

"Holy fuck Zal Finn you scared the crap out of us.!" Lissa finally managed to say, to which a confused Zal Finn just asked, "Why?"

"For the exact same reasons you always scare the crap out of people, you look like everyone else!" Lissa stammered.

"I do not look like everyone else!" Zal clarified, "I have a pink GameCon shirt on because I'm the event planner of this event. I am head of GameCon! And… you're right. I look like everyone else. This is maddening!"

Zal Finn was hurt, but Lissa gave her a hug, a bellybutton ring, and an apology. The demeanor of Zal improved.

"Why wasn't Caela standing alone at the ramp? I just remembered I was curious about that.," Lissa inquired to who she was pretty sure was the real Jenn Ericks.

"Um…" the Jenn Ericks who was the real one (Lissa had guessed right this time) "he wasn't alone. He was talking to me before you guys interrupted us."

"Of course! It makes sense now" Lissa felt foolish now but kept talking. "But… why?"

"Because he was talking to me about what I should say to that Sweet Hippolyta. I was stalking her earlier, but she didn't notice me when I went up and said hi. She just asked directions to the corsets!" confessed Zal Finn.

Anders, had the answer. "Now, I don't really know a lot about women, I will be honest here, but what I do know is that if you want Hippolyta to like you, you should be yourself. Looks are not as important as what is on the inside, and you are really sweet on the inside!"

Roodg added, "Also, you should tell her that she has an amazing rack!"

Everyone had agreed that all things considered it was a pretty good plan. Zal Finn thanked them all with a sweet hug and ran off to do one, or both, of those things.

Their next stop, according to the map, was for autographed pictures of various cute kittehs. It wasn't a stop they would make under normal circumstances, but these were free kittehs. Anders had settled on a nice picture of cats playing poker when he felt a rather hard slap on his back followed by a hearty laugh.

"Why if it isn't a lad, a lass, and a Roodg all together! I have been looking for you three!" said the slap.

When they turned they were not surprised to see Palcath, but they were surprised to see Palcath. It was a flesh and blood Palcath, dressed completely in a full set of spot on cosplay Palcath gear. Had he been shorter, and looked like a dwarf he would have been twins with himself.

"Wow Palcath, "Roodg said while admiring a particularly good pectoral plate, "you look just like Palcath!"

"Well thanks… uh… Roodg! I made it myself!" Palcath said as he proudly displayed his creation.

Lissa chimed in with a hint of suspicion in her voice, "You made this yourself?"

Palcath may have been slightly deflated at that moment, Anders wasn't sure. But if there had been a *Girl Who Thought I Was Cool But Now Doesn't Because I do Cosplay Animation* in real life, Palcath would have used it. "Yeah," he stammered.

Lissa's eyes bulged out slightly, "Wow! These are great. Normally I think this stuff is lame, but this is the nicest suit of Armour I have ever seen."

Palcath was lifted up from his depression as quickly as he had sunken into it. "Why thank you fair maiden, it ought to be, I am a professional blacksmith after all."

When people thought he was kidding, Palcath proved them otherwise, using his phone to show pictures of all sorts of Armour and weapons that he had produced for television and movies.

Lissa reached into her portfolio and handed Palcath something, "I feel sort of lame giving you this now since your stuff is so good and in movies and everything, but I made you a *Last Boss Shield* bracelet."

Palcath whistled while he looked at the bracelet, "Your attention to fine details in this is exquisite. Truly a masterpiece. Would you mind if I showed this to a few people, lass? There were talks about an official Annals of Gentalia line of items, and even some mention of a television series. Would you like to come to the meeting I have tomorrow?"

She agreed before Palcath had even finished his sentence, and even flat out kissed him, sexy-like. Palcath was happily thinking about Lissa cosplaying Lissa, with all her leather and laces. He would suggest making her a cosplay outfit as soon as possible (to help her get on the television prop crew of course).

"What all do you have left? I got here early and am finished, so I can show you anything you lad, lass, and Roodg missed." Palcath happily suggested.

Lissa replied without thinking, "I am pretty sure we've done everything and met everyone."

Roodg disagreed, "No, we haven't met Max yet, or gotten those *Caution Step* albums Gliint talked about!"

"You haven't met *Caution Step* yet?" Palcath's eyes widened, "So you don't know?"

"No, we know that *Caution Step* is here, we just told you that," Lissa said while rolling her eyes.

Palcath grabbed Lissa by the arm, "No you don't understand. You can't go meet *Caution Step*! You must never go there!"

Lissa got a competitive look in her eye. She nearly yelled, "Like Flaming Pit I am not going to go give those assholes a piece of my mind!"

Palcath realized he had said the wrong thing, but it could not be helped. He lead them to the line up for *Caution Step* albums and autographs. Roodg, and Anders got into the line up eagerly. This was free and *Caution Step* was Sawesome. Lissa got into the line up after a few others had snuck in ahead of her, which did not make her pleased. Palcath stayed on the other side of the velvet rope to watch nervously. This was going to be crazy. He tried to stop her several times, but she was not going to back down.

Anders was smitten by the lead singer Trip Hazard, who said nothing important and smiled as if he was already bored with the endless supply of geeks he was pandering to. Ashler Waldenmyer looked much better than the last picture Anders had seen of him on the celebrity news, and while Ashler did take much longer to think of what to write on his photo Anders chalked that up to the fact that the poor guy had just gotten out of rehab and was likely still shaky. Such a shame what happens to celebrities. Gunner M. Jefferies also was a bit shocked to see Anders, and smiled at him kindly, which made Anders a little weak in the knees if he was to be honest with himself.

Anders stood there lost in his own little *Caution Step* fantasy. He felt someone pulling on his arm. It was gentle at first, but by the time he had snapped out of this daydream it was starting to hurt. Anders was confused as to why Roodg was doing that and asked. Roodg insisted that Anders need to look at the autographs, saying that it was beyond important.

Anders read the first one out loud. "Thanks for playing. - Trip Hazard." He rolled his eyes. That wasn't important.

Roodg nearly slapped him, "No, read the other one!"

Anders read the second one. "I'm sorry for all the trouble I caused you. Please don't stop being a nice guy. - Ashler Waldenmyer." Anders thought about that one, "I don't get it."

Palcath nudged Anders. "No, the other, other one!"

Anders read the last one. "Had a great time adventuring with you Dragon Cultist! Who would have thought you were a real person? Hugs and Flexes - Gunner Maximus Jeffries."

Anders couldn't believe it. All this time he had been adventuring with a member of *Caution Step* (intimately at one point)! He thought of something better. Lissa, the girl that had been credited with the creation of *Caution Step's* most famous song, who had cheated on Ashler Waldenmyer, with Gunner Mr. Max Jefferies no less, was in the line up to meet *Caution Step*. Palcath was right to try and stop this.

Lissa reached the front of the line by pushing the budging group of snots aside and got her finger poised and ready for waving. All three band members changed colours to various shades of 'oh crap' when they saw Elizabeth Collins approach them. She got herself nice and angry and started to yell. "I need to say to you no talent hacks that I am... that I am... so mad at all of you... and that... I am mad for..." Lissa sighed and continued, "I wanted to say that I am sorry. I am sorry Ashler for cheating on you. I am sorry Gunner for blaming you when it was my idea. I have no right to be mad at either you, but writing that song about me was pretty low, and it hurt."

Ashler stumbled to his defense. "I didn't think it was going to be a song. Trip stole my diary and used the words. I wouldn't have done it otherwise."

Gunner put his arm around Ashler, their friendship had been patched, "Yeah, I was so surprised when Ashler told me yesterday that the song was about you! Lizzy is a nickname for Elizabeth, I had no idea. I could see why you'd be mad at us!" Typical clueless Max.

"So all this time I shouldn't have been mad at all three of you, I should have been mad at only Trip? Good to know!" Lissa accentuated her statement with a big slap to Trip's face. Security could not interfere as her badge was laminated, and ranked even higher than Trip's.

Gunner chimed in, "For the record, I'm still sorry about all this Ashler, and to you too, Lizzy. You know, I met a girl that is a lot like you lately. It's odd really how much you remind me of her."

Lissa replied, honest and oblivious, "I hope you two will be happy."

"Nah," Gunner replied, "I'm pretty sure she likes my fellow adventurer dwarf bro better!" With that, Lissa understood everything, and her mind was forever broken. She walked away a stunned drooling wreck of a thing.

Palcath was the first to reply, "Now we have done everything here."

Anders politely disagreed, "No, we haven't met Fourni yet!"

Palcath shook his head, "That brother of mine. He would be late to his own funeral. Do you know that it took the lad over an hour to pick an action figure?"

Now it was Anders turn to be shocked, "Fourni is your brother!?"

"Didn't you know that? I totally knew that," Roodg said matter of fact.

Palcath chuckled again, "Yes, the lad certainly is."

Anders needed to know, "Then why isn't your nickname Bro?!"

"Because my name is Manfred and that is an obvious way to go with it?" shrugged the cosplay dwarf.

"Manfred? Your name is Manfred?" Lissa's shock level increased against impossible odds.

"Either way," Palcath said, "the lad is going to be too late to join us for the announcement. He says he will meet us after they reveal the big Annals of Gentalia news."

The lights flicked as soon as Palcath finished speaking, signaling the announcement was starting. Palcath could claim divine intervention all he wanted, but everyone knew the truth was that he had memorized the schedule of events.

The stage lit up and Charlie took command of the crowd. He was not wearing anything with Ni Hao Bunny© on it, which slightly disappointed Anders.

"Thank you for coming everyone, and welcome to GameCon."

"First of all I would like to dispel the rumours of Tornado Tech Games getting sued. They are 100% true. Thankfully, due to the fact that this was already a rated M game and you all had to be of legal age to play it in the first place, we got off the hook and the suit was dropped!"

"Now, I am sure you all are curious as to the fate of this game; your game. I can say with honesty that looking at the various outfits people are wearing, seeing the crazy turn out for this event, and seeing all seven internet memes related to Gentalia Ogre loincloths, that you people like this game exactly how it is! Don't you?"

Anders was surprised by the volume of the cheering from the crowd. Apparently, there were a whole lot of perverts out there. He cheered right along with them.

Charlie continued, "If you want to keep playing, we just need you to sign an amended playing agreement. We promise to fix the big problems, and even have some exciting content coming down the pipe. I'll turn you over to my head programmer to give you some of the details…"

Roodg was pulling on Anders' arm again. Anders looked over to see Roodg pointing to the woman with frazzled hair, bottle-thick glasses, and a frumpy red sweater with a picture of two cats playing in leaves on it.

Roodg said hastily, "Oh my Charlie... she is..."

Charlie continued again, "Miss Eleanor Edna Lynn."

Lissa tried to be more surprised, but she couldn't. "Crazy skirt?"

Palcath understood now and explained. "She is the one responsible for secretly programming the world to be her personal sex romp! Her, the head programmer! All this time she was right under our noses. I can't believe it."

No one else could either, E. E. Lynn was responsible for making this game what it was, and despite the fact that she was off her nut insane, they would have to thank her later. They really didn't pay much attention to what Eleanor said, the only key point they heard was that a real crafting system was going to be implemented, new art, monsters, items, and guilds! When she turned over the presentation to her head artist and 3D modeller to show off some of the sexy near gear, it was Roodg's turn to have an exploded head!

"No way! The head artist. He talks just like Cinnamon! He wasn't a computer program. He was a real dude that she was forcing to live insider her virtual vagina!" Roodg couldn't even. "What kind of messed up relationship must they have?"

"I know!" Palcath squealed with delight! "They are adding crafting and guilds! I'm so excited for that!" (Palcath hadn't heard Roodg)

After the presentation, and the traditional resigning of the gameplay agreements, Anders made it his mission for them to find Fournimer before they had to go to the fancy dinner with head staff and the *Caution Step* concert. He made Palcath text him, and they would all meet by the least busy vendor stall, the one that sold cute kittehs, but Fournimer refused to meet there due to centaur trauma. They met at the coffee mugs instead.

Palcath pointed out his brother, Anders was the one who got to be shocked this time. It was the dude that he had helped earlier in the day. Bernhard was no longer wearing his jacket, but was still wearing his scarf, likely for dramatic purposes as it wasn't even remotely cold in the building. Anders walked over and Bernhard stood up from the bench he was on, he looked as stunned (and stunning) as before.

Anders had to take the lead, "Hello Fourni, it's me."

"Yes, I know. I saw you before," Fournimer replied completely dumbfounded.

"Why didn't you say anything?" Anders asked with a pouty lip.

"Because," Bernhard Fortinbras continued, "when I saw you I couldn't believe it. You looked so much like the Avatar that I had fallen in love with that I couldn't even speak. Except... well..."

"I'm wearing clothes? My ears aren't pointy? I'm not as fat as Kray?" Anders guessed.

"No, except that your eyes aren't protagonist green," Fournimer smiled.

Anders stammered a little "You really noticed that my eyes were a different colour?"

"Of course I did! Eye colour is supwe important in fantasy books."

"I'm sorry to disappoint you." Anders blushed a little.

"Why would I be disappointed? You know that I am all about the colour blue!" Fournimer smiled.

Anders smiled and jumped into Fournimer's arms. In the real world Fournimer's kisses did not produce cartoon hearts or explosions, but when their lips touched for the first time, Anders he knew for a fact that the little love hearts had broken through the fabric of reality and appeared above their heads.

◊ THE END ◊

Roodg said, "Aw! That was super cute!"

Want to read more about Anders, his friends, and their sexy adventures? You totes can!

They all show up as cameo characters in the Tales of Gentalia series!
They are prequels so you should probably read them first! Wait a round, damn. Oh well!

For more exciting adventures you can always visit the Annals of Gentalia official website (and later delete your browser history) and see what is up!

www.annalsofgentalia.wordpress.com

AUTHOR'S NOTE

Here is some advice that you never thought you would hear and for good reason: Don't set a precedent for dedicating your books to jokes. It sounds like an absolutely great idea (and it honestly is) but you will find yourself with a problem: How do you actually thank people who helped you when writing the books?

The answer is: The Author's Note! A page at the absolute end of the book that nobody will read anyway except people that might be thanked. Seriously, no one but the most dedicated readers will read this page. It could be about anything really, so here is a fun sentence about fancy hats. Fancy hats are sawesome!

There are so many people I would like to thank, and all of them coincidently worked as unimportant GameCon employees!

Darcy: Thank you for being the absolute first person that found out I was writing with your mad detective skills, beta reading absolutely everything multiple times, and helping with sexy power brainstorming sessions.

Jay: Thank you for not thinking I was absolutely mad when I started off our first conversation with theories of Hydra-Cock (you just thought I was hilariously mad)! Thank you for beta-reading everything and providing additional silly jokes to the series!

Jessica & Bethany: Thanks for beta reading and for showing me that all readings of these novels must be done with friends using silly voices. (Try it yourself, it is great!)

Amanda: Thank you for providing a gentler side to the novels, I do appreciate it! Thanks for even reading it, I know it makes you blush!

Vanessa: Thanks for beta reading like an absolute boss, and being a great super fan.

Christina: Thank you for suggesting that I write some smaller works and tie them to the main series. You inspired the Tales, and I ♥ them!

Lucas: Thank you for having a horrible argument with me about how someone couldn't start writing a book. Without your arguments that it couldn't be done, I never would have started to write these books to prove you wrong!

And to everyone else I missed, including Ben: Thanks so much for reading!

Thanks again!

- CB Archer

www.ingramcontent.com/pod-product-compliance
Lightning Source LLC
Chambersburg PA
CBHW051511250626
47156CB00001B/48